Someone's Watching

(The Stourbridge Serial Killer)

Steve Barnbrook

Acknowledgements

Karen Taylor

Patricia Lewis

Sean Jones

To Karen, my bluntest and harshest critic thank you for your time and effort

To Pat and Sean, thank you for your time and insight

Contents

1

Is Anyone There?

"Try flashing the headlights again" said Claire impatiently.

"It's no use there's no one here" Fraser replied "I've never seen it so quiet. This place is normally buzzing on a Thursday night; perhaps we should try somewhere else?"

"We haven't got enough time; my old man finishes his shift at ten o'clock, so I need to be back in the house before he gets home. We'll just have to get on with it and hope somebody turns up."

Claire then pulled down her knickers to her ankles and bent over the bonnet of Frasers battered old Ford Mondeo. This was their favourite dogging spot, Stourbridge Park; you could normally guarantee a good audience and plenty of willing participants. It was well known throughout the local area and it was advertised on a number of dogging websites. It was also common knowledge with the local residents. Tonight, however was disappointing with not a soul in sight even though it was a perfect night for it. It was a warmish balmy evening; the moon wasn't too bright which meant you got a good view if you were quite close, but it also provided a slight cover of anonymity.

Claire was an attractive brunette. She had been indulging in dogging for a number of months after being introduced to it by Fraser who had been doing it for several years. He was known locally as a bit of a pervert. They had met via an on-line chatroom for swingers and they agreed to meet in a local pub called The Bush which was frequented by swingers, doggers and any other sexual deviants you could think of. She had quickly progressed from simply watching to being watched and then joining in group sex, the more the better, one after another. She could not explain even to herself exactly why she derived pleasure from such depraved practises. She just knew that the first time she tried it she was amazed; the exhilaration and sexual excitement she felt, it was like nothing she had ever experienced before. Whether it was the exhibitionism or the clandestine manner and the sense of danger of being exposed she just didn't know. What she did abhor however was the feeling of disgust and self-contempt after it was all over and finished. She kept telling herself after each time that it would be the last time, but it never was, and she was always drawn back to it again and again. So why did she do it she asked herself? She simply didn't know she just knew that this was something that filled some deep-rooted need within her, something she could not get from her husband, even though he was quite a nice respectable good looking athletic bloke with a normal sexual appetite but also boring as hell.

Whilst Fraser on the other hand was completely different, he was a fat sweaty slob but sexually adventurous. He was into swinging, dogging, group sex, in fact almost anything. She knew he fucked lots of other women apart from her, but she wasn't particularly bothered. She was using him to satisfy her cravings just as much as he was, perhaps even more so but it was difficult to imagine two more completely different people.

Claire's face was pressed hard into the bonnet of the car they had been waiting there so long for someone to turn up that all the warmth from the engine had gone and she could feel the metallic coldness against her cheek it gave her goose pimples and sent shivers down her spine.

Fraser with his trousers round his ankles wasn't affected by the chill in the air he had plenty of layers on the upper part of his body and the fat in his legs and his huge backside provided him with ample insulation he continued to penetrate her, grunting and groaning. This made quite a hideous sight and it is difficult to understand why anybody would want to see such a spectacle.

8

"Is anybody watching yet can you see anyone?" asked Claire hopefully.

"No there's still nobody around" panted Fraser; his wheezy breath interspersed with bouts of phlegm like coughing fits.

The years of overeating junk food the total lack of exercise and his huge beer belly were taking its toll on him. He was sweating profusely, the beads of which were falling from his forehead onto the back of Claire's neck. This sent a shiver of disgust through her body, no wonder they call him smelly Fraser behind his back-Claire thought. She realised now more than ever that her only pleasure from all this was the perverted idea of being watched, especially by strangers and that part of her perversion was being fucked by someone as fat and smelly as Fraser. In normal circumstances she would not look at him twice. She thought to herself I'm a good-looking woman with a fit body and well educated a bloody teacher for Christ sake.

"Well if there's no-one else about get it over with quickly" Claire shouted.

"Okay" Fraser grunted he didn't need to be asked twice and he began to thrust away as fast as his fat unfit body would allow.

Claire closed her eyes and tried to block out what was happening. She began to realise now more than ever that the one and only kick or thrill of excitement that she ever got from all this was the thought that someone was watching and that with the total lack of onlookers she found it quite repulsive and received no pleasure or satisfaction at all and she felt sick to her stomach. She promised herself that this would be the very last time; never ever again would she subject herself to such vile and degrading abuse.

She repeated again for Fraser to hurry up if there still wasn't anyone watching, all she wanted to do now was to go home she could feel a tear slowly rolling down her cheek.

Fraser didn't reply because his exertions at trying to speed things up had left him panting for breath and with his heart beating wildly out of control, it was all he could do to keep thrusting away let alone spare enough breathe to speak.

Fraser was quite wrong however about being on their own. Someone was indeed watching them and had been for quite some time. He was also blissfully unaware that from the cover of the shrubbery their every move was being closely and secretly observed. Fraser was also ignorant of the fact that this someone had now left the cover of the undergrowth and had stealthily and silently made their way across the carpark and approached the pair of them and they were now standing immediately behind him within touching distance, close enough to smell the sweat his fat body was exuding. Fraser was getting more and more worked up as he began to approach a climax his breathing became more and more strained with his heart pounding fit to burst.

"Hurry up Fraser I'm begging you" pleaded Claire.

"Fucking have it bitch" he grunted. "Fucking have it" he repeated. Louder and louder he began moaning and gasping for breath, thrusting away as fast as he possibly could then he let out a short loud wail. He stopped his thrusting motions and became quiet, the breathlessness subsiding. His body now bent over double resting on the back of Claire.

The tears were now in full flow dripping off Claire's cheeks and dripping onto the bonnet, thank fuck for that thought Claire, I just want to go home I've had enough of all this. Claire then felt the full weight of Fraser on her back she wanted to wipe her tears away but she realised it would do no good the tears kept coming and were cascading down her cheeks forming a salty liquid pool on the bonnet she knew that as quickly as she could wipe the tears from her face they would be replaced, she would wait until it's all over stand up sort herself out and walk away forever.

Fraser's weight had her firmly pinned down, she knew he was always like this after he had ejaculated he was so unfit he needed a breather before he could move. She endured it for a while before it became too much making it difficult for her to breathe. "For fucks sake Fraser you're squashing me stand up; you've got all your weight on me if you've come get off me come on Fraser, get up now" she repeated impatiently.

Claire was now becoming increasingly pissed off with Fraser as she squealed out in agony. She was completely unable to move, stuck between the bonnet and smelly Fraser's fat sweaty body that was pressing down and almost smothering her.

"Fraser get off me I can barely fucking breathe" she managed to utter whilst struggling with the weight compressing her chest making it more and more difficult for Claire to get her breath, this had now changed from severe discomfort to excruciating pain and she could stand it no longer.

She shouted again as loud and as venomously as she could manage given her shortage of breath caused by her limited chest movement "Get off me you fat fuck. You're hurting me, fucking move."

Fraser did not respond or make even the slightest movement but simply laid there completely motionless, as much as he would have liked to do as Claire was asking him to do and move to relieve the pressure and pain she was suffering he was unable to move at all, the long thin metal spike that had been driven through the back of his neck had severed the main artery that supplies blood to the brain. His airway was blocked and the damage to his cranial nerve was causing complete paralysis. His larynx had been punctured, rendering him unable to speak or breathe properly.

Claire who was completely unaware of what had happened to Fraser was now comprehensively and utterly trapped between Fraser's fat and increasingly smelly body and the cold hard metal of the car bonnet. Unable to move or even turn her body round she started to panic. Oh my god she thought what if he has had a heart attack or a stroke or something what do I do, what can I do. I can't even move I daren't cry out for help the humiliation of being found in this position would be more than she could bear.

Her heart began to race in fear; a feeling of terror and hopelessness began to grip her body and course through her veins. She was completely helpless unable to do anything as she felt the coldness of the steel spike that was now being driven through the back of her neck and severing her cranial nerve. She tried to cry out, but the spike had been plunged with such speed and force it had penetrated clean through the front of her throat, through her larynx and into the bonnet of the Mondeo.

She desperately wanted to scream out for help, but something was preventing her from doing so something was lodged in her throat and she realised that it needed to be removed so she summoned up all her strength and energy and attempted to raise her arms towards her throat. She gathered up every ounce of strength in her body that she could muster but still her arms wouldn't move, she realised why she couldn't move her body because of the weight of Fraser but why couldn't she move her arms, what on earth is happening she thought.

Then the chilling realisation dawned on her, there wasn't a gap between her neck and the bonnet, whatever it was in her throat was also embedded in the car. She had in effect been nailed to the cold lump of metal and impaled like in a crucifixion, her arms remained spread over the car resting in a cross like position and there she remained.

The grotesque sight of two pathetic half naked doggers spread-eagled and completely incapacitated over the car bonnet cast an eerie silhouette in the half moonlight. The only sound to be heard apart from the gentle night breeze blowing through the leaves in the nearby trees was the low rhythmic gurgle of air escaping from the now helpless bodies as it fought to break through the slow trickle of blood that was gradually flooding into their lungs. Neither of them able to do anything other than come to terms with the terrifying acceptance of their impending fate and the shame they would bring on themselves and their loved ones when they were found in this position their lives were slowly ebbing away, neither of them able to comprehend fully what had happened to them but both knowing they were slowly and simply approaching the end of their time on earth in the most agonising and humiliating manner.

Then there was silence.

2

The Unkindest cut of all

Detective Constable Oliver Latifeo, better known as Oli to his friends and colleagues was ambling along the street casually strolling towards Stourbridge Police Station. It was a warm summer's day and he was enjoying the bright morning sunshine whilst pondering what to do with his day. Breakfast was first on the agenda of course, then later maybe a wander around the town at lunchtime and do a spot of shopping, anything but police work. It had never been his intention to join the police force, he would much prefer a more relaxed career, one in which he could blend into the background and put his feet up. He wasn't a fan of hard work or indeed any work at all but pressure from his Italian parents who wanted him and the rest of the family to blend in and become part of the community having immigrated to England some years earlier had sealed his fate.

His parents were immensely proud that their son was a member of her majesty's constabulary and took every opportunity to tell all and sundry about their brave upstanding son who worked tirelessly protecting the public. In reality however Latifeo had managed to find himself a nice little easy post where he could get away with doing as little work as possible. Today being a prime example, he should have reported for duty two hours ago but instead he had spent a couple of extra hours in bed with his girlfriend Sam Gail.

He had been seeing her for some while; she was a stunner, a small petite gorgeous blond with a slight but perfectly formed incredibly sexy body. She had an incredible magnetism about her, a kind of alluring charm and he would do anything for her to please her. His wife on the other hand was quite plain and dull with all the personality of a dishcloth; he had only married her because of pressure from his parents. They had singled her out for him as the safe stay at home marrying kind who would supply the much-wanted grandchildren and he couldn't be bothered with all the hassle of standing up for himself against his parents so like his police career his fate was sealed.

DC Latifeo strolled into Stourbridge Police Station having spent the night with his girlfriend the excuse he had given his wife was that he was working overtime on a secret undercover assignment.

His wife wasn't exactly the sharpest knife in the box Latifeo thought but it suited him. He could tell her anything no matter how ludicrous it was, and the silly cow would swallow it, hook line and sinker. What a stupid bitch he thought, he would have much preferred to make a life with Sam she was the type of woman he wanted the sort he craved after she was exciting and fresh there was something about her that he couldn't get enough of.

She was fantastic in the sack but it wasn't just the great sex she had an attraction that he simply couldn't explain but he knew deep down it would never happen because he simply couldn't be bothered with all the work and complications and the grief he would get from his parents that would be involved in splitting up with his wife, he just wanted an easy life and at this moment in time he had the best of both worlds. He reached the police Station and walked in nonchalantly and made his way towards the CID office. He was late, but then he always was. It was never a problem on earlies no one else was there to notice what time he came in. As he walked past the front desk and exchanged a good morning with the desk staff, the duty sergeant said, "You had better shake a leg, the DCI has been looking for you he is doing his nut."

Latifeo was taken aback by this "But he's never here this time of the morning" Latifeo replied "what's the bloody hell is happening?"

16

"We've got two dead bodies in the town park" the desk sergeant replied. "Oh fuck" thought Latifeo as he hurried along the corridor towards the DCI's office.

Latifeo was well known in the Station to be bone idle, doing just enough work to get by. Today being a perfect example, he should have reported for duty at six o'clock as the early turn CID cover, but he was never there before eight knowing full well that no other CID officer could check on him as they wouldn't appear much before nine but this time it had backfired. Just my bloody luck he thought, his mind was racing now to prepare excuses for the inevitable grilling he was about to get from the DCI.

Frank Twead was known to be a useless twat, unable to detect his own arse. He was famed throughout the force as a complete buffoon. Some of the ludicrous decisions he had made during police operations had made him a laughing stock among rank and file, but he was also known as a particularly nasty bastard, especially if you didn't do what he wanted no matter how ridiculous the order may be. Rumour is that he only got the DCI's post because he was a member of the funny handshake brigade and he was now stuck in the post unable to progress further because of his incompetence and his problems with alcohol dependency which was common knowledge amongst rank and file but never acknowledged officially by the hierarchy.

Latifeo made his way towards the DCI's office. The entire nick was alive with excitement and he had never seen so many staff at this time of the morning. He waited outside the door to DCI Frank Twead's office steeling himself for an imminent rollicking whilst running through in his mind some of the excuses and answers he had thought for the inevitable questions concerning his whereabouts.

"Yes sir" he said as he entered the DCI's office. The DCI deliberately stared at him without saying a word knowing that this would make Latifeo feel ill at ease and unsettle him; eventually when he spoke he was very matter of fact.

"I assume you've heard that we have a possible double murder in the park? What I want is you there ASAP to make sure the SOCO's don't cock the scene examination up. I'll be there later on to take charge is that understood?" Twead eyed him a fixed steely gaze whilst waiting for the reply he knew he had unnerved him.

Latifeo wasn't expecting this, he assumed he would have received a severe tongue lashing and it took him a while to respond he eventually cleared his throat and replied. "Yes, sir I'll go and supervise the scene and make sure the correct procedures and protocols are observed. I'll get a vehicle and go straight there."

Latifeo then left the DCI's office and made his way to the rather less palatial CID department where he located the keys for the duty CID vehicle he knew in the back of his mind that he had been let of the hook far too easily; this wasn't Frank Twead's style. The vehicles were parked in a secure compound at the rear of the Police Station. Latifeo was scanning the compound searching for the battered old Ford Escort that had been twice round the clock and was literally falling to pieces. It was however the only vehicle they had; it was a bit of a disgrace for it to be used a police vehicle.

He was all the time cursing his luck of being rumbled coming in late; no one normally saw the DCI until lunchtime after his hangover had subsided. The DCI hadn't said anything to him, but he knew he had made a mental note of it for future reference. Having found the keys to the vehicle he made his way outside to the rear of the Station and saw the battered old wreck parked in the far corner. Still cursing his luck as he approached the car he heard someone trying to attract his attention.

"Oli" came an excited shout from the far side of the compound. "It's me Shirley"

"O fuck" Oli muttered under his breath.

WPC Shirley Wallows was continually aspiring to have an attachment to the CID department much against the wishes of most of the office. She was considered to be hard work and a bit dense.

"I've got an attachment, starting today" she beamed.

"Congratulations but I'm sorry I've got to go now we've got a job on in the park" and with that he climbed into the car and sped off towards Stourbridge Park and to the crime scene thinking to himself that's all we fucking need a split arse in the office.

The park was quite close to the police Station and Latifeo parked the car on the roadway outside and walked through the main entrance and found the crime scene just a short distance in. The scene was cordoned off by blue and white police do not enter tape and two uniform officers were standing guard. Latifeo approached the uniform officers and registered his arrival on the scene log. He could see the two people in white paper suits. One was a SOCO; the other one Steve was the crime scene manager. They were both busy examining the scene and taking their forensic trace samples. One of the uniform officers outlined the appropriate route to Oli saying, "The common approach path is to the right following the line of shrubbery."

"Thanks" he replied as he bent low under the police tape and made his way towards the scene.

The common approach path or CAP was a standard police method of ensuring minimum cross contamination of the scene if everyone who needed to visit the scene walked the same route.

The crime scene officers were well known to all the officers at the Station including Latifeo. They were notorious for their macabre ghoulish behaviour and blasé attitude to horrific or grisly scenes. This being the result of countless examinations of dead or dying mutilated bodies and most probably acted as a form of safety release from the nightmarish images that these scenes inevitably conjured up. A kind of pressure relief valve commonly referred to within the job as black humour. They were both serving police officers, but everyone referred to them as either Steve or Dave and this suited them. Neither of them was a stickler for authority nor respecting rank structures and they adopted a laid-back approach, they were considered part of the furniture.

The reason they had both opted to get out of uniform duties and to work in forensics was because dealing with dead bodies was infinitely more preferable than fighting with and rolling about on the floor with the Friday night drunks then having to repeat the procedure the next day by fighting with violent football hooligans, there were much better ways to spend a Saturday afternoon. Dealing with dead bodies could be quite gruesome but at least they couldn't shout or scream at you or try and give you a good kicking. The worst they could do was to occasionally make your stomach turn or give you a restless night especially if the cadaver was that of a baby or a young child but they were thankfully few and far between, most murder or suicide victims were adults and they could be dealt with by adopting an air of detachment and concentrating on the job in hand whether it was conducting a post-mortem examination or a fingerprint identification.

They had both quite often crossed swords with senior officers during investigations especially the current DCI with his crackpot ideas concerning crime scene examinations. He refused to listen to anyone else and for some reason believed that because of his rank he knew better than the experts who had been highly trained in forensic examination and strategy. Some of his decisions had become legendary among the force as sources of amusement, not least because of the eagerness of the SOCO's to make sure that as many officers became aware by whatever means as quickly as possible of his latest outlandish crazy ideas.

When the scene first came into view Latifeo was stunned 'Jesus Christ' he thought. He stood there for a moment unable to comprehend the sight before him. The bodies were still in situ bent over the bonnet of a blue ford Mondeo, a pool of blood had congealed on the floor between the male victim's legs, his trousers were round his ankles showing a horrible white fat arse. There was obviously a body pinned beneath him and the car bonnet, but it was difficult to see. It was mainly obscured by the pale lifeless flabby body sprawled on top of it. He began to feel a bit sickly; he was not good at dealing with dead bodies let alone the macabre sight that was laid out before him.

The SOCO's were busy taking crime scene samples. Oli recognised them straight away and was relieved to see it was Dave and Steve. This meant that because they were old hands and used to this type of thing he could leave it with them and he could disappear knowing they could be relied on not to grass him up to the DCI. Dave and Steve had both noticed Latifeo approaching and were well aware that he was quite squeamish and weak stomached. They gave each other a devilish grin as he neared the scene. As he got closer he shouted from a distance "What we got lads?"

"Hiya Oli" was the reply from Dave. Latifeo was updated with the information established so far that the couple were both married though not to each other and the vehicle belonged to the deceased male. Arrangements had been made to inform their spouse's, a cause of death had not been established but based on the temperature of the corpses and the onset of rigor mortis they had both died sometime late yesterday evening.

"Could it be natural causes or a suicide pact" enquired Latifeo.

"Highly unlikely" said Dave and Steve simultaneously.

"How can you be so sure if you've not established a cause of death?"

"Because" replied Steve "apart from being dead, the bloke has had his cock chopped off. I think we're dealing with some sort of pervert."

"Holy shit" Latifeo cried as he tried to stifle a stomach wretch.

"Looks like it's been sliced off with a Stanley knife or something similar. Put a scene suit on and you come and a have a closer look." encouraged the SOCO's.

Latifeo thought about this. It should be the correct thing to do, the DCI had after all told him to supervise the SOCO's but there were two problems with this. One he was very tickled stomach when it came to dead bodies and he didn't want to embarrass himself by throwing up all over the crime scene and secondly, he hadn't got a clue what to do in relation to forensic scene examination, or any kind of forensics when it came to it. So as usual he looked for a way out where he could do the least amount of work.

Latifeo could feel the bile rising up from his stomach. He took a deep breath and said "I'm going to the café. If the DCI turns up tell him I'm doing an area search. Do you want anything bringing back?" Oli asked. The more ghoulish of the two SOCO's Dave replied with a grin "I'll have a sausage sandwich with plenty of tomato ketchup."

"Very fucking funny" said Oli "I'm sure you're not right in the head you bloody weirdo."

Oli made his way back past the uniform officers guarding the scene and told them "If the DCI turns up, tell him I'm doing an area search and conducting initial house to house enquires."

He did not go to the café or make any house to house enquires and had no intention of doing so, he knew the DCI was unlikely to turn up, so he simply made his way to his girlfriend's house, the house he had just left within the last hour to go to work. Her house was literally right opposite the park just a few short yards away, so he left the CID vehicle parked where it was. He casually strolled up the garden path towards the front door. This was something he had done several times before, but he normally did it under cover of darkness and his visit would normally be pre-arranged with Sam. When his girlfriend Sam opened the door to him she was struck dumb at first and obviously surprised to see him, she then composed herself and hurriedly and nervously looked around to see if anyone was watching.

"What on earth are you doing back here so soon and in broad daylight? You know you are supposed to call me first." She was standing in the open doorway still dressed in her nightgown.

"It's okay; calm down it doesn't matter if anyone sees me you'll never believe it but there's been a double murder in the park opposite. If you look out of your bedroom window you can probably see the crime scene."

She hurriedly ushered him in and they quickly made their way upstairs and peered out of the window towards the park. They could just see some of the blue and white police tape sealing the area off. Although most of the scene was obscured by bushes and shrubs the same foliage that was used by the doggers to obscure their activities from general view.

"That place is used by the perverts" Sam said.

"I know" he replied. "It looks like a couple of sexual perverts are the victims. You'll never believe it but the bloke has had his cock chopped clean off."

His girlfriend shuddered and said, "I don't know how you can deal with something like that it would turn my stomach."

"It doesn't bother me" Latifeo said in a macho type voice. "You need to be made of strong stuff in my line of work, that's why I've been made the lead investigator" he lied.

"Anyway, you're taking a chance coming to the front door in daylight what if someone has seen you?"

"Already thought about that" he said. "I will simply say that I am doing house to house enquires and for the foreseeable future I can be seen in this area without raising suspicion. After all I am the lead investigator in the case. Also, this investigation will give me a great excuse for pretending to work odd shifts and overtime, rest day workings and so on."

"I'd still feel more comfortable if we stick to our usual routine so make sure you call me next time and every time" she added.

"Okay relax, I'll phone you as normal if that makes you feel better. I'll have a lot of spare time now with this murder investigation. In fact, I'm in no hurry now" as he began to undo the cord of her dressing gown and push her gently towards the bed, the bed they had only got out of less than an hour ago.

Back at the crime scene the SOCO's had now been joined by the pathologist, Dr Chuman. Dave had seen the pathologist approaching and whispered to the other SOCO. "Chuman is just booking himself in the scene attendance log. Don't turn around yet but you want to see the state of him."

Both SOCO's had worked with the pathologist several times before, both at crime scenes and at post-mortems. He was always invariably hung-over but neither of them had seen him in such an awful state as he was in now. His eyes looked like the proverbial pissholes in the snow, his face was like a pickled beetroot and he seemed to have the shakes. They thought to themselves he doesn't look much better than the fat dickless corpse draped over the car. The SOCO's greeted him and began to outline the crime scene detailing the samples they had already taken.

The crime scene manager Steve said "The bodies were found at four o'clock this morning. I started to examine the bodies about four-thirty. There was a little warmth left in both the bodies and rigor mortis was just beginning to set in so I guess that would make time of death about eleven last night."

The pathologist agreed "Has death been certified?"

"Yes" replied Steve. "The paramedics pronounced life extinct at four-forty for both bodies. The guy's penis has been cut off, quite a clean cut perhaps using a Stanley knife or something similar and there is considerable blood pooling on the floor. The guy most probably bled to death. I haven't found any other injuries on him and there is no obvious injury to the female."

"Looking at the size of him he could well have crushed her to death" said the pathologist. "Is anything known about them?"

"Not a great deal yet. Initial enquires have established that they were both married but not to each other."

"Jealous husband perhaps" said Dr Chuman "And she may have been unintentionally asphyxiated by the weight of his body. In that case I've seen enough, I'll leave you to take the samples and I'll arrange the post-mortem for two o'clock. I will see you at my office at one-thirty to discuss your findings. I'll appreciate it if you can have the photographs ready prior to the PM. See you later."

At that the pathologist left the scene, he endorsed the scene attendance log and left the SOCO's to continue with their examination.

"What a waste of time he was" Dave said to Steve. "I don't know why he bothers to show up at all. He didn't examine the body or do fuck all."

"I'll tell you why he comes to the scene" said Steve "Because he will now invoice for his attendance and it will probably be more than our weeks wages put together that's why. He always makes sure that he signs the scene attendance log so religiously so that he has a record just in case of any comebacks. You and I are in the wrong job mate."

3

Hair of the Dog

Frank Twead sat in his office; his hangover from the previous night's drinking session was still raging through his head. What he needed was hair of the dog and a couple of hours sleep.

What a time to get a major enquiry he thought, he was finding it difficult to focus. His first priority on anything he was ever involved with was self-preservation. He ran through his actions so far that day. The scene was being examined by the SOCO's and he had also sent Latifeo there to supervise, even though he knew he was useless but if anything went wrong any major slipups or mistakes then he could shift the blame on them. He had tasked a detective sergeant to set up an incident room and a detective inspector to allocate actions, so once again any mistakes he had someone else to blame. He paced the floor in his office, his hands were becoming clammy and he was becoming more and more impatient and restless his head wouldn't clear and it was difficult to focus.

He sat back on his chair and tried to relax but he knew it was futile he knew exactly what the problem was and how to fix it, fuck it he thought I can't wait any longer and he got up from his chair walked over to the door of his office and locked the door. Returning to his chair he opened the top drawer of his desk and took out a bottle of Famous Grouse and half-filled a whisky glass with its contents. He stared at it for a moment before swallowing the entire contents in a couple of gulps. The hit was immediate, he then settled back in his leather chair with a refill sipping it at a more genteel pace and waiting for the alcohol to do its magic and ease his throbbing hangover. After half an hour and half a bottle of whisky the DCI felt relaxed and was able to focus on the day's events and review what actions he had taken. Oh, shit he suddenly thought, I've forgotten to arrange the post-mortem and to update the superintendent. His mind began to race thinking of who to blame for the oversight. The DCI then picked up his mobile phone from off his desk and pressed number one on his speed dial. The call was answered within a couple of seconds with "Hello Frank how's your head?"

"I feel like absolute shit" he relied.

"I assume you are ringing about the bodies in the park?" asked the pathologist.

"That's right H" said Frank "I've just realised that I have not made any arrangements for the PM and I'll have the bloody superintendent on my back soon the interfering twat."

"Not a problem" Chuman replied "I've scheduled the PM for two o'clock this afternoon. I arranged it with your SOCO's, it shouldn't take too long so I'll see you in the pub about four o'clock and give you the result."

"Great that will fit in just right with the six o'clock briefing. See you later" said Frank who feeling more relaxed set about polishing off the remains of his bottle of whisky.

Hubert Chuman and Frank Twead were lifelong friends and had grown up together. They were in the same class at school and had been in a few scrapes and misadventures together. They had shared a lot of common interests over the years as they grew up and still did to this day. The common interest they both shared now did not concern the type of interests they had shared when they were young up such as music, girls, sporting activities etc., but something entirely different. Their one and only shared pastime these days revolved around the pub and how much alcohol they could both throw down their necks. They were both extremely heavy drinkers and they would drink at any and every available opportunity. This had brought them even closer together over time as the only people who can tolerate a habitual drunk is another drunk. Their propensity for drink had reflected in both their personal and professional lives, neither of them was married or had any children. They both lived alone with no outside interests and both continually made mistakes and errors of judgement concerning their jobs.

Frank was feeling more at ease now after having spoken with his mate Chuman so he sat back in his chair and realising he had finished a complete bottle of whisky he opened his desk drawer and took out another bottle and poured himself another large whisky, he felt his eyelids becoming heavy knowing that in a few minutes he would doze off as he did on a regular basis for half an hour or so. He quickly finished his last glassful, leant back and closed his eyes his breathing became deeper and louder until the sound of gentle snoring took over.

Shirley Wallows had risen deliberately early for her first day on attachment to CID and had spent a lot of time selecting her outfit for the day. She wanted to make sure that she looked the part to give her confidence a boost. Her self-confidence had taken a bit of a battering since joining the police force; it was still very much a male dominated work place and unless you happened to be extremely attractive then police women were considered to be second rate.

Shirley wasn't unattractive, but she could not be called a stunner. She certainly wasn't a head turner just sort of average, but she was level headed and intelligent. She knew she had the ability to be an efficient and competent officer, but she would have to negotiate her way through the macho male environment and their persistent put downs. It was something she had needed to do during her upbringing and she was determined that she would not let these archaic sexist attitudes interfere with her career.

As she had left her tiny bedsit where she lived on her own and made her way to the Station early that morning she had continually said to herself 'be confident, be strong I can deal with anything they can throw at me.' She was now glad that she had made that extra special effort that morning because as part of the CID she automatically became a member of the murder incident room and was just about to receive her very first major incident briefing. She had tried her best to speak with her new colleagues in CID but the only one who bothered to reply was Latifeo and that was only a fleeting couple of words in the carpark when he was on his way to the murder scene but despite that she was determined to stick it out and become part of the team.

The DCI having woken from his alcohol induced nap strode bullishly into the briefing room having just the right amount of alcohol running through his body for him to be able to function efficiently. "Everyone settle down quickly so we can get started" he announced.

The parade room at Stourbridge Police Station had been turned into and was being used as the incident briefing room. Extra chairs, desks and filing cabinets had been shipped into the department from force headquarters and the I.T. Department were busy installing extra phones and desk top computers. There a feeling of excitement in the air, this was the most interesting and serious crime to have happened in Stourbridge for many a long while and indeed for most of the personnel gathered to take part in the investigation. It was by far the biggest thing they had ever been involved in. In addition to all that was the possibility of unlimited overtime and for Latifeo the chance for extra sex sessions with his girlfriend.

The briefing began with introductions and the pairing up of detectives to work as enquiry teams; this was always a tense time especially now as WPC Wallows was on attachment to CID and no one particularly wanted to work with her. Latifeo kept repeating in his head 'anyone but her, anyone but her.' A visible sigh of relief from the CID staff in the incident room was blatantly obvious when it was announced that Wallows was being paired up with Latifeo. Through clenched teeth and with a forced smile he nodded towards Wallows whilst thinking stupid bitch. Wallows returned the gesture thinking it could have been worse, there are a lot of other officers who wouldn't give her the time of day but at least Latifeo did his best to be a little bit civil and hide his disappointment, she was fully aware that she was not a popular choice for the CID attachment and an even less popular working partner. She had sensed the sigh of relief from the rest of the room when they realised that she wasn't their partner. She and Latifeo had received their orders; they were to accompany the SOCO's to the mortuary that afternoon to assist with the post-mortems. Other teams of detectives were allocated tasks including interviewing the respective spouses of the deceased and house to house enquiry teams. An office manager was appointed who would be responsible for the day to day running of the incident room.

Twead then wound the meeting up. "The next briefing will be at six o'clock sharp, no excuses for turning up late now everyone get cracking." He then shouted across the room for everyone to hear "before you go I want to see you in my office Latifeo."

Latifeo nodded in acknowledgement towards the DCI thinking what a prick, this is going to be about me coming in late this morning. He couldn't even ask me privately. He had to shout it out in front of the entire murder investigation squad. It's just typical of him to embarrass me.

He followed the DCI into his office but before he had a chance to even take a seat the DCI boomed. "Where the fuck was you this morning? You were the early turn detective and you were two hours late."

Latifeo had been expecting this and had his answer ready "I came in early and went into the interview room to do some paperwork because it's quiet there. I only found out when the desk sergeant saw me that you were looking for me." Latifeo had invented the story of being in the interview room in the cell block because it was soundproofed and there was no Station internal loudspeaker system in there to avoid unwanted audio being recorded when interviewing suspects on tape.

"Don't bullshit a bullshitter. This is a major enquiry and I don't want you taking the piss. That's why I've put you with that useless bitch Wallows so you can't pull any of your disappearing acts. You will have to keep an eye on her make sure that she doesn't do anything stupid or drop a bollock is that clear?"

Suitably admonished Latifeo replied "Yes sir" thinking to himself at least I get here sober not like you, you drunken git. He left the DCI's office with his tail between his legs and feeling deflated. He needed to build his self-esteem back up somehow. He needed to impose himself, assert his authority on someone, someone who couldn't really fight back, he instantly thought of Wallows. She was an easy target and the trip to the mortuary that afternoon would give him the perfect opportunity.

4

Don't Faint my Dear

Latifeo and Wallows were sitting in the mortuary office having a cup of tea with the mortuary technician. The room was quite small and scruffy with odd bits of mismatching furniture here and there. The smell coming from the post-mortem examination room was filling her nostrils with a strong pungent odour. Her heart was pounding, and she felt a little nauseous of the prospect of seeing a human body being dissected. Latifeo sensed Wallows unease and decided that this was his opportunity to put the wind up her to make her fuck up and hopefully she would be booted out of CID and he could return to his normal routine.

"You'll be okay" he said "You just need to know what's going to happen so that there are no surprises in store. I'll just run through the procedure with you."

"That's very kind of you" said Wallows with a smile.

He was giving the impression to everyone that he was trying to reassure Wallows about her first forthcoming post-mortem. No one knew that in reality what he really wanted was for her to fuck up good and proper and maybe pass out, scream or cross contaminate some samples. Something he could use to humiliate her when they were at the evening briefing with the ultimate goal of getting her removed from the enquiry so that he could go back to working on his own. He didn't like working with anyone else let alone a woman, it cramped his style. Some of the skives and dodges he did whilst working were off the menu with Wallows in tow.

"It's nothing like you see on the telly you know, it's not like Quincy with his little scalpel making small neat incisions. The first cut is with a big fuck off knife and it goes from just under the chin all the way down to the groin. Then the body is opened up to expose the ribs. It looks just like a side of beef that you would see hanging from a hook in an abattoir. The ribs are next, he snaps them one by one with a massive pair of shears and you can hear each of the bones cracking one by one."

Latifeo could see Wallows face begin to change colour. He could see her cheeks puffing out as if she was trying to prevent herself from throwing up. Latifeo was just about to push Wallows further to see if he could make her sick when he saw Steve the crime scene manager and Dave the SOCO walk into the office both dressed in white paper suits, overshoes, latex gloves and face masks. They were carrying two further suits which were thrown in the direction of the two officers shouting "Come on get these on and we're ready to go."

"I'll just go and hang my coat up in the cloakroom" Latifeo said "I'll be right back."

Whilst waiting for him to return Dave whispered in Wallows ear "Don't worry about anything you will be ok. I assume that dickhead has tried to wind you up? But all you need to do if you don't like anything is just turn your head away for a while and take a deep breath. We will do all the work. We won't ask you to do anything and if you want a good laugh to relax then watch Latifeo trying to struggle into his paper suit."

"Ok thanks I'll try but what is that awful strong smell?"

"That's formaldehyde. It's a constituent of embalming fluid that's injected into the dead bodies to stop them decaying. It's extremely potent, just smelling it will make your skin itch and irritate your eyes. What it does is it kills off all the bacteria that's present in your body, in fact it would just kill anything"

Dave then gave her an extra strong mint and said, "Put this in your mouth just before you enter the examination room it will help."

Just then Latifeo walked back in the room and began to un-wrap his paper suit which came in a clear plastic bag. Wallows did the same with hers and quite quickly donned it, zipped it up and then watched in amazement as Latifeo huffed and puffed and struggled like a madman to get his arms and legs into his suit. It looked like the reverse of someone trying to extricate themselves from a strait jacket. She now understood what the SOCO meant about having a laugh. Latifeo wasn't a particularly big man but he was a reasonable size and the SOCO's had obviously given him a suit that was ridiculously undersized for him. The legs of the suit finished halfway between his knees and his ankles, the arms were likewise way too short and after eventually pulling the front zip up everything was so tight that he looked like he was going to explode. Even his head and face were bright cherry red looking as if they were about to pop, Wallows didn't know if this was caused by the tightness of the suit or the exertion used to get into it, but he looked absolutely ludicrous.

She then realised how much more relaxed she felt, the nausea in her stomach had gone along with the butterflies and she walked into the examination room with a confident smile on her face. She also understood now why the SOCO had given her a mint because she could no longer smell the horrible chemical smell that had made her feel queasy before because It was masked by the extra strong menthol vapour of the sweet.

The SOCO's glanced up at the two officers as they entered the room. It was a good job they had face masks on thought Wallows because judging by their eyes when they saw the ridiculous looking Latifeo they were both pissing themselves. One of them looked at Wallows and gave her a quick wink of his eye.

The examination room contained four white ceramic tables. On one lay a white body bag that was still fully zipped up whilst on the furthest table was the body of the male murder victim who had been removed from the body bag. The SOCO's were busy photographing the clothing and then removing each item one by one, packaging, sealing and labelling them. Wallows was surprised at how quickly the SOCO's worked. They had obviously done this many times before and each SOCO knew what their part was in the process. Once the clothing was fully removed the pathologist began an external examination whilst all the time talking into a Dictaphone, the SOCO's keeping pace with him. They were photographing the relevant areas and locations on the body; again, it was obvious that they had also worked together on a number of occasions and everything seemed to function like clockwork.

The body was that of a middle aged white man. He was quite fat, especially his stomach which could best be described as a beer belly. The colour of the skin was white and pale at the top but a mixture of dark blues and purple and blotchy at the bottom. Wallows eager to take an active interest in the examination asked why this was. The pathologist tutted raised his eyebrows and gave her a derisory look and said, "Have you ever heard of gravity?"

"Of course, I have" she replied.

"Well" said the pathologist "the heart is no longer pumping blood round the body therefore the blood flows to the lowest part of the body. This body has been lying on his back and so the blood has flowed there which accounts for the discolouration."

"Thank you, sir," said Wallows.

"I am now going to begin the internal examination, you are not going to scream, or faint are you my dear" asked the pathologist condescendingly at the same time as producing an enormous looking knife. Wallows caught the smug look on Latifeo's face; he was obviously enjoying the fact that the pathologist was blatantly mocking her. Wallows didn't reply she just shook her head and decided to keep quiet for the rest of the exam. 'I only asked a simple question she thought and now he's treating me like the village idiot'.

The first cut was exactly as Latifeo had described it. Starting from just below his chin all the way down to his groin stopping slightly above where his missing manhood should have been, it looked surreal to see a knife inserted deeply into a human being and it was difficult to come to terms with it even though the body was dead it was still a gruesome sight. The body was then opened up giving access to the ribs. Wallows was determined to tough it out given the embarrassment she had already endured. She took a deep breath and tried not to show any trepidation or weakness even when the ribs were cut away making the most awful cracking sound. She was aware that Latifeo was still looking at her trying to see any signs of weakness. After the ribs were removed with what looked like large garden pruning shears, the internal organs were removed and examined one by one then handed to one of the SOCO's. They then weighed them in what looked like a butcher's scale and entered the weight of the relevant organ on a white board. Particular time and attention was paid to the neck area and a lot of long words that Wallows had never heard of were spoken into the Dictaphone.

Time was now going or seemed to be going super slow and Wallows thought there cannot be anything else left to do and it will soon be over. She had managed to come through it in reasonably good order aside from the disparaging and humiliating remarks that she had borne the brunt of. The pathologist then walked to the far side of the examination room and Wallows breathed a sigh of relief. It's over; I've done it, no throwing up or screaming. I've done it she thought.

Wallows said to one of the SOCO's "That was quite a horrific sight. I didn't think it was going to be as bad as that but at least it's over now, I've survived my first post-mortem."

"Yes, nearly finished" he said, "Well done."

"Nearly finished!" Wallows said incredulously "What else is there left to examine he has already been totally gutted."

Then she heard it behind her. She had taken her eyes off the body whist speaking to the SOCO's but as she turned back round towards the body she was suddenly awestruck at what she was looking at and what it was doing.

"Oh my god" she said and turned her gaze back to Latifeo just in time to see him turn grey, go completely glassy eyed and then pass out stone cold on the mortuary floor. The pathologist shook his head in abject disgust at the sight of Latifeo sprawled out on the mortuary floor. Wallows looked to the SOCO's for guidance.

"What shall we do with him?" She asked.

The CSM Steve looked at Latifeo flat out on the floor, thought about it for a moment and replied, "fuck him."

"He'll come around in a bit" added Dave "He's not banged his head or anything and you can see him breathing. We'll just crack on with the second PM" and that's exactly what happened. He was left in a crumpled heap on the mortuary floor.

Wallows took a deep breath and prepared herself for what was about to come. She had been reasonably okay for most of the post-mortem, but it was what was happening now that she wasn't prepared for and this part of the examination really unsettled her, it was the most frightening and stomach churning procedure imaginable. It was what had caused Latifeo to pass out; she had been quite proud of herself that she had coped with it especially given Latifeo's reaction. When both the post-mortems were complete Wallows and the SOCO's were in the mortuary office downing a much-needed cup of tea. Latifeo was still half dazed and woozy slumped in an armchair slowly coming back to life.

"I wanted to ask the pathologist some questions" Wallows said to Dave one of the SOCO's "but he was treating me like a bloody kid, it was quite embarrassing the way he spoke to me especially when I asked about the skin discoloration on the body I mean what sort of reply was that when he said have you heard of gravity?"

"He is a bit of a prick" said Dave "Mind you it's a wonder he could perform the PM at all. He was on the piss with the DCI Frank Twead last night, both of them bloody legless apparently, they're well known for it. The pair of them have been seen in some right drunken states over the years, god knows how they get away with it that's probably why he couldn't be bothered to explain hypostasis to you."

"Hypostasis, what on earth is that?" asked Wallows with a puzzled look on her face.

"It's the discoloration of the skin due to the pooling of blood in parts of the body following death. The skin becomes blotchy sometimes called livor mortis. It normally begins a couple of hours after death, the skin turns a dark blue or purple colour which is termed lividity then at around five or six hours the blotches merge together but if you press the skin it will turn white but later on after ten to twelve hours the lived colour remains even if you apply pressure."

Enthralled Wallows replied, "That's fascinating, does that mean that it can be used to determine the time of death?"

"It can be but it's a bit of a crude and inaccurate method. The best evidence obtained from examination of the hypostasis is to determine if the body has been moved after death for example if a body is moved after hypostasis has set in and placed in a different position or turned over then the discoloration would be in the wrong place"

"Thanks for that Dave that was really interesting. Why couldn't the pathologist have answered me that way?"

"Apart from him being somewhat pretentious, thinking that he is a cut above us he has probably got the mother of all hangovers and he can't wait to get back on the piss again but even given all that, the way he spoke to you was particularly rude and condescending but don't let it bother you it's just the way he is, now what else was it you wanted to ask?"

"It concerns the swabs he took from the bloke's arse. Why did he do that?"

Dave replied "He will have taken the swabs to establish any sexual offences. He is supposed to do a high one inside his arse, a low one and a perianal one that means near the anus, but he's so piss poor, if you noticed he just took them from one place on the outside of the anus, he's just to idle to bother to do them properly."

"Thanks Dave" said Shirley "So what happens with the swabs then, I assume they go on the DNA database?"

"Yes, that's right. They'll be searched against the main database and then if needed sometimes against the immigration database, and against the police elimination database."

Wallows looked surprised "I didn't think they were allowed to do that. I thought the police DNA database was only used to eliminate unidentified DNA at a scene. To eliminate traces accidently left at a scene by an officer?"

Dave smiled and said "They are not supposed to search against them. They tell you when you give your DNA for inclusion, that it won't be used for searching crime scene samples but believe you me they are."

The pathologist then entered the room and began without any introduction to brief the team on the initial findings. "The conclusion from the PM together with the crime scene examination indicates that the male deceased died due to exsanguination as a result of major trauma to the genital area. The cause of death for the female is compressive traumatic asphyxia due to cracked ribs causing the lungs to haemorrhage as a result of pressure on the upper torso. No other wounds or trauma were evident on either cadaver. Swabs and blood samples will be sent for toxicology and deoxyribonucleic acid testing. DCI Twead will be notified when those results are known but I don't expect them to alter the initial findings."

The pathologist then left the room without a further word, not even allowing any questions to be asked or thanking the team for their help. Shirley thought the lads were right when they said he was a bit of a prick. She would have liked to ask the pathologist what all the long words meant and if he could explain the cause of death in language she could understand but she was not going to give him another chance to humiliate her, so she kept quiet.

She looked towards Steve with a puzzled expression "What on earth did all that mean?"

Steve replied "In plain language what he said was, that the guy bled to death from the injury in his groin i.e. his cock being chopped off. The technical term is exsanguination and the female was crushed to death by the weight of the bloke on her back causing her ribs to crack and puncture her lungs."

"You did alright today" Dave said to Shirley "much better than that dipstick" looking in the direction of Latifeo who was now beginning to come around.

"I didn't feel too bad except right at the very end. I couldn't believe what he did with that circular grinder or whatever it was" Shirley replied.

"That's called a vibrating saw. It cuts bone but not tissue. When he's done a complete circle round the skull, he uses a small chisel to separate the two halves of the skull, so he can then scoop out the brain, it is the most gruesome part of the PM I suppose."

They then watched as Latifeo raced to the sink as he began to wretch and heave having listened to the description of the procedure that had caused him to pass out.

"We're going back to the nick" said the SOCO's "Can you make sure that he cleans the mess up from the sink before you leave otherwise the technicians won't let us use this office again?"

Shirley nodded and said "Okay, see you later."

5

Not Such a Big Deal

The incident room at Stourbridge Police Station began to fill up, it was nearly six o'clock and everyone involved in the murder enquiry had assembled in the makeshift briefing room. The room wasn't nearly big enough to comfortably accommodate the amount of staff that was crammed into it. The room was normally used as a parade room where the handful of duty shift officers would assemble at the start of their tour of duty and receive any criminal intelligence and get their allocated tasks and beat areas for the day. People settled down and sat wherever they could, on top of desks filing cabinets, or anything they could perch on. Sat at the table at the head of the room was the detective chief inspector together with the superintendent and a detective sergeant.

The briefing began with the DCI first calling for quiet, he was obviously not comfortable with being in charge of a murder investigation with the responsibility, duties and moreover the pitfalls and the scope for possible cock-ups that it entailed so he overcompensated by being as loud and officious as he could be.

Twead began "The briefings from now on will be at nine am and five pm. I will not tolerate any excuses for none or late attendance. I am the senior investigating officer. DS Courtan is the incident room office manager, you will liaise with him to receive your actions and Superintendent Gibbs will be the overall strategic commander. I want you to be succinct and to the point at these briefings, no waffling or time wasting. We will start with the scene examination."

Steve, the crime scene manager stood up and began to outline the significant findings from the forensic examination of the murder scene.

"The bodies were reported to the police control at 04:00hrs. I arrived at the scene at 04:30hrs. The scene is the main carpark at Stourbridge Park. It is a well-used and maintained park with plenty of facilities for children and adults during daylight hours. However, in recent years from late evening it is well known as a local dogging site. I don't think I need to explain what dogging entails. It would appear that the two deceased were engaged in some form of sexual activity. There was a little warmth left in the bodies and the onset of rigor mortis was just beginning to manifest. This would indicate that death occurred sometime yesterday evening. I would estimate somewhere in the region of ten or eleven o'clock. Please be aware everyone that this is purely estimation and cannot be relied on to be totally accurate, but it does gives us something to work to."

Steve paused then continued "The pathologist Dr Chuman concurred with this approximation of the time of death. They were both in a state of semi undress with their underwear around their ankles and they were bent over the bonnet of a car. The female was pinned to the bonnet underneath the male. No sign of any violent struggle was evident, and no defence wounds or injuries were visible on the victims this would indicate that both victims were caught unaware and the male may have been incapacitated by some form of blunt trauma to the back of the head, this will need to be verified at the post-mortems. The male person had however suffered major trauma to the groin area, his penis having been cut off. The resultant wound appeared to be uniform and neat indicating a sharp implement such as a Stanley knife or something similar. A large pooling of blood was evident immediately beneath the wound which means the male was probably alive during this period of blood loss. The penis as far as I am aware has not been found. Various swabs and fibre tapings have been taken from the scene and the bodies; the results of which will be fast tracked at the forensic lab."

44

"Thanks Steve" said the DCI. "Now we will have the post-mortems, Latifeo if you please."

Latifeo swallowed nervously and stood up. He had been desperately trying to work his way round his pathetic performance in the mortuary and make it appear as if he had actually done some detective work. He began to describe the supposed extensive house to house enquires he had made and the comprehensive supervision of the crime scene examination.

"Latifeo" boomed the DCI derisorily "you have been asked to brief us on the PM nothing else, so get on with it."

Having already seen the pathologist in the Chequers Pub in Stourbridge within the last half an hour, Twead knew full well the result of the PM and he was also well aware of Latifeo fainting during the first PM and knew he wouldn't have a clue what the results were, but it gave him the opportunity to embarrass and demean him in front of an audience.

"Yes, sir with regards to the PM, I detailed WPC Wallows to be the reporting officer."

"Latifeo" he boomed once again "you were the one I designated to take charge at the PM. I did not give you permission to pass it onto a split arse WPC. I will see both you and Wallows in my office straight after this meeting." Even for Twead the use of the term split arse was way over the top this was a throwback from the sixties and it caused a few eyebrows to be lifted including those of the superintendent who decided to let it slide for the present.

Latifeo sat down having been suitably humiliated. Wallows stood up and said, "I could brief everyone with reference to the PM result sir."

The DCI then began to rant and criticise the standard of professionalism of the pair of them indicating Latifeo was falling far short of what was expected of him and that for Wallows to try and give the PM result was utter nonsense because she was inexperienced and only a policewoman who was getting fanciful ideas about her capabilities. It was said in such a pompous embarrassing manner that she found herself once again totally humiliated. This had been twice within a matter of a few hours.

Wallows sat back down on her seat aware that everyone was looking at her and that she would be the butt of further locker room jokes. The DCI then gave the initial PM report to the assembled personnel himself, or as much as he could remember from the conversation he had whilst having a drink or several drinks in the pub with his mate Dr Chuman.

The resulting effect of the PM examination led most of the incident room personnel to surmise that the male was murdered by some nutter or jealous husband perhaps and the weight of him on the females back caused her accidental death. Everyone secretly hoped that it was some random nutter meaning it would be harder to solve and the length of the investigation and the unlimited overtime it bought with it would last considerably longer.

The next to give their report were the search team. Their task had been to search the area around and in the vicinity of the crime scene. The sergeant in charge of the search team gave details of how the area was divided into sectors and how the position of each of the recovered exhibits was plotted in relation to the crime scene. Among the numerous exhibits recovered for forensic examination were cigarette butts, drinks containers, beer bottles and cans etc. Basically, anything that could yield DNA or fingerprints. One exhibit that he was particularly pleased about was a pornographic magazine found in the bushes. This could yield fingerprints and DNA as could the other exhibits, but the most exciting aspect of this exhibit was a clear footwear impression on the front cover. SOCO had identified the impression as belonging to a Magnum safety boot. These were quite a popular brand but apparently there was enough detail there to compare it against any suspect's footwear.

"That's something to start with. I want you Oli to co-ordinate forensic submissions and update me on the progress and results."

Latifeo smiled and nodded his head in agreement; his mind already racing trying to figure out how he could use this to his advantage. Only trouble he thought was 'I don't know jack shit about forensics.'

"Who's the team liaising with the victim's spouses? We'll have you next"

Detective Sergeant Grant Courtan stood up to address the room. In addition to his duties as office manager he was also expected to conduct some enquires himself. He was a well-respected capable detective with 22 years' service and he had worked on a number of serious investigations. He was popular with his colleagues; his Achilles heel however was his well-known attraction to the fairer sex; this had led to the break-up of his marriage some years earlier. He considered himself to be quite a lady's man and he had a somewhat inflated pompous opinion of himself where the ladies were concerned. The other member of his team had been recruited into the murder incident room because of her training as a family liaison officer or FLO for short.

An FLO is an experienced officer who has been trained to communicate with the family of a deceased person who dies in traumatic circumstances. Their responsibility is to gather material from the family in a manner which contributes to the investigation plus provide support in a sensitive and compassionate manner in accordance with the needs of the investigation. Grant had not been happy with being paired up with anyone for two reasons, the first being that it took the limelight off him and he liked to be the centre of attention and secondly it cramped his style in some of his non-police activities, so he decided to utilise her as little as possible and would give her mundane office jobs to keep her out of his way. They had been assigned to deal with the spouse of the deceased female.

Grant Courtan detailed the result of their enquires. "The husband of the deceased, Trevor Pickes has told us that his wife was not at home the previous night when he returned from work late; he works for the local council as a housing repair officer, so he retired to bed. He only became concerned when he awoke this morning and she wasn't there. He hadn't reported her missing as he assumed she had gone for a night out with one of her friends and for whatever reason had stayed the night. She normally went out every Thursday but had always come home. He thought she may have gone straight to work. She was a teacher at the local high school."

"How have you confirmed the identity?" the DCI asked Courtan.

"We have used personal papers on the body and photographs at the address for the initial I.D. He was then taken to the mortuary to do a visual confirmation of his wife Claire."

The SOCO's looked at each other in an air of resignation and disbelief. They both realised that this must have been done before the post-mortem. This would therefore compromise any trace forensic evidence recovered which could prove crucial especially if the husband were to become a suspect.

Courtan concluded with "A statement has not been taken yet. He was too distraught, so this has been arranged for tomorrow."

The team assigned to the male deceased were two detectives both long in service but unfortunately short in intelligence. DC Frank Fergas and DC Robert Peeves. They always teamed up together on major enquires for a number of reasons; they were both good friends and It would allow them both to do anything they wished to, no matter how inappropriate or unethical their actions were, sometimes bordering on illegal. Police rules and regulations certainly went straight out of the window. They were both massive binge drinkers and even bigger grab a granny fanatics; they were famed for trying to shag anything that moved no matter how ugly or gross. In fact, the uglier the better as this gave them a greater chance of success.

There were a number of nicknames the duo had including dumb and dumber for obvious reasons, mincer and marcher because of the way they walked; one would swing his arms like he was on a parade ground whilst Mincer walked like he was on the catwalk and trying to hold something between his butt cheeks. Another popular nickname for them was Laurel and Hardy, this was based initially on their appearance as one was short and fat the other being thin and puny plus they were known as a pair of clowns. But the one most commonly used behind their back was invariably dumb and dumber.

Frank Fergas stood up and gave the briefing. "The deceased Fraser was an ex pub landlord who had quit the profession under a cloud concerning financial irregularities. This had apparently left him with a few enemies from various individuals who had been left out of pocket. He had been working locally as a barman and he and his wife were living literally hand to mouth. He had told his wife that he was working yesterday evening and was expected home around midnight. When he failed to show his wife assumed he'd had a lock in at the pub where he worked, and she went to bed. Initial identification had been done by personal papers on the body. We would have taken her to the mortuary for formal I.D., but she was too upset so that has been arranged for tomorrow am."

The DCI was intrigued by the possibility of enemies of Fraser and this would fit in nicely with the current theory that he was the targeted victim and Claire was an innocent but unlucky consequence. The briefing having concluded, all the teams were awaiting their allocated actions. This was standard in a large-scale enquiry; everyone being given tasks on an action sheet which when complete were updated and fed back into the incident room.

Once Wallows and Latifeo had received their allocated actions they both sheepishly stood outside the DCI's office waiting to go in and get their impending bollocking. On entering the DCI's office, they found him remarkably calm, he invited them both to take a seat. Both Latifeo and Wallows felt uncomfortable at this more relaxed change of attitude and they both knew some bombshell was about to be dropped.

"The reason I have asked to talk to you is because of the direction this case is taking. It is becoming clear that the real victim was Fraser, the females demise was a consequence of Fraser's murder. He was known to have enemies with his recent financial problems, so we find out who his enemies were, and bingo case solved. We are not dealing with a serial killer so I'm downgrading the operation and

49

reducing staff numbers. I'm cutting the number of enquiry teams and pulling the covert observation teams on potential dogging sites. I am trimming the team down to a more investigative core led operation. This means you pair will return to normal duties. Oli you are the late turn detective starting tonight and WPC Wallows you are the late turn WPC also starting tonight."

"But sir, I've waited a long time for this attachment and I've only been here two days" Wallows replied.

The DCI stood up and stared Wallows in the face and with a look that said 'How dare you question my decision' he snarled. "We are dealing with real police work here and it needs to be done by real policemen not some split arse that is only good enough to make the tea and parade around the office with a shiny new handbag."

Humiliation complete Wallows and Latifeo turned around and left the office. Wallows was almost in tears borne out of frustration having been degraded once again. Latifeo felt slight relief, he had expected much more retribution given his recent performance and he could still however use this to his advantage after all his wife didn't know he had been taken off the murder squad and he could use this to see his girlfriend more often.

6

Making an Entrance

Wallows had been teamed up with a probationary constable on the late shift. She knew the score and that she was baby-sitting in effect. It was a pairing no one really wanted and that was why it had been given to her. She was aware that they would be tasked with all the boring basic jobs and every call where a female was involved which would include the policeman's nightmare callouts referred to as domestics. They would normally involve a husband or partner beating up their wife or girlfriend. The general scenario would then be to arrest the husband or boyfriend, get him to the nick and book him in start the mountain of paperwork. Then halfway through the wife or girlfriend would drop the charges, the paperwork would go in the bin, he would be released, go back home and beat her up again. She was still determined to get back into CID but for now she was stuck on this shift with this spotty teenage useless probationer who was literally straight out of training school and still wet behind the ears.

They were on the high street when the control room operator gave them their next job. They had already been given a number of tasks via the control room, including beggars making a nuisance and some illegal parking. All of which had been a waste of time as both the beggars and the vehicles had moved on prior to them arriving on scene. This call they were now given to deal with was a domestic dispute. The original call had come in from a next-door neighbour who could hear shouting and screaming from the adjacent house. The location was a run-down rough council estate not far from the centre of town and Wallows knew the area well. She answered the call and gave an eta of ten minutes. As they walked to the scene the probationer looked a little uneasy. Wallows tried to put him at ease by running through their plan of action.

"The first thing to do is to speak to the neighbour to obtain details of what has happened. Then we will knock on the door, hopefully it will have all died down by then. Give them both words of advice and if it's all calm leave them to it. We'll then go back to the nick write it up and have a meal break."

"Okay" replied the spotty teenager looking slightly more relaxed.

As they approached the scene this plan went to rat shit straight away. As they neared the two adjacent properties they could see the occupants of the informant's address standing on their doorstep and it sounded as if world war three was erupting in the house next door. They quickened their pace mindful that a number of local residents were watching them. This was to give the impression that they actually gave a shit and were responding as fast as they could to someone in trouble. As they knocked on the door the neighbour who had reported the incident shouted that there were young kids in there. There was no answer from the initial knock on the door, so they knocked again. All the time the continual sound of screaming and crying and the crashing of furniture becoming louder and louder, still no answer.

A crowd had gathered outside, and they were now becoming quite agitated. "There are kids in that house don't just stand there like a pair of wet cunts, do something" they shouted.

"We need to get in there" said Wallows, "We'll have to kick the door in."

The probationer took it upon himself to have a go at bashing the door in. He took a few steps back, steadied himself and then ran full pelt at the door hitting it with all his might. This resulted in him rebounding off the door, losing his balance and falling over the small wooden fence that separated the two houses. He then collided into and flattened the neighbour, the one who had made the initial call to the police. She was now flat out on the floor with the probationer lying on top of her. The door was totally undamaged not a single dent or even the slightest of scratches. The probationer stood up embarrassed and red faced aware that everyone was watching him. The adrenalin and anger were now pumping through his body and leaving the informant neighbour poleaxed on the floor he stood up clenched his fists, took a deep breath, stuck his chest out, and attempted to vault the small wooden picket fence that he had just fell over in order to have another go at the door.

Unfortunately, he didn't actually clear the small fence but instead caught his foot in between two of the wooden vertical slats causing one of his size nine boots to get wedged stuck. His momentum carried him through the fence and with a splinter and a crash the fence was totally demolished. The probationer was heading face first for the garden path his foot still wedged in a segment of the fence. He attempted to put his arms out to break his fall, but he was too slow. His face or more specifically his nose cracked off the pavement with a sickening thud.

When he stood up he looked a pitiful sight, his crisply pressed new uniform was torn tattered and filthy and his helmet had flown off and was floating in the ornamental duck pond in the front garden. His face was flushed and like the colour of beetroot and he felt completely humiliated in front of this jeering hostile crowd. His nose was totally smashed all over his face with blood pouring out of it and down onto his chin and reaching his uniform. Part of the wooden fence he had obliterated, was still stuck round his lower leg. The amassed crowd of onlookers stared in amazement not knowing whether to laugh or cry it was beginning to resemble a scene worthy of the keystone cops.

Wallows couldn't believe her eyes when she saw him preparing to have another go at shoulder charging the door. This time he took a much longer run up. He went back as far as the pavement and took a few deep breaths. He made a facial expression similar to a New Zealander all black rugby player doing the Hakka and screamed at the top of his voice. The crowd were transfixed in eager anticipation and began to chant as he made his charge at the door. The surreal sight of a member of her majesty's finest, dishevelled covered in blood and snot and screaming like a banshee sprinting as fast as he possibly could towards the door. As he neared the door his pace increased, and the crowd thought with this speed and aggression, he is either going to smash the door or himself to smithereens. Two more steps and he would be crashing through the door, the screaming reaching a crescendo and with a mighty heave he launched himself into the air letting out a final ear shattering scream. The crowd all held their breath as this young policeman was flying through the air like some sort of demented super hero. He finally in full flight reached the door at the exact same moment as it swung wide open having been unlocked by one of the occupants.

It was a young frightened looking little girl, but it was too late for the probationer to stop. He continued on with his flight straight through the open door like superman going over the top of the young girl's head who was now stood holding the door ajar looking up into the air with astonishment as a policeman came flying over her head. He then smashed full on into the wooden balustrade at the foot of the staircase which he then rebounded off and succeeded in knocking himself out cold. He now lay completely prostrate and spread-eagled on the hallway floor. The crowd began to shout and cheer, hysterical laughter rang out, people clutching their stomachs. They were laughing so much tears running down their cheeks and then the crowd began to clap.

Wallows was stunned for a moment unable to move or decide what to do, she only came back to reality when she realised that the shouting and screaming coming from inside the house had intensified even more. She looked at the frightened little girl standing in the doorway as she entered the house and scrambled over the body of the probationer still flat out on the floor and headed in the direction of the screaming. At the end of the hallway a door led into the main room of the house from where the screaming was emanating. As Wallows pushed the door open she saw a woman being held by her throat pinned up against the wall, her feet dangling off the floor. She looked to be in an awful mess, bloodied and bruised, the room looked like a bomb had gone off, broken furniture everywhere with empty beer bottles littered all over the place.

The owner of the hand that was pinning the woman to the wall belonged to a huge brute of a man. He was unshaven, scruffy with long unkempt greasy hair, his massive arms covered in tattoos, sporting a big pot beer belly hanging over his trousers. In his free right hand was an empty beer bottle that he held by its neck, this was raised in the air above the poor terrified woman who screamed as it was brought down with tremendous force and smashed on the top of her head, glass shattering everywhere. Blood began to cascade down her face and over her brow into her eyes; his hand was now firmly gripping the remains of the bottle by the neck and he pulled his arm back preparing to smash the jagged end of the broken bottle into the screaming woman's face.

Wallows had gotten close enough to make a lunge for his arm and she managed to get hold of the one that was holding the smashed beer bottle and although she had managed to prevent him from shoving it into the woman's face the guy was so strong that he began to toss and throw her about whilst she clung on. He smashed her body against the living room wall, time and time again, but she was determined to hold on to his arm to prevent him using the bottle to slice open the terrified women's face. She was being flung from pillar to post like a rag doll.

"Drop the bottle" Wallows screamed. But he was like a man possessed, he slammed her against a display cabinet, the glass smashing and the contents spilling onto the floor and breaking. Wallows realised she could not hold on to his arm much longer and he wasn't going to drop the bottle, so she sunk her teeth into his arm and bit down as hard as she possibly could until she could feel bone against her teeth.

The monster of a man shrieked in pain, let go of the bottle and with his free hand aimed a punch at Wallows head. He didn't connect properly but caught her with enough force to send her reeling across the floor and into a dining room table with enough force to cause it to collapse. Slightly dazed and before she could get to her feet he was standing directly over her. He had lifted the television set over his head and was shouting "You fucking pig." He prepared to bring the TV crashing down on her head. Wallows instinctively curled up into a ball protecting her head with her arms waiting for the impact. The tattooed monster was then suddenly and violently shoved into the wall causing the TV to crash onto the floor, it was the probationer. He had come around and had charged into him and was now on top of him raining punches on the back of his head.

Wallows grabbed her handbag and removed her handcuffs before jumping on the back of the monster and managed to put one cuff on one of his massive wrists. The probationer took hold of his other arm and tried to move it towards the handcuffs, but the guy was too strong. Unbelievably the guy then stood up with the probationer hanging off one arm and Wallows off the other. He then started swinging them round bouncing them off the walls, neither of them able to reach their radios to summon help. This is getting desperate thought Wallows he is going to beat us both to a pulp, then suddenly from nowhere the bruised battered and blood-soaked wife jumped on the monsters back and began digging her long sharp fingernails into his face leaving long deep scratches streaked with blood all over his cheeks and brow.

This proved enough of a distraction to force him to the floor and eventually between the three of them managed to get the remaining handcuff on. All three of them sat on his back keeping him firmly pinned down whilst they got their breath back. With the monster now shackled and incapacitated on the floor they summoned a police vehicle to take him into custody and began to regain their composure. The monster's wife then took full advantage of her husband's incapacity and began to literally kick the shit out of him, kicking him violently and repeatedly about the head.

Wallows and the probationer looked at each other as if deciding what to do about it. They realised that what they were trained to do and what they were supposed to do which was to restrain the woman, after all they had a sworn duty to protect everyone alike. They hesitated for a moment, looked at each other and then said simultaneously "Fuck It" and joined in; aiming a few well-placed kicks to his head and groin and together with his wife the three of them gave him the beating he deserved. When they had finished kicking the living daylights out of him and he lay there battered and bruised and covered in blood with most of the fight and resistance from him gone they stopped. Wallows got the monsters details from his wife, so she could get a head start on the necessary paperwork and checks that had to be done for all prisoners. The prisoner transport van had arrived and as Wallows left she told the monsters wife that she would be back later that evening to take a statement and he was then manhandled into the back of a police van.

Once in the police Station they waited in the queue of prisoners and officers waiting to be booked in by the custody officer. "You can have this one" said Wallows "as it is your first arrest you just need to tell the custody officer the circumstances of what happened and that he is under arrest for assault. Obviously don't tell him we kicked the shit out of him after he was handcuffed."

When it was their turn they went in the custody office. It was a small room with a large desk behind which the custody officer stood whilst he listened to the officer's report and if he accepted the charge which was nearly always a formality he completed the custody record and the prisoner was led through a steel door leading to the main cell block. The custody officer beckoned them to come in, it wasn't someone Wallows recognised, and she was quite surprised how short the sergeant was. He was very broad, but he could barely see over the top of the charge desk. Wallows and the probationer stood either side of the prisoner and related the facts to him who accepted the charge. He took a long knowing look at the arresting officers with their dishevelled uniforms, the redness of their faces and their generally unkempt knackered appearance. He could picture the scene in his mind, he envisaged two young inexperienced officers who were simply doing their job to the best of their ability and had received a battering at the hands of this huge toe rag.

"I assume he was a bit of a handful" asked the custody officer, both arresting officers nodded to confirm this.

He then addressed the prisoner and said "I am accepting the charge of assault, you will now be taken into custody whilst the officers complete their enquires. Do you understand?" The prisoner made no reply just gave him an aggressive stare. The custody officer took up his pen, looked at the forms in front of him, looked at the prisoner and said "Name?"

The prisoner raised his head, looked straight at the custody officer staring him straight in the eyes and replied slowly and deliberately "Fuck off."

The custody officer did not bat an eyelid or indeed give any reaction at all, but simply placed his pen back on the desk and looked up at the arresting officers and asked, "Do you have all his details?"

"Yes sarge, his name is Stan Gutthy. We have all his relevant details including criminal records office number." Wallows replied.

The custody officer then stood up to reveal an absolute giant of a man. Wallows had assumed that he was already standing but he had obviously been sitting down behind the charge desk on a tiny chair giving the impression he was quite a small man, but it was in fact the exact opposite. He was so huge it was if the room seemed to descend into darkness when he came from behind the desk and approached the prisoner whom he completely dwarfed and whose cockiness had now been replaced with a look of horror especially when he was picked up unceremoniously by the scruff of his neck and dragged like a sack of rubbish through the steel door into the cell block. Wallows and the probationer stood there complexly awestruck at the sight of what they had just witnessed, the huge violent thug that had been swinging both of them around from his massive arms had gotten a taste of his own medicine he had been lifted off his feet by someone twice the size of him, the astonished frightened look on the prisoners face showed that this was something he had not experienced before.

For the next few minutes all that could be heard from the cell block was crash, bang, wallop and the occasional thud of something crashing into the wall. Then it all became quiet and the custody officer returned from the cell block and straightened his tie which was slightly askew, sat behind his desk and he was supplied with the necessary prisoner details for the completion of the custody record. When all the required paperwork was completed Wallows and the probationer retired to the police canteen for a well-deserved cup of tea over which they discussed the circumstances of the arrest.

"My name is Ben by the way" said the probationer "Ben Whyte. Now tell me what happened in the custody block. Is it what I think happened?"

"I hope so" said Wallows "Did you see the look on his face when the custody officer stood up, I thought Gutthy was going to shit himself. He's the biggest bloke I have ever seen, he totally dwarfed that monster who threw us around from pillar to post. I know you are young in service, but I hope you realise that if we were ever questioned about it then we saw nothing untoward take place, a bit like when we kicked the shit out of him after we got the handcuffs on him. We do what we have to do and sometimes we have to bend the truth a little do you understand"? Ben nodded his head to signify he understood and they both continued to drink their tea in silence. Tea finished Wallows left to return to the address to obtain a complainant statement leaving Ben to complete the rest of the paperwork.

Latifeo walked down the garden path leading to his girlfriend's house. This is fucking great he thought, I'm not working on the murder enquiry which means I don't have to do jack shit, but the wife still thinks I'm working on the murder incident room, so I can come and go as I please. He knocked on the door and waited, when there was no answer he knocked the door again a bit louder this but time still no answer. He knocked a third time and eventually he heard movement from inside. When Sam answered she said, "What the fuck are you doing here I've told you before you must let me know when you're coming around."

"Well I'm here now" he said as he invited himself in and walked into the hallway. Latifeo thought how great she looked even though he had come around unexpectedly and caught her on the hop; she still looked stunning, hair, make-up, sexy lingerie the works.

"I've got an hour before I have to be back at the nick, we've got time for a quickie."

Sam replied "I'm not in the mood I've got a headache and I'm tired. I just want to go to bed. It'll have to be another time and make sure you call next time, so I can make sure no one's watching. I don't want the neighbours talking."

Latifeo wasn't happy with this and did his best to talk Sam round into changing her mind but she was adamant, and it became clear that she wouldn't budge so Latifeo reluctantly agreed and gave Sam an unwelcome peck on the cheek and left. He was feeling a bit pissed off as he made his way back to the nick. He had felt extremely horny and had been looking forward to bending his girlfriend over and relieving himself. She's probably coming on that's why she was so tetchy. I'll just have to go back and shag the wife tonight he thought.

Sam checked that she had locked the front door, turned the downstairs light off and made her way back to bed. She took off her negligee and hung it on the door hook and admired herself in the full-length mirror. She was very proud of her looks and her figure. She ran her fingers through her hair and plumped it up, checked her make-up and slid back into bed.

"You can come out now" she shouted.

The walk-in wardrobe door opened and out stepped Grant Courtan.

"Has he pissed off yet?" he asked.

"Yes, he says he is going back to the nick but that was a close one. I've told him to call me next time, but I don't know if he will take any notice of what I've said."

Grant thought about it and said, "I'll make sure his movements are monitored whilst he's on duty that should give us a bit of warning."

Grant decided to get back into bed and resume what he was doing before being disturbed by that insufferable needy little prick Latifeo.

7

Gas, Gas, Gas

Wallows was awake early, she was still bruised and battered from last night's altercation with Stan Gutthy, the horrible twat of a wife beater. She cringed when she remembered the fiasco of gaining access to the address and the idiotic buffoonery of Ben Whyte, the green as grass probationer. He did step up to the mark when it started to get rough though so credit where it's due. They had given that monster of a bloke a hell of a kicking when they had eventually gotten the better of him. She smiled to herself when she recalled the image of Gutthy being lifted of the floor by the giant custody officer, the terrified look on Gutthy's face was one she would remember for a long time it had lifted hers and Ben's spirits to see him get his comeuppance.

She eased her aching body out of bed unable to remove the mental image emblazoned in her memory of Ben flying through the air as the front door opened and knocking himself out when he hit the foot of the stairs. She thought how she could handle it differently next time. There were strict guidelines laid down of how to deal with a confrontation which basically dictated that the minimal amount of force should be used and that is what they had done, they had followed the rules but following this procedure had resulted in both her and Ben receiving a bit of a pasting. Pepper spray next time she thought stuff the protocol, just gas the cunt straight away and be done with it.

Suddenly her mobile phone began to ring, unusual for this time of the morning she mused as she dragged her aching body across the room to the dressing table where her phone was on charge. She could see Latifeo calling on her screen and thought why on earth he is ringing me, especially at this time in the morning; it's not even six o'clock yet. An excited Latifeo blurted out excitedly "We're   back in"

Wallows couldn't quite understand what he meant "What do you mean we are back in, back in where? What on earth are you talking about?"

Latifeo still shouting at a fever pitch said "There's been another murder in the park, same as the last one. A man and a woman killed at the same dogging spot shagging over the bonnet of a car it looks like the same M.O as the first one. Everybody is being re-called back to the enquiry; looks like we've got a serial killer on our hands. I'll see you at the nick as quick as you can get there" he then rung off.

That's a result thought Wallows, to get off shift work and straight back into CID in the murder incident room. I just don't think I could take many more beatings like last night. She hurriedly got ready and made her way into work.

Wallows arrived at the police Station shortly after seven o'clock. She felt good to be out of uniform and back in plain clothes especially with a murder incident room running. It also meant that she was unlikely to be involved with another incident like last nights; the place was already rammed to the rafters with personnel from across the entire force. She had never seen so many police in one place before. The buzz of excitement could be felt in the air, the mood had changed completely, and the investigation had escalated from trying to catch a murderer to a serial killer. This is not now an interesting and serious local murder but what could be the start of a series of murders attracting national attention.

The instructions for the assembled staff were to remain in the nick to await a briefing by the DCI. The gossip among the assembled staff was the arrival of the force detective superintendent and the furore that had been heard from the office of the DCI. Rumour had it from the staff who had been in the Station when the superintendent arrived was that the DCI was getting the biggest bollocking of his life and they were right. The detective superintendent had received the early morning call from the chief constables press office and had been told in no uncertain terms to get his arse into gear and supervise that useless twat Frank Twead and take charge of the operation. The national press was already all over this and the last thing the force needed was more bad publicity. They had recently been slated not only by the dailies but also by the coroner in a recent investigation whereby all the CID from across the division was on the piss at a re-arranged party and an acting CID officer had been on call. This officer was known for his enthusiasm, but he lacked any investigatory skills and was famed for a number of stupid statements including asking a pathologist at a post-mortem examination if the deceased was alive at the time of death. The pathologist had looked at him in at the time with a puzzled expression and decided to shake his head in disbelief and just ignore the question. No one had ever fully fathomed out what he meant, and this statement had as quickly as lightning spread throughout the force.

The briefing had been delayed due to the detective superintendent's involvement and had been re-scheduled for nine-thirty. Latifeo and Wallows were at a loose end, they like the rest of the staff had come into work early as instructed but until they received their tasks from the briefing they were left kicking their heels. From the end of the corridor coming from a room used to show CCTV and other digital images they could hear the sound of laughter and giggling. Latifeo beckoned to Wallows to follow him down the corridor to find out what all the excitement was about. As they walked in they could see a large projector screen in one corner of the room, it was playing a clip from You Tube. The assembled crowd were in fits of uncontrollable laughter as they watched the antics on screen.

Wallows stood there mouth agog with astonishment as she saw what was being shown on the screen, she began to feel herself colour up in embarrassment. The clip showed Wallows and the probationer

65

Ben Whyte trying to gain access to the premises at the scene of lasts nights domestic. It culminated with the sight of Ben flying through the air straight through the open door and colliding with the bottom of the stairwell knocking himself clean out. The clip must have been taken by one of the onlookers on their mobile phone thought Wallows and uploaded to You Tube. At least I didn't come out of it looking too bad, but Ben is never going to live that down. He is stuck with that for the rest of his career, but I have to admit it was incredibly funny. The video clip had been put on a loop, so it was continuously running time after time. Wallows had seen enough, she decided to seek out Ben to pre-warn him about the video.

Ben was in the parade room when she found him. This was the room that was now being used as the temporary incident room, he was busy doing paperwork. He like Wallows looked a bit the worse for wear after last night's fight with the wife beater.

"Is that the paperwork from last night's arrest?" asked Wallows as she approached Ben.

He looked up at her "Yes. I'm nearly finished."

"What did you charge him with in the end? To my way of thinking it should be grievous bodily harm. When I went back and saw his wife to get a statement from her I saw what a mess she was in. He had really knocked her about something terrible. She couldn't see out of one of her eyes, it was completely closed and swollen, and she has lost a couple of teeth. But I assume as normal the custody officer would go for the easier option and only authorise actual bodily harm instead."

"They wouldn't authorise anything" Ben said somewhat dejectedly "his wife came in the nick while I was processing him and dropped the charge. I even asked about the assault on me and you, but I was told that unless either of us had a broken bone or some other serious injury it wouldn't be worth it, so I had to let him go. He was laughing his head off when I showed him out."

"Unbelievable" shouted an exasperated Wallow's. "After that bloody fight and the hassle, we had and all the bruises and punches we got. He walks away Scott free."

"Not exactly Scott free" said Ben "I think they must have given him a good battering in custody. He looked a right bloody mess when he was released from the lock up."

Wallows replied, "Well at least that's some consolation I suppose."

"A bit I guess" said Ben "but I think he is used to being in some pretty serious scraps. I did some digging into his previous convictions, apparently he is a bit of an enforcer and he works for local gangsters and thugs to put the frighteners on people or inflict some sort of beating."

Wallows then went on to give Ben the heads up on the You Tube clip, but he was already aware of it. He had come to work early that morning even though it was his day off and it was already being shown as he walked in. That was why he wanted to complete the paperwork quickly and book off duty and try and forget the whole previous evening's events.

Wallows remained in the incident room which for the time being was empty of staff which allowed her to relax in the quietness and ponder on lasts night's fiasco. She was battered and bruised as was Ben. His confidence and enthusiasm for the job had taken a massive hit, he was plastered all over You Tube and he was only just taking the first few steps in his career. He was already well on the way to becoming as cynical as some if not most of his more experienced officers. What a shame she thought, and she wouldn't be surprised if the wife beater had gone straight back home and given his wife an even worse beating.

The briefing began at nine-thirty sharp; a much-berated sheepish DCI opened with the initial run down of what had happened during the night with the second murder which was pretty much a carbon copy of the first one. His every word was obviously being closely monitored and scrutinised by the superintendent and everyone in the briefing room was aware of this.

The superintendent had already made a number of changes including much more detailed and in-depth actions. He had immediately despatched DS Grant Courtan to the scene to make some initial fast track enquires, namely to identify the victims and establish any possible connection between them and the victims of the first double murder. He had arranged for a criminal psychological profiler to be brought in and he had made provision for a different pathologist to be used to conduct the post-mortem examinations. It was well known that the Superintendent Tony Gibbs did not rate Dr Chuman. He thought of him as incompetent and a bit of a drunkard but on the other side of the coin it was just as well known that that Gibbs had an eye for the pathologist he had replaced him with and she was single and quite a looker.

Wallows and Latifeo were given different actions. Latifeo was given the task of liaising with the psychological profiler and Wallows was instructed to arrange for the fingerprinting of the cadavers from the first murder, something which the DCI had overlooked the first time and had been picked up by the superintendent. Wallows hadn't got a clue how to fingerprint a dead body, so she had been told to meet the SOCO team at the mortuary when they had finished today's murder scene examination. This was now the most serious incident that almost everyone working in the incident room had ever been involved with. It was a boost to their ego and would be a talking point for years to come even if the killer was never caught or convicted. Just to have been involved in the case gave you canteen bragging rights for years to come.

Detectives were busy collecting their allocated actions and getting ready to start their day's enquiry when the Station duty inspector came in and spoke with the DCI and the superintendent. The number of officers working on the daily shifts had been badly depleted due to extra staff being seconded into the incident room and it appeared that the Inspector was asking for help from the incident room personnel.

When Wallows was summoned over to speak with the DCI people were visibly relieved that is was her and not them who may be recalled to shift work. "Have you made arrangements with SOCO to fingerprint the bodies yet?" the DCI asked Wallows. She told the DCI that she was to meet the SOCO's at the mortuary at midday before the post-mortems on the second murder victims and they were going to show her what to do.

"In that case you can help out the shift for a couple of hours; they have a domestic incident and no policewoman on duty. It shouldn't take long and make sure you're finished in time to meet the SOCO's."

Wallows went with the duty inspector who explained they had a complaint of a domestic related incident. The operational support unit were being utilised because of staff shortages and she should liaise with them at their vehicle in the Station carpark where they were expecting her. This won't be too bad thought Wallows, at least she was with a support unit which consisted of a sergeant and five officers so there would be no problem with the physical part of it any rough stuff then they would sort it out.

All the officers on the unit were trained to deal with violent confrontations and they were waiting for her in the back yard. She jumped in the back of their riot van and off they sped. Wallows didn't pay much attention during the journey her mind was elsewhere. She was thinking about her task later in the mortuary. How on earth do you fingerprint a dead body she thought?

"We're here, everybody out" shouted the unit sergeant "make sure you bring the door key with you."

The door key as it was jokingly called was a big heavy metal bar with handles on the side. It was used to smash your way through a door, you swing it hard near where the door lock is located, and it nearly always gives way within a few strikes. Wallows couldn't believe it when she stepped out of the van "Oh Christ" she said.

"What's the matter?" asked the sergeant "you look worried"

"I was here last night dealing with a domestic. We arrested the husband for beating his wife up, he didn't get charged because she withdrew her complaint, but she was in a right mess. He'd really beaten her up badly."

There was no noise coming from inside as the sergeant knocked on the door. He waited for a moment and still no noise, no sign of any movement from within. He looked towards the officer holding the door key and nodded towards the door. The officer stepped forward, took a couple of practise swings and then with a thud hit the door about half way up on the left-hand side near the door lock which gave way immediately. He then stepped back allowing the rest of the unit to pile through the doorway. Shouting police at the top of their voices, one by one they entered. Wallows and the sergeant were the last ones to enter the house; all the other officers were now gathered in the living room the scene of last night's fight with the wife beater.

The room looked like a bomb had gone off, wrecked tables and chairs, television smashed to pieces, pictures and ornaments broken and strewn all over the place, but no one was looking at the state of the room. They all stood in silence looking at the broken and battered body of a female lying prostrate and motionless on the floor surrounded by a huge pool of dark crimson blood. The wall above her head was also heavily bloodstained; it was congealed into a gooey sticky mess with long streaks and rivulets stretching as far down as the skirting board that had now dried. You could clearly see clumps of hair and fragments of bone and body tissue embedded within it. The sergeant put on a pair of latex gloves and turned the body over trying to disturb it as little as possible. She had now been rolled gently onto her back and facing upwards as he knelt down beside her and took a deep breath and began to look for any sign of life. After a brief examination he looked up towards the rest and said solemnly "I can't feel a pulse anywhere, and she's not breathing. She also feels quite cold as well; I think she may have been here some time."

Wallows joined the sergeant on the floor, she was kneeling down beside by the body on the opposite side from the sergeant. "Oh my god" she said, "There's a massive hole in the side of her skull. He has literally beaten her brains out, that's what the tissue is in the mass of blood plastered all over the wall."

"There was a young girl here last night" Wallows said urgently to the sergeant "we need to find her."

Two officers were told to search the house for any sign of the husband and the young girl. As the two officers began to climb the stairs Wallows shouted after them telling them to be careful because he was a big horrible extremely violent nasty bastard and he's doesn't give a shit for uniform. The force control room was updated with the present situation and they began to arrange for the necessary specialist back up to attend and the DCI to be informed that they had what appeared on the face of it a domestic murder.

The two officers began to search the upstairs rooms mindful of what Wallows had said. The first room appeared to be the parent's bedroom, there was an unmade double bed; the bedclothes were lying half on the floor and half on the bed. It looked as if someone had been dragged forcibly out of it; the bedside cabinet was on its side and was several feet away from its original position by the bed. The rest of the room looked relatively undisturbed. The room was searched, under the bed, in the wardrobe and anywhere that was possible to hide but no sign of the wife beater who'd now become a wife killer.

Next was a tiny dirty little bathroom "how do people live like this? What a filthy shithole" said one officer to the other. Before the other officer could reply they heard something coming from one of the rooms and their pulses began to race. The officers looked at each other in silence with an acknowledgement that they had both heard the same noise and that it had come from the room at the end of the corridor. One armed himself with pepper spray whilst the other took out his extendable baton. He extended it to its full length as quietly as he could and they carefully almost on tiptoes walked along the corridor making as little noise as possible.

Trying to keep their breathing under control as they neared the door both officers' hearts were beating fast, adrenalin pumping through their veins. Then they heard the sound again, it was only a low muffled sound, but it was definitely coming from inside the room, this is it they thought crunch time. They stood outside the room with baton raised and pepper spray at the ready pointing towards the door with a thumb poised firmly on the activation button on top of the pepper spray canister. They remained outside the door listening intently for any further noises, but everything was ominously hushed nothing else was heard from inside the room but both officers were certain that the noises they had heard previously emanated from within that room and that someone was in there.

"Perhaps he is hiding somewhere in the room" one officer whispered to the other.

"You could be right" came the hushed and somewhat nervous reply. "Fuck it; I'm not taking any chances."

The officer with his extendable baton drawn replaced it silently back into its holder and his Taser stun gun was withdrawn from its holster, he held it in a two-handed grip at chest height with arms outstretched.

"We'll go in after three" mouthed the officer with the Taser "take no chances, first sign of trouble spray the bastard."

A couple of deep breaths later and it was one, two, three then bang, the door was kicked through. Both officers shouting and screaming "Armed police, armed police put your hands in the air."

The Taser was rapidly sweeping the room left to right in front of them, behind them but he was nowhere to be seen. The officer with the Taser began to panic; he started shrieking out loud "Where the fuck is he? Where the fuck is he?"

The officer with the pepper spray franticly scanned the room and then noticed out the corner of his eye a slight movement within the bed.

"He's behind you he screamed."

The officer turned around towards the bed and fired in one movement at the same time as the warning shout "gas, gas, gas" went out from the other officer.

This was the standard operating procedure to be followed when discharging pepper spray, something that was practised time and time again in training. It was chiefly for the safety of other officers or personnel in the proximity.

Wallows and the rest of the team downstairs then heard the most tumultuous uproar and commotion coming from upstairs. Shouting, screaming, swearing, cries of agony and the sound of objects being smashed and furniture being knocked over and crashing to the floor and the sound of bodies bouncing off walls. It was like all hell had broken loose.

"Looks like they've found him" said the sergeant as they all began to run up the stairs towards the pandemonium. Then a scream from one of the officers in the bedroom sent a chill down the spine of everyone running to their assistance.

"He's shot me, he's fucking shot me. The fucking bastard he's shot me."

The rescuers continued to hurtle along the corridor and piled into the bedroom all pumped up with a mixture of fright and anger and a feeling of gung-ho comradery ready to get stuck into the fray to save their colleagues. When they all burst into the room ready for action they were suddenly halted in their tracks and they all stood there dumbfounded trying to make sense of the bizarre scene that unfolded in front of them. Both officers were on the bedroom floor rolling about in agony. One of them still had hold of the Taser stun gun which had been discharged in his right hand; his left hand was holding his face as tears were running down his now red and inflamed nose and face.

"Oh my god" he cried "the fucking pain." This made his body curl up into a foetal position and caused both of his hands and fingers to tightly clench, this in turn activated the Taser again and sending another few thousand volts into the recipient at the other end. The recipient of the electric charge was not the wife beater however but was the officer with the pepper spray who had somehow managed to pepper spray himself and his colleague. He had discharged pepper spray everywhere in reaction to being accidentally shot with the Taser when his mate had turned around suddenly and shot immediately in panic.

The officer who had been shot with the Taser had one hand on his chest where the Taser had struck him and his other hand on his face where he had sprayed himself. He then suddenly went into an uncontrollable fit of violent and jerking spasms and began screaming. Someone then shouted out "he's still got his finger pressed on the trigger" and an unrelenting charge of electric volts was still being pumped through his mate's body. When his fingers were finally prised off the trigger both officers lay curled up on the floor and both were completely poleaxed and unable to move continuing to cry out in pain.

It was difficult to imagine a more surreal and pathetic sight. Two operational support constables whose primary function was to deal with difficult and violent confrontations who had received extra intensive combat training in the use of police issue self defence equipment yet somehow, they had unbelievably managed to pepper spray and Taser each other.

The room was sparsely furnished. There was a small wardrobe which was now on its side and smashed to piece's, a small dressing table with a chair that had suffered the same fate as the wardrobe lying in a broken pile of rubble and a bed. Peeking out from under the bedding was the face of an utterly bewildered small child; it was a girl, the same girl Wallows had seen the night before, the girl who had opened the door for them. Thank goodness he can't shoot straight thought Wallows otherwise he would have Tasered her. It was obviously her movement that had spooked those two clowns, fortunately she appeared to be unharmed more by luck than judgement thought Wallows and said to herself. "This is what should really be on You-Tube. These two incompetent idiots who had managed to shoot and pepper spray each other having been panicked into doing so by a five-year-old girl."

Wallows sat in the operational support vehicle sipping at a cup of tea together with the rest of the unit. They were parked on the street outside the murder scene. The unit had been told that they were shortly to be stood down; the two officers who had gassed themselves were stood outside facing into the breeze in order to help cool the burning sensation in their eyes and face. They had both declined a hospital check-up or any other first aid this was because they didn't want to draw attention to what had happened but wanted to hush the whole sorry episode up. They had asked the rest of the unit to keep quiet about it to spare them any embarrassment to which everyone agreed.

Wallows smiled to herself when she heard this, she knew their promise to keep schtum was absolute cobblers. She had seen what they had done whilst the two buffoons were rolling about the floor in agony; they'd all taken out their mobile camera phones and clicked away merrily, it wouldn't be long before the images would be displayed on the internet or some social media websites she thought.

The crime scene itself was now under control. There were two uniform officers Stationed at the front door taking details of personnel entering and leaving the scene and recording such details on the scene log. The pathologist Sally Drice together with the crime scene manager, who had both come directly from the double murder scene in the park were inside assessing the potential evidence and trying to establish exactly the sequence of events and decide upon the forensic examination strategy.

Wallows had been told to wait for them to finish and accompany them to the mortuary, so she could complete her task of fingerprinting the first two murder victims. Whilst drinking her much welcomed cup of tea with a little time on her hands she reflected on the whole sorry debacle and her thoughts turned to the young girl who to all intent and purposes was now parentless. Her mother had been beaten to death and her dad would on his way to prison if and when he gets caught. The girl was now in the care of social services which fair play to them had arrived quickly on scene when they were made aware of a vulnerable five-year-old whose mother had just been murdered. Wallows felt a feeling of empathy with the poor mite as she recalled parts of her own upbringing and for a while her mind was elsewhere trawling through past events in her own childhood.

She snapped out of it with a start when the sergeant shouted "Shirley" and handed her some vehicle keys. "Me and my lads have been stood down" he said. "We're going back to the nick. The CSM has asked me to tell you to wait in the SOCO vehicle until they've finished in the house. He reckons about an hour."

Wallows got in the passenger seat of the SOCO van and got her mind back on the job and waited for the crime scene manager.

8

Coffee and Cake

Grant Courtan had been given the job of organising the house to house enquires in relation to both the double murders. These had now been given the nickname of the 'dogging deaths.' He had produced a standardised crib sheet with a list of questions to be asked of any and all potential witnesses. Copies of this crib sheet questionnaire had been issued to the entire enquiry officer teams that had been allocated to him. Each of the teams had each been given specific streets and premises to canvass. He had however kept one particular location for himself, the location where he was now knocking on the door in eager anticipation. Sam Gail opened the door and Grant went in. "Before you say anything I'm working house to house enquires on the murders in the park. There's no danger of that idiot Latifeo turning up because I have arranged for him to babysit the psychological criminal profiler, so we'll be undisturbed."

She replied, "Well I was actually in the middle of doing something; everything doesn't just revolve around sex you know."

"What's got you so worked up?" asked Grant.

Sam showed him into the living room where spread over the dining table were numerous bills, invoices and demands for payments "I'm struggling to pay all these bills" Sam explained.

Grant whose initial plan was to pop round for a quickie thought to himself, I haven't got time for all this crap and wracked his brains to think of the quickest way to resolve this and get her upstairs and into bed.

"Look" said Grant "I'll tell you what if it helps at all, the money I give you each week to help you out I'll start to put a bit more in."

"I don't think you realise how much I struggle to keep my head above water. These bills keep going up all the time and I only have a few students each week, giving piano lessons doesn't pay that well you know. A little bit of extra money won't go very far" replied Sam.

Grant who had been feeling as horny as hell when he arrived felt even randier now looking at Sam. She was a fantastic looking woman and had an incredible body. Curves in all the right places and she was unbelievable in bed. She was game for anything, even the really mucky stuff and was without doubt the best sex he had ever had. Even though he was quite a player and had more than his fair share of women she was by far the best and she was looking as sexy as ever. She was wearing an incredibly tight little black dress; he was now beginning to feel desperate with frustration and felt like a dog on heat. I need to do something to get her into bed quickly he thought, his head now being ruled by his genitalia.

Grant blurted out in desperation "I'm earning a fair bit of money with overtime on these murder cases, if I give you an extra hundred quid a week will that help?" A big beaming smile appeared across Sam's face, she didn't say anything she just took Grant's hand and led him upstairs towards the bedroom.

Sam had known exactly what she was doing, she realised by the look in Grant's eye as soon as she had answered the door to him that he was feeling horny and that most blokes think with their cocks instead of their brains when they want sex. She had deliberately dressed in a sexy revealing outfit and applied her make-up and done her hair to get him going so that she could get what she wanted and what a result an extra hundred pound a week. I'll give him an extra special shag today with a few treats thrown in she mused, that'll seal the deal.

After the most rampant sex he had ever had Grant lay back in bed totally exhausted; sweat dripping down his back, muscles aching. I must have given her the shag of her life he thought, her moans and groans of pleasure were non-stop and the cries of ecstasy at the climax was ear shattering. Together with the other stuff she was doing to me she must have thought she had died and gone to heaven. What a bloody stud I am he silently congratulated himself. He turned to Sam and saw her smiling from ear to ear; he thought how content she looked.

"How you feeling?" he asked.

Sam replied "absolutely fantastic, I feel like I've been fucked by a train but a bit tired and I'm aching all over. I just need to relax for a while." She gave him a peck on the cheek and rolled over on her side. That should satisfy him for a while she thought, keep him well and truly on the hook. god it had been hard work though he was absolutely useless in the sack, he couldn't find an erogenous zone if you drew him a map. And all the pretend moaning and screaming I had to fake was draining, even that idiot Latifeo is a much better shag than Grant and he is no great shakes but at least he's got a reasonable sized cock on him unlike that little tiddler Grant's got between his legs, its looks more like a chipolata than a cock. But never mind, it was worth the play acting for an extra hundred pound a week. She let out a sigh of contentment at she thought of the extra money.

Grant heard the gentle sigh coming from Sam, he puffed his chest out and he had the grin of someone who had just been told they had won the lottery. He silently again said to himself yes what a fucking stud I am. "I'll need to go soon" said Grant "I've given myself the job of doing the house to house enquires in your street. It shouldn't take long though, I've got a pre-prepared list of questions so it's just a case of ticking a few boxes and then I need to go back to the nick."

Sam asked, "Do I need to fill one of those forms in?"

"No, I'll fill one in for you" Grant said.

"What was that thing you talked about when you came in earlier, a psychologist or something?"

Grant then explained about criminal offender profiling and how it helps to identify the type of person the offender is likely to be and so narrows down the search criteria, and how he had been brought in on the order of the superintendent who in turn had been told by the chief constable to take charge of and start running the operation because the Detective Chief Inspector Frank Twead was so bloody useless.

"So, what's Oli's involvement with it then?" She asked.

"The profiler is not local, so he won't know where or how to find or access things or anyone. It's just to take the guy around and show him how he can make arrangements to speak with any officers or personnel. It's a piece of cake, basically a child could do it but at least it will keep him out of the way. Anyway, it's time for me to go, I'll see you as we arranged."

"Make sure you do" said Sam "I can then arrange to give my music lessons and also make sure that there aren't any nosy neighbours in their front gardens because I don't want any gossip. Okay?"

"Okay" he said in an exasperated voice.

"I mean it" she said, "only on the days we agreed and call me just before you get here so I can check out and see if the neighbours are about."

"Is that why you've got those binoculars on the window sill in your bedroom?"

"Well I'm not trainspotting am I, now go" she answered whilst ushering him towards the door. She had to bite her lip to stop herself bursting into a fit of the giggles when she thought what she should have said the reason for the binoculars were. I should have said I use them to search for his tiny little cock.

Grant strolled along the street with a smug confident air thinking how great he had been. No wonder women can't resist me he mused as he knocked on the front door of the first address on his list and put his mind back on the job.

Sam was tidying away the pile of bills that were spread over the table when her mobile vibrated in her pocket; she looked at the caller ID and saw it was Latifeo. She answered the call and he said he wanted to know if he could pop round because he had a couple of hours free. Sam gave him the okay and hung up. She went back to the pile of bills on the table, she smiled as she spread the bills back out again. It was a good job I hadn't thrown them away she thought, after all they are only old ones. They had been paid months ago. Thank goodness Grant didn't have a close look at them; hopefully Latifeo won't look at them either. She then began the process of making herself up and squeezing back into her little black dress to await the hapless horny idiot who hadn't a clue what was in store for him.

Wallows was now on her way to the mortuary, she was in the back of the pathologist's Mercedes. The crime scene manager was travelling in the front, he had left his vehicle at the domestic murder scene for the SOCO's to use so they were travelling in style. This is the sort of car I want Wallows thought and one day I intend to get one. In the front they were discussing between them the crime scene they had just examined. When listening to them describing the scene it all seemed quite straight forward, however when they began discussing the two double murders in the park and the techniques that they had used that became a lot more complicated.

The complicated phraseology they used Wallows had never even heard off let alone understood what they meant. Terms like palynology mycology and blood pattern analysis left her completely in the dark. She did feel however a little more relaxed this time than she had on the way to her first trip to the mortuary. It had given her confidence a boost because she had managed to come through it reasonably okay whereas Latifeo with all his cocky showmanship had passed out on the mortuary floor. She also felt some relief that she wouldn't have any dealings with Dr Chuman who had completely humiliated and belittled her last time. When they arrived at the mortuary they used the same technician's office as before to prepare.

Steve, the crime scene manager said to Wallows "Shirley I've got Dave on his way to show you how to fingerprint a cadaver. To save time can you get your PPE on and get the male victim of the first murder out of the fridge and make sure his hands are clean. If they aren't use some soap and water on them and dry them with paper towels. Are you okay to do that?"

Wallows replied, "Yes no problem I'll get straight on it."

She thought it's nice to be trusted, to be able to do something without all the condescending behaviour and not being spoken to like you was a child. I'm also getting to know some of the terminology as well PPE, personal protective equipment and cadaver means a dead body. In the part of the mortuary where the individual fridges housed the cadavers Wallows removed the body of Fraser or fat Fraser as he was now constantly being referred to. She examined his fingers, they appeared to be quite clean but a little greasy and so she decided to wash them. Near to the sink she could see hand wash and a small bowl, so she filled it with warm water and using the soap began to clean his cold dead fingers. It was the first time she had touched a dead person and she thought she was going to be sick, but she took a few deep breaths to calm herself down and carried on.

She was surprised at how cold the fingers were and also how incredibly stiff and immovable they had become, they were clenched almost into a fist. Goodness knows how they can be fingerprinted in that state she thought. After she had dried the fingers with paper towels she sat down at a small table, put her handbag on top and waited for Dave. From where she was sitting she was able to see through into the post-mortem examination room where on the tables were lain the bodies of the other two murder victims ready to be examined. She could hear the post-mortem team making their way into the examination area; the team consisted of the pathologist, a couple of SOCO's and Steve.

Steve approached "Dave is running a bit late; he'll be here in about half an hour, you might want to watch the PM while you're waiting; she is completely different to Chuman. You'll probably find it quite interesting, oh and just a tip, you should only bring into this area something that you can either dispose of afterwards or completely sanitise so it's best not to bring your police handbag in."

"I'm sorry about that, I didn't think. It's probably because I always have it with me everywhere I go. I must remember next time" she replied.

"No harm done but it would be a good idea to wipe it down with the sanitiser before you leave" he said.

Wallows nodded in acknowledgement and appreciated the fact that she had been told in a manner that didn't humiliate or embarrass her. She then began to watch the team at work. Steve was right thought Wallows, she works completely differently to Dr Chuman. It felt like I was in an abattoir watching him at work but Sally Drice was much more precise and meticulous in what she did and paid a lot more attention to detail.

When Dave arrived he said, "Sorry I'm late Shirley, I see you've got the body out ready." Wallows explained how she had cleaned the fingers because they were a bit greasy and that the fingers were completely stiff and curled up, so she didn't know if it was possible to fingerprint them.

"Not a problem" said Dave as he opened his mortuary box and began to lay various pieces of equipment next to the body. "The first thing to remember is that any consumables we use like packaging material goes in the bin before we leave this room. That includes your paper suit and gloves etc., anything else like fingerprint powder and brushes goes back in this box and they are not used on anything outside the mortuary."

Wallows was then handed a fingerprint brush loaded with powder and was asked to apply the powder to the ends of the fingers and the palms of the hands. She was about to say that she couldn't because the fingers were curled up but before she did, so Dave wrapped both of his own hands around the deceased's and pressed both of his thumbs into the back of the deceased's hands. This caused the deceased's fingers to open up like a flower head giving easy access to the finger tips and palm. After a few unsuccessful attempts she managed with the help of Dave to lift and place on acetate sheets ten fingerprint lifts and two palm impressions. Dave checked each lifted print, looked at Wallows and announced "Not bad for first time, they'll be okay for identification purposes. Right let's put Fraser back and get the next one."

After completing the fingerprinting of the second body they returned back to the technician's room and were now sipping their obligatory cups of tea. Wallows asked Dave "What happens to the fingerprints now?"

Dave explained how if a person's fingerprints were on file they would be compared with the database. If they were not on file, then you have to get some prints for comparison. You would normally do a fingerprint examination of their home address and compare against them. In this particular case he added, these people aren't known so an examination of their home address needs to be done but that would be arranged by the SOCO Department.

"Do you mind if I ask another question?"

"No not at all, go ahead" said Dave.

"You hear, especially in the media about fingerprints being planted, but how can you do that? I mean you can't exactly chop someone's finger off and use it to touch something so that it leaves a fingerprint, can you?"

"The easiest way to do it would be to fingerprint something that you know somebody has touched, like the teacup you're drinking from now. Take a lift of that fingerprint with low adhesion tape just like we did from the body and then use the print on the tape to plant it where you want to. You would not use powder though you would simply rely on the natural sweat from the body."

"Blimey that sounds easy" she replied.

"You can do the same with DNA, similar principal all you need is a swab. Again, use your teacup as an example, run the swab around the lip where you'll get traces of saliva and then wipe that somewhere else. Saliva is not a particularly good example though because most of the saliva would stay absorbed in the swab and you would only start off with a small amount. Other body fluids would be better, and an even easier way would be to use the object itself. Once again use your teacup as an example. If you left your cup here in this room and it is not washed up or cleaned at all then all someone has to do would be to pick it up taking care not to leave their own DNA or prints on it and leave it at a crime scene. What you need to remember is that if DNA or fingerprints are found at a scene it doesn't automatically mean that the person was there but something they have come into contact with has. Obviously in most circumstances the trace evidence is there because the person, whether a suspect or victim was actually there but it could also be planted to frame somebody or set them up. It's highly unusual but it is possible."

Wallows was completely enthralled by this "That's absolutely fascinating. It's something you would never even think about, this scenes of crime stuff is so interesting. Do you have any attachment opportunities in the department? I would love to spend some time learning all about it?"

Dave replied, "I know there have been attachments in the past, the best one to speak with about it would be Steve."

After thanking Dave for all the information, she decided it was time she was heading back to the nick to get ready for the five o'clock briefing. She enquired if Dave was returning also but he had been told to hang on there to assist with another post-mortem after the double murder victims had been examined; it was a domestic where the wife had had her brains bashed in. Wallows explained that she had been involved with the incident and how after locking the husband up they couldn't charge him because two hours later she had withdrawn the charges.

"Bloody hell" said Dave angrily shaking his head in disbelief. Before she could ask what, the matter was Dave outlined a conversation he had with Steve concerning the circumstances of the woman's death. Because the death was recent and in a warm place where the temperature was constant it meant that the pathologist by taking the temperature of the body and other factors could give an accurate time of death. By comparing it with the timings you have just given me it looks like the poor woman was dead within less than an hour of him being released from the police Station. He must have left the nick, gone straight home and battered her to death immediately. It makes you wonder why we lock them up in the first place."

Wallows felt awful, she couldn't get the thought out of her head that she could have done something else. Something more to help that poor woman and if she had done then she may still be alive. She took a slow walk back to the police Station, she needed time to think to try and make sense of the events of the last few days. She suddenly realised how hungry she felt, it was mid-afternoon, and she had not eaten a thing all day. She decided to take a detour through the park and take advantage of a recently opened up-market café called No 92 Coffee Lounge that sold the most delicious, albeit calorie laden cakes and other chocolate coated goodies. That'll pick me up she thought ironically it is only fifty yards from the still cordoned off murder scene.

As she approached the main gates to the park she saw Latifeo at the front door of a house directly opposite, the front door opened, and he was just about to go in. She was about to shout to him but changed her mind deciding that he was obviously doing something in connection with the murders and it wouldn't look very professional if she were to shout to him from some distance away. Besides she was now desperate to get something nice to eat and drink to satisfy the rumbling in her stomach. Wallows ordered something to eat and drink and found a nice secluded table next to a large window facing into the park. As she was waiting for the waitress she gazed out over the park, to the right she could see part of the children's play area and an outdoor gym. Straight ahead was the bandstand and to the left she could see the trees that surrounded the carpark. She could just make out through the trees some of the police barrier tape flapping in the breeze that was still in position round the murder scene. She then realised that the house that she had seen Latifeo entering would give a great view of the carpark scene of the murder, I wonder if he is looking now.

Latifeo was indeed looking at a great view; it was nothing to do with the crime scene though. The view he was looking at was dressed for now in a tight, figure hugging little black dress. What a fantastic sight he thought, it was well worth giving her some extra money to help pay those bills that she was struggling to pay.

The waitress placed the food and drink that Wallows had ordered on the table in front of her. It was an extra-large frothy coffee with all the trimmings and a huge slice of chocolate fudge cake with a great big dollop of fresh cream on the side. What a fantastic sight she thought.

Both Wallows and Latifeo continued to savour the delight in front of each of them until the temptation became too strong for them to wait any longer and they both indulged themselves.

9

A Right Cock-up

Stourbridge Police Station was rapidly beginning to fill with detectives, uniform officers and a whole host of civilian staff and other specialist's in readiness for the five o'clock briefing. The enquiry was now gaining momentum. The Station was full of reporters and news media personnel not just the local reporter who would occasionally stroll into the Station from his office a few yards away on the opposite of the road with his pencil and note book on the off chance that there was anything happening that was worthy of reporting on to fill a few vacant columns in the once a week edition. These were completely different animals, these were the big boys with all the paraphernalia that came with it. Cameramen, lighting technicians, even make-up artists to make sure that the face of the media didn't have a shiny nose, the lot. This double, double murder enquiry had gripped the imagination of the whole country and it was big, big news.

Wallows was rehearsing what to say if she was asked about the fingerprinting of the bodies. Pretty straight forward she thought, she felt reasonably relaxed especially with that naughty but nice scrummy piece of chocolate fudge cake in her stomach. Also, she had not been humiliated or embarrassed by any senior or more experienced officers and she was relieved that the pathologist Chuman who had belittled her at the post-mortem had been temporarily replaced by Sally Drice who appeared to be much friendlier and a lot less pompous and condescending. She like most of the assembled staff in the briefing room was stood up because of the vastly increased numbers of personnel and the size of the room which simply couldn't accommodate any further chairs. From her position she could see Latifeo across the other side of the room; he looked like the cat that got the cream. He must have been allocated some interesting or important action Wallows thought. She tried to attract his attention, but the incident room was so jam packed he couldn't see her waving her arms at him. I'll speak with him after the briefing she thought, she was intrigued about what actions he had been given and what he had been doing at the house opposite the park.

The superintendent and the DCI came into the incident room and took their seats at the table at the head of the room. The amount of staff on the bosses table had swelled in numbers, in addition to the incident room manager and WPC Gail Tomaso who had been assigned directly to the superintendent apparently because of her short hand abilities so she could take notes and minutes of meetings and strategy planning discussions. It was nothing to do with her stunning dusky Mediterranean looks and her hour glass models figure of course, it was just administration reasons. There were two other people who Wallows didn't recognise and surveying the faces of everyone else in the room she wasn't the only one.

The superintendent opened the briefing by introducing the new members on the table. Edward Barista the first person to be introduced looked like some sort of nutty professor. He obviously wasn't the type of person who made much of an effort with his appearance. His grey curly hair was all over the place, it looked like he had been dragged through a hedge backwards and then been zapped with a few thousand volts of electricity. His non-co-ordinated and ill-fitting clothes would have disgraced a charity shop, but the most striking feature by far was his little piggy eyes that appeared to be squinting through the most incredibly thick round spectacle lenses that were perched on the end of his nose. One of the arms was attached to the frame with some sort of sticky tape and they were obviously loose because every few seconds he would put one of his fingers in the centre of the frame and push the specs from the end of his nose right back flush to his face. This then made his little piggy eyes look enormous as if he was peering through a high-powered magnifying glass then because they weren't a secure or tight fit to his head they slowly slid back down the length of his nose where they remained for a while until he once again pushed them back to the top of his nose. This was a process that was continually repeated; it looked like a cross between the late comedian Eric Morecombe who on stage was continually pushing his glasses back along the bridge of his nose by pressing his finger on the centre of the frame and a Les Dawson character, Cosmo Smallpiece who wore very similar looking thick lensed round spectacles. This was the criminal psychological offender profiler who had been brought in by the superintendent. Not that he or anybody else thought that he would do any good or make a worthwhile contribution to the investigation but more to basically cover his own back against any recriminations concerning the supervision of the enquiry if it all went tits up.

The other person on the table to be introduced to the room was the force senior press and media liaison officer. He was a completely different kettle of fish to the offender profiler, a tall and athletic looking type with striking good looks and a shock of thick blonde hair which together with his clear bright blue eyes ensured he got plenty of admiring glances and eyelash fluttering from all the young free and available females in the room as well as some of the not so available. His responsibility would be to not only liaise with the press and media but to help the DCI together with the psychological profiler to formulate a press strategy.

A comprehensive and effective press strategy could assist the investigation tremendously in a number of ways, crucial evidence could be established, and new witnesses and important evidence may be to light. People could be eliminated from the investigation but most importantly the possibility of suspects being identified. There were two very important factors to be remembered and strictly observed, the first one was to keep the press and media onside. You need their willing co-operation it was important to give them up to date information and it was their job to print and report the news in a manner that sells newspapers and attracts the public's attention. If they were continuously fobbed off with what were commonly referred to as holding statements such as 'The police are dealing with an incident that is being treated as suspicious and we are making an appeal for witnesses and information' then you will soon lose their co-operation because this type of information will not sell newspapers or excite the imagination of the paying public. This may lead to them making up their own version of events or they may seek to obtain inside information with the help of a few backhanders in plain brown envelopes.

The second incredibly important thing to remember is never to give full and exact details of the modus operandi or M.O. as it is informally better known as, because later statements made by a suspect or a witness or even a hoaxer can be evaluated against what would have only been known by the offender. This could prove vital especially in the later stages of the investigation and may mean the difference between a successful prosecution and a case being lost on a technicality.

Most serial killers repeatedly use the same method to disable or kill their victims, such as Peter Sutcliffe aka the Yorkshire ripper who used a ball-peen hammer to incapacitate his victims by hitting them over the head before stabbing them, sometimes in such frenzy it had the effect of disembowelling them. Kenneth Erskine aka the Stockwell strangler who strangled his victims using one hand, all this could help police to identify specific murders committed by an individual or identify a series of connected murders. In some cases, it has helped to rule out suspects who have falsely claimed to be the killer. It was for this reason that the superintendent had decided to utilise the help of the force press officer who he knew would be well versed in this area as opposed to the DCI who was famed for opening his mouth before engaging brain and not considering the consequences.

"Right" bawled out the DCI "if we are all here we'll make a start."

The office manager interjected explaining that scenes of crime had informed him they would be about half an hour late reason being was that they were finishing off at the mortuary.

"We'll still push on and we can have their input when they get here. We've got a lot to get through and I'm sure you are all aware that the national news agencies have descended upon us and we have a news conference scheduled straight after this briefing which can't be delayed because they have deadlines to meet in order to air tonight and make the morning papers. So, we'll kick off with Grant who's co-ordinating the house to house enquires, but first can you tell us if you have identified the bodies yet and have you established any connection between them and the first victims. I want you to make it brief, relevant and to the point, we've no time to hear non-essential information."

"Yes sir" said Grant mindful now of sticking to the essentials and cutting out the additional waffle that he had prepared to try and give extra weight and importance to his part in the investigation. "The victims have yet to be formally identified but from papers on the bodies and the DVLA check on the vehicle they were using they are believed to be a married couple named Adam Dores and his wife Peri. The papers in their possession have given us where they work, and their respective positions and I have made some enquires there. They are both employed by the local authority in the social services sector in high ranking positions. He is the regional children's and young person's senior service co-ordinator and she is the local supported living scheme manager. Because of their profession's they are both subject of CRB checks so obviously neither of them have any criminal convictions and they are well respected members of the local community. Their home address is in the Hagley area about two miles from the first victims address who lived in the

Oldswinford area. I haven't established any direct link between them and the first victims other than it would appear that they may well have been interested in and possibly engaged in public displays of sexual activity."

He outlined the detailed questionnaire he had produced and issued to all his officers, the specific area being canvassed and the estimated time it would take to complete. Obviously, some addresses and premises weren't occupied during the day and arrangements had been made for enquiry teams to re-visit that evening, and he would begin analysing the data that evening for any useful information. Grant was thanked for his contribution and the briefing continued in the same manner.

The intelligence department reported that they had been liaising with other forces to establish any similar offences or possible suspects, and to date nothing had been received back. No connections had been found between the two pairs of victims, enquires concerning any possible enemies or anybody holding a grudge had not revealed anything.

Everyone was going through the motions and achieving the same results which when it came to it amounted to a big fat zilch, no new leads, no new suspects and no new promising lines of enquiry. The investigation was still in its infancy and a lot of information had to be looked at, evaluated and assessed for potential evidence or the promotion of any new lines of enquiry. But the longer the initial breakthrough was in coming it made it harder to investigate and less likely to have a successful outcome. It also had an effect on the moral and appetite of the investigators to fully commit themselves fully to the job in hand.

The mood in the incident room was becoming a little lacklustre. The initial sparkle and gusto had begun to diminish albeit ever so slightly however the superintendent and the DCI could sense it. They realised they needed some positive input, the press officer was also thinking that something was needed to give the press to keep them interested. At this rate all they had for them was that they were making enquires. Superintendent Gibbs enquired of Detective Constables Fergas and Peeves as to the progress of their specific enquires. They had been given the action to engage with members of the dogging fraternity to find out as much as they could about them and establish any links between the killings or possible suspects.

Detective Frank Fergas outlined their initial actions so far and that they had made contact with various groups within the Stourbridge area, they explained that had been slightly overwhelmed by the sheer number of organisations and groups dedicated to dogging. Some of them had been quite reticent to divulge details but others were only too happy to tell all. They all seem to link together with and overlap with other sexual preferences such as swingers, flashers, gangbangers, voyeurs and many more. A meeting had been arranged with one particular group that evening in a local pub in the Oldswinford area which seemed to be the centre of the swinging scene and it was also very close to the location of the park where the two murders occurred. The group they had arranged to meet were open and willing to co-operate they didn't think it wise to do so over the telephone but preferred to do it face to face.

"Well let's see if you can make in-roads into these groups and develop some leads and pay particular attention to finding any links between the two sets of victims" said the DCI.

Fergas was unsure whether the DCI was simply making a statement or was asking a question that needed a reply. Fortunately, before Fergas had decided if he needed to reply or not the crime scene manager together with a couple of SOCO's entered the room. They apologised for being late asking if the message re their overrunning at the mortuary had been received, the reply was that they were aware of it and thanked them for their warning.

"Have you got anything of interest for us Steve?" asked the superintendent.

"Yes" came the reply, "we have a lot of new information from the post-mortem examinations and some of the previously submitted forensic exhibits." Thank god for that thought the superintendent and the DCI, at last some sort of result.

"When you're ready Steve" said the superintendent who at the same time looked towards Tomaso to impress on her the need for her to take comprehensive notes. He also added "I don't know if you are aware, but we have scheduled a press conference straight after this briefing, so I realise that you may have a lot of information to go through, but I would appreciate if you could cut it down to the essential points." Steve nodded his head and began to brief the room with the forensic and evidence up-dates.

"We've got quite a bit to go through, but I will cut it down as much as I can sir" said Steve. He continued "We have performed three post-mortems on murder victims this afternoon. The first one I think you need to be made aware of is a domestic incident not connected to the murders in the park."

The DCI spoke "if it's a domestic then it doesn't concern me, the superintendent or members of the senior CID team and certainly not the incident room staff. It can be dealt with at divisional level I can allocate a suitable detective inspector unless there is something particularly outstanding about it."

"I'm afraid there is sir, shall I continue?" asked Steve.

"Go ahead" said Superintendent Gibbs.

Steve nodded and began to detail the scene examination from the domestic murder. "It's believed to be a husband and wife. The husband returned home whilst his wife was asleep in bed. It would appear from the marks on her ankle that she was pulled out of bed causing the back of her head to strike the bedroom floor and she then sustained an injury to the upper rear left side of her head. She was then forcibly dragged along the floor towards the bedroom door. She was obviously struggling at this point and managed to grab hold of a bedside table. This was dragged along the bedroom floor with her, but she must have lost her grip after a few feet. She was then further dragged along by the ankle down the stairs on her back this is substantiated by traces of hair blood and tissue that were evident on each step as her head struck them. There are further signs that she was still struggling whilst being manhandled down the stairs. There were finger-marks on the bannister where she had tried unsuccessfully to grab hold of it and on the opposite wall there were smeared trails of blood that would appear to be from the fingers on her right hand in a desperate attempt to try and halt her descent down the stairs. Similar marks were evident along the hallway to the living room where she either stood up or was most likely hauled to her feet and held upright by her throat. Bruising to her neck from finger and thumb marks indicate she was held by the assailant's left hand, it was at this position where she was violently punched about the side of her head and jaw. The blood pattern analysis of the blood-stained wall behind her indicated she was being struck from the left-hand side of her face. There were seven teeth knocked out and the jaw broken in three places and the lower jaw had become completely detached from the upper jaw. Her head was then repeatedly struck against the living room wall fracturing her skull. This continued even after the fracture, thus causing severe brain damage. The extreme level of force used also caused one of her eyes to become dislodged from its socket and whilst still attached to the optic nerve, the eyeball itself was resting on her cheek. The height of the blood staining and the impact point with her skull on the wall did not correlate with the victim's height, i.e. the area of bloodstaining on the wall was a lot higher than the victim's height. In simple terms ladies and gents, it would appear that she was held aloft with a hand around her throat and suspended in the air like a rag doll with her feet approximately 12 inches off the floor. She was then repeatedly and incredibly violently punched by the assailant with his right hand until the lower part of her jaw was basically demolished and became completely detached from the upper jaw, then whilst still being held aloft; her head was then repeatedly smashed against the wall. The cause of death was a brain haemorrhage and severe head trauma."

A quiet hush had descended over the incident room, the atmosphere was somewhat sombre, some of the staff had turned a little grey whilst others just reflected and tried to imagine what that poor woman must have gone through. What a waste of a life and a horrible painful way to die. No one in the room spoke; it somehow seemed to be the respectful thing to do, to give the poor woman some mark of respect in her passing and after an uncommon eerie lengthy pause, the DCI spoke in hushed tones.

"A particular violent and nasty death" said the DCI "but that doesn't explain why we need to be aware of it."

Steve continued "because of the stable conditions in the house i.e. the constant temperature and the pathologist's examination at the scene, an accurate time of death was established. It was very close to two o'clock in the morning and according to our custody record that I have just checked this was approximately one hour after the suspect was released from police custody after having been arrested for assaulting his wife."

At this both the two senior detectives put their head in their hands in disbelief "how much more is going to bloody happen" said Superintendent Gibbs in exasperation under his breath.

Steve finished by saying "which obviously now becomes a death in police contact requiring a referral to the Independent Police Complaints Commission."

In reality Twead and Gibbs realised that it also meant a much more detailed and in-depth investigation than would normally be required for a single domestic murder. It would need the deployment of a wealth of extra staff which they simply didn't have. The department was already at breaking point with all detectives and ancillary staff allocated to either the serial murders incident room or backfilling the spaces and positions left behind by those staff. Twead looked absolutely furious as he venomously shouted out, "why have I not been informed of this? Who was the arresting officer?"

Steve replied, "I think the arresting officers were probationer Ben Whyte and WPC Shirley Wallows."

The DCI then stood up and launched into a relentless, sustained and vitriolic verbal assault on Wallows. It continued for what seemed an age. Twead's voice increasing in intensity and ferocity, his face looking as though it was about to explode with rage, the air turning blue with the number of expletives being echoing round the room. He concluded with "I should have been notified immediately of this. Even a complete and utter idiot should have realised that. I'm beginning to think I may have to reconsider my decision to allow you an attachment to the CID."

Wallows stood there in a state of shock. She was frozen solid to the spot as she tried to speak but was unable to, even if she could think of anything to say she couldn't have said it. All she could think of and all that was going through her mind was how embarrassed she was. Of all the times she had been belittled, criticised and made to feel pathetic and useless this was by far the worst. All the eyes in the room were upon her, some seemed to share her embarrassment, and some felt uneasy at the tirade of abuse they had just been witness to. Others found it quite comical and a few even let out a giggle or two.

The ferocious verbal onslaught and her feeling of complete isolation was compounded by her prominent position in the room. She had been forced to stand up because of the shortage of chairs and the area of the room where she stood was on a slightly elevated platform. She felt like she was some sort of sacrifice being held up on display at some sort of ritualistic altar, surrounded by a pack of bloodthirsty minded vultures.

Superintendent Gibbs eyed Frank Twead with a fixed steely gaze as if to say enough is enough, cool it. The DCI took the hint and sat back down there then followed an uneasy hiatus in the briefing the deafening silence was eventually broken by the support unit sergeant.

"I think I may be able to shed some light on the communication breakdown sir" he said.

"Yes, go on "said Gibbs.

"I was in charge of the support unit at the scene sir; the incident was originally reported as a possible domestic. We were being utilised because of shortage of staff and the possible assailants' known violent behaviour and his sheer physical size. When we entered the premises and found the body of the deceased, WPC Wallows identified it to me as that of a female that she had dealings with the previous evening when her husband was arrested for assault on her and later released because of the wife's withdrawal of the complaint and her refusal to press charges. In light of this information sir, as soon as the scene was made secure I informed the com's room. I told them that the possible domestic we had been assigned to was now a murder scene and that it related to an incident at the same premise the previous evening whereby the husband had been arrested and subsequently released from custody.

I requested that this information be relayed to you sir and I was assured that it would be. It looks like there's been some sort of hiccup or breakdown somewhere in the comms room.

The DCI remained silent. In addition to perpetuating his reputation for being an overbearing bully; he had also been made to look like a bit of a fool. His public annihilation of Wallows had been completely unwarranted and totally unjustified. His anger should have been directed elsewhere, the responsibility for the break down in communications, would appear to emanate ironically from the communications room.

"We can allocate some resources to this. I'm not sure where from though at the moment and arrange for the I.P.C.C. to be informed but right now we'll hear the rest of the forensic input please Steve" said Gibbs.

Wallows was still reeling from the now established unwarranted and completely undeserved public humiliation meted out to her by Twead, her emotions were now gradually shifting from ones of utter embarrassment to anger she was fuming at the lack of any kind of apology from the DCI even though he and everyone else in the room knew it was no fault of hers and that she had done everything she was supposed to in those circumstances. The worst of it all was the frustration of knowing there was nothing she could do about it she just had to suffer in silence.

Steve stood up and began to thumb through his briefing notes to pick up where he had left off, he had assumed some sort of reaction from Frank Twead, but that incredible outburst beat all expectations by a long long way. The room was still in a state of subdued silence and even as he began to give the forensic brief he could feel that he hadn't got the room's full attention and that most people's minds were still focused on the spectacle they had just witnessed. Steve cleared his throat and began.

"The double murder scene in the park today was very similar to the previous double murder. It would appear that the couple were engaging in a sexual act at the same location which everyone is now fully aware of is a dogging spot. Once again, the male victim has suffered an injury to his groin area and his penis had been removed. The victims unlike the previous couple had come to rest in different positions than the previous two whereby the male was pinning the female to the bonnet of the car. On this occasion both bodies had come to rest on the ground adjacent to their vehicle. I won't go into the examination of the bodies at the scene as this is covered and explained in greater depth at the post-mortem. Because of the location of the bodies on the ground then asphyxiation of the female caused by the body weight of the male victim pressing on her back was ruled out."

Detective Frank Fergas stood up and interjected asking "How can you be sure of that? It may be that she was killed by the male pressing on her back and then later on falling to the ground?" Frank sat back down with a self-satisfied smug grin on his face. He had only asked the question to try and discredit the validity and accuracy of the scene of crime examination and moreover to discredit Steve himself. He was renowned as a bit of a prick that had an overinflated sense of his own self-importance and at every turn would do his utmost to undermine the efforts and achievements of others. Some people found this quite surprising given that he was as thick as a brick. Most people steered well clear of him though because of his reputation as being an informant for the DCI mainly concerning

101

other colleagues and supposed workmates whom he wouldn't hesitate for a moment to stab in the back.

Steve replied "The scene examination in particular the blood pattern analysis on the ground adjacent to the bodies meant that we were able to discount asphyxiation as the cause of death. I hope this answers your question Frank?"

Frank stood up again and in a condescending manner said, "No it doesn't because as far as I'm aware you can still bleed whether you're bent over a car or lying on the ground."

Frank sat down with an even bigger annoying smug expression on his face and looked to Steve for an answer. Steve was thinking to himself the little prick is being even more of an annoying twat than normal however I will give him his answer in a clear non-technical friendly and helpful manner without showing any sign of agitation that will show everyone what an ignorant interfering idiot he is.

In a calm controlled voice Steve replied "Frank, I feel confident that all present here in the room realise that a person has the ability to bleed irrespective of whatever their body position or orientation is, however the body's position in relation to the blood splattering distribution has a significant impact upon the size shape and patternation. Blood exuded from the body whilst standing in an upright position would result in a different size, shape and direction of individual and collective blood spots, splatters and patterns than that of exuded blood from someone who is stooping, bending, genuflecting, sitting, or in a prone position. This will also affect the spread the pooling, saturation, distribution, dispersal and amount. The time of death and the position of the body at the time of death will also have a significant effect on all the aforementioned indicators and is a major factor to be considered and analysed. There are also a number of other factor's to be considered, including the extent and type of trauma and in an outside scene such as this the strength of the wind, the wind direction and ambient temperature. From the information I have just outlined concerning blood pattern analysis examination I hope you can all appreciate that it is an intricate and complex area of forensic examination and that a scientifically trained and qualified forensic blood pattern analysis expert can establish a lot of vital information. Including the conclusions, I have given at the start of my briefing specifically that asphyxiation can be excluded as cause of death in this instance."

Frank who was now beginning to regret asking the question and was sinking fast with the weight of the information he had been given was looking for a way out and to save face at the same time and as a last resort said, "Well don't you think the professional thing to have done would have been to use a scientifically trained blood pattern analyst then?" Frank thought brilliant fucking got him now, he had examined the scene entry log and he knew the only people who were registered to be on scene were the pathologist, Steve and Dave. There was no mention of anyone else there.

"The examination was conducted by a scientifically trained and qualified blood pattern analysis expert" said Steve who was still doing his utmost to reply in a courteous manner and hide his annoyance even though what he really wanted to do was to kick Frank's teeth down his throat

Frank was not going to let this go "Well who was this so called scientific expert, because on the scene entry log there was only you, a SOCO and the pathologist at the scene?" Frank sat down, leant back in his chair and in the most arrogant manner looked around the room with the biggest smirk on his face so far.

Wallows was fascinated by this verbal jousting between the two of them, this was more like a personal grudge match rather than an incident room briefing and it served to shift the rooms attention away from her.

Steve replied "The scientific fully accredited blood pattern analyst expert who conducted the examination was me. I am listed as an expert on the home office register of accredited blood pattern analysts." Steve then sat down awaiting Franks reply but nothing was forthcoming, and Frank remained firmly fixed in his seat. Wallows smiled, game set and match to Steve she thought.

103

"For goodness sake" shouted the superintendent at Frank "unless you have anything of significance to say then stay seated and stop asking ridiculous questions about a subject you are obviously completely ignorant of."

Gibbs knew why Fergas had tried to look like the all-important I am, it was because he was trying to impress the gorgeous female sitting next to him which he had failed miserably to do so, and it had somewhat backfired on him making him look like a right wanker. Anyway, Frank had no chance of making any in-roads because Gibbs had seconded the stunning Gail Tomaso as his personal assistant for the duration of the murder investigation, rank has its privileges he thought. Gibbs nodded his head towards Steve indicating for him to continue with the briefing.

Steve resumed "The bodies were discovered early in the morning and I and the pathologist were on scene at 04:30hrs. The time of death parameters the pathologist Sally Drice has estimated based on the body temperatures and the beginning of the onset of rigor mortis as between 01:00hrs and 03:00hrs. The scene of the immediate area yielded very little as the area had been examined at the time of the previous murder and anything and everything that could yield forensic evidence was recovered then. The cause of death I will give during the post-mortem examination report. It would appear from initial enquires from identities in their pockets and the vehicle registration that they were husband and wife. The post-mortems revealed that the male suffered severe trauma to the groin area as previously stated, his penis was removed. The method with which it had been removed was similar to the previous murder victim's penis removal in that it had been sliced off with a sharp bladed instrument, in one movement as before. His penis has however been recovered."

This startling piece of information grabbed people's attention immediately and made everyone in the room sit up, all eyes now trained on the crime scene manager eager to hear what was coming next. "His penis has been recovered from inside his mouth; it was wedged deep into his oropharynx just short of his laryngopharynx. In simple terms it was forced into his throat almost as far as his voice box. We still need to confirm that the penis found is his by means of DNA but having examined the trauma to the cut end of the penis, it also has been sliced with a sharp bladed instrument we are therefore quite confident that the penis is his. We now come to the most significant and interesting finding revealed during the PM. It relates to an injury to the deceased's neck, there is a deep penetrative wound, the puncture wound's point of entry originates from the rear of the neck. It had penetrated numerous vessels and nerves including the internal jugular vein and the internal carotid artery. The laryngeal and trachea were punctured, together with the oesophagus and pharynx. The phrenic nerve was also damaged which is significant because it can cause paralysis. There was evidence of trauma to the larynx and the recurrent laryngeal nerve, both exhibited extensive trauma this can result in paralysis of the vocal folds better known as the vocal cords or voice box. The instrument inflicting this injury is estimated to be at least six to eight inches long, approximately two to three millimetres in diameter and would need to be constructed of a hard-rigid material such as metal or steel. To summarise, the victim's neck has had something similar to a six-inch nail driven through the back of his neck all the way through and exiting the front of the neck causing extensive internal trauma that most probably resulted in body paralysis and loss of speech. This would not cause death at this point however the cause of death which could have taken some considerable time would result from the blood flow filling the airway and eventually this would completely block the airway. The victim may well have been aware of this happening but would have been unable to do anything about it as they most likely would be incapacitated. Had they been able to move then the blockage could have easily been avoided or cleared."

Superintendent Gibbs then asked, "So if I understand this correctly, the victim lay on the floor fully conscious and slowly choked to death because he couldn't move his head to spit the blood out?"

"That's basically it" replied Steve "It would have been a slow agonising death."

"Interesting" said Gibbs "Does this mean then we can assume the female was killed first otherwise she could have helped him move his head to get rid of the blood?"

"I don't think we can make that assumption sir" said Steve.

"Why can't we?" retorted Gibbs.

Steve replied, "Because we have found the exact same injury to the female as well sir, she was probably incapacitated and suffered the same slow death."

The superintendent and the DCI then exchanged a few hushed words that the rest of the room were not privy to and they both began to nod in agreement. The superintendent spoke and said, "Both I and Frank agree that in view of this information then it may be prudent to re-examine the original murder victims."

"I thought that might be the case sir, so the pathologist and I took a non-invasive look at the other two victims." said Steve.

"And?" said the DCI urgently.

"Both bodies are exhibiting the same small puncture type entrance wound at the rear of their necks" replied Steve "and what's more sir" Steve continued "I can see something lodged at the back of the male's mouth."

Oh my god thought Frank Twead, my pisshead pathologist mate Chuman has really cocked up this time. I will have to warn him somehow before the shit hits the fan but even, so I can't see him wriggling his way out of this one. It looks like he's totally fucked this time, it's a wonder he hasn't been caught out before this he is so incredibly pissed all the time he can barely see the bodies let alone examine them.

"Can you arrange the post-mortems for first thing tomorrow please Steve?" asked Gibbs.

The crime scene manager nodded his head and added, "Yes sir, I've already pre-warned the pathologist that you might request them. I will contact her as soon as the briefing is finished."

"Well as far as I'm concerned, this briefing is over, unless anybody else has got some more earth-shattering information?" He surveyed the faces in the room and was met with blank expressions.

"Next briefing nine o'clock tomorrow morning. Thanks everyone" shouted the DCI and the room began to empty.

10

A Swinging Time

The briefing had overrun by quite a while leaving but a few minutes for the press liaison team consisting of Gibbs, Twead, Barista and the press officer to formulate their strategy. They were all gathered in Frank's office discussing how to handle the press and what to say to them in light of the new game changing information. They had all agreed that the exact details of how the victims were murdered or the cutting off of their penises should not be disclosed but that they could elaborate on the dogging angle. That would give the press something to excite the imagination of their readers and sell their newspapers like hot cakes. Besides which this was already common knowledge, so they would already be aware, and we could also use it to make an appeal from the dogging community for information.

The press was now assembled in the incident room, a sweep of the room had been made beforehand to ensure no sensitive material was on display and a uniform presence was there to keep an eye out and deter any over inquisitive reporter delving where they shouldn't. The full cross section of the countries media was assembled from the big national dailies to the lowly local Stourbridge paper that had sent the full might of their one and only reporter with his trusty pad and pencil. But the main focus of the media circus was the lead reporter from the national news the one and only Spenser Wark. The most revered personality in the media industry.

The superintendent opened the press conference with the usual patter given on all these occasions. He welcomed everyone, thanked them for coming and said he looked forward to working closely with everyone in a spirit of co-operation etc. etc. he then handed the chair to the DCI to give the brief.

The normal run of the mill information was given to the media, dates times location of murders, a brief description and background of the victims, the general reassurance that everything possible was being done to protect the public and there was no cause for general alarm. He elaborated somewhat on the sexual theme; this was to give them something juicy for their headlines to keep them placated. He made a two-pronged appeal for information, one for anyone who had seen any suspicious behaviour in or near the park including sighting of vehicles that may have appeared out of place. The other appeal went out directly to members of the dogging community to come forward with any information; he had to word it tactfully and didn't refer to them as doggers just as people who frequented the park at the relevant times.

The DCI together with the press officer answered all the media's questions without any real problems and everything seemed to be going along swimmingly, the press officer gradually assuming the lead role of taking questions whilst Twead sat back and began to relax thinking about the drink he was going to have as soon as they were finished. His head was splitting he was a little dehydrated and he was beginning to get the very slightest onset of the shakes, this bloody enquiry he thought is playing havoc with my drinking regimen. Just as Twead thought the conference was coming to an end Spenser Wark took centre stage, he stood up and waited for a moment giving the cameramen sufficient time to focus on him and his intended target and with practised ease gave a long enough dramatic pause to secure everyone's attention.

"This is a question for Detective Chief Inspector Frank Twead" announced Wark. Oh, fuck thought Twead trying not to show any emotion. He and Wark had previously had quite a notorious and public war of words which Wark had won hands down giving him an abundance of headline grabbing blockbusters leaving Twead bathed in embarrassment and his career advancement in tatters.

"Do you think it is right and proper that in such a high profile horrific series of murders on members of the public that a detective who classified the death of three down and out street sleepers as non-suspicious deaths and completely missed the connection between what are now being investigated as a series of murders of vulnerable members of society. I am referring to op sithens of which you were the senior investigating officer which to my knowledge because of the failure to make the appropriate initial enquires still remains unsolved."

Before the DCI could reply Gibbs interjected stating that since operation sithens the chief constable had reviewed certain procedures and practises and had implemented a force wide training initiative to combat any similar future issues. The deaths were subject to a coroner's investigation and it would therefore not be appropriate to discuss the incident further. Could he please make sure any further questions relate directly to and only to the present enquiry?

The rest of the gathered media representatives were now taking a back-row seat to Wark, they were well aware of the pecking order and they didn't want to get on the wrong side of him. Gibbs had been quite incisive and had been expecting something like this from Wark and had this pre-prepared stock answer to stop him in his tracks. Wark himself was also a consummate professional and he also had the foresight to anticipate negative replies and rebuttals, so he always kept further ammunition in his locker.

Wark replied "Thank you for that superintendent, I am fully aware that the coroner is conducting a review into your forces actions. The question however did not relate to details of the incident it related to the competence of one of your senior investigating officers and the appropriateness of appointing them as the senior investigating officer."

Twead's embarrassment was now turning into anger and frustration. I would love to wring his fucking neck he thought, and this anger was obvious from his facial expression, even the normally snobby air of unflappability of Tony Gibbs was being pushed to the limit.

Wark continued "Can you confirm chief inspector, if the cause of death was blood loss caused by the removal of the penis and has the second male victim also had his penis removed?"

Twead was not ready for this and he was astounded that Wark was aware of this fact which had been deliberately and religiously kept under wraps, he could not think of a way around the question and so simply answered "I am not at liberty to divulge any specific information relating to injuries to the body."

Wark gave a knowing smile as did most of the rest of the assembled media. His refusal to answer was as good as a yes; they all knew that the feeble non-committal replies from Twead meant that Wark was spot on the money and that there was some element of truth to the penis removal angle. With that the superintendent declared the press conference over and the assembled media began to disperse to file their reports. The press liaison team adjourned to Twead's office to discuss the implications of the briefing debacle. Twead was absolutely fuming "that bastard Wark" he said.

"Hang on a bit Frank" said Gibbs thoughtfully, "lets analyse this; he's referred to op sithens. Now if I recall correctly that was the police covert name for the op, the name given to the media and the public was op habstrom. Also, we have not overtly revealed that the victim's penis has been removed. We need to figure out how Wark is getting his information."

"Sounds to me like he has an informer somewhere" said Twead.

"That's exactly what I'm thinking" said Gibbs. Gibbs dismissed the press officer and Barista asking them both to meet again at eight o'clock the next morning to discuss any overnight developments. When they had both left the office. Gibbs asked Twead "Any news from the covert teams who are keeping observations on the victim's spouses?"

"So far nothing but I've arranged for the teams to brief us at seven o'clock tomorrow, I think it would be a good idea to keep the covert ops to just between ourselves" Twead replied.

"I agree Frank, I'll see you here in the morning and we will need to decide on how we find out who is Wark's source. Have a think about it overnight." Gibbs then left the office.

About bleeding time thought Frank, he then walked over to the door and locked it. Returning to his chair he opened his top drawer and took out a bottle of whisky, without wasting time he poured some into a glass and took three huge swigs straight from the bottle, the alcohol quickly began to take effect and he began to relax. The withdrawal symptoms from a few alcohol-free hours were beginning to dissipate as he poured himself another large tumbler which he downed in one then repeated the process until the entire bottle was empty. He would normally now open another bottle, but he had already arranged to meet his mate Dr Chuman and he would have to give him the heads up on the second victims PM results at least give him a chance to try and find some way to dig himself out of the shit he would be in.

Fergas and Peeves parked the CID Mondeo in the pub carpark; they had arranged to meet a group calling themselves the Oldswinford swingers. Initial contact had been made through an on-line dogging site and even after explaining who they were and that they were investigating the murders in the park the group appeared to be only too willing to co-operate and it was on their suggestion that they meet in the pub. It was a small local village pub only a short distance to the scene of the murders and it was in an area where everyone seemed to know everybody else. As they walked in and ordered drinks at the bar they were spotted immediately by the group they had arranged to meet, and they were beckoned over. The group had gathered at the far corner of the pub, there were about a dozen in number and the lead figure for the group; a huge obese woman introduced herself and gestured with her arm to indicate that everyone else seated around the tables were some of the group members. Peeves immediately took a seat next to the fat swinger; he was in his seventh heaven. He had a fetish for big brassy women and this fat swinger fitted the bill perfectly. She looked to be aged in her mid-forties, weighing somewhere in the region of twenty-five stone with peroxide blond hair. She wore a tiny short bright red skirt which exposed folds of milky white cellulite riddled fat thighs spilling over the top of her fishnet stockings, her skimpy top revealed rolls of belly fat resting on her lap and her enormous breasts were lying on top of her belly and were barely contained within a ridiculously tight top. Her make-up was piled on so thick it could have been applied by a builder's trowel, bright red lipstick with equally bright matching long fingernails, the amount of eye makeup made her resemble a panda bear with pantomime long curly black eyelashes.

Fergas could barely conceal his amusement, he was fully aware of Peeves and his fat fetish addiction, but this was taking his perversion to the absolute pinnacle and to witness his best mate totally and utterly besotted by this huge grotesque spectacle of a woman who had reduced Peeves to a compliant all obeying slobbering wreck was more than he could stand, and he erupted into uncontrollable laughter with tears streaming down his face. Fergas himself wasn't particularly choosy but even he would think twice about taking on this monster. Peeves was well aware of Fergas pissing himself but wasn't overly concerned he was in his element. Peeves was deep in conversation with the fat swinger, she was outlining the pleasures of sexual deviations and Peeves was enthralled. "So, tell me exactly, what is it that people get out of it?" he asked

"It depends" she said "different people get different kicks out of it. For instance, I like people to watch me, I get a kick out of getting someone sexually excited especially if it is someone I don't know or haven't seen before. A couple of weeks ago there was quite a few of us, I was bent over a car bonnet being fucked by a complete stranger, there was another six or seven guys again all complete strangers standing in a circle around us. Some were just watching, some were wanking, it was absolutely amazing. The buzz if gave me I felt like I was some sort of sexual superstar being able to excite all these guys just on my own. Is that the sort of insight into the dogging community you are looking for officer?"

Peeves replied "Firstly call me Robert or Rob if you prefer and yes this is exactly the type of inside info we need so we can understand what we are dealing with"

She continued "There's a lot more to it, you get lots of different people with all sorts of sexual preferences. Do you want me to continue?"

Peeves nodded and said "Yes go on"

"Well" she continued "You see the girl over there, the one talking to your mate, she likes something completely different. She's very attractive so she pulls the blokes really easily and that's part of her fetish. She'll pull a couple of blokes at the same time get them going, all sexually excited so they are feeling really horny and talk them into having a threesome which is not so strange you might think. But what she will do is gradually manipulate the situation bit by bit and by revealing to them her sexual fantasies to get the blokes into a frenzy and encourage them to do things with and to each other, that's how she gets her kicks."

"What does she get them to do to each other?" asked Peeves, who was absolutely fascinated by the information the fat swinger was divulging.

"She'll push them as far as she can get them to go; it could be as tame as getting one of them to touch the other or both of them to touch each other while she watches. Or much much further, she is remarkably persuasive and most times very successful. But the thing to remember in all these things is that everything is done with the others consent, no one is ever forced to do anything they don't want to. A lot of doggers just want to watch, like that guy over there,

Walter. He gets his kicks by watching, he doesn't touch anyone or let anyone touch him. He doesn't even touch himself while he's watching, he might get quite close at times in order to get a good view but that's as far as he goes."

The fat swinger also gave details about individuals who watched from a distance, they didn't become directly involved in the dogging but would skulk about in the bushes, so they could barely be seen but obviously got their kicks from watching from afar, probably wanking at the same time, but they would never reveal themselves. Sometimes there would be one or two or sometimes several individuals scattered throughout the shrubbery. The site where they were most prevalent was Stourbridge Park, the scene of the murders. This was probably because of the number of trees and shrubs that they could use take cover.

"Did you know a couple called Fraser and Claire?" asked Peeves.

"If you mean the couple that got murdered then the answer 's yes they were quite well known" she replied.

"Can you tell me what you know about them? "Peeves asked.

She gave it some thought and was racking her brains trying to bring to mind what she knew about them then replied "They started showing up a few months ago. At first, they would just watch and then gradually they became more and more involved. She was very attractive and most of the blokes used to fancy her, he was a bit of a pig though he was known for being quite smelly which I and a lot of the others found a big turn off. They fairly soon progressed to performing sex acts on each other whilst others watched and eventually onto full blown sex in front of everyone. More recently she was having sex with a few strangers while he looked on; I think her kick was the humiliation she suffered. I think she got turned on by it which is again not as uncommon as you might think. After she had shown up a few times I suddenly remembered that I had already met her and her husband"

Peeves said "The person she was with was not her husband"

"Yes, I know that" she replied, "I knew her from school she was a teacher at the local high school. I worked there occasionally as a supply teacher and I spoke with her a few times mostly in the pub after work. She quite liked a drink and that's putting it mildly. I'm sure it was then that the conversation got around to dogging and I told her all about it she seemed to get a little excited about it. She mentioned she would like to try it but would have to do it when her husband Trevor was working late shifts; he worked for the council as some sort of emergency repair man. I spoke with him a few times when he came to pick her up from the pub, he would stop for a drink occasionally. I thought he was a bit weird, there was something creepy about him. It's difficult to define exactly why but he seemed a bit of a loner, an outsider he just didn't seem to fit in."

The conversation continued as did the flow of drinks. Everyone wanted to chip in with a bit of information and swap stories and give ideas and opinions about the murders and what sort of person the killer must be. As the evening wore on the group were becoming more animated and the situation started to get gradually louder and more raucous as the drink began to take effect. Peeves then asked her "Did you know the other murder victims the husband and wife Adam and Peri?"

"Yes, I knew both of them; they weren't much liked though they were both a bit standoffish. They thought they were better than us especially the husband he was very pompous and controlling"

"What do you mean by that exactly?" asked Peeves curiously.

She went on "He would only join in if it suited him. He seemed to prefer the younger girls, they were the only ones he would have a dabble with. It was different with his wife though she had to have sex with whoever he chose for her, she wasn't allowed to decide for herself he totally dominated her, and she would comply with everything he told her to do without question. Neither of them socialised with us, they never came here to this pub to have a drink with the rest of the group. I think his wife Peri might have wanted to, but she had to do whatever he said I think they use to drink in some sort of hoity-toity wine bar."

Peeves replied, "That's interesting, can you tell me if there is any connection that you can think of between them and Fraser and Clare anything at all?"

"Not as far as I'm aware, in fact I can't even remember them meeting each other they tended to turn up on different nights and I don't think they were the type of people who would socialise with each other."

"Can you think of any reason why someone would want to kill them?"

She thought again for a moment and replied "Like I said, Adam was a bit of a pain but certainly not enough for anyone to want to kill him. The general feeling amongst everyone is that it was some random maniac and they were in the wrong place at the wrong time."

Peeves nodded in agreement with this hypothesis as he together with the rest of the investigation team were of the same opinion. With the alcohol still flowing freely and more people beginning to relax some of the rest of the group then began to chip in with their opinions and snippets of information and the general conversation began to flourish. Peeves had gotten a lot of useful intelligence from a number of the group including a comprehensive list of local dogging sites and the best nights and busiest times. He had also gotten himself as horny as a stoat and he was becoming more and more infatuated by the fat swinger.

He couldn't see his mate Frank and he assumed he had taken the swinger he had been talking to outside to try his luck see what was on offer, so he thought he might push his luck as well. He sat back down and re-engaged her in conversation. He started by giving her a bit of flattery about how sexy she looked and the inevitable ultimate bullshit about how young she looked when she had revealed her age to him and that he didn't believe her, and she was obviously much younger. She took the bait straight away and gave Peeves a few saucy come-ons of her own and reminded him that her forte was getting guys excited. He gave her some more compliments about her figure, notably her huge breasts, she took it a stage further and with a drunken giggle she twisted and turned her torso around until her breasts were more or less completely exposed.

His drunken sexual urges had now overtaken his common sense and he began to fondle the biggest mounds of flesh he had ever seen before burying his head deep in between them. When he eventually surfaced for air he saw that most of the group were now indulging in drunken acts of either exposing themselves or groping various bits of everyone else's flesh and body appendages people oblivious to the fact that they were in a public house.

"What would your husband say if he knew about this" asked Peeves.

She answered "He likes to watch that's how he gets his kicks from watching other blokes doing things to me and I mean anything. If you don't believe me, you can ask him yourself he is sitting next to us."

Peeves looked at the tiny bald headed insignificant guy who had been sitting next to him all night but had not said a single word and he still didn't say anything he just sat there, took a sip of his drink and gave Peeves a little smile. What the fuck is happening thought Peeves; this is all becoming a bit crazy. He looked around the area of the room they were occupying; everybody was doing everything to everybody else. It was like a scene from a vintage porn gangbang movie. Things were starting to escalate out of control he thought.

The drunken revelry was shattered by the sound of Frank Fergas screaming like a banshee making his way awkwardly towards Peeves as quickly as he could whilst trying to pull his trousers up which where halfway between his knees and his groin. He was closely followed by the female dogger whom he had been speaking to earlier together with another male both of who were in a dishevelled state with their clothing in disarray. Peeves looked on in astonishment as Fergas approached him and as Fergas began to speak the room suddenly lit up with the most incredible flash of light. Then it became a series of bright flashes, everyone realised they were all being photographed by what were obviously press photographers. Immediate panic and pandemonium ensued and a mass stampede of drunken sexual deviants in various stages of undress began rampaging towards the exit knocking over anything and everything in its path. Glasses, tables, chairs and photographers were all caught up in the melee, everyone desperate to get out as quickly as possible and avoid being snapped and possibly exposed by the tabloid press.

Fergas and Peeves didn't need to speak to each other they immediately ran for and made it to the CID Mondeo and quickly guided it out of the carpark as fast as possible scraping a bollard on the way causing a large indent in both the front and rear passenger doors, but they didn't dare stop or even look back at the mayhem spilling out onto the carpark.

"What on earth happened to you? Why were you screaming like a lunatic when you ran back in the pub?" Peeves asked Fergas.

He didn't respond straight away but seemed to be deep in thought for a while. When he eventually replied he was very matter of fact with his response. "It was that bird, she was a bit weird and she freaked me out a bit that's all."

Peeves began to push him a little and asked "What was the matter with her? She looked alright to me. I thought she would be just your type?"

Fergas snapped back at him and replied sharply "She was just a bit weird and that's all there is to it, now just drop the subject and get us back to the nick so we can dump the car and then get our story straight for tomorrow."

Peeves let the subject drop, he was also anxious to get the CID car back to the nick; he was well over the drink drive limit, but he got pulled over by uniform he would be alright they wouldn't breathalyse a detective on duty but if he got in an accident even the slightest prang then it meant an automatic breath test. That's why they hadn't stopped when they scraped the bollard in the carpark, they would simply ignore that and if no one noticed the damage to the car straight away they would shift the blame to someone else. They drove back to the nick in silence with Peeves mulling over what the fat swinger had told him about the swinger that Frank had been ensconced with and her strange fetish still trying to work out what had happened.

11

Eyes On

Frank Twead was slowly coming around. He tried to open his eyes, but he couldn't, it was if they were glued together. His head was a complete mess; he needed to try and think where he was and what had happened. He tried to focus but the excruciating pain in his head made it impossible, it felt as if a pneumatic drill was pounding away inside his head trying to break out of his skull. One eyelid was eventually forced open just enough to allow some light in he shut it straight away when the beam of light exploded at the back of his brain. He tried again and squinted towards the direction of the light that was searing into his head and burning at the back of his skull.

He realised he was in his office sitting in his chair slumped over his desk, every bone in his body ached. The blinding light that was flooding into his face was his office desk lamp which was pointing straight at him. He shut his eyes and began to piece together the previous night's events. He remembered he had fully downed a bottle of whisky that was almost full as soon as the superintendent left his office.

Then he met his mate the pathologist in the pub where he told him about the results of the post-mortem on the second murdered couple and how a cursory examination of the initial murdered couple had cast doubt on the conclusions he had given as the cause of death and a second PM would be taking place. He had initially been surprised at how calm Hubert had been when he told him the news; it was if he had been expecting it, but then Hubert opened up to him partly to ease the burden of carrying his guilty secrets on his own and wishing to get it off his chest to somehow ease his burden. This need was fuelled by the loosening effect on his tongue caused by the quantity of alcohol they had both consumed. He had told him that he had long since resigned himself to the fact that the countless mistakes that he knew he had been making over the years would eventually catch him out or come back to haunt him.

He realised that his pathology examinations had become gradually more slipshod and less detailed than they should be; in some of his more lucid periods he had reflected on some of the horrendous oversights and misdiagnosis's he had made due in the most part to the state his excessive drinking had left him in and his desire to complete examinations as quickly as possible to start drinking again.

One in particular had initiated a murder enquiry he had misidentified red and purple marks to the front of the neck as a sign of bruising leading to strangulation. Fortunately, no one was ever convicted but the case still remained on file as an unsolved murder. It was only a chance conversation with a detective in the case some considerable time later that he became aware that the body had been found lying face down and the marks were in fact 'pseudo bruises'. These were caused when the blood pools naturally after death from the effects of gravity.

He also opened up about the recent examination of three tramps whom he had wrongly concluded died of natural causes and he was now reasonably sure were the result of foul play. These cases were familiar to Frank but despite knowing what they both should do now they had decided to keep quiet about everything. Frank had a special interest in the deaths of the three tramps he had also failed to do his job and simply dismissed them as non-suspicious. The coroner was looking into these deaths, but Frank had already been assured unofficially that the enquiry would find nothing untoward and the enquiry would be allowed to fizzle out. No one was really bothered about the deaths of three down and out smelly tramps anyway; there was no pressure from any family members because none had been found so who cared.

It was worrying to Frank however about what the meddling press maestro Wark knew about it and what issues he may raise. The drink then had begun to take hold and they had both then ignored these startling revelations and set about getting completely pissed which they managed to do extremely successfully. At the end of the evenings session when the pub called last orders and no more drink was available, Hubert had got into his motor to drive home.

Twead had returned to his office and opened another bottle of scotch for a swift nightcap. It was all starting to make some sort of sense, but he still couldn't understand why he felt so incredibly hungover. He then put his hand on his forehead as one would do to shield your eyes from bright sunlight and opened his eyes after he had scanned the room and his eyes had become used to the light and he could manage to focus, he looked around his desk he realised why he felt so bad. Lying on its side in the middle of his desk amongst crime files and assorted paperwork was a bottle of scotch. It was the one he had opened when he was already totally pissed to have a nightcap, amazingly it was completely empty. The clock on the wall was showing a little after six o'clock, it was going to be a busy day he needed to get his act together; there were a lot of things scheduled.

His normal routine when he had fallen asleep in his office was to freshen up in the Station toilets; he would either splash water on his face or time permitting use the shower. Frank opened his desk drawer to retrieve his washbag that he kept there for just such occasions; it was nestling next to an unopened bottle of scotch, the last one left in the drawer. He made a mental note to restock sometime that day. He thought for a second and then took a long hard stare at the unopened bottle "Fuck it" he said out loud and reached for the bottle cracked it open and took a hearty couple of swigs before making his way to the shower room.

At seven o'clock DCI Frank Twead and Detective Superintendent Tony Gibbs were having an unofficial undocumented and unrecorded meeting with two covert officers. Both the officers had been secretly assigned to keep observations on the spouses of the first murder victims. It was completely without lawful authority as the laws regarding this type of surveillance required special permission under the Regulation of Investigatory Powers Act, otherwise known as RIPA. They realised that the criteria to grant covert surveillance and or phone tapping would not be met in these circumstances, so they had decided to do it completely unofficially.

The covert officers had been pre-briefed to keep their activities totally clandestine and, in the event, that they were shown out they were to simply state that they just happened to be there by pure chance. The information concerning the movement and activities regarding Fraser's wife was mundane to say the least, she was what was normally referred to as a stop at home. She rarely went out anywhere had no visitors to speak of and more importantly her phone calls that were being tapped illegally did not show any unusual or incriminating behaviour and certainly nothing that would connect her in anyway with the murder of her husband.

When it came to Claire's husband however this was completely different. The covert officer Pete explained that Trevor Pickes in his role as an emergency repair man for the local council had access to a council pick-up truck which when not working he drove for personal use. Pickes was seen leaving his house and getting into his pick up shortly after nine the previous evening. The vehicle had been followed at a safe distance; he had driven to four separate locations before eventually being lost. The places visited in order were Wassell Grove Pedmore, Oldswinford Park, a supermarket in Netherton and finally Morfe Lane Kingswinford. Pete paused for a moment when he saw the look on the senior officers faces they had turned to face each other both with smiles stretching from ear to ear and then they returned their attention back to Pete eager to hear more.

Pete said, "I can see by your reactions that I don't need to tell you that all these places he visited are well known dogging sites."

He then outlined what happened at each site. At the first two sites he was able to get a vantage point where he could see what Pickes was doing. Pickes got out of his vehicle looked around and then disappeared into the bushes so that he was hidden from view, his position would have given him however a good clear view of any activities that may take place. At both sites there was no sign of anybody else or anything happening, he stayed around ten minutes then left. At the third site, the supermarket he parked in a corner of the carpark. He didn't get out of his vehicle and again it was all quiet and nothing was happening, he waited for a few minutes then drove off. The fourth location Morfe Lane Kingswinford is a small narrow country lane so in order not to show out Pete explained he had to drive past and park some distance away. Pete cleared his throat and announced, "Now this is where it gets really interesting."

"Hold on a bit" said Frank as he got up from his chair and walked over to his office door withdrew the door key from his pocket and locked the door. "That's so we won't be disturbed or get any interruptions, now go on" he said as he settled back into his chair in hopeful anticipation.

Gibbs and Twead had unconsciously moved their chairs closer to Pete's. This meant that he could talk in a hushed more secretive voice; it was if they were naughty schoolboys about to hear some smutty story or gossip that no-one else was privy to. With their full attention Pete recounted what happened next.

"After parking so far away to avoid showing out it took me about ten minutes to walk back to the scene. The country lane where Pickes vehicle was parked was very narrow barely wider than a single track. Vehicles approaching from opposite directions would need to use the refuge areas located at varying intervals to pass each other. There is no street lighting there or anywhere else nearby, also there are no houses or farm building in the area so the number of vehicles that use the road must be minimal. It is very much a lonely isolated stretch of road and fortunately for me the night was cloudy and overcast so it was extremely dark giving me good cover as well as not casting shadows. I circled around the back of the location and approached the scene from the direction of the woods. I don't know if you are aware, but I am a level four crops trained operative meaning I'm an expert in covert surveillance in rural surroundings. This allows me to get up close in this type of countryside setting without detection. From some distance away, I became aware of some activity taking place, it was coming from a clearing in the forestation situated between me and the country lane where I had last seen Pickes' vehicle. As I edged closer I could identify two vehicles both with their sidelights switched on and four persons near one of the vehicles."

After a sip of water he continued "Each time I moved closer I made a visual reconnoitre of the scene using night vision goggles and an audio sweep with a specialist listening amplifier. From about forty yards away I identified another area of low level noise that was not emanating from the where the vehicle's and the four persons were. I had to remain static until I located the position of the origin of the second noise and identified it with visual confirmation. When I pinpointed the target area I had to change direction to approach this second site from a rear aspect, when I obtained maximum optimal position I had a clear line of sight of the three areas of interest. The furthest away from me in a straight line was the country lane and then came the two parked vehicles together with the four people. Then next closest to me was the second area of noise interest. I could see both the vehicles and could identify that the four persons were one female and three males. The female was in a state of undress and bent over the bonnet of one of the cars whilst the three males in a state of semi undress took turns penetrating the female. Then the closest area of interest to me I could clearly see Trevor Pickes. He was positioned in a manner and location that afforded him a view of the dogging scene but he himself was hidden from the view of the doggers. His trousers were down around his ankles and in one hand he held a pornographic magazine and with the other he was masturbating whilst watching the scene. It was at this point when a vehicle sped into the clearing from the direction of the country lane at speed with headlights on full beam youths were hanging their heads out of the vehicles windows and they were making shrieking noises and shouting obscenities towards the vehicle. Then they did a handbrake turn and sped off in a cloud of dust as quickly as it had arrived. It appeared to be teenagers messing about having some fun at the expense of the doggers, this obviously curtailed the activities and they hurriedly adjusted their clothing and retreated to their vehicles and drove off. This had also unnerved Pickes who backed away from the clearing deeper into the woods until he was just a few feet away from me. He was that close to me that I could hear him breathing and despite him looking around the area he failed to see me almost right behind him. He then went back to his vehicle after a short while and drove off. When I returned to my vehicle that had to be parked some distance away, he was long gone; this was now eleven-fifteen, so I drove back to keep observations on his address arriving at eleven-thirty. He arrived home in his vehicle at one-twenty-five and went inside so there is a missing period of approximately two hours, I then concluded the observations."

Gibbs then spoke "thanks for that technical explanation Pete, some of the jargon I didn't fully understand but what is blatantly clear is that this bloke is a full-on pervert. He obviously gets his kicks from covertly spying on other perverts, doggers and the like and wanking off in the process. Judging by his activity last night he's obviously very active so the chances are he probably caught his wife in the act of being shafted over the bonnet of a car and in a fit of jealous rage killed them both. He will have done the second murders to divert any suspicion away from him and lead everyone to think we have a serial killer on the loose."

"It all seems to make sense" said Twead "now then Pete it goes without saying that this does not get repeated ever. The evidence we have obtained is by illegal inadmissible means and we would all be

129

in the shit if it came to light, so we need to find some other way to use it and create a legitimate and legal source, but myself and the boss will sort that out. The pornographic magazine that Pickes had, did you manage to see what its title was?"

"I did better than that" Pete replied "Pickes dropped the magazine on the floor when the speeding car came into the clearing, so I recovered it for examination. The title of the magazine is Desire and it looks like some sort of specialist dogging contact magazine."

"That's great work Pete. Is that everything?" asked Gibbs.

"Not quite" replied Pete "there's more. He also received and made some interesting phone calls. I haven't made any written records for obvious reasons."

Gibbs nodded his head and said, "quite right Pete good idea; we wouldn't want any documentation falling into the wrong hands we'd all be for the chop if that happened."

Pete continued "The gest of the conversations between him and his callers concerned dogging or more accurately the act of covertly spying on doggers. They discussed the best locations to spy on them and where the hiding places that give the best view at each location. They also made arrangements to meet up at various dogging sites."

Twead asked "Did you manage to obtain any telephone numbers or names so that we can do some follow up enquires?"

Pete replied. "I couldn't retrieve or identify the incoming or outgoing telephone numbers because of the restricted type of phone hacking that I had to use, to go to the level of obtaining numbers requires a different technique which can sometimes be traced back to the hacking source. With regards to names none of them give their real identities they all use nicknames. Trevor Pickes uses the name Sneaky Peaker, laughable I know but somewhat accurate if you think about it."

Gibbs looked at his watch, it was seven-thirty "I think that's all we have time for now we need to prepare for the morning briefing so thank you both for your efforts and we will see you here same time tomorrow."

The covert officers then left the office and the Station separately and as quickly as possible so as not to draw attention to themselves. When they'd left the office and Gibbs was confident that there was no one in possible earshot he looked purposely at Twead and spoke slowly and in no uncertain terms. In a manner of fact way that underlined the rank structure implying I'm the superintendent and you're my subordinate chief inspector. "As far as I'm concerned he is our man. I want you to do everything and anything to nail that bastard pervert and when I say anything I mean anything; do I make myself clear Frank?"

This wasn't said in the form of a request or instruction this was a direct specific order. Frank knew exactly what Gibbs meant. Trevor Pickes was to be arrested, tried and convicted for the dogging murders whether the evidence was there or not and if it wasn't there or couldn't be found then it needed to be fabricated, planted, made up invented or whatever it took for the charges to stick and there were no holds barred. Gibbs had appointed himself as judge, jury and executioner.

12

A Word in Your Ear

The morning briefing began with Fergas and Peeves giving their update on their efforts to gain information and an insight into the world of dogging. Fergas outlined the meeting with the Oldswinford doggers and explained how there were different genres and types of sexual deviants within the group and they all got their sexual thrills from different sources. Some like to watch, others like to participate or encourage others to do so and so on. Gibbs and Twead's ears pricked up when Fergas mentioned the type who likes to remain hidden in the background and watch covertly from a distance. Fergas did not mention the debacle that the meeting had descended into and he was hoping that it would fade away without becoming public knowledge especially the damage they had caused by scraping the CID car against the bollard.

"Oh, there was one other piece of information from the meeting" said Peeves.

"Go on" said Twead.

Peeves outlined what he had been told about the first victims Claire and Fraser and how Claire was known to a leading member of the doggers via the local high school where they both worked. When he detailed what had been said about Claire's husband concerning him coming across as a bit weird and a bit of a loner Twead could barely believe his ears he wanted to shout out we've got the bastard and would have done so if Gibbs hadn't intervened and said, "That's a job well done lads" and gave Twead a hard-piercing stare.

Twead knew that he had nearly jeopardised the investigation by almost shouting out in his excitement and it was only the timely intervention of Gibbs that had stopped him. The rest of the briefing was routine nothing of any particular interest was forthcoming. Peeves continued with what he had learned about the second victims husband and wife Adam and Peri and him being a bit of a domineering bully and that no connection had been found between the murder victims, but this was falling on deaf ears because as far as Twead and Gibbs were concerned they already had their man it was just a case of how to get him. They were just about to wind proceedings when the SOCO team entered the briefing room. They had just returned from the second post-mortem examinations on the first victims. Gibbs said "Hello guys we were just about to complete but if you're ready we'll have your input. I assume you've got the results of the second post-mortem on the first murder victims?"

"That's right" said Steve.

Twead knew what was coming, he expected the second post-mortem to completely discredit the findings of Dr Hubert Chuman's initial examination and this would probably spell the end of Chuman's career. Twead said "If you can outline your results as succinctly as possible Steve please just outline the relevant points that we need to know for us."

"I'll be as brief as I can sir, I just need a couple of minutes to get my paperwork in order." Whilst Steve was preparing his paperwork Gibbs said to Twead "You almost blurted out something when it was revealed Claire's husband is a weirdo, remember we cannot divulge or give any indication that we have any information on him. Anyone with half a brain would figure out that we are conducting covert ops and that would fuck everything up so think before you speak. Remember total secrecy is paramount is that message understood?" Twead nodded and realised he had been so close to making a complete hash of things.

Steve then began his brief. "The initial post-mortem finding concluded that the male person had died from exsanguination as a result of major trauma to the genital area. In other words, he had bled to death as a result of having his penis cut off, his penis was not found. The cause of death to the female was given as compressive traumatic asphyxia as a result of pressure on the upper torso again in simple terms she was unable to breathe because of the weight of the dead male on her back crushing her. The second post-mortem was ordered because the causes of death to the second pair of victims were so different and they both died as a result of unusual specific injuries. The pair had both died because of a deep puncture type wound to the back of the neck causing severe trauma to the internal jugular vein and the internal carotid artery, the laryngeal nerve together with the trachea the oesophagus and the pharynx, the vocal folds had also suffered severe trauma. To summarise in simple terms the victims died as a result of an object something similar to a six to eight-inch nail or metal spike being driven through the back of their necks, the resultant damage would cause paralysis and loss of speech. They would then slowly bleed to death because they were unable to move or cry out for help. The male victim in addition had his penis cut off and inserted into the back of his throat. The re-examination this morning of the first victims shows that they also suffered the same traumatic injuries to the neck. These injuries were missed in the first PM and the cause of death was also misdiagnosed they were in fact killed and died in the same manner as the second pair of victims. In addition, the male victim's penis has been found in the back of his throat. This makes the killing of both pairs of victims identical."

Twead knew this was the final nail in the coffin for Chuman not only had he given the wrong cause of death he had missed the injury to the back of the neck and how on earth had he managed to miss the guys penis stuffed down the back of his throat.

Shirley Wallows had listened with interest to the account of the second post-mortem. She remembered the humiliating way Chuman had treated her and she had also seen the completely different approach in the way he conducted his post-mortems in comparison

135

with pathologist Sally Drice, she seemed much more methodical and thorough than his offhand casual manner. While she was still thinking about the possible repercussions for Chuman, Grant Courtan approached her and said "I've been told to tell you that the DCI wants you in his office in thirty minutes"

"Have you any idea what he wants to see me for?" asked Wallows with a worried and slightly puzzled expression.

Courtan replied "I haven't got the faintest idea, I've only been told to give you the message, but I shouldn't worry he wasn't his normal miserable self he seemed quite jovial and upbeat for a change."

Wallows thanked him and made her way to the police canteen and sat there nursing a cup of tea. She had been intending to have something to eat as she had not had time for breakfast before she had left home for work but now she had lost her appetite. Despite the assurances from Grant Courtan about Twead's demeanour the hunger in her stomach had changed to a feeling of queasiness. She was wracking her brains to think of any possible reason why she had been summoned to Frank Twead's office. She kept her eye on the time; she didn't want to be late for whatever awaited her. It wouldn't be good news she was pretty certain of that.

Ten minutes to go she started to feel sick with worry, her stomach was churning. She told herself not to be so stupid; she could handle all the streets could throw at her, the drunks who wanted to fight everyone especially uniform police. The violent criminals and the constant abuse and name calling. All this was no problem to her, but she hated the constant humiliation and belittlement from senior officers and people in positions of power, people like Twead and Chuman. One last look at the clock it was now time to go. She stood outside Twead's office took a deep breath and decided to put on a brave face and not let him see she was so nervous. She knocked on the door then walked straight in trying her utmost to exude an air of confidence. She strode purposely into the centre of the office but was then taken aback, she looked around the room and she had not been prepared for what she saw. What on earth was this all about she thought?

"Take a seat Shirley and we'll get started" said Twead.

Shirley sat down; still perplexed by what she was seeing as this was not what she was expecting. She thought she was in for some form of criticism an embarrassing telling off or some form other form of humiliation, but this certainly wasn't that. In the office were the DCI, DS Grant Courtan, DC Latifeo and DCs Frank Fergas and Robert Peeves.

Frank Twead addressed the assembled officers "Thank you all for coming, you are all obviously curious as why you are here. I have personally selected each of you for a special operation. But before I go any further and prior to giving you the details of the operation I want assurances from each and every one of you that you will not reveal any single detail or one iota of information concerning the operation. That includes not telling anyone that you are working or attached to a special unit. If anyone feels they would not be able to comply with that condition, then please feel free to leave the room and carry on with your normal duties. If you wish to remain then do so but that is on the understanding that you have accepted these conditions, have I made myself clear?"

Twead then slowly looked around the room and eyed each individual officer in order to illicit a positive or negative response.

"You can count me in sir" said Latifeo. Fergas and Peeves both nodded their heads to indicate acceptance and then all attention was on Wallows. The situation had caught her off guard, in the space of a few minutes she had gone from having butterflies in her stomach in the expectation of a severe reprimand to being invited to work on a special operation. She tried to speak but her mouth was so dry nothing came out. She coughed to try and clear her throat and at the same time nodded her head to indicate she wished to be part of the team.

"Right, you are all now committed to the operation and I will repeat again the conditions you have accepted are that you tell no one else outside of the officer's present in this room any details whatsoever or that such operation exists. I will now hand the floor to Grant, please pay careful attention."

Grant Courtan stood up and with a bundle of papers on a clipboard stood by the white board situated in the corner of the room and addressed the room.

"First I will give a very brief rundown of the investigation so far. We have two double murders in the same location the main carpark in Stourbridge Park. The method used on all four victims is identical, they were all murdered by the insertion of a thin bladed weapon through the back of their necks to such a depth that it completely penetrates their necks all the way through to their larynx or voice box as it is more commonly known. This damages vital nerves and causes immediate paralysis, so they cannot move, and it renders them unable to speak or make any sound at all. In simple terms they have slowly internally bled to death and because of the paralysis it may also cause suffocation if the blood flow blocks the airways and they can't move to clear the blockage. Background and intelligence checks have been made on all the victims to try and establish any links between them or reasons why anyone would want to kill any of them and this is what we have so far. The first male victim Fraser was an ex pub landlord who because of some of his shady business practises has upset a lot of people in short what he did was to borrow a lot of money from various sources including friends, family and business associates immediately prior to declaring himself bankrupt thus negating the obligation for him to repay any of the money which he is believed to have hidden away somewhere this obviously could well make him a target. The woman murdered with him Claire was a school teacher she was apparently well liked and respected she had no criminal convictions or outstanding debts and apart from the fact that she was having an affair with Fraser if that's what you call it we can find no obvious reasons for her to be a target, but I will come back to her shortly neither of them had any children. The second pair of murder victims were husband and wife Adam and

138

Peri Dores they were both professional people and started their careers in the social services sector mainly involving children and worked their way up the ladder culminating in both of them having high ranking managerial positions. They are quite well off with no obvious debts or money worries and they have both received awards and recognition for their charity work within the social care spectrum, especially in aid of deprived children as well as within their own local community. He is known to be somewhat domineering particularly towards his wife and he is known for getting his own way but there is nothing in their background that we have found that could suggest that they were a target. They have one child Cambion who is presently away studying at Durham University. Background checks on him reveal he has no criminal convictions and is not a member of any subversive groups he seems a normal well-adjusted young man enjoying university. Enquires will continue into the victims and their respective backgrounds but these will be conducted by detectives within the main incident room we will be concentrating our efforts elsewhere. This investigation is codenamed overbrant; it is an operation within an operation. It still directly relates to the two double murders in the park. But our team has however one primary objective, we will direct our attention to and conduct enquires targeted at one specific individual. I have received credible information that implicates this person as responsible for both double murders."

The team sat there in total silence, completely and utterly enthralled by what they were listening to. It was common knowledge to all and sundry within the incident room that the enquiry had made no in-roads or established any productive lines of enquires and to date no possible suspects had been identified. Everything seemed to have stalled so to be directly involved with investigating the possible killer as part of a small team was absolutely incredible; this was something that each and every one of the team could take so much kudos from in the future especially if they were successful. What the team didn't realise was that they had been handpicked by Twead because he knew that he could control and manipulate each one of them and they would do exactly what he directed them to do. Not one of them had the backbone or spirit to question him or defy his instructions.

Grant Courtan wiped the briefing board clean before continuing. "I will be writing some briefing notes on the white board" he said, then added "but it will be wiped clean before we leave this room there is to be no permanent record made of our enquires or actions by anyone no one is to make any notes or document what we are doing at this moment in time it is imperative that there is nothing that can be traced back to our activities I hope I have made myself clear." He waited for a moment for this to sink in then continued. "Shortly after eight o'clock this morning I was contacted directly by telephone to my landline, this is significant because the call did not come through the switchboard but direct this means that caller was aware of my number. They also knew me by name without me offering it. I would surmise that the caller is one of my informants but for reason or reasons unknown they did not want to identify themselves."

Latifeo asked "If it was one of your informants then wouldn't you be able to recognise their voice?"

Courtan replied "Normally yes I would but they deliberately disguised their voice. They were using some sort of voice scrambler, it made their speech sound similar to a Doctor Who dalek, you know the sort of thing - we will exterminate you etc."

Fergas then chipped in "Can we not trace the number Grant?"

"Already looked into it and there is no way we can retrieve the originating number" said Courtan.

Wallows said "But we can get the voice recording of the conversation, all incoming calls to the Station are automatically recorded. I know this because one of the girls in admin received an abusive call last year and the recording was used in the court case perhaps we could get it examined forensically."

Courtan nodded his head towards Wallows with a look of approval for thinking outside of the box and replied "That's good thinking Shirley but it's a no go, the only calls that are recorded are ones that go via the switchboard. The same reason as why we can't trace the call but well done these are the sort of idea's we need. I'll now outline the contents of the call and give you your allocated actions without a written record or recording of the conversation I can only give you the general information. The caller stated that the person responsible for both murders was Trevor Pickes, the husband of the first murder victim Claire Pickes. He further stated that he is a pervert who gets his kicks from secretly watching sexual activities such as dogging. He has access to and uses in his activity a council pick-up truck that he uses during the course of his employment and he also uses it for personal use."

Peeves then interjected "We have some information concerning Trevor Pickes; we had a meet with members of a swinger's club in Oldswinford. The wife of Trevor was known to them as a participant in the dogging activities, she was also known by one of the group as a work colleague at the local school where they both taught. The husband was known to them when they would go for a drink after work and her husband would come to pick his wife up from the pub and joined them occasionally for a drink or two. He was described as being a bit odd something weird about him, which coming from a leading member of bunch of sexual swingers is saying something."

"Yes, I picked that up at the briefing" replied Grant "but there is no suggestion that he was known to the group as a swinger or dogger or took part in any of their sexual deviances is that correct?"

"Yes" replied Peeves "No one said they saw him during the sexual stuff only at the pub when he came to collect his wife after work. His wife was always with the bloke who got murdered during the dogging they referred to him as fat Fraser."

The expression on Grant's face was beaming he looked as if he had just won the lottery "It looks like it's all fitting together nicely, we've got a cheating wife who goes dogging in the park with another

141

bloke or maybe even several and a husband who didn't take part and probably didn't even know anything about it but like to secretly watch without anybody knowing he was there. He may have stumbled across a couple bent over a car in the park watched for a while and then realised he was watching his cheating wife being fucked over the car bonnet by her boyfriend and hey presto the bloke has flipped and done them in? He probably did the second murders to shift any suspicion away from him and make it appear there is a homicidal maniac on the loose, so it looks to me like this anonymous info is spot on. I've allocated you all specific areas to investigate. Frank and Robert, I want you to enquire with his friends, associates, work colleagues etc. Find out anything and everything concerning his behaviour and movements. Is that understood?" Frank and Robert both nodded.

Grant then looked towards Wallows, she sat up expectantly eager to find out what her part in the undercover enquiry was to be. She could feel butterflies doing gambols in her stomach, a different kind of feeling to that when she thought she was in for a roasting this was sheer excitement this was an adrenalin rush like she had never felt before.

"You Shirley, probably have the most difficult and potentially the most important part of our investigation. You could possibly give us the breakthrough we need." Grant then paused for a moment to emphasise the importance of what he was about to say. "The information we have been given is that Pickes contacts other perverts who also like covertly watching displays of public sexual activity, he contacts these people through a sexual contact magazine called Desire. The participants usually use pseudonyms; Pickes uses the name Sneaky Peaker."

Wallows listened intently to this as did the rest of the team. This was fascinating they all thought, this was edge of your seat stuff and what's more they were the only one's privy to this information. This also gave it all of a more enigmatic and ego boosting quality.

142

He went on "Your role Shirley is to infiltrate this group ideally by placing your details in the contact magazine and getting him to make the first move. If he doesn't or if it will take too long to get an advert included, then you will have to contact him direct via his advertisement in the magazine although this would be our second choice. I will make enquires with the magazine to find out the time constraints."

Shirley's mind was racing, this is what proper undercover police work is all about she thought, this is why I joined the job. "Grant, what do I need to do about contact details and false names?" Shirley enquired.

"I'll get you an unregistered pay as you go phone, the only people to be given the number apart from me and you will be whoever tries to contact you it will be safer that way. You will need a pseudonym and a cover story; I will leave that with you."

Latifeo was beginning to feel a little left out not having been given an allocated task "What will I be doing?" he asked a little impatiently.

Twead who had been silent so far throughout the briefing replied "You will be partnering Shirley, this could be quite dangerous, and you need to look out for her and provide a level of back up for protection if needed. In addition, I also want you to still act as liaison officer with the criminal profiler; this will also assist in maintaining your cover. That also applies to you pair" directing his gaze at Peeves and Fergas. "You can still continue your enquires with the swinger's organisations again maintaining your cover."

Twead then stood up saying "Grant will give you each help and any other details that you need. I have other matters pressing. I want you all to start immediately is that understood?" Everyone in the room gestured their agreement. "I want to see you all for a private team debrief at eight o'clock this evening in my office. If any of you have anything personal arranged then cancel it, you will all be there no exceptions."

Twead then left the room. He went back to his own office and entered with a self-satisfied smug look spread across his face. "Hook line and sinker, they've fallen for the lot exactly as planned. In fact I didn't even have to guide them towards the conclusion they pieced it all together themselves" Twead said with aplomb after he had closed his office door.

Superintendent Gibbs who had been waiting for him gave an appreciative nod and replied, "Excellent well-done Frank now sit down and fill me in with all the details."

Twead then outlined how he had assembled a small team of officers; he had handpicked each individual because he knew they would all do as he said without causing much fuss. He had the ability to exercise full control over all of them. The information had been given via an anonymous source to Grant Courtan, who is under the belief that the source is one of his informants. Then there was the info from Peeves about Pickes being a weirdo that's when they put two and two together and figured Pickes accidently came across his wife being fucked by another bloke whilst doing his secret watching fetish and killed them both. A few more things still needed to be drip fed to the team such as a few sightings of Pickes council van near the crime scenes and a bit of forensics thrown in for good measure which I will set up Shirley Wallows or Latifeo to find and the jobs a good un.

"Sounds fine so far Frank" said Gibbs "but just a couple of questions, how was the information conveyed to Courtan? And is there any possibility that it could be traced back to our unauthorised surveillance?"

With a self-congratulatory look spread all over his face Twead replied "Completely untraceable Tony, I phoned Courtan's landline direct not through the switchboard so the originating number cannot be identified and the call would not be recorded. He couldn't recognise my voice, I used one of those scrambler devices, you know the sort? The type you can get off e-bay or amazon for just a couple of quid and Courtan is so full of himself he actually thinks it's one of his informants whose voice would have been known to him without the use of the scrambler, what an arsehole. As far as I can remember the only informant he ever had was a down and out drunk who would tell him where the other down and outs were stealing their booze from. In addition to this I have told them all that this is a secret operation and they are to tell no one anything at all, not even that such an operation is in existence but I know that idiot Latifeo can't hold his own water. He will blab his big mouth so I have kept him as the liaison officer with the psychological profiler whom he will tell in supposed confidence all about Pickes, how he is bang to rights and give him all his details and information. If I know Barista he will use this to make up a profile to suit him and then he will supply it to us. He will give us some cobblers as to how he compiled the offender profile, he won't have a clue that I have set him up to give me the profile I want and that should be the icing on the cake."

Tony Gibbs stood up with all the cocky presence of a man who had just gotten exactly what he wanted. Confident in the knowledge that he would be taking all the credit for a successful conclusion to a major murder enquiry and receive his due recognition and enhanced future career prospects from the chief and that if anything were to go wrong and the operation went tits up the buck would be passed all the way down the line as far as possible away from him. Gibbs then reached inside his jacket pocket to retrieve his vibrating mobile phone and Twead heard him say "Yes you can bring the car round the front and take me to force HQ." Gibbs turned his attention back to Twead telling him "I'm on my way to brief the assistant chief constable. My driver is waiting out front so keep me up dated of any major developments please Frank."

Gibbs then strolled out of the office with a swagger as if he owned the place without even having the courtesy to wait for a reply. Twead knew what Gibbs was doing but he wasn't overly concerned, he can go and get his perks if he wanted including using his position to appoint himself a so-called driver who just happened to be the stunning looking WPC Gail Tomaso. She wouldn't normally look at Gibbs twice or give him the time of day if he wasn't a detective superintendent. The affair between the two despite their attempts to conceal it was common knowledge throughout the Station and beyond. It was plain for everyone to see that he was using his position and she was manipulating the situation with her good looks and her hourglass figure envied by all the female staff and lusted after by every red-blooded male in the job. But Twead wasn't particularly bothered by all this he was happy just as long as he got left alone to enjoy his own perks and he knew exactly where he could them.

13

Unhealthy Take Away

Twead sat back and relaxed in a high-backed leather chair in the local Wetherspoons, his best mate pathologist Hubert Chuman was coming back from the bar with a tray of drinks for them both. As he lay their drinks down on the table, two pints of Foster's lager and two large chasers of Famous Grouse Scotch whisky he said, "Well here's goodbye to my career" and sunk the first large whisky down in one. Twead also drunk his scotch down in one but in silence, he simply couldn't think of any words of comfort to say to his mate. He had told him straight away of the results of this morning's second post-mortem on the bodies in the park which had completely discredited his original findings and conclusions.

Chuman looked despairingly into the air, his gaze apparently transfixed by the huge chandeliers suspended from the ceiling "Do you know" he said, "In all the times we have been coming in here I have never noticed the chandeliers and look at them, they are absolutely stunning and they are gigantic enormous great things."

As Wetherspoons go, Chequers in Stourbridge High Street was one of the nicest in the chain. It was well laid out with large floor to ceiling front windows looking out over the main ring road flooding the entire bar with bright cheery sunlight and combined with the really high ceilings with numerous expensive looking glass droplet chandeliers dotted all over it gave the pub a relaxing feeling of space and openness.

"If I can miss them it's no wonder I couldn't see a puncture wound to the back of the neck but how on earth could I miss a prick that has been stuffed into the back of a corpse's throat?"

All Twead could think to do was to go to the bar and get another round of drinks for them only this time he left out the lager and got them four large scotches. He handed over a twenty-pound note to the barmaid and whilst waiting for his change he saw some of the national press sitting in one corner, they had made this pub their base ever since they had descended on Stourbridge a few days ago like a pack of baying wolves he thought all eager for blood especially that twat Wark.

He will have a field day when he hears of the results of the second post-mortem Twead thought to himself, he will absolutely crucify Chuman and he always somehow found out about almost everything. Money talks I suppose he mused, he decided he couldn't be bothered to wait for his change so shouted to over to the very attractive team leader barmaid to put the change in the charity box and he returned with the drinks. Almost as soon as the drinks were put on the table Chuman had grabbed the first one and downed it in one again. This is going to be a heavy session if he is going to drink that quick Twead thought, he realised that he needed to get his mate engaged in conversation to try and slow him down a bit. "The national press is over there including that fucking twat Wark; he gave me a right slating in the nationals over those vagrant deaths a few months ago."

"They'll have plenty to say about me then when they find out about the second post-mortems" he bemoaned.

Twead replied "they don't necessarily have to find out; we won't volunteer it and if they are not aware of them taking place they have no reason to make any enquires. You might get away with it."

"I've already been suspended Frank, I got the phone call from the PDB a few minutes after you called me this morning, it will soon become common knowledge and the press will want to know why, that's why I feel like getting totally pissed."

"Who are the PDB?" Twead asked.

"They are the Pathology Delivery Board; they oversee the provision of forensic pathology. The slightest whiff of a complaint or a procedural error and they are right on your case and it's normally an automatic suspension, I've got seven days to appeal."

"Not a good idea to get pissed here" Frank said "it's too open, everyone can see in plus those tossers from the press. They'd love to write about me and you having a few drinks irrespective of the fact that most of them were already half pissed when we walked in. If it was just the local Stourbridge news lads we'd be okay but I don't trust the big boys they would do anything for a story. Let's go over the Wagon and Horses on the other side of the ring road no one can look in there."

Another reason Twead didn't like getting pissed in the Chequers was because it was next door to the police Station which could obviously cause him a few problems. He hadn't said as much to Chuman because it sounded a bit of a selfish reason on his part for leaving the pub and he knew his mate was feeling bad enough, so that's what they did and resumed their drinking in the Wagon and Horses downing pint after pint of Wychelms 'Katy' cider which at 7.4% packed quite a punch even for the most seasoned of drinkers. As the drink flowed Twead and Chuman's mood fuelled by the alcohol became less sombre and a bit more upbeat. Chuman asked how the enquiry was progressing and Twead told him they had a strong suspect and told him all about Pickes whom he was sure was the murderer and that within a couple of days they would have him in custody and charged.

"That should take some of the press attention of me then, they can focus on him" said Chuman.

"Yes, you're right Hubert; it'll give me some breathing space as well. They'll be too busy sniffing out and interviewing his family and friends and digging up old schoolmates and works colleagues and doing all that sort of crap."

Twead banged the table several times with the palm of his hand in an excited manner and with a devilish look in his eye he said, "I've just had a great idea, I think I can find a way how we can shift the blame for the post-mortem cock-up, excuse the pun, away from you."

Chuman sat bolt upright and then leant forward on the table top between them and stared at Twead in a semi drunken state of hopefulness. "We can shift the blame to the SOCO's and to Latifeo."

"Go on I'm listening" said Chuman.

"Well" he began "I instructed Latifeo to take charge forensically at the post-mortem and to instruct the SOCO's and I can say that I gave him some detailed instructions and advice. You know full well I didn't actually give him any advice at all because as you are aware Hubert, I haven't got a clue what to do at a post-mortem and I know jack shit about forensics. Latifeo hasn't got the faintest idea either that's why I chose him so that if the wheel comes off as it has done in this case there is someone else to carry the can. Latifeo was frozen rigid when I told him to take charge forensically, he was so shaken up he wouldn't have been able to remember what I said to him. In addition, I can make up and type some backdated briefing notes that I supposedly read to him, including giving him the responsibility for instructing the SOCO's in the searching the body for the penis to include clothing and body orifices. You will need to help me and tell me what to write. We can also include in those notes that I have discussed this with you and that you are aware that the SOCO's will be responsible for searching for the penis. Also, I know that Latifeo fainted, passed out cold on the mortuary floor so you can say that as the senior medical person there your immediate attention had to be given to him and that you assumed the other personnel in attendance were doing what they had been told to do in an efficient and competent manner. The SOCO's will obviously say they were not briefed to search for the penis but I know Latifeo he will say that he remembered the briefing exactly and that he did instruct the SOCO's. They will then argue amongst themselves. The attention and focus will be directed completely away from you or I and the blame will end up with one of them. What do you think of that as a plan?"

Chuman was stunned, he just stared at Twead with a look of amazement combined with disbelief on his face and he said nothing for a while as he thought through and contemplated what he had just heard. His look of amazement slowly transformed into a huge smile when he said, "My god you are such a devious bastard Frank Twead, what a fantastic idea it's absolutely brilliant let's do it, but first I'll go and get us some drinks in and then I can tell you what to put in your made-up briefing notes."

Chuman then went up to the bar and came back with two large expensive single malt whiskies "Twenty-five-year-old drop of the good stuff to celebrate" he said and placed one in front of Twead and said, "Cheers Frank, here's to imaginative thinking."

Frank lifted the glass and held it out in front of him and clinked glasses with a now greatly rejuvenated and smiling if somewhat pissed hopefully to be shortly re-instated pathologist. Twead's mobile phone rang just as the amber gold was put to his lips. He tutted and began searching through his pockets not able to remember where he had put it. With his senses dulled by the considerable quantity of alcohol he and Chuman had thrown down their necks he couldn't locate the source of the infernal racket, he continued searching eventually realising it was in his inside jacket pocket, scrambling to retrieve it from his pocket he manged to then drop it on the carpet where it duly bounced under the table. Twead then uttered a string of obscenities and curses as he dropped to his knees and then began to crawl under the table on all fours in search of the incessantly ringing and now incredibly annoying contraption.

"DCI Frank Twead" he boomed out into the elusive mobile as soon as it was in his grasp. No reply "DCI Frank Twead" he shouted out again even louder, still no reply he then realised he had not pressed the receive button in his drunken state. With little light and on all fours under the table he could not see it so he just started pressing anything until eventually a voice on the other end answered him.

"This is the control room sir, we have a possible hostage situation and you are the on call trained negotiator. The incident is in Mill Race Lane, an officer is being held on the roof of a building under construction can you give me an eta?"

Twead was trying to think fast, trying to clear his head. He knew there was no way out of it, the force only had two trained negotiators and the other he knew was on holiday sunning himself on the Costa Brava. Mill Race Lane was a couple of minutes' walk from the pub so he gave the reply "eta twenty minutes." I must try and sober up he thought, I'll go to the toilet and splash some water on my face.

He shook his head and then tried to jump to his feet completely forgetting that he was under the table, he succeeded in knocking the table over sending the expensive malt whisky together with a couple of pints of cider into the pub carpet smashing the glasses in the process. He also managed to knock Chuman off his chair leaving them both prostrate on the soaking wet carpet surrounded by the glass remnants. The pub landlord came running from behind the bar thinking that there was some sort of fight going on. When he saw who it was he wasn't too surprised; Frank Twead was a regular customer and he had seen him in similar drunken states before.

"You okay Frank?" asked the landlord, both he and Chuman had now managed to get to their feet and replied that they were. Twead also added that he would pay for any damage even though the table had been knocked over when he had tripped over a rip in the carpet he lied.

"It's just a couple of glasses" came the reply "don't worry about it, be careful of the broken glass and I'll get something to clean it up."

Twead made his way to the toilet and was splashing water on his face desperately trying to sober up. Because he was such a prolific drinker he was better and quicker than most at sobering up given all the practise but even he was struggling this time. He put his mouth under the tap and drunk as much as he could stomach of the tap water. He returned to the bar where Chuman had got himself another drink and was seated at the bar. "I've got to go" he told him "Call me tomorrow about what we talked about." With that Twead as he always did sidled out the side door of the pub that emerged into a small side street.

Mill Race Lane was in an industrial estate on the outer edge of the ring road a few hundred yards away. It housed a number of industrial units, plumber's merchants, vehicle tyre outlets amongst others. It was also home to a few indoor kiddie's entertainment and play areas, trampolines, climbing frames, go karts and the like. There was an undeveloped area immediately adjacent to the main Stourbridge ring road and several new buildings were under construction. They were mainly some of the more prolific fast food outlets such as a drive through McDonalds and Costa Coffee; these were already built and open for business. Several others were in various stages of construction.

Building land in Stourbridge was in short supply caused mainly by short sighted town planners in the sixties authorising the building of a ring road which not only completely surrounded the town centre but also strangled it and prevented or at the very least stifled any possibility of expansion. Stourbridge ring road was notorious for its number of fatal accidents and near misses when pedestrians had tried to run the gauntlet of three lanes of fast moving traffic emerging from tight blind bends. There had already been a vast increase in reported near misses caused by the newly opened McDonalds that was located diametrically opposite the other side of the ring road to a college causing hordes of young students due to the absence of a pedestrian footbridge to take their lives in their hands by sprinting across the road in order to get their Big Mac lunch or to simply congregate there as this had apparently become the new meeting place for youngsters.

Twead was aware of these problems as several complaints had been received at the Station from motorists and pedestrians alike all wanting to know what the police were going to do about it. He also realised that this meant that there would be a large audience at the hostage scene with an unobstructed view of the incident and would witness how it was dealt with. He and other officers' actions would be put in the spotlight, he was a little uneasy at the thought of this knowing the amount of alcohol he had consumed but the fresh air hitting his face and the nervous adrenalin rush was beginning to kick in and his head was clearing fast. He was filling his mouth with extra strong mints that he kept constantly in his pockets for such occasions in an attempt to hide some of the smell of the alcohol. He was cursing the fact that he had volunteered for and attended a hostage negotiator course some months previous. He had only done so thinking it would be an easy week with plenty of opportunities to indulge in his favourite pastime, that of getting pissed. In the distance Twead could see the flashing blue lights of a number of emergency vehicles, not only police but ambulance and fire service. The obligatory police 'do not enter' barrier tape had been put in place and most of the personnel from Stourbridge Police Station had turned out and were now surrounding a building which was still under construction. The ring road had been sealed off to motorists and blocked by a line of traffic cars which had solved Twead's first problem of how to get across the road without getting himself wiped out. The first person to approach Twead was Shirley Wallows.

"What we got Shirley?" Twead asked

"What's happened sir is the suspect for the domestic murder Stan Gutthy was seen coming out of the Duke William pub in Coventry Street and when he was approached he ran over here pursued by the young probationary Ben Whyte who originally locked him up for the initial domestic assault. The guy has climbed on top of this building here which is still under construction via the scaffolding. I think it's going to be a new KFC takeaway and the officer has climbed up after him. We have not heard or seen anything of either of them since."

"How many officers are up there? Do you know Shirley?"

"Just the one as far as I know sir and as far as we can tell there is no one inside the building."

"Is there any access to the roof from inside the building or any other way?" he said eyeing the building looking for entry points.

"I don't think so but I can't be certain" Shirley replied.

Twead who was sobering up fast pressed number one on the speed dial of his job mobile having just remembered that this gave him direct emergency access to the control room. It was answered immediately with "control room emergency."

"This is DCI Frank Twead. I'm on scene at the possible hostage situation at Mill Race Lane. Can you tell me what resources do we have on scene and which are on-route?" he enquired, trying to speak as soberly as possible. The controller clicked onto the computer screen that displayed the list of resources allocated to the incident and relayed the information to Twead. The list read like a who's who of police specialists, every available man and his dog as the saying goes had turned up or were on their way. It was difficult to imagine what and how some of these skills could be put to use in a possible hostage situation, they ranged from a firearms team to police dog handlers. But this was the norm for any major incident everyone wanted to get in on the action. One team Twead thought would be useful was the special ops unit; he knew they were trained in a number of skills that could prove useful including forcible door entry, working at heights and angry man techniques.

He gave Wallows instructions to contact the special ops team and get them to liaise with him. Twead was racking his brains thinking back to the principles of hostage negotiation, he was remembering back to the time spent sitting in the lecture room head invariably always splitting with horrendous hangover thinking about his first drink as soon as the days lessons finished. From somewhere in the back of his mind he began to recollect some of what he had supposedly learned. Principle one, make contact; principle two, establish a rapport with the hostage taker as he was dredging the odd piece of information from the depths of his booze ridden brain he heard a shout emanating from the roof of the under-construction Kentucky Fried Chicken building. On top of the roof was the suspect for the wife killing Stan Gutthy, he was standing at the edge of the building clutching a can of extra strong lager whilst swaying from side to side as he put the can to his mouth and swallowed.

Twead shouted up to him "I'm Detective Chief Inspector Frank Twead. I need to speak with you but you need to step back from the edge of the building."

In a loud drunken slurred voice came the reply "I'll stand where I fucking want to you cunt, now fuck off you piece of shit."

Twead thought oh well that's contact made I suppose but before he could reply he could see another person on the roof. They were crouching down behind a ventilation shaft at the rear of the building. He could see the outline of a police uniform, he assumed this to be Ben the probationary constable that had chased him and followed him up on to the roof. Twead was anxious to keep hold of Gutthy's attention in order that he wouldn't spot the officer hiding behind him.

"The special ops unit will be here in a few minutes sir, they are just getting into their protective gear" said Wallows.

"Great" said Twead "but first I want you make contact with Ben. I think he's on the roof hiding just behind that ventilation shaft."

Wallows took out her radio and began speaking into her radio, "What do you want to tell him sir?"

"Tell him to get himself down here" said Twead.

Wallows tried and tried again but no reply, she then tried to call the control room to relay the message but still no reply. It suddenly dawned on her that her radio wasn't working.

"Hurry up with that bloody call" Twead shouted impatiently.

In a panic Wallows said, "I think my radio is dead, a flat battery I think I'll get someone else to do it."

She then ran over to where Latifeo was trying unsuccessfully to chat up an attractive new recruit who had been tasked with cordon duties. "Oli" she shouted as she neared him "I need you to send a radio message to Ben who is up on the roof. It's from the DCI."

Latifeo looked round in annoyance at having been interrupted in his attempt to use his charms to move in on this pretty and as yet innocent young WPC. Who on earth did she think she was giving orders to me he thought the bloody stupid handbag carrying splitarse. Not wishing to piss the DCI off he half-heartedly and with some reluctance begrudgingly agreed to send the message, as he did so Wallow's dashed back to tell Twead that the message had been passed. Twead was busy in the middle of briefing the special ops unit he had tasked them with gaining access to the roof and subduing Stan Gutthy.

The special ops team were infamous for having a somewhat gung-ho attitude to dealing with situations and this was just up their street, a huge violent thug wanted for murder shouting and cursing at the top of his drunken voice with orders to basically sort him out. The only down side was that this was in full view of a large audience, the students from the college opposite had gathered on the ring road and would witness everything that went on even more worrying was the press. They had set up on the edge of the cordon with all their cameras and high-tech equipment and zoom lenses. In normal circumstances a local reporter from the Stourbridge news would show up and if they really pushed the boat out a photographer with a stills camera, but because the national press was firmly encamped in Stourbridge because of the murders they were quickly swarming all over the place.

Twead scanned some of the faces of the press most of them he had seen earlier in Wetherspoon's and he couldn't fathom out how quickly they had found out about the ongoing and unfolding situation. Even though he was still somewhat drunk Twead was trying his best to think on his feet, his main aim in life and likewise in his police career was to always do as little as possible and engineer situations in a way in which he could shift all blame and responsibility away from himself for any potential cockups. This was his reasoning for tasking the ops unit to deal with and giving them the responsibility for getting the violent nutter down from the roof, he would of course claim all the credit and the glory if the situation went well whilst the ops unit would get pushed way into the background. He could also reverse back faster and quicker than a First World War army general in the event that everything went pear shaped leaving other people to carry the can.

The special ops unit consisted of a sergeant and six constables and they had made their way to the rear of the building out of sight of the drunken nutter on the roof and were beginning to slowly and cautiously scale the scaffolding. Armed to the teeth with Tasers, pepper spray, speed cuffs, extendable metal batons, body army, bullet proof vests, and the rest of the elaborate protective ensemble it resembled a scene from some over the top American swat movie or Robocop. The situation seemed to now be in some sort of limbo the drunken nutter was shouting, swearing and threatening everyone down below.

"Come on you cunts, come and get me you fucking wankers." There was no reply from Twead he just stood and watched and listened along with the country's press, hundreds of onlookers and every King Edwards college student who had positioned themselves on the ring road to the drunken tirade of abuse coming from the roof of the Kentucky fried chicken shop. Everyone looking intently wondering what was going to happen. The state of limbo seemed to last an eternity. A caravan takeaway snack bar which had been a permanent fixture in a lay by on the ring road adjacent to the college was doing a roaring trade in bacon sandwiches especially as the newly opened McDonald's was sealed off within the police cordon.

The more adventurous in the crowd had gone into the Duke William pub which was nestled between the college and the bacon butty caravan and had emerged with copious pints of Cradock's real ale forming quite a large merry gathering the size of which was increasing with the speed that the bar staff could pull the pints that were being taken outside. This crowd now fuelled by the reassurance of a beer or two in their bellies and some more in their hands were now chanting even louder than the drunken nutter on the roof their abuse directed spasmodically between the drunk and then increasingly the police.

The silence was suddenly broken by the sight of PC Ben Whyte emerging from behind the cover of a ventilation shaft at the rear of the Kentucky roof running headlong towards Gutthy with baton in hand. The crowd began to roar and cheer at this development, some action at last shouts of 'go on my son' and in a pantomime fashion 'Watch out he's behind you.'

Ben now running at full steam decided to launch himself at Gutthy from behind before he became aware of anything and with a huge cry began his leap to overpower the ranting and raving obnoxious moron. The nutter alerted by the crowd's cries turned around to see Ben flying through the air towards him, Gutthy had enough time to simply raise his arms and catch the flying police officer like a babe in arms and held him in a bear hug as if he'd caught a prize-winning fish. He turned around to show the crowd laughing uncontrollably as the young officer began in vain to flail his arms and legs in a frenzy to wriggle free but it was obvious this young officer had been caught like a rat in a trap and was completely trapped in the arms of this huge man who dwarfed the officer like some huge animal holding and showing off his newly captured prey. Ben was trying to swing his baton but because the movement in his arms were so restricted it resembled a naughty child trying to smack his parent because they had been refused some treat or other.

The crowd were now in fits of hysterics at the sight of this monster showing of his catch. This in turn encouraged the monster to play to the crowd and he began to swing his prey round and round and then to the delight of the assembled masses began to engage in a mock dance with his captive something resembling a waltz on the edge of the roof, this continued for some time much to the amusement of the crowd who were roaring with laughter. Then to everyone's horror things then took a terrifying twist. Gutthy had become tired of his mock dancing and took things to another level he manoeuvred Ben from his position of being clasped close to his chest and twisted him round one hundred and eighty degrees until Ben was now completely upside down. He then grabbed him by his ankles and moved closer to the edge of the roof then whilst holding him upside down dangled him over the edge of the roof. Ben then began to scream and plead with his captor. These screams of terror seemed to delight Gutthy as he then began to swing him from side to side. The mood in the crowd changed from one of frenzied excitement to one of sheer horror and panic as they watched this poor young police officer being held upside down by his ankles from the edge of the building pleading and crying for his life. As he watched the drama unfolding and realising it could soon turn into a tragedy Twead thought all his nightmares were happening at once, desperate to do something to maintain his self-preservation policy he beckoned Latifeo to him whom he knew had a working radio. It was his intention to tell him to radio the ops unit and tell them to hurry up; this would have the effect of shifting blame to them if they didn't get there in time to save their colleague.

Latifeo had been keeping one eye on the events and the other on the young WPC he was still trying to chat up. He rushed over to Twead when he saw his arms gesturing him over not wishing to incur his wrath and said, "Yes sir."

Twead said "I want you to send a radio message to the ops team; they are scaling the building from behind."

"No problem sir" he replied, "I have already sent the first message you wanted to Ben to tell him to get him down but it looks like he has failed."

"You sent what you fucking idiot?" shouted Twead in amazement.

Latifeo shocked and surprised by this coughed and spluttered and uttered the reply "I only repeated what you said about getting him down so I simply said what you had ordered and told him to get the nutter down."

"You bloody stupid dickhead" came the reply "The order was to get himself down not the fucking nutter."

Things were going bad to worse for Twead. An officer was in danger of losing his life, his pleading and crying were being filmed and recorded in every detail by the national press who were no friends to him and would certainly not do him any favours in their reporting of the incident. The ops unit were taking an age to get to the top of the building and his drunken state had now turned into an instant hangover and it was his job to sort it out. He grabbed the radio from Latifeo but before he could talk a radio message came for him from the ops team. In a hushed voice the sergeant said, "Me and my men are on the roof, what are your orders sir?"

Twead replied "He has hold of PC Ben Whyte by his ankles and is dangling him over the edge of the building you need to sort it out quickly."

The ops unit reply from the sergeant put the onus squarely back in Twead's court. "The operational procedure as dictated by the force management manual states that the protocol in these circumstances are that we do not approach the suspect as this could endanger life. It states that negotiations are initiated and maintained between the suspect and the hostage negotiator i.e. you sir."

Twead thought the smart arsed shithead, trust him to know the fucking manual back to front. He couldn't even argue the point with the sergeant because he had barely read the manual let alone remembered any of it. His option of shifting responsibility and blame had spectacularly backfired on him, this time and he knew he had to somehow negotiate with the nutter to try and save his officers life. He shouted up towards the roof "I am Detective Chief Inspector Frank Twead I need to speak with you."

"I've already told you to fuck off once" came the reply from the now guffawing nutter.

"I want you to release the officer immediately" shouted Twead.

Wallows heart went in her mouth and she looked at Twead, she was about to tell him of the ridiculousness of his request. She was

161

quite fond of Ben, he was one of the only officers and quite possibly the only officer who had shown her any level of respect unlike all the other officers who treated her like some sort of second class lowlife who was there to be abused and belittled, but before she could speak the response came from Gutthy.

"You want him released you can fucking have him released detective chief fucking inspector."

Gutthy then held the screaming officer at arm's length over the edge and said "bye-bye, your boss wants me to release you" he then let go of his grip and Ben went hurtling towards the ground below. The bloodcurdling screams coming from the falling officer sickened people in the crowd, there was now no cheering or chanting but a hushed silence interspersed with several screams. Even hardened veteran police officers had to turn their face away as they saw their screaming colleague with arms and legs flailing franticly falling helplessly towards the concrete floor.

14

Do me a Favour

It was eight o'clock at Stourbridge Police Station; Frank Twead was preparing to give a briefing to his small secret team with reference to the incident with Ben Whyte on the roof of the Kentucky Takeaway. "Right first off concerning this afternoon's incident there is to be no smart remarks or comments, we were all there, we all know what happened and if anyone has anything to say or any questions say them now or keep quiet."

Twead scanned the assembled members with a slow and deliberate gaze making intense eye contact with each individual as he went around the room asking everybody one by one if they wished to pass comment. Grant Courtan, Frank Fergas, Oli Latifeo and Robert Peeves all in turn shook their heads in a negative response. There were lots of things that they all wanted to know but the tone of Frank Twead's voice made it quite plain that it would be in their best interests to keep quiet.

"How about you Shirley?" asked Twead

She replied "Just one question, how is Ben? Is there any update on his condition?"

As this was a fairly innocuous question Twead's tone of voice changed and the intense stare softened. This was not a criticism of the incident just a simple welfare enquiry. "Ben is in intensive care at Russell's Hall Hospital, he has suffered numerous injuries in the fall including several broken bones. His condition is described as critical but stable."

"Has he regained consciousness yet?" Shirley asked.

"Not as far as I am aware, the last update was that he was still in the same unconscious state as when he was recovered from the skip and I think we can all thank god that was where he landed. I think we can all imagine what would have happened if he had landed on his head straight onto the floor. Now if there are no more questions we will get on with the briefing" Twead said this in a tone of voice that more or said end of conversation.

The room fell into a hushed silence indicating that no-one dared ask anything else. Twead nodded towards Grant as a signal for him to start the briefing. With a blasé air of self-importance Grant stood up and for dramatic effect slowly made his way to the head of the room and opened the leather-bound folder, flicked over a few pages and began.

"In compliance with your orders sir and to make an immediate and speedy start I have made enquires with the editorial staff of Desire magazine to enquire about inserting an advertisement and basically the next issue is already set for print. It goes out in a few days and as it's a monthly issue it would take approximately five weeks for a new advert to be seen which is obviously too late for the enquiry. So, I decided we would make direct contact with our suspect Pickes via his previous magazine entry, so over to you Shirley."

Shirley like the other members of the team felt a trifle nauseated at Grants subservient demeanour towards Twead, especially in his opening comments of 'in compliance with your orders sir' but she like the others did well to hide it. She joined Grant at the head of the room and began to give her brief, unlike him she recounted what progress she had made without any embellishment or unnecessary false flattery. Twead and the rest listened intently and were surprisingly impressed with what she had done. She had contacted the suspect via the phone number given in his previous magazine advertisement entry indicating that she was responding to him because she shared a common interest of covertly spying on people engaged in dogging and other sexual acts but didn't have the confidence to do it on her own and he has agreed to meet her that evening and take her to a dogging spot.

Twead spoke up "Sounds good so far Shirley, have you got a false name and nickname?"

"Yes, sir I have" she told Pickes "My name is Lilly Drake. With reference to the nickname I have made enquires with people and organisations with similar fetishes the technical name for this one is Scopophilia, it is defined as obtaining sexual pleasure whilst watching other people naked or having sex usually without their knowledge. Participants are commonly known as jags and apparently your personal nickname which everyone has needs to reflect your particular fetish. I will give the nickname eye of the snake if asked."

Twead although not wishing to show it was becoming increasingly impressed with what Wallows had to say and his opinion of her began to shift he used to think of her as did the others as a handbag carrying useless bitch. "What about security?" he asked, "are you wired up?"

Grant Courtan then interjected "We were unable to get any covert radio equipment or tracking devices sir, the technical ops department will only supply or release that sort of high tech gear when they are given an operational name and as this a secret unsanctioned op then I couldn't make an application for any. But I have allocated and liaised with Latifeo who will be contactable nearby via her unregistered mobile phone to make plans for her safety."

Grant then looked at Latifeo raising his eyebrows indicating for him to outline his action plan. Latifeo glad to have a speaking part at last began to outline his strategy and procedure for keeping Shirley safe.

"The location for the initial meet is the layby on the Hagley Road, near the Badgers Sett pub. Shirley will then get into the suspects' vehicle and go in that same vehicle with him to a dogging spot in Uffmoor Wood, there are several different dogging spots in those woods and he didn't specify which one he was going to. There is nowhere to observe the vehicles at the layby so I intend to park up in

Uffmoor lane at the first parking place so they will have to drive past me to get to any of the dogging spots so I will then be able to follow at a discreet distance and park up nearby. Shirley will have my phone number on redial in the event of any trouble and if she is unable to use her phone she could just press the vehicles horn or shout and scream and I will be close enough to move in straight away."

When Latifeo had finished Frank Fergas was next up, he spoke for himself and Robert Peeves. This was not unusual it was if they were joined at the hip and couldn't do anything without each other it was little wonder that the two detective constables had attracted so many derisory nicknames. He began with their conversation with the Oldswinford swinger's association, in particular their reference to the deceased's Pickes wife who could only participate in dogging when her husband was working the late shift with the council and had to be home before he returned from work.

Twead interrupted impatiently "We have already heard this before how does it further the enquiry?"

Fergas replied a little embarrassed at being halted mid flow "Well sir we have spoken to his manager at the council who by the way also thinks Pickes is a bit of an oddball, he has given us details of his recent work rosters. He mainly he works mostly day shifts he also is rostered to work a number of late turn shifts starting at four o'clock until midnight. During these shifts he is responsible for emergency repair work in his own area and adjacent areas. He is a general handyman but his specialist trade is as a carpenter. He has access to a council van which is quite distinctive because of the council markings on the side. He technically shouldn't use it outside of work hours for his own use but they are aware that he does and they simply turn a blind eye, it is the only vehicle of this type in the area. There are other vehicles in the fleet similar but they are based some distance away and they cover their own areas. We have compared dates with when his wife was dogging and when he was supposed to be on late shift and the two do not tally but best of all the icing on

166

the cake is we have read through his statement about his whereabouts on the night of the murder. He stated he was at work on the late shift and guess what; he wasn't even at work it was his day off."

Fergas then sat back down next to Peeves both with stupid smug grins on their faces as if they were god's gift to police work and they had single headedly cracked the case. Grant knew that Fergas had that piece of incriminating information and also knew that he would try and save it until the end of the briefing so that it had maximum impact and made him and his shadow Peeves look good and as he was in charge of the briefing he had allowed him to do it. He had however some further even more vital evidence himself and he decided that this was now the perfect time to reveal it to top those pair of twats and make him look top dog. He stood up and in a false slightly condescending manner congratulated dumb and dumber on their detective work.

He then said, "I have some evidence as a result of my extensive enquires that further incriminates our man Pickes and co-ordinates all the other small pieces of information that we have heard." Grant by deliberately referring to other small pieces of information had belittled dumb and dumbers input. He continued by saying "Pickes council van has been sighted by three different and independent sources who all place his vehicle parked for some considerable time at a location less than forty yards from the first crime scene at the approximate time of death. In addition to this we have one sighting of his vehicle at the scene of the second murders."

Fergas and Peeves were totally pissed off with this information even though it was enough to put the final piece in the puzzle and Pickes was as good as bang to rights, but they were more bothered that their thunder had been stolen than the successful outcome of the investigation.

Twead on the other hand was over the moon after today's debacle on top of the Kentucky Fried Chicken shop which he knew would require some serious answers, this would push all that into the background. He was just about to solve the biggest, most serious and high-profile murders Stourbridge had ever seen and he would make sure that he got the credit for it. He had already as was his nature begun to work round the two mistakes he had made at the scene. The first one was his ambiguous order via Wallows and then Latifeo for Ben to get himself down and the second when he said release my officer. The only witnesses to those two mistakes were Wallows, Latifeo and Ben himself. No-one else was in earshot when he uttered the words release my officer.

It would be better for him ironically if Ben had died. They could blame Ben for tackling the nutter in the first place. Twead, Wallows and Latifeo could say that he was clearly told to come down and not put himself in danger and the release my officer comment would never be mentioned. He could control Wallows and Latifeo but if Ben woke up and remembered details of the incident he could spoil things. Anxious now to get his next drink Twead stood up and in order to move things along he began to close the briefing by giving a summary of the evidence amassed against Trevor Pickes "So to re-cap so far the evidence we already have. We have a motive; his wife has a fetish for dogging and has sex with strangers on a regular basis. He has a fetish for covert voyeurism what was it you called it Shirley, scopophilia? Is that right?"

Shirley nodded to indicate it he had pronounced it correctly and he continued. "And it is highly likely that he saw his wife engaging in these acts. He is described by several individuals as being a bit weird, his shift patterns at work do not correlate to when his wife has been engaging in dogging. His alibi of being at work at the time of his wife's murder has been disproved and in addition his vehicle was seen parked near the scene of the murder at the estimated time of death and also at the scene of the second murders. His post murder behaviour has been somewhat strange in that he doesn't appear to be grieving and even more unusual he is continuing to engage in his fetish. I think we have got enough to pull him in for questioning however we will wait and see what we can gain from tonight's meeting with Shirley. So, unless anybody has anything to add this meeting is adjourned. Good luck for tonight Shirley and I will see you all at seven o'clock tomorrow morning." With that Twead immediately left the room, everyone assembled knew exactly why he had departed so quickly they all knew he was desperate for a drink.

Twead sat in the corner of Chequers pub. What a day he thought, totally pissed at lunchtime, knocked over a table in the Wagon and Horses and one of his officers thrown off a roof. Fortunately, it had ended well after Ben had been dropped off the building the special ops unit had overpowered Gutthy and with the help of the fire brigade and their hoist he had been bought down safely and had been subsequently charged with one count of murder and one of attempt murder off the young officer.

The biggest result of the day had been the evidence gathered against Trevor Pickes and Twead was now back in his favourite place the pub, downing his third pint. He was joined by his mate Dr Chuman; he looked a bit worse for wear after today's drinking session.

"Bloody hell you look rough" said Twead as Chuman sat down and placed two large whiskies on the table one for him and one for Twead.

"I feel it" replied Chuman,

"I had a few more after you left, I was that pissed I couldn't remember where I parked my car, I had to get a taxi. I have managed to write those post-mortem briefing notes for you though. I have emphasised that you instructed Latifeo to brief the SOCO's to search for and recover the penis and that you and I agreed it. I have also drafted out my letter of appeal to the PDB, I'll use these briefing notes as the basis of the appeal so as soon as the blame is shifted to the SOCO's I'm hopeful my suspension will be lifted, but they will probably contact you for confirmation on the briefing notes so will you be able to back me up?"

"Yes, no problem" Twead replied "but I need you to do me a favour as well."

Chuman looked a bit puzzled but replied "Of course I will. What do you want?"

Twead leant closer to Chuman anxious not to be overheard and whispered, "It's best not to discuss it here I'll tell you later." They agreed to meet the following day to discuss things further, but for now they were both content to resume their favourite pastime, that of getting pissed.

15

A Walk in the Park

Wallows got into the unmarked police car in the back yard of Stourbridge Police Station, she was now beginning to feel a little nervous her trepidation was also tinged with an overwhelming sense of excitement. This was the biggest, most important enquiry she had ever worked on and in the space of a few short ridiculously hectic days she had gone from being a uniform officer who normally gets assigned to the boring humdrum tasks such as looking for lost kids, typing up other officers reports or even worse making the tea for everyone else in the office to someone who was going under cover on her own to try and implicate a suspected serial killer.

She had been briefed what to say and do by Grant Courtan, it had been made easier because no recording equipment was to be used so even if she said something that was out of place anything that could be construed as entrapment it wouldn't be on record. She had rehearsed what to do in the case of an emergency and had practised using the speed dial button on her phone to alert Latifeo, she was even able to press the button whilst the phone was still in the pocket of her denim jeans. From where they had arranged to meet there was only one way to drive to Uffmoor woods and that was via Uffmoor lane, this was where Latifeo would be parked and as soon as they drove past he would follow at a discreet distance and when we stopped he would position himself as close as possible so what could go wrong.

Latifeo as planned parked in the first layby in Uffmoor lane and waited for the pre-arranged phone call from Wallows to say that she was leaving the police Station, he was feeling really pissed off with the way the operation had panned out. He thought he would have been able to sneak off and see his girlfriend Sam a bit more often, but he had not had chance to do so for days as he had been assigned tasks and things to do by Grant Courtan which meant he was always busy during the evenings and was invariably working nowhere near his girlfriend's house. It'll all change soon he thought, he knew Twead was notoriously impatient and that he already had enough evidence to arrest Pickes especially when he receives the psychological criminal profile from Barista that he knew he was preparing. Twead had judged Latifeo correctly and he had rightly predicted that he would tell the profiler all about Pickes and as such Barista would compile his profile to fit whilst denying any prior knowledge of the suspect.

"Hi Shirley, are you setting off now?" Latifeo asked as he answered his phone.

"Yes" she replied, "I'm just leaving the carpark now, I'll be at the meeting point in ten minutes."

Latifeo trying to sound concerned said "Remember the signals if there is any trouble I'm in position in the first layby in Uffmoor lane on the left-hand side so you should go past me a couple of minutes after you meet up with Pickes. Good luck, speak later."

Wallows drew up in the layby on the main Hagley Road. Pickes was already there and she pulled up behind his council van. Her heart was beating fast and her stomach began to churn, pull yourself together she thought; concentrate on what you have to do. She checked that her mobile phone was in her pocket, took a deep breath, got out of her car and locked it and approached the council van. Pickes got out of his van and walked towards Wallows, she suddenly lost her nervousness and adopted a confident air as Pickes neared her.

"Hi" he said, "Are you Lilly?"

"Yes, that's me" she replied

"It's very nice to meet you, my names Trevor." He then opened the van passenger door and invited her to get in. Wallows got in and closed the door behind her. She was surprised at how filthy and messy the inside of his van was, everything was covered in dust, the seats were stained and the foot well was littered with empty food packaging and drinks cans. There was a horrible damp musty smell which made her feel a little nausea. Pickes joined her in the vehicle and began to ask her all about herself and what particular pleasures she liked. Wallows was prepared for this and had her lines well-rehearsed, she told him that she got excited by the thought of secretly watching people having sex. She explained that she had never had the nerve to do it but some years previous she had accidently whilst walking in Warley woods saw a couple having sex in the bushes and that's when she realised that it was a turn on for her.

Wallows began to realise why so many people referred to him as weird, there was something not right with him, he was creepy to say the least and he didn't seem to show any emotion. The expression on his face stayed the same all the time, his eyes were unblinking and gave out a horrible cold relentless icy stare that sent a shiver down her spine. She decided to turn the tables and began to ask him some questions, but he was unresponsive especially when Shirley asked about any girlfriends. He simply shrugged his shoulders and told her he didn't have any girlfriends, he was incredibly unemotional for a man who had just lost his wife he didn't mention her once. This wasn't going to plan Wallows thought, they had all reasoned that Shirley would get in the van and they would straight away drive to the dogging spot, but she had been in the van now for at least twenty minutes and Pickes was still asking questions and showed no signs of letting up.

Wallows tried to speed things up and enquired when they were going to watch at a dogging spot. Despite her best efforts to get going Pickes wasn't budging and continued to ask about her fetish what did she like to look at, was it men or women or both what was

173

her preference. The confidence was ebbing away from Wallows now and this was gradually being replaced by a feeling of foreboding. But at long last Pickes started up the van and pulled out of the layby, he drove along the dual carriage way a short distance towards the island where he needed to turn right to enter Uffmoor lane. He slowed down at the island and indicated right, Wallows confidence was now beginning to return as they would shortly go past where Latifeo was parked and she wouldn't feel so isolated. This confidence was short lived however when Pickes didn't take the right turn into Uffmoor lane but went straight past the turning and was now driving back along the dual carriageway. She was trying to think fast, she was now quickly being separated from her only source of back up, did Pickes realise who she was did he know she was undercover police? In the calmest voice she could manage she said, "I thought we were going to Uffmoor wood, isn't that what you said in our telephone conversation?"

"Have you not read the Stourbridge news tonight? The National Trust has closed all the carparks and access points; it is because of all the complaints of anti-social behaviour, dogs running wild, drug dealing and of course dogging. Apparently, it is the first time something like this has ever happened in the country, closing the access to public spaces. I blame the drug dealers and dog owners I mean the doggers aren't doing anybody any harm are they? The only thing they are interested in is enjoying themselves; don't worry though I know plenty of other good sites."

They were now heading down a country lane towards a place Wallows knew as Wassell Grove. This put them about a mile away from Uffmoor wood, her mind was now racing trying to decide what to do.

"If there are any cars parked on the left-hand side down here then we are in luck" said Pickes as he slowed down when he neared a small clearance. The site was empty however; there were no vehicles or any sign of life or any movement in the bushes. Pickes didn't say anything but continued driving in complete silence Wallows heart began to sink this was not supposed to happen.

Much to the annoyance of Grant Courtan his mobile phone began to ring, he thought about answering it but decided to ignore it and continue with what he was doing.

"Aren't you going to answer that?" Sam Gail asked as she lifted her head up from the kitchen table. Grant pushed her head back down on the table and continued thrusting away in her. He just about managed to say "If it is important they will phone back" as he increased the pace prior to ejaculating. He let out a self-satisfying moan of pleasure and Sam who was never impressed with Grant's lovemaking thought time for a nice cuppa. As soon as he withdrew from Sam she stood up and walked to the kettle and flicked the switch just as Grants phone began to ring again. This time he answered it whilst at the same time trying to unsuccessfully put his penis back in his trousers. Sam looked at the pathetic sight of Grant awkwardly thumbing the buttons on his phone in one hand and trying to put his tiny little pecker away with the other.

"What?" Grant shouted angrily into the phone. "You must have missed them somehow, what I want you to do is drive round all the carparks and potential dogging sites and find that fucking van and do it quickly. I'm on my way" he then hung up.

Sam looked at him, she could tell by his shouting and the concerned look on his face that something was seriously wrong "What's the problem Grant?" she asked.

Grant shook his head as if in disbelief "It's that useless idiot Latifeo, he was supposed to be the back-up for a female undercover officer in a murder suspects car and he can't find them. He has probably fallen asleep or has been distracted by using his phone or something. Either way he has fucked up. I am going to have to sort it out I might see you later, but I will give you a call."

He then hurriedly picked his car keys up of the hallway table and started out the front door, waving goodbye. "Can I give you a word of advice Grant?" she shouted. Grant turned around and screwed up his face as if to enquire what she meant by this.

"I think you will probably look more professional and be less embarrassed if you were to do one thing for me" she said. Grant gestured despairingly with his hands and arms outstretched thinking I haven't got time for this nonsense and with some irritation he said loudly and impatiently "What do you want me to do for you?" She approached him and looked straight into his eyes and calmly with a cheeky grin on her face said quietly "What you can do for me Grant is to put your prick back into your trousers."

"Oh shit" he said as he turned his back in embarrassment when he realised that his manhood was hanging out of his fly. He quickly adjusted himself and said. "That could have been embarrassing I'll call you later." Sam was trying to control herself until she shut the door and she then burst into an uncontrollable a fit of hysterical laughter, he was right about one thing it would have been embarrassing especially with his tiny little pencil dick.

Wallows was now somewhere in the Staffordshire countryside in a small country lane. She had no real idea of the exact location, but she was in amongst a clump of bushes standing next to Pickes. They had a clear view of three couples in a carpark in various stages of undress. They were all taking turns with each other, swapping partners every few minutes and performing various sex acts on each other. Pickes seemed to go into a sort of catatonic state; he was totally transfixed by the sight in front of him. She realised that he must have been here a number of times before because he knew exactly where to go for the best view and knew how to get there without being seen. Pickes then spoke in a hushed voice "Can you see ok?" he enquired.

"Yes, I've got a great view" she replied as she was trying to feign some sort of excitement. Pickes continued to speak with her as she tried to pretend to be getting a sexual thrill out of what they were doing, the expression on his face had completely changed from being almost expressionless to one of someone who was totally enthralled with the situation.

Wallows suddenly then felt sick to her stomach as she saw what Pickes was doing, his gaze was alternating between eyeing the doggers and then looking at her whilst he spoke with her. All the time he was furiously masturbating with a horrid distorted lecherous expression on his face. He was obviously getting extra pleasure from Wallows being present whilst they watched the doggers and he tugged himself off at the same time. Prior to Pickes fully satisfying himself, the doggers had finished what they were doing and had got dressed and were getting into their vehicles ready to leave. Wallows could see the disappointment in Pickes face even though he was continuing to masturbate she decided that this was now becoming too dangerous and she must do something to get out of this predicament.

"Do you know anywhere else where we can go?" She said trying to sound enthusiastic at the prospect of another dogging site. Pickes appeared to be pleased that she wanted to go and look at another dogging site and with a smile excitedly said, "Yeah I know loads of places come on let's go." He put his penis back in his trousers and they made their way back to his van. When they set off he said, "It's really nice to have someone else to share this with."

Wallows was trying to get her bearings as they were travelling, she roughly guessed that they were heading back towards the Stourbridge area and as they continued she recognised more and more of the landmarks along the route. When they were back in the Stourbridge area Wallows felt a little easier if she had to use her phone to call help at least she would be able to tell Latifeo exactly where she was.

Pickes parked the van and said, "This is my favourite spot to watch dogging, it's normally quite busy and you can get really close without being spotted and get a good view."

Oh my god thought Wallows this is Stourbridge Park, the scene of the murders. Pickes parked the van on the main road near the entrance gates and got out. Wallows got out of the van quickly as she followed Pickes into the park and through the undergrowth towards the carpark where the dogging usually took place. She quickly realised why this was his favourite spot, it was possible to get extremely close without detection and like he said you got a really good view of what if anything was going on. There was no one there at the moment but Pickes suggested that they wait a while to see if anybody turned up.

Sam Gail had been looking out of her bedroom window towards the park where Pickes had parked his van and she saw the two occupants get out and walk in the direction of the main entrance. She studied the van for a while, she couldn't figure out why but something about the van was niggling at the back of her brain. Then she realised why, she ran downstairs and picked up a form that Grant had left on the kitchen table and took it back upstairs with her and began to read it. The form was a pro-forma questionnaire and it concerned vehicle sightings. Grant had filled out the various sections and had left it with her and requested that Sam should sign it. The form basically said that she had seen a council van parked outside her house adjacent to the park on a specific time and date; she knew this was the time and date of the second murder.

She hadn't actually seen anything but Grant still wanted her to sign it. Sam looked at the description on the form and it exactly matched the van that had just pulled up. She began to piece things together, if that van that Grant wanted me to say I saw was involved in the murder and if an undercover police woman was with the murder suspect then that was the two people she had just seen but what on earth was going on. Should she tell Grant or should she bide her time and see what happened next, she thought about it for a while and decided to sit and watch.

Wallows and Pickes were still secreted in the bushes but no one had as yet turned up. "How often do you come here?" asked Wallows

"At least two or three times a week" He replied.

178

Wallows decided to push him a little "And what sort of things have you seen?" she continued.

"I've seen loads of things happen here I will tell you about them in time." It was said in a tone of voice that indicated that he wasn't going to divulge anything else and that he didn't want to be asked anything else on the subject for the time being.

They hung about in the bushes for a further twenty minutes when Pickes suggested that they call it a night as there was still no sign of any action and that he would give her lift back to the layby so that she could collect her vehicle.

Sam watched as they both got back into the council van and drove off still not knowing what to do so she decided to keep what she had seen to herself for the time being whilst she gave it some more thought.

When Wallows eventually got back in her car she breathed a sigh of relief she was glad that it was over, and she could relax a little. As soon as Pickes had driven away from the layby and was out of sight she rang Latifeo to let him know what had happened. Latifeo and Courtan were travelling in the same vehicle, they had been scouring the area for her and she heard Courtan shout in the background "Shirley make your way back to the nick and we can have a debrief."

Shirley replied, "Okay see you in about ten minutes" and she pulled her vehicle out of the layby.

16

You Scratch my Back

Stourbridge Police Station seven-thirty a.m.; Twead had a thumping hangover as the rest of the team came into his office. He and his mate Dr Chuman had really tied one on last night after drinking until closing time in Wetherspoons they had then both returned to Twead's office and continued drinking, eventually polishing off a bottle and a half of scotch whisky. Chuman had crawled into a taxi in the early hours of the morning whist Twead stayed in his office until literally passing out; he had once again drunkenly slumped over his desk not awakening until seven o'clock. He tried his best to focus and concentrate on the briefing despite the incessant pounding in his head.

Grant Courtan opened proceedings and began to outline the undercover operation from the previous night. He, Shirley and Latifeo had agreed between them not to mention the initial cock up when they lost contact with Shirley for some considerable time. "We have made some in roads into the type of character we are dealing with" he said and then invited Wallows to elaborate.

Shirley went through her liaison with Pickes. "The first thing you notice about him is that he is incredibly creepy, it's difficult to put into words exactly as to why he comes across so strange but I can understand why so many other people have referred to him as a bit weird. He is extremely emotionless, the expression on his face doesn't alter and he shows no feelings at all. He speaks in a repetitive monotone voice, doesn't smile and worst of all the most frightful thing about him is his intense staring unblinking eyes.

Pickes seems to know and has visited every dogging site in the local area. He says he goes two or three times a week. He knows exactly where to park and how to get close to the action with a good view without being seen. We went to a couple of sites but only saw sexual activity at one, it was somewhere in Staffordshire, I think it was near Kingswinford. This was where I saw him change his complete persona. It was as if he becomes possessed when he sees any sort of sex acts, he was acting like some sort of crazed demon wanking fast and furiously, I thought he would break the bloody thing off. The second site we went to which he referred to as his favourite spot, the one he visited the most often. The place we went was Stourbridge Park. He showed me his secret vantage point in the undergrowth which was incredibly close to the murder scenes. He also told me that he had seen loads of thing at that location and that he would tell me more in time."

With this information Twead forgot his hangover for a while; the evidence was piling up against Pickes. "This is all good stuff, well done Shirley. Now I want you all to write everything up quickly and get it to me this morning including those vehicle sighting reports" he said glancing towards Grant.

With the meeting concluded the team left the office leaving a now more upbeat Twead who decided that this progress deserved celebrating as he opened his desk drawer and took a couple of long swigs out of his half full bottle of whisky then filled his mouth with extra strong mints. He logged onto his computer and saw an e-mail with an attachment from the criminal profiler Barista. He smiled to himself when he began to read the attached report, it was the psychological profile of the killer and it fitted Trevor Pickes perfectly. He knew he had been right to give Latifeo the job of his liaison officer and he knew the blabbermouth would secretly tell Barista all about their suspect. He was just about to congratulate himself by taking the bottle of whisky from his desk but just at that moment an extremely irate detective superintendent burst into his office. Tony Gibbs was absolutely fuming, he threw a copy of that day's newspaper onto Twead's desk and said, "The Chief has had my bollocks for breakfast; we have been made to look a laughing stock by the national press especially that prick Spenser Wark."

Twead read the headline news on the front page 'Swinging Stourbridge Sleuths'. There were a number of pictures; the first being one of PC Ben Whyte being swung upside down by his ankles over the edge of the Kentucky Fried Chicken takeaway by this beast of a man Gutthy. The text associated with the picture portrayed them as keystone cops. Twead shook his head with disbelief; he knew Spenser Wark was a complete asshole but this going too far.

Twead said angrily "Something needs to be done about this article and the reporter. For goodness sake a young brave officer is in a critical condition fighting for his life and they show a picture of him being dangled from the roof."

"The chief has already made a complaint to the independent press standards organisation but we need to tread carefully, read the article on the next page" Gibbs replied.

Twead thumbed the page over and could scarcely believe his eyes, what a pair of idiots he thought. The accompanying pictures showed a chaotic scene inside a public house with a number of individuals both male and female in various stages of undress trying to flee the from the photographers. Some of the faces had been deliberately obscured by inserting a black bar across the eyes but unmistakably two off the persons in the picture with clothes in a state of disarray and trying to escape from the cameras were officers DC Frank Fergas and DC Trevor Peeves. The officers weren't named individually just referred as Stourbridge police detectives, the article read like a carry-on film list of double-entendres. It was written in a manner to cause maximum humiliation to the force.

"The problem we have" began Gibbs "Is that if we make a too vigorous complaint about the officer shown dangling from the roof it increases the publicity around the debacle in the pub which is being described as a more or less police endorsed orgy. What we desperately need is something major to grab the headlines; to divert attention away from this bloody mess. So, tell me, how is the investigation into the serial killings going? What evidence do we have on the suspect Pickes?"

Twead perked up at this and Gibbs could tell it was going to be good news. When a much-relieved Gibbs was given the full update on Pickes especially his alibi being disproved and the covert work by Wallows he immediately said, "Right get the bastard in straight away and let me know immediately and I will arrange for a press conference in time to make the evening news."

Gibbs was now on a high, he knew that this would ease the pressure on him from the Chief and even whilst still speaking with Twead he was dialling the Chief to relay the news. When he had finished on the phone Gibbs said to Twead "One other thing Frank, we have obviously got someone who is giving information to the press. The number of times they have turned up to incidents almost as quick as we have and the debacle in the pub with the swingers and those two bumbling idiots dumb and dumber means they have someone on the inside. I want you to find out who it is, I want their bollocks on a plate and quickly."

Twead nodded and said, "I'll put Grant Courtan on it; he's a nosy bastard and seems to know everybody's business."

Gibbs then left the office, his parting words and the manner in which he said them left Twead in no doubt that his future depended upon it and that he would have to do whatever it takes using any means available legal or otherwise.

Grant Courtan acting on Twead's orders began to gather the team together in his office. With the exception of Latifeo, the team were now assembled in Courtan's office. Wallows and dumb and dumber were talking amongst themselves speculating as to why they had been summoned to this impromptu meeting. Grant bounded into the office; the team could tell by his upbeat demeanour that something big was in the offing.

"Thanks for coming so quickly" he said as he looked round the room "Has anyone seen Latifeo?"

They all shook their heads. Wallows replied "The last time I saw him was at the briefing this morning. Maybe he's with the criminal profiler, shall I go and check?"

"If you would please Shirley and be as quick as you can, we have some urgent actions to do and it needs all of us."

Wallows went in search of Barista and found him in the incident room. He was reading through the latest intelligence reports on the serial killings. The guy gave Wallows the creeps he was pleasant enough but there was something sinister about him she couldn't put her finger on why exactly, but she knew a lot of other people thought the same way.

"Hi" she said, "I'm looking for Oli, have you seen him, or know where he is?"

"I saw him this morning but he told me he had some urgent business to attend to and I haven't seen him since."

Wallows not wishing to engage him in conversation for longer than she had to said, "Thank you" and turned to leave the office as she reached for her mobile and punched in Latifeo's number.

"That bloody phone" shouted Latifeo.

"Don't stop now" came a muffled cry from Sam whose face was being firmly pressed into her pillow.

The phone continued to ring again and again "Oh fuck it, I've got to take it" and he reluctantly picked up his mobile from the bedside cabinet. Hello, DC Latifeo speaking."

"Oli this is Shirley. We are all needed for some form of urgent briefing, we've been trying to get hold of you for ages. Where are you?"

Oli trying to think quickly said "I'm at the err bank. I've got some things to sort out" he lied.

"Well you had better sort it out quick and get back. Courtan will do his nut soon. Are you okay? You sound out of breath."

"I'm okay" he replied "I'll be back in ten minutes" he then hung up. By now Latifeo had gone completely flaccid and had slipped out of Sam.

"You may as well put that little floppy thing away it's no good to me like that" laughed Sam.

A cursing and slightly embarrassed Latifeo got dressed in a hurry and dashed downstairs. Sam shouted down to him "Don't forget that bill Oli; it's on the table by the door." Oli picked up a utility bill off the hall table, he had agreed to help Sam out financially after she had told him how short of money she was and found herself struggling to pay household expenses.

Grant Courtan was obviously somewhat peeved at Latifeo's tardiness, he would have been absolutely livid if he knew the real reason and what he had been doing. His annoyance quickly abated though when he began to brief the team about what they were about do "You will all be pleased to know that the reason I have called you all in is that we have the green light to go and nick Pickes on suspicion of murder. He is to be arrested as soon as possible so here's the plan and your individual duties."

Courtan began to outline each officer's specific duties and responsibilities. Dumb and dumber were to be the arresting officers, Wallows and Latifeo were responsible for searching his house and vehicle whilst Grant himself would be the interviewing officer. They had an hour to get themselves prepared before they set off.

Twead met Chuman in the carpark of Russell's Hall hospital at the pre-arranged time of eleven-forty-five; this was in order that their conversation couldn't possibly be overheard.

"I'm not sure about this" said Chuman nervously.

"Listen Hubert, we have no choice. I can help you and you can help me, we can get each other out of the shit." Chuman took a deep breath and they both made their way into the hospital.

Russell's Hall Hospital was a large affair it had replaced several other local hospitals that were now all mothballed. The ones that were still operating were in a limited capacity which meant as a result this was an extremely busy place and it was quite modern with good facilities.

Twead followed the directions to the ward on the third floor and entered the private room where Ben Whyte lay. He scanned the room and realised that Ben was on his own and there were no visitors present. It was a light airy room with a large south facing window that allowed the sunlight to flood in. It was well decorated and the walls were painted a pale pastel blue colour which gave a feeling of serenity and calmness. There was a large comfortable high-backed chair with a large fluffy cushion adjacent to the bed.

He sat down and made himself comfortable then studied Ben for a while noticing that he was lying completely motionless he didn't even blink an eyelid. He began to talk to him even though he was in a coma, this was on medical advice. It wasn't fully known or understood why and there were different schools off thought on the benefits of talking to people in an induced coma but the general census of opinion was that familiar voices somehow stimulated certain areas of the brain in coma patients. Ben was wired up to and attached to a vast array of machines and monitors that were checking all his vital signs, they emitted a constant rhythmic almost soporific sound and his breathing was being helped with the use of an oxygen mask.

The consultant had previously explained to Twead that the reason for putting Ben in a barbiturate induced coma was to reduce the metabolic rate of brain tissue as well as the cerebral blood flow. With these reductions the blood vessels in the brain narrow, decreasing the amount of space occupied by the brain and hence the amount of intracranial pressure. Everything was state of the art; the high-tech equipment was automatically doing everything for him. In the unlikely event that anything went wrong then loud warning beeps and flashing lights were instantly relayed to the nurses' Station that was constantly monitored by a member of the nursing staff. They in turn would immediately activate the emergency alarm and medical assistance would come running.

The consultant had been pleased with Ben's progress and had already started the process of bringing him out of the coma; this was expected to take between twelve and seventy-two hours.

Twead continued talking in a low quiet relaxing voice and related the experience on the roof of the KFC. "I admire your bottle Ben, it must have taken a lot of courage to try and tackle someone twice your size. You are a credit to the force but if that stupid idiot Latifeo had got the message right or if I hadn't said that ridiculous comment to let you go then you wouldn't be in this mess. The dilemma we have now is that if this gets out I will be in the shit, but the only witnesses within earshot of me telling him to let you go are Latifeo, Wallows and you. Now the only problem left is you. I can control what they both say and do, in fact they have already made their statements which don't implicate me in any way but if you wake up and say the wrong thing then everything could go tits up, if you understand my meaning. So, you must realise that it's nothing personal, I've nothing against you but I have got to do what I need to do to protect myself, so no hard feelings there's a good lad."

He looked at his watch it was twelve noon exactly. He stood up and went closer to the bed, reached over and stroked Ben's face "You are a true hero, your parents quite rightly will be extremely proud of you as will all your friends and colleagues back at the nick." Twead then slowly removed the oxygen mask from Ben then placed it on his pillow. He picked up the large cushion from the armchair he had been sitting on and gently placed it over Bens face pressing down hard. Twead was surprised when he detected movement from what he thought would be a docile, lifeless body. He had not expected this and Ben must have been closer than the doctor estimated to coming out of his coma Twead thought. Ben had managed to move his arms upwards and took hold of either side of the cushion trying to push it away from his face but he was as weak as a kitten. As he increased the downward pressure Twead said in a gentle voice "Shush now don't fight it not long now and it will be all over. Its sleepy sleepy time now just relax." What little fight left in

Ben was diminishing and his efforts and movements became weaker and weaker.

"That's better" said Twead "That's a good lad; it's nearly over. You know it's for the best." Twead looked at his watch; it had been four minutes since he had placed the pillow over Bens face. There had been no movement from him for the last two minutes and all the monitors had been displaying warning signals. Twead had done his homework, he knew that after four minutes Ben would be technically brain dead and even if he were to be resuscitated the damage to his oxygen starved brain would be irreversible and he would at very best be basically a cabbage. He certainly wouldn't be able to do or say anything that could reveal what actually happened up on the roof. Twead replaced the pillow on the high-backed chair plumped it up and checked his watch ten seconds to go and then he would run out of the room shouting for help.

He took one last look back at Ben and thought poor bastard. Bang on time he could hear the alarm bells ringing from the nearby nurse's Station and the sound of feet pounding along the corridor as assistance was hurrying on its way. He dashed out off the door and shouted with a sense of urgency towards the approaching medical staff "Quickly, quickly something's wrong."

He then ran back into the room and to his horror realised he had forgotten to replace the oxygen mask on Bens face, it was still on the pillow where he had placed it. He ran around the bed and quickly tried to grab the mask but only succeeded in knocking it to the floor, he bent down and scrambled to recover it and clumsily pulled it back over Ben's now lifeless face managing it with a split second to spare before the staff together with the crash cart burst into the room.

"You will have to leave now" shouted one of the staff as they all went about their well-rehearsed resuscitation techniques. Twead said nothing he just did as he was told and left the room. As he passed the nurses Station he could see Chuman shuffling some paperwork together before casually strolling back into the main corridor. They met up again in the main hospital carpark. "Perfect timing" said Twead "what excuse did you use to get into the nurses Station?"

"I left some paperwork there earlier and I simply pretended to be looking for it. I'd left it near the emergency warning panel so I flicked the switches off and hid the panel with the papers while I thumbed through the paperwork. It was a close call to switch them back on at the right time though she was looking straight at me but fortunately the phone rang with a few seconds to spare so she had to turn around to answer it."

Twead said "I'm going back in now, I've got to do my concerned employer bit. I will see you later in Wetherspoons and we can discuss what I need to say to the pathology delivery board and how we can further stitch up the SOCO's and Latifeo. It's like I always say Hubert you scratch my back and I'll scratch yours."

17

Keystone Cops

Grant had been left in no doubt by Twead that the arrest of Pickes had to go smooth without any slip-ups and that he would be held responsible for any mistakes. He had not been surprised at this, it was just the way things worked in the force. All the pressure together with the shit that goes with it got passed down the chain of command whilst all the praise and accolades got passed upwards. In addition to his team he had also enlisted the help of the special ops unit, they would be useful if it all kicked off or they needed to batter the door in to gain entry.

A covert surveillance vehicle had already been sent to sit outside the address to establish if Pickes was at home or not, they had already reported back almost immediately that they had sighted inside him inside his premise. They would remain on scene to check to see if he stayed there, if he left they were prepared to follow him. All the teams left the Station at the same time travelling in convoy; they had all been tasked and briefed back at the nick as to each person's specific task and it had been emphasised the importance of completing a smooth and successful operation.

Pickes lived in a modest semi-detached on a busy main road across from a small local hospital not far from Stourbridge Football Club. Parking wouldn't be a problem; they had agreed to park on a section of tarmacked area surrounding a kitchen showroom, there was always ample space there with the exception of match days. The arrest team were now outside of Pickes house, they double checked with the covert surveillance team to confirm that Pickes was still inside and when they replied that he had not been seen to leave the covert team wished them good luck and with their job done they left the scene. Everyone on Courtan's order alighted from their vehicles on-masse and made their way quickly to the target address.

Three of the special ops unit went around to the back of the house in case he tried to make a run for it, the rest of the ops team who had the battering ram with them went to the main front door which was situated at the side of the house with dumb and dumber and Courtan. Latifeo and Wallows remained in their vehicle parked out of sight some distance away, they would be called in after the arrest to search his premise and vehicle when he was safely in custody.

Wallows was pleased with this as she didn't particularly want to see Pickes. She felt a little embarrassed following the previous night's undercover sting and she was unsure how he would react if he saw her and realised she was a police officer and that he had been set up. Courtan knocked on the door and waited, they all stood there in silence for a while. There was no reply from inside so Courtan knocked for a second time but a little louder, again no answer so he knocked for a third time.

"Get ready with the door key" he told the special ops unit, and the officer with the battering ram stepped forward. Courtan bent down and opened the flap on the letterbox and shouted through "Trevor Pickes, this is the police I want you to open the door we need to speak to you." Still no answer, they all looked at Courtan waiting for him to make a decision. He bent down once more and shouted as loudly as he could through the letterbox once again.

"This is the police, this is your final warning if you do not answer the door we will break it down now open the door immediately." The officer with the battering ram approached the door and readied himself; he was looking at Courtan waiting for the go ahead when he indicated to Courtan him with a nod of his head that he needed to look behind him. When he turned around he saw the postman walking down the garden path towards them, the guy with the enforcer put it down resting it on the floor.

"You will need to come back with the post another time mate we are in the middle of dealing with something here" shouted Courtan in the direction of the postman who frustratingly continued walking towards them. "What a prick" Courtan whispered under his breath just loud enough for the team to hear.

"I'm not here to deliver the post" he said to Courtan. With a little irritation in his voice he replied, "If you're not delivering the post then how can we help you?"

"Well" he retorted "I was just walking past and saw you lot here and I assumed you're here for the occupant because if you are you might like to know he has just climbed out of his downstairs window and is now running down the road towards the football ground."

"Holy fuck" shouted Courtan looking towards the sergeant in charge of the special ops team and screamed at him "Don't just stand there get after him."

The three special ops officers immediately gave chase including the one who had been holding the battering ram which he dropped to the floor and joined in the chase. It landed on its end and bounced slightly then toppled over horizontally ending up directly on the end of Courtan's left foot causing him to immediately collapse to the floor in the most extreme agonizing pain that shot through his foot and travelled up his leg. He began rolling about on the floor clutching his foot and cursing and uttering expletives in the direction of the special ops officer that was now running full pelt in pursuit of Pickes. Dumb and dumber went around the rear of the premises stating they were going to get the rest of the officers, in reality they had to get out of Courtan's sight because they could barely contain themselves at the sight of him on the deck incapacitated holding his foot and swearing and yelling out in pain.

One of the three ops officers had climbed the back fence to access the rear of the premise and then unbolted the gate for the others. Dumb and dumber strode quickly through leaving the gate ajar anxious to put some distance between themselves and the ridiculous sight of the prostrate screaming Courtan so that he wouldn't hear the guffaws and hysterical laughter that they were doing their best to contain. They could not hold themselves together any longer and once in the back garden   they both exploded into fits of laughter trying their upmost to muffle the sound by placing both hands across their gaping mouths. The tears began to stream down their cheeks. The ops team looked at them with a bemused quizzical expression; the response they got was finger pointing towards the direction of the open gate. Curiosity aroused all three of them walked towards the open gate and peered out. They all realised immediately what had happened as the battering ram was lying on the floor adjacent to Courtan's foot which he was clutching in obvious agony. This was too much for the ops unit and they also joined dumb and dumber in uncontrolled hysterics. The level of laughter increased as they all revelled in the situation and became more amused at the sight of each other all unable to control themselves.

The noise they were making so was intense that nobody heard the growling and menacing snarling coming from the ferocious dog that had been excited by the furore and had jumped over the fence from the neighbouring garden and was now heading for the officers. The Doberman pinscher saw this wild howling group as a threat and with teeth bared running at full speed launched itself towards them. Complete and utter chaos then ensued the crazed dog biting anything and everything it could. Ripping chunks of flesh from arms and legs the hilarity immediately turned to horror, shouts of laughter were replaced by screams of terror as the attack increase in intensity. The smell and taste of blood sending the dog into a blood crazed frenzy.

One of the officers had removed his CS spray from its holster and began spraying the dog completely emptying the canister the officer couldn't believe his eyes it was having no effect whatsoever. The dog just continued with his attack all the officer had succeeded in doing was gassing one of the ops team who was now rolling about on the floor in agony clutching his face. Frank Fergas who was now on his back sprawled across the floor hands clasped around his leg trying to stem the flow of the sticky claret substance that was oozing from the gaping wound just below his knee shouted, "CS spray doesn't work on dogs, use your baton."

The dog then received an almighty kick under his rib cage sending it flying through the air landing on the chest of Fergas. The dog as is his instinct went for his throat, Fergas just in the nick of time managed to put his hands up to protect his neck from being mauled and grabbed hold of the beast's neck. With the ferocious teeth just, a few inches from his jugular he held on for dear life summoning up all his strength knowing that if he let go his throat would surely be ripped out. The snarling jaws were now covered in a white foamy mess and they began to drool pouring out over the terrified face of Fergas. His grip was beginning to loosen and he knew he couldn't hold on much longer.

Another officer also put his hands around the dog's neck, a baton was repeatedly being cracked off the back of the dog's head and after several blows the dog's ferocity began to wane slightly. With one officer grasping the dog preventing it from biting anyone else the rest of the team picked the dog up and as if they were swinging a child by a wing and a leg in a playful manner they swung the dog and on the count of three let go and hurled the vicious beast high and handsome over the garden fence towards the front door. One officer then immediately shut the gate to prevent the dog getting back in.

"Thank god for that" shouted Peeves, examining the tear to the back of his trousers exposing his fat backside. "Where on earth did that fucking thing come from?" Before anyone could reply they could hear the spine-chilling screams coming from some other poor soul being mauled by this out of control monstrous dog.

"Courtan" somebody shouted, "He must be attacking Courtan." They opened the rear gate and could see the defenceless officer on the floor being savaged and bitten time and time again. With batons drawn they ran towards the dog intending to somehow beat it senseless. But before any blows were struck a loud voice shouted, "armed police step away from the dog, move." They could now see a police marksman crouched on one knee looking through the sight of his Heckler and Koch MP five aiming directly at the dog whilst at the same time his firearms colleague who was brandishing a Glock 17 Pistol was ordering Courtan to stay still. Then they heard the sound of a fierce some crack as the officer squeezed the trigger of his sub machine gun sending a 9mm round into the dog's skull tearing a huge hole in its head where its brain used to be. The force of the shot blasted the dog clear of Courtan and it lay there motionless on the floor with half of its head missing.

The officer with the Glock hand gun walked towards the dog cautiously and when he was directly above it fired three close range shots into the main body of the lifeless animal. Everyone was stunned into silence, what on earth had just happened it was something nightmares are made of. No-one spoke for a while and they each examined their wounds inflicted by the dog. It was the firearms officer who eventually breached the silence "I've ordered an ambulance for you all, I'll take care of things here it's a good thing we were passing goodness knows what carnage that bloody thing would have inflicted."

The armed response unit had been on patrol in the area due to a recent spate of terrorist attacks in Manchester and London and every police force in the country had raised its armed response capabilities. Whilst they were waiting for the ambulance Courtan was trying to cough up and spit out some of the dog's brains that he has swallowed when the dogs head had exploded and much of the rest of it was splattered all over his face. When he was able to speak he tried to make radio contact with the rest of the team who were in pursuit of Pickes but he didn't receive a response.

The team had chased Pickes along the main road past Stourbridge football ground and towards the canal side bonded warehouse. He had a considerable head start and as the officers saw him turn right into Canal Street they didn't hold out much hope of finding him but continued giving chase. Wallows and Latifeo were sitting in their vehicle waiting for the call to begin the search wondering why it was taking so long for them to be contacted. Shirley whilst sitting in the

196

passenger seat of the car had used the time to fill out as much of the pro forma documentation as she possibly could. She lifted her head out of the pile of papers on her lap just in time to see Pickes run past their vehicle towards the canal. He was being pursued by three uniform officers some distance behind.

"Jesus Christ its Pickes" she shouted. She scrambled out of the car as quickly as possible, paperwork scattering all over the place and began to give chase. Latifeo who was not so quick or as keen to give chase got out of the vehicle much more sedately by which time the rest of the pursuing team had joined him. All four now resumed the chase but the three officers were now reduced to a walking pace even so they were still outpacing Latifeo who deliberately lagged behind. They had seen Wallows follow Pickes in-between two disused buildings so they split into two pairs and encircled the buildings. They now had Pickes trapped; they edged around the buildings as quietly as possible trying to control their heavy panting of their breath that the chase had given them.

As they approached the last corner Latifeo could hear the sound of gravel under foot, he signalled to the officer that someone was nearby. He put his finger to his mouth and then signalled for the officer to go past him towards the noise. Typical CID thought the uniform officer; they were always shrinking into the background especially when there was a fight or any chance of physical violence. The officer edged silently around the corner of the building only to be met with the sight of Wallows emerging from the other direction with the rest of the team. They all looked around wondering where on earth Pickes had disappeared to and thinking what to do next.

"It looks like you've lost him" said Latifeo to the group always quick to shift any possible blame away from himself "I'll go back to the vehicle and tell Courtan what has happened while you try to find him."

Latifeo was running through in his head what to say to Courtan, whatever he said it needed to reflect badly on the others and show him in a good light. He was mulling the possibilities over in his head as he neared his vehicle and to his astonishment saw Pickes opening the driver's door and climbing in. As the vehicle started to move Latifeo was near enough to grasp the front passenger door handle and he began banging the window shouting at Pickes through the window. This had the effect of panicking him into swerving and accelerating at the same time causing the vehicle to skid across the road and mount the pavement and crash into the window of a Chinese takeaway restaurant demolishing the entire shop front in the process. Bricks flew in all directions; the window had shattered showering glass everywhere and a fish tank inside the takeaway waiting area had been knocked over flooding the floor which was now covered in tropical fish that were flapping their fins furiously. The two customers in the shop waiting for their chicken chow Mein and sweet and sour pork balls were cowering in one corner together with the owner. They were all covered in building debris and in a state of complete shock and bewilderment.

Pickes put the vehicle in reverse gear and floored the accelerator. The engine began to scream and the rear wheels spun round at an alarming rate, the vehicle however was going nowhere it was resting on the pile of debris from the demolished brick wall causing the wheels to be suspended in the air. Realising the car was stuck he got out the vehicle and jumped over what was left of the takeaway counter and into the kitchen knocking over scalding hot pots and pans and covering the floor in half prepared food. He ran through the emergency exit door and found himself on the canal towpath, Latifeo having no choice but to chase after him.

They were now running along the canal tow path back in the direction they had come from and back towards the rest of the team. Latifeo was aware of this and thought that if he kept far enough behind him then the rest of the team could arrest him and he could take the credit. That was until Pickes who must have been aware that he was running back towards the rest of the police suddenly jumped over the canal landing on the far towpath. Latifeo in a sudden but unusual split-second show of bravery but most probably fuelled by the thought of the kudos of capturing the murder suspect single handed also attempted to jump over the canal. He leapt for all he was worth, muscles being stretched to the limit, heart pounding, flying through the air, arms and legs outstretched he managed to land gracefully smack bang in the middle of the canal immediately sinking up to his waist in the most vile and putrid stinking canal water.

Pickes had turned around to see if he was still being chased when he saw the hapless detective stuck in the water. He knew he was safe for the time being anyway and stopped to regain his breath. Latifeo's legs were submerged in the foul gooey mud and he tried to lift them one by one to get himself out. But despite his best efforts he could not lift either of his legs, he tried harder and harder and when he realised that he was completely stuck in the mud unable to extricate himself he started to panic and began shouting for help. He continued struggling and then the chilling realisation hit him; he was slowly sinking lower and lower in the mud and fast. The water level had already gone from his waist to his chest and was still rising at an alarming rate. He began to scream with all his might the water level now having reached his shoulders. He was continuing to struggle but this was causing him to sink even faster. The water was now up to his chin.

Latifeo began to cry knowing that in a few short moments the water would be above his head and he would be no more. He coughed and spluttered as the foul-tasting water entered his mouth, he tilted his head back slightly to keep his mouth out of the water and took a couple of deep breaths but that wasn't effective for long as he continued to sink. He shut his mouth as it went totally under water and he began to breathe through his nose, with his mouth under water he could no longer shout to attract attention all he could think to do was to wave his arms in the air. Then with his nose now under water all that could be seen of him now were the petrified eyes of a man staring up to heaven with all hope lost.

He quickly became completely submerged thoughts running through his mind of how a dying man is supposed to be able to see his entire life flash before him in the final moments. His lungs were now bursting, he knew he wouldn't be able to keep his mouth shut much longer and his natural bodily responses were telling him to breath out, expel the air from his lungs and refill them with clean fresh air. What is the quickest way to finish it he thought, take a couple of lungful of dirty water as speedily as he could perhaps then it would be all over. He held on for as long as he could but when he couldn't take it anymore he decided it's time to go it's all over he said to himself as he opened his mouth and took his first gulp of filthy canal water, please let it be quick he said in a silent prayer to himself. The filthy water flooded into his lungs and he felt like his stomach was about to burst when he suddenly felt his body begin to rise upwards, someone or something had taken hold of his arm and was pulling him to the surface. Within a second his head was completely out of the water and he opened his mouth and spewed out the stomach full of canal water he had swallowed and took several deep breaths of fresh air.

"Thank god, thank god" he cried as he found his arms draped over a wooden plank. It was a little difficult to see at first, his eyes stinging from the pollutants in the dirty canal water but he could make out that the plank was traversing the two opposite towpaths. He could see Wallows with some uniform officers on one towpath and some uniform officers on the opposite side. He looked up to see the face of his rescuer, his life saver standing on the plank immediately above him as he squinted slightly and found himself staring straight into the eyes of his saviour Trevor Pickes.

18

Bang to Rights

Courtan sat in Frank Twead's office; he had been summoned there as soon as Twead had finished making arrangements at the hospital and the coroner's office in respect of the now deceased Ben Whyte. Stan Gutthy had now been further charged with the young officer's murder. Courtan had a cast put on his broken foot and several stitches in some superficial dog bite wounds together with a tetanus injection. He had long given up on how he could put some sort of spin on the arrest of Pickes; it had been absolutely catastrophic complete and utter pandemonium and he had resigned himself to receive the biggest bollocking of his life. The only saving grace had been that when Pickes went back to pull Latifeo out of the canal saving him from a watery grave he had been surrounded and so he gave himself up peacefully and was now incarcerated in the police cells.

In the initial interview concerning his wife's murder and despite Pickes denying the charge Courtan had managed to implicate him with some clever questioning. Twead strode in the room purposely and sat behind his desk eyeing Courtan for some time before speaking.

"My instructions to you Grant were to arrest Pickes with as little fuss as possible and I wanted everything to go smoothly. What on earth happened? How could something as simple as an arrest go so horribly wrong?"

Courtan shrugged his shoulders and replied, "I just don't know how so many things went wrong, it was just an unlucky bizarre sequence of events."

Twead flicked through the report on his desk and appeared to be counting something in his head and then stood up and gave a precis of the report. "So as far as I can tell and please correct me if I am wrong but we seem to have the following. An escaped murder suspect, one officer suffering breathing problems as a result of being gassed with CS spray, a further six officers including you treated for various bite wounds inflicted by a dog, this same dog had to be shot dead by armed officers and whose brains were plastered all over your face. You also have a broken foot; a police car was then stolen because it had been left insecure with the keys in the ignition and a Chinese takeaway restaurant demolished by the stolen police car. The owner of the takeaway in addition to several customers all badly injured and suffering from shock. We have a demolished tropical fish tank together with dozens of expensive dead tropical fish. One officer almost dying after swallowing half of Stourbridge canal who then had to be rescued by the escaped suspect whom you had lost in a foot chase from his home address. Now tell me, have I missed anything out DS Courtan?"

He stared straight at Courtan but he made no reply, he just hung his head and shook it indicating that he hadn't. Twead continued "And your explanation for all this mayhem and carnage is that it was unlucky."

There followed an awkward silence as Twead paused awaiting a reply, Courtan however said nothing as there wasn't a single thing he could think of to say to offer any measure of mitigation for the fiasco. Twead broke the stony silence by saying "The only redeeming factor is that the focus of attention is not on this arrest but on the tragic death of one of our colleagues. This will give you a little breathing space to progress the interview. How are you getting on with Pickes? Is he co-operative?"

This eased a lot of the pressure off Courtan's shoulders; he could now deliver some good news. "Well sir he is still denying it" said Courtan "But I have asked him a series of questions that I can prove his response to them are lies. I haven't further pushed him in those yet but I will resume the interview shortly and turn the screw."

"What sort of thing can you disprove?" Twead asked enquiringly.

"Firstly, is his alibi for the night in question, he states he was working which we know to be false. He wasn't at work it was his day off. He denies using his van outside work and says he has no knowledge of any dogging spots or ever visiting them and he has never heard of the contact magazine in which he placed an article plus a number of other things. He obviously isn't aware that we have so much evidence against him but by far the most significant comment is when I asked him about his wife. I said to him that he didn't seem particularly upset at his wife's death. His remarkable reply in which he drops a huge clanger has probably sealed his feat."

Twead was now all ears and Courtan had his full attention and he was urged to go on. "In his reply when I asked him about not being upset about the death of his wife he said he was extremely upset and that he couldn't get the picture out of his head at the thought of her lying dead and motionless across the car and that he continued to have nightmares about it."

Twead's face showed his excitement at this statement he was almost fit to burst "That's it" he said "we've got him as it was never revealed how she actually died. No-one knows that she was found dead bent over the bonnet of a car. He has to have been there so conduct your further interview and get him charged tonight."

At last a smile came across Twead's face "Has he asked for a brief yet?"

"No not as yet" came the reply.

"Well push him as hard as you can before a brief gets involved and tells him to go no comment and make sure you record on the custody record that he has been asked several times if he requires a brief and that he has declined."

203

Pickes hadn't in fact been asked several times it had just been once and that was in a very offhand casual manner. The exact words as he was being booked in were, you can have a solicitor if you want but I don't suppose you want one, do you? Before Pickes could think what was being asked of him and before he could reply his response had been recorded as negative and he was being led away to a cell. Courtan knew he needed to do as Twead said and he would arrange for the custody record to be amended accordingly. Courtan internally breathed a sigh of relief, Twead was now firmly focused on getting a result with Pickes and everything else would fade away into the background and be forgotten. "I'm just waiting for some forensics updates and then I will continue with the interview."

"Okay" said Twead "I'm going to a meeting now give me a call and keep me updated."

Courtan knew full well that Twead didn't have a meeting to go to and he was in fact on his way to the pub so he just replied, "Yes sir, will do."

As Twead left the office Courtan was feeling quite pleased with how things had turned out, he had been expecting to be on the end of a much bigger more verbose roasting than the one meted out to him. Perhaps it was the death of Ben Whyte that Twead had been more concerned with Courtan thought or maybe something else that he wasn't aware of either way Twead wasn't his normal overbearing bullying self but it was still good news for him.

Back in his own office his team were already assembled, they had just found out about Ben Whyte and were in a sombre mood. Wallows had found herself more deeply affected that the rest and she was on the verge of tears but was somehow managing to keep it all together. The team were looking a bit the worse for wear after today's series of events. Dumb and dumber had come off the worst of the team, both had a number of wounds in their legs and arms that required stitches with Peeves having further dog bites to his backside. Latifeo had a few minor cuts and bruises where he had fallen over when he was chasing the stolen CID car that he had left the keys in the ignition. His worst injuries however weren't fully known, the damage done to his lungs caused by the filthy canal water only time would tell. Wallows wasn't physically injured but the rest of the team could see quite plainly that she had been deeply affected by the death of Ben Whyte.

Wallows pulled herself together and began to itemise the evidence she had retrieved from the house and vehicle search belonging to Pickes. She had completed the search on her own as Latifeo had been receiving treatment at the hospital. Wallows read through her house search documentation and outlined the articles recovered; perhaps the most significant material was the sheer amount of contact magazines, most of them concerned with voyeurism and more specifically scopophilia watching other people having sex.

"The guy must have a serious addiction to this stuff" said Wallows. "The magazines number in excess of one hundred" she continued. "I also recovered a laptop; this is now being examined by I.T. and they will have a full report in a couple of days. A video cassette tape that was seized and has been viewed is interesting and it is what is referred to as a snuff movie." This caught the attention of the group.

Frank Peeves asked, "Is it a genuine snuff movie Shirley, does the person actually die?"

"No" came the reply "It looks as if it is a simulation but it shows a darker side to his perversion." Wallows then moved onto the vehicle search, the council van that he used for personal use. "This is where it starts to get really interesting" said Shirley.

The group were now on the edge of their seats especially Courtan who was looking for evidence that would strengthen the case for Pickes to be charged which he had to do to get Twead off his back. Wallows showed the room two sealed evidence bag then detailed what they contained.

"The first one is an ordinance survey map. In addition to showing roads it also gives locations of parks and woodlands etc.

205

and various areas have been circled with a pen. I have made a separate list of them all and it appears to be a complete map of every dogging site in the Midlands, each one has been allocated a number. The second one is a note book and it gives a description of each of the numbered dogging sites, the best place to stand and the busiest times and dates for each site. There are also contained within this notebook a number of selfies, he seems to have taken his own picture at a number of dogging sites, all the photographs are automatically timed and dated and displayed at the top of the photograph."

Wallows then paused for a while and drew a deep breath; the group realising something good was coming.

"It also contains times and dates of the sites visited" and with a huge smile on her face she said "And I know what you are all thinking and hoping and the answer is yes. His records show that he was there the night of the murder and at the appropriate time including a timed and dated selfie of himself."

The room burst into applause whooping and cheering. They all knew they had their man and more than enough evidence to convict him, what an incredible irrefutable piece of evidence; a timed and dated selfie taken at the murder scene. They all stood up patting each other on the back and shaking hands. Courtan let everyone celebrate for a while and then appealed for calm so he could continue; slowly they all bought their exuberance under control and began to settle down. Before Courtan could continue Wallows said "There is just one more thing, I also recovered something from his tool box. The technical name for it I have been advised is a bradawl"

Fergas shouted "What on earth is a bradawl?"

"A bradawl is an implement used by carpenters to put holes in wood to make it easier to insert screws, it consists of a wooden handle attached to a long thin round steel spike which fits the pathologist's description of the murder weapon. Scenes of crime have sent it for testing, it is being fast tracked and we will have the results in forty-eight hours."

Trying for as much impact as he could Latifeo had kept his information to the very end, he wished he hadn't now because they all knew they already had enough evidence to charge him and his input was now a little superfluous.

"I've got the forensic update on the magazine left at the first crime scene, it has his fingerprints all over it and the SOCO's have compared the footwear impression on the cover with the shoes that Pickes was wearing when he was bought in and they are also a match."

No-one was overly interested in what Latifeo had to say because they all knew they already had more than sufficient evidence but Courtan made a note of this saying "I'll add that to the interview schedule; now can everyone get busy please and make sure your reports and paperwork are complete. I will interview and charge Pickes and then I think we can all go somewhere to celebrate."

Pickes wasn't looking overly concerned when Courtan walked into the interview room; he seemed more interested in the contents and make-up of the room. It was a purpose-built interview room; the walls were completely soundproofed and the only furniture there was a small wooden table with four chairs. A state of the art voice recorder was on the table with a number of microphones situated at various angles to capture all words spoken by anyone in the room. Courtan decided to go straight for the jugular and cut through the niceties. The tape recorder was switched on and Courtan went through the formalities stating the times dates and persons present etc.

"Trevor Pickes, I remind you that you are still under arrest and I will be asking you questions in regard to the murder of your wife Claire Pickes. You earlier stated in this interview that at the relevant time and date of your wife's murder you were in fact working in your capacity as an emergency handyman for the local council. Enquires have revealed that this is not correct and I have a statement from your employer stating that you were not employed that day it was your day off. For the purpose of the tape I am showing Mr

Pickes a certified copy of his employer's statement. What do you have to say to that?"

Pickes still didn't look particularly worried but simply replied "I must have made a mistake."

Courtan asked "Where were you on the night of your wife's murder?"

Pickes replied "I can't remember, but I was nowhere near that park."

Courtan decided to begin to push him.

"Your vehicle was seen parked adjacent to the murder scene at the appropriate time could you tell me where you were?"

Pickes began to lose his air of confidence slightly but still replied "I can't remember but I didn't go in the park."

Courtan began to turn the screw "For the purposes of the tape I am now showing Mr Pickes two exhibits, one is a pornographic contact magazine and the other is a writing pad recovered from Mr Pickes vehicle. The contact magazine has numerous traces of your fingerprints and on the front cover there is an imprint from the sole of your left shoe. The writing pad found in your vehicle has an entry in it giving details of you visiting the murder scene at the time of the murder; do you still deny being there?"

Pickes expression had now completely changed. He had not been expecting anything like this and he now began to realise that the police must have been making enquiries into him for some time. He didn't reply for what seemed like an age, when he eventually blurted something out he said, "No comment I want to see a solicitor" and sat back and folded his arms with an attitude of defiance.

Courtan smiled he knew that he had got him, he was well aware that a solicitor would now advise him to go no comment to any further questions. He leaned over towards the tape recorder and completed the formalities including the fact that the suspect now wanted a solicitor and that the interview was now suspended until the arrival of legal advice. He then switched the tape recorder off.

Frank Twead was just downing his fourth pint of lager in Wetherspoons as his best mate and his now co-conspirator to murder Dr Hubert Chuman walked up to the table with a pint and four large glasses of whisky.

"It's double congratulations" said Chuman smiling from ear to ear.

"How so?" asked Twead taking a large sip of Famous Grouse.

"Well thanks to that report you put in shifting the blame to the SOCO's. The threat of suspension has been lifted. The PDB are quite happy that it was no fault of mine.

"That's a result" Twead said as he raised his glass towards Chuman's and after clinking them together their first large whiskies were downed.

"What's the other piece of good news" he asked curiously.

"The second is I have completed the post-mortem examination on Ben Whyte and given the cause of death as heart failure bought on as a result of the induced coma. It doesn't occur that often but it is not totally uncommon. The coroner is happy with that and so are the hospital staff as it takes any pressure off them as there is no need to examine the care and procedure administered so there will be no fuss or any questions raised by anyone." They both then downed their second large whisky in one gulp.

Back at Stourbridge Police Station Courtan was liaising with the duty solicitor or to be more accurate a solicitor's runner. This was normally a person with a little legal training. They were used by legal firms in order to avoid one of their solicitors having to suffer the inconvenience of being called out at odd hours although the firm would still charge at the full going rate for a fully qualified solicitor. In this case it was an ex-police officer from Stourbridge whom Courtan knew well. He was an ex detective sergeant and he had worked with Courtan many times. Once the details of the evidence against Pickes in respect of the murder of his wife and two other victims were outlined to him the runner said "Well he's obviously guilty, I'll see if he wants to confess. If not, I'll tell him to go no comment because I assume you are going to charge him anyway and then me and you can have an early night, job done."

An hour later a frightened confused Pickes was in the charge office where he was formally charged with the murder of his wife and then remanded in police custody to appear before the magistrates the next morning. Courtan relayed the news to Twead whom he could tell by his slurred speech that he was already half pissed especially when he let out a loud drunken whoopee and congratulated Courtan but also added as a warning that he expected the relevant associated paperwork to be completed ASAP before abruptly hanging up. Courtan had wanted to give Twead some of the more finite details of the interview he wanted to blow his own trumpet and bathe in the glory of charging a serial killer but it began to dawn on him that Twead simply wasn't bothered about anyone else he only cared about himself and his booze so feeling a little deflated he replaced the receiver.

There was plenty of time for the completion of the paperwork so he decided to join the rest of his team in 'The Bank' which was a newly opened bar in the centre of Stourbridge. The premises of an old bank that had been refurbished they had chosen for their celebration because it was little used by police officers and they wanted a little bit of privacy.

Their mood was a little subdued what should have been a cause for a huge celebration had been tainted by the untimely and tragic death of their fellow officer PC Ben Whyte and before the first drink Wallows stood up and proposed a toast to their fallen colleague. The atmosphere lightened after a few drinks and the conversation flowed in a relaxed fashion. Courtan had his mind on other things there was something not, quite right? He couldn't put his finger on it but he felt a little uneasy. The enquiry had gone really smoothly perhaps too smoothly, maybe that was it or was it Frank Twead's behaviour. He felt as is something was wrong but he couldn't put his finger on what, he convinced himself he was being over analytical and pushed it to the back of his mind and continued with the celebration.

19

A Nice Little Earner

Courtan had stayed the night with Sam Gail. He had been too drunk to perform but he had been bursting to tell her all about the result of the enquiry into the serial murder and although he shouldn't have he told her all about Pickes and how his clever interview techniques had cracked the case and secured enough evidence to charge him with murder.

He was quite surprised at how much interest she had shown and the number of questions she asked and this pleased him even more, the fact that she showed an interest made him feel more important and he gave her every last detail until he had fallen asleep in bed mouth wide open and snoring like a jack hammer. In the morning he woke with the after effects of the previous night's drinking session. He hadn't drunk a great deal but he wasn't a regular drinker so it affected him more than most but he felt the celebration was worth it. They had managed to solve the biggest crime Stourbridge had ever seen and he and the rest of the team had played a major part in the investigation. He knew this would strengthen his chances of future promotion. He would have preferred to have had a lie in and sleep it off but he had been assigned to attend the magistrate's court for the initial appearance of Pickes so that he could report back with the result to the incident room.

As he left he gave Sam a kiss on the doorstep and he took a brown envelope out of his inside pocket "I almost forgot. I'm making a lot of extra money from this enquiry so here's a little bit extra to help you with the bills." He handed her five hundred pounds in crisp fresh notes, gave her another kiss and left shutting the door behind him on his way to court.

Courtan's head was still pounding as he sat in the magistrates' court but he soon forgot about it as he watched when Pickes was brought up from the cells below the court into the dock. He eyed him up and down carefully; he looked completely different from the previous day. He was now pale and weary and looked as if he had aged overnight. He seemed to be in a state of shock and not fully aware of what was happening to him. His face was expressionless and he showed no emotion as the charges of murder were read out.

He said nothing other than to answer to confirm his name; his defence brief then automatically entered as was the normal procedure in these circumstances a plea of not guilty. No bail was applied for and Pickes was remanded in custody to appear before a higher court as magistrates do not have the power or jurisdiction to deal with cases of murder.

Courtan thought he saw Pickes beginning to sob as he was led back down the steps by the court officials returning him to the holding cells where he would be held pending his transfer to HMP Birmingham. The whole thing was over in a matter of minutes and it all seemed a bit anti-climactic thought Courtan as he left the court and made his way to the Station.

A press conference had been arranged for midday at Stourbridge Police Station. The morning papers had not been able to report on it because of the time of charging of Pickes late last night. It had been after the deadline required for early edition newspapers, therefore the force and the chief constable wanted to make as big an impact as possible in order to divert away from some of the bad publicity that they had been subject to recently. The chief constable was scheduled to attend personally as he was not one to miss out on what he referred to as positive publicity and he would make a point of opening the briefing. Everyone was busy getting everything ready and the Station was a hive of activity.

Courtan having returned from the magistrate's court needed a bit of peace and quiet to nurse his sore head, his hangover was really beginning to kick in and he was sitting in his office quietly drinking a coffee when surprisingly in walked Twead who took a seat at the desk opposite Courtan. "Good morning sir I wasn't expecting you this early. Is everything okay?" asked Courtan.

"Couldn't be better" came the reply "I just wanted to make sure everything went as expected at court this morning."

"No problems at all. Pickes has been remanded to Birmingham prison pending his next court appearance at crown court."

"And how are you progressing with the other enquiry I gave you Grant, have you any idea where the leak is coming from?"

Courtan shook his head and simply replied "Not as yet. I have a gut feeling who I think it is but I don't have any evidence."

Twead stood up and turned for the door to ensure it was shut and locked, he then returned to and leant over the desk almost face to face with Courtan and whispered "What is your gut feeling? Just give me a name, that's all I want just a name" he then stared expectantly.

Courtan took a deep breath and in a whispered voice said "Latifeo." No further conversation took place and Courtan watched Twead leave his office his mind obviously mulling over this information and what to do with it. Courtan sat back and closed his eyes, there was still an hour before the conference so he decided to try and relax and let his headache ease off.

Pickes was in his own personal hell. In the brief time since he had arrived at HMP Birmingham he had been constantly threatened with violence and sexual abuse by other inmates, even the ones that didn't threaten him with violence would whisper the word 'pervert' in his ear as they walked past him. There was a distinct lack and presence of uniform prison officers and this had made him feel very uneasy. He had been allocated a cell on his own and although he was allowed to wonder the wing if he wished to he decided he would be safer in his cell. As he lay on his bunk he was thinking back through the last twenty-four hours. In hindsight he thought he would have been better off telling the police the truth but that was too late now. His first concern now was how to stay safe and not get beaten up or sexually assaulted.

Then suddenly the unlocked door to his cell opened and a gang of prisoners burst in, two of them positioned themselves at the door and kept a look out. Before Pickes could shout out or scream to get a prison officers attention or some help four of the men rushed in and in an obviously well-rehearsed move had pinned him flat on his back on his bunk. One was on each corner gripping him by the legs and shoulders whilst another man shoved a bundle of rags deep into his mouth. Pickes's eyes were wide open in terror his heart was thumping like crazy and he had an awful churning in his stomach as he watched what he assumed to be the leader of the group approach him. He saw him take something out of his pocket, to his instant horror he saw it was a toothbrush; it had been altered and attached to the handle was a long thin razor type blade. In his other hand he held a pair of metal pliers.

Pickes tried to struggle but he couldn't budge an inch, he was locked in a vice like grip forced down on to the bed. The apparent leader of the group, an evil looking man with a horrid sickly grin and big bulging eyes was sporting a scar running diagonally across his face from forehead to lower lips that had sliced through an eyeball and nose. This demonic looking man could see and sense the fear and panic that was gripping Pickes and he took obvious pleasure in this.

He put his finger to his lips telling Pickes to keep quiet and stop struggling. He nodded towards the men holding Pickes legs and then both of them began to pull down Pickes trousers and underpants until they were round his ankles and exposing his genitalia. He then spoke in a slow and menacing voice "I am now going to remove this from your mouth and I want you to keep completely quiet do you understand me?" The terrified Pickes nodded his head in compliance.

"Because if you do shout out it will do you no good, no guard will come running to rescue you. If you make the slightest sound I will take hold of your tongue with these pliers yank it out of your mouth and slice it clean off. I will then cut your dick off and shove it down the back of your throat just like you did to those poor bastards that you butchered. Do you still understand?"

Pickes nodded once again his eyes bulging from their sockets in sheer fright. The razor blade held in his hand was placed close to Pickes face and aimed near the centre of his quivering mouth. With the other hand he slowly began to remove the rags from his mouth until they were clear and Pickes could breathe slightly easier. He didn't speak for a short while he just stared unsmilingly and intensely at Pickes in an obvious threat for him not to make a sound or cry out. He then spoke "Listen carefully. As a remand prisoner you are not subject to the same amount of monitoring as the rest of us, the rules are more relaxed. You will therefore be able to smuggle certain things in and out of here. We will tell you what to do how and when. Are we still understanding?"

Pickes again nodded. With the razor blade still close to his face he was further told.

"Failure to comply with what we tell you to do will result in another visit from us and we will not be as friendly as we are now. Tell anyone about this and we will be back. Remember we can get to you at anytime and anywhere. I take it we are still understanding?"

Pickes couldn't nod his head this time because the point of the blade was now pressed against and was touching his eyeball and if he were to move a hairs breadth the blade would pierce his eye. After a few seconds the blade was removed from his eyeball and with a last menacing look they all left leaving Pickes alone in his cell half naked and unmoving on his bed. Frozen with fear Pickes didn't move immediately, when he was eventually able to move he pulled his trousers and underwear up got off his bunk and curled up in the corner of his cell in a foetal position and then began to sob uncontrollably like a small child. He was so terrified; he lost control of his bodily functions and a puddle of foul smelling urine formed beneath him.

The press briefing at Stourbridge Police Station had gone well, the chief constable gave his usual non-descript address during which he thanked everyone for their hard work, dedication and professionalism. He gave reassurances to the members of the public stating that thanks to the hard work and professionalism of his officers the serial killer that had terrorised Stourbridge residents was now safely locked up behind bars. He congratulated everyone on a successful operation but still managed to claim most of the credit for himself.

Twead didn't have a speaking part as most of the details of the operation and any questions were directed towards Gibbs who like the chief constable was doing his best to claim as much of the credit as possible. He had even managed to involve and give credit to Gail Tomaso who had now earned the nickname of the superintendents bit of skirt. The rest of the team looked on exasperated, they had done the hard work, they had taken the risks and got the result and yet the hierarchy were claiming all the glory. Unbelievable thought Wallows, none of us have had the slightest of mentions and it's as if we didn't exist. She looked towards Latifeo who he acknowledged her glance and she could tell he was thinking the same as her.

Twead had been monitoring what the press had to say and what questions they were asking, he had been expecting some sort of comeback over the fiasco of the arrest of Pickes especially from that prick Spenser Wark but there was no sign of it. Somehow the press had not been given any information on it which fitted in with Courtan's theory that Latifeo was the leak because Latifeo wouldn't want it to be known that he had to be saved by the person he was trying to arrest he would simply keep quiet about it. Twead was getting bored now and his mind began to wander, he was mulling over recent events and how well things had turned out. The serial killer locked up, the wife beater had been caught and charged and there would be no comeback of his mishandling of the KFC rooftop incident, the only witness being poor Ben Whyte whom he'd murdered and got away with it.

Rumours and allegations regarding the previous enquiry into the death of three tramps had simply faded into the background and all attention was being focused on everything else that had happened. Things were now back to normal so he could get back into his daily routine of getting drunk at every available opportunity. He was trying to remember how many bottles of whisky he had in his desk drawer, he vaguely recalled two bottles and a few slurps left in another bottle that would do for tonight he thought. He was thinking so much about how drunk he was going to get that he almost didn't notice that the briefing was more or less finished.

The press hurried off to prepare their editorials whilst everyone else engaged in celebratory back slapping and mentions of commendations. Courtan had gone back to his office a bit pissed off that he hadn't been mentioned during the press conference and he was staring at the pile of paperwork that had amassed during the Pickes enquiry. Knowing it was his job to make sense of it and prepare the prosecution file for court he realised that it would give him some manoeuvrability to divert some of the credit and kudos towards himself. Just then the door to his office opened and in strode Spenser Wark, Courtan looked nervously behind Wark anxious to see if there was any one in the corridor that had seen him walk in.

"What are you doing here? This isn't what we agreed."

Wark smiled and also looked around to check that they were alone and he reached for his inside pocket and removed a thick brown envelope which he handed to Courtan.

"Careful" Courtan said as he quickly took the envelope and stuffed it into his inside pocket. "Haven't you got to get in touch with your news desk and give them the story?" Courtan asked.

"Already done, nothing was said at the conference that you hadn't already told me I only went for the sake of appearances."

"We need to be careful" Courtan said in a hushed voice. "Twead knows that someone is leaking information to the press, fortunately he has asked me to investigate it and I've already hinted that I think it could be Oli Latifeo and he seems to have swallowed that, so from now on we stick to our arrangements and meet at the Windsor Pub where nobody knows us. Okay?"

Wark shrugged his shoulders and half-heartedly agreed. In reality he wasn't overly bothered whether Courtan was outed or not as he sensed that Courtan was coming to the end of his usefulness anyway. After Wark had left the office Courtan began to have regrets about accepting money for information. He knew that Wark now had a hold on him and could manipulate him; he also knew that he couldn't trust him. Wark had nothing to lose if it all came out it was not a crime to give money for information but it was a crime for a police officer to receive it. Wark would be alright, he would continue on in his job as normal, perhaps even get some sort of bonus but Courtan knew full well that he would lose his job and possibly face prosecution for misconduct in public office. However, since he had started receiving wads of money he realised he was now dependent upon it. He certainly couldn't maintain his relationship with his girlfriend Sam. He knew she was really appreciative of the money and willing to show that in sexual appreciation. What a complete and utter fuckin mess how on earth did I manage to get myself trapped in this mess he muttered under his breath.

20

Whisky Galore

Pickes remained in the corner of his cell still curled up in a ball like a frightened little child. He had to find a way to get some protection but he was so terrified he couldn't think straight. His head was spinning with thousands of nightmarish thoughts and his body was shaking uncontrollably. He was hoping and praying that his cell door would be locked soon so he knew he would be safe if only for a short time, but that may give him the peace he needed to clear his head and think straight.

He heard a noise at the cell door, he expected it to be the prison officer who would be locking him in and affording him some much-needed rest bite from this ever-present fear that kept churning away at his stomach. He wondered if he dares ask the prison officer for help or just say nothing to him and think things through in his mind first before saying anything. Immediate horror and panic then gripped him when he saw who had entered his cell. He recoiled further and pushed himself back harder into the corner as he saw not the prison officer but someone he had seen recently in news bulletins.

It was the wife killer Stan Gutthy, the person who was seen on national television dangling a petrified young police officer from the roof of a building by his leg before dropping him to the floor and now he was standing in his cell. He was a huge beast of a man, he dwarfed the other prisoner who was standing at his side, a weasel like scruffy little runt who resembled an inbred retard with horrible skin, dirty greasy hair and horrid disfigured black and yellow teeth.

Pickes was shaking like a leaf, he looked up towards the two men and began to beg "Please, please don't hurt me." He tried to plead with them some more but he couldn't get his word's out because of his uncontrollable crying and shaking.

Gutthy found this highly amusing and began to laugh out loud like some giant pantomime ogre; the little one had a sickly evil looking smirk on his face. Both of them were getting an incredible kick out of the enormous amount of terror that they were bringing to Pickes just by their presence. The little one acting on a signal from Gutthy knelt down next to Pickes and grabbed his head from behind with both arms holding his head in a vice like grip. With him unable to move his head he wanted to shout out as the huge imposing figure of Gutthy neared him but he knew it would do him no good. Pickes tried to look away as Gutthy unzipped his fly and took his penis out and said to his sidekick "Hold the stupid little shit still."

He was now standing directly in front of Pickes whose crying had now turned to a whimper. Gutthy began to laugh and guffaw, louder and louder as he began to urinate all over the defenceless Pickes spraying him with a hot foul smelly stream of liquid that was soaking into his hair, skin and clothes. Pickes was silently praying to himself wishing it would stop. He then felt two hands inserted into his mouth the fingers of which were curled round the inside of each cheek which were then forcibly pulled apart. With his mouth now gaping wide open the stream of putrid urine was now being aimed directly into Pickes mouth. He began to choke and gag as he tried to close his mouth but was unable to so. In response his head was tilted backwards and upwards towards the spray and his mouth was being forced ever more open. He thought the pressure exerted on his mouth would rip his face apart. His mouth was now completely full of the foul-smelling liquid he tried to cough it out but couldn't. It was swirling around the inside of his mouth and over his tongue and as he was forced to swallow the acidic fluid which burnt the back of his throat making him wretch and splutter. It seemed to last an eternity, on and on and all he could do was just sit there and take it.

When at last it was all over the smaller one of the two inserted his urine-soaked fingers into Pickes mouth and ordered him to suck them dry. It was all he could do not to be physically sick as he felt the dirty wet grubby fingers at the back of his mouth. Then he heard the menacing threat again being repeated and whispered with a threatening evil tone into his ear "This is a gentle warning, a little reminder of what you have already been told remember we can get to you at anytime and anywhere don't forget it." They then left the cell giving him one last long lingering stare as he curled up into a ball in the corner of his cell quivering uncontrollably unable even to cry any longer.

Twead emptied the last dregs of whisky from its bottle half filling the tumbler on his desk, raised it to his lips and downed it in one huge gulp. One bottle down and one to go he thought as he opened his desk drawer and took out another full bottle of Famous Grouse and unscrewed the cap. His intention was to get absolutely blind drunk, his best mate Dr Chuman had a meeting with the pathology delivery board early the next morning to confirm the lifting of his possible suspension so he couldn't run the risk of getting slaughtered, therefore Twead was forced to celebrate and drink on his own. Things were now beginning to return to normal, there were no outstanding major enquires, all his cock-ups and mistakes had been successfully covered up and his best mate's career was back on track. He was free to indulge again in what he liked to do best, which was to sit back, do as little work as he could possibly get away with and drink as much alcohol as humanly possible.

His enquiry team however were doing the exact opposite; they had to put in extra unpaid hours of overtime busy beavering away preparing the murder committal file and the associated paperwork. The only drinks being consumed by them were constant cups of hot coffee to keep alert and stay awake.

Latifeo stifled a yawn as he lifted his head up from the paperwork on his desk and looked towards Wallows, attracting her attention he said "I wonder what Pickes is doing now? It's strange but I can't help for some reason feeling a little sorry for him."

Wallows replied "He'll be tucked up in his cell now waiting for lights out I suppose, it's only natural you feel that way after all he did save your life when he pulled you out of the canal. We were all too far away from you to get there in time. I shouldn't worry about him he's probably relaxing on his bunk while we are stuck here doing all this paperwork." Wallows couldn't have been more wrong.

Pickes was still curled up in a ball in the corner of his cell whimpering occasionally then all of a sudden, his heart went back in his mouth when he heard the cell door slowly begin to open fear was racing through his body and he thought he was about to soil himself again in fright. When he entered the cell Pickes almost cried with joy and relief when he saw it was a uniformed prison officer.

"Ten minutes to lights out" he said and he turned to walk out. Pickes dashed over to him and begged for his help. "Please help me I need some protection, I'm not cut out for this. Can't you put me in some sort of segregation away from the other prisoners" he pleaded. The prison officer looked at the pathetic, frightened, piss-soaked specimen in front of him and couldn't help but feel sorry for the poor wretch. He knew by the sorry state of him that something had gone on so he asked if Pickes had been assaulted or threatened in any way knowing full well that even if he had been beaten up or abused that he like everyone else would be too frightened of repercussions to say so. Pickes shook his head in response and simply looked at the prison officer silently pleading for help. This was the normal expected reply; the prison warder had seen and heard it hundreds of times before. It was the worst and most dangerous thing a con could ever do in prison to grass on somebody and it would be the equivalent of a death sentence.

"Look, the only way you can be segregated is being put on rule 45 for your own protection but basically you need to be either a child killer or molester, a police officer or a potential suicide risk. And as far as we are aware you are none so what I suggest you do is get into bed and try and get some sleep."

Pickes stood there in silence as he saw his possible saviour turn and walk out the door and then lock it behind him. He felt a little safer now that the door was secure and he sat on his bunk thinking what to do. He could think clearer now he knew he was safe for the next few hours but he realised that he needed to do something straight away. He thought about what the warder had said and the phrase potential suicide risk began to repeat in his head. That was it, that was what he needed to do, he had to prove that he was at risk of killing himself, a potential suicide risk. He monitored each and every time the spy hole opened in his cell door and he saw an eyeball staring through it. It was regular as clockwork give or take a few seconds, every twenty minutes without fail.

Pickes took off his piss sodden shirt and ripped it into strips and made a makeshift noose that fitted loosely around his neck. He turned his bunk bed on end so it was sitting upright and attached the other end of the noose to the top metal leg of the bed. He looked at his watch; there was ten minutes before next check-up so he practised his position. He soon realised that this would not pass for a genuine suicide attempt, the noose was not tight enough and his feet could reach to the floor. The only way he could do it and make it look convincing was to use a knot that tightens up when weight is applied to it. He quickly set about tying a taut-line hitch knot; this is a knot that is used by lorry drivers to secure loads to vehicles so that if the load moves whilst in transit as it invariably does sometimes then the knot gradually tightens. It was a technique he had learnt ironically enough when on a council run vehicle health and safety training course.

He knew that once the knot was on then it would not be possible for him to remove it but he had used this knot hundreds of times and he was aware that the tension applied was extremely gradual and he could last a long time before it would begin to restrict his airway. He shortened the rope to the minimum length he dared risk and his feet could just about touch the floor using his tip toes.

He waited until the twenty minutes was nearly up and applied the rope round his neck and when he heard the sound of footsteps on the landing nearing his cell he pulled the knot securely around his neck whilst still leaving sufficient slackness for it not to affect his breathing. Then he waited and watched for the peep hole in the door to open. He was waiting and expecting to hear the sound of the alarm being raised when the warder saw him hanging there but no sound came. No bells ringing no sound of feet running along the landing had he seen the peephole open or had he missed it when he closed his eyes for effect. He checked his watch; it was already one minute past the twenty that had been adhered to rigidly for the last couple of hours.

Perhaps the warder had looked in and not paid attention, if that was so it would be another twenty minutes before he came around again. Don't panic he thought I can easily keep control for that long. It would take the knot a long time to tighten and it would only tighten if he moved about, if he kept perfectly still he would be okay. He tried to keep his breathing under control and settled down for the forthcoming twenty minutes, after what seemed an age Pickes could hear footsteps walking along the landing. He checked his watch and he was bang on time again exactly twenty minutes. He heard the footsteps get louder and louder as they neared his cell and then incredibly he heard them get quieter and quieter until they began to fade as he walked past and away from his cell. Oh my god he thought the warder has stopped looking through the peepholes, he is just walking the landing. I need to shout to get some attention; he then stupidly moved his body so his that his head and more importantly his mouth was facing towards the cell door in order to project his voice. But as he did so the sudden movement caused the knot to tighten, only slightly but enough to restrict his vocal chords and prevent them from giving out any sound. Pickes began to panic and as he did so he could feel the noose taking more of a grip round his neck, he struggled with the knot to try and undo it but he knew from experience that this would not be possible and all he was succeeding in was doing was increasing the tension on his neck. Stay still he said to himself, keep calm he knew now his only hope would be to remain completely still for the remainder of the night until the morning when the cells were opened, otherwise it would be a slow lingering and painful death.

Courtan looked at his team, it was clear that they were extremely tired and it was beginning to show. He didn't want people making mistakes at this stage of the enquiry so he decided to wind things up for the evening. "Okay guys" he shouted "I can see we're all getting knackered so I'm calling it a day. Go and get some rest and I'll see you all back here at eight in the morning. I know it's been a long day but I do appreciate your efforts, thanks a lot everyone I will see you all in the morning."

Whilst everyone else quickly left the Station, Wallows went to the women's locker rooms. She was feeling a bit grubby and wanted to freshen up. The facilities were quite good; the showers were spacious and clean with plenty of hot water and there was a seat and a mirror where she could sit and apply some fresh make-up. She took her time getting ready as she wanted the rest of the team to leave the police Station. There was something she wanted to do without the rest knowing. It had been two extremely long and tiring days for Wallows but the rewards had been worth it. She had achieved a lot in the short time she had been attached to CID and she could now feel a little more respect coming from her fellow officers, there was still a long way to go to get the full credit she thought she deserved but it was a step in the right direction. She looked at herself in the mirror, considering the time I have had and the hours worked I think I look pretty good she told herself. She touched up her make-up once more, ran her fingers through her hair, checked her handbag and made towards the door. She put her ear against the wooden panelled door and listened for a while to establish that the corridor was empty and when she was satisfied she left the room.

Twead had almost finished his second bottle of whisky and he was beginning to feel the effects of them. The drink was taking hold of him but what the heck he thought he deserved it. Then an unexpected knock came on his door, Twead quickly downed his last swig of whisky and secreted the bottle back into his desk drawer. "Come in" he shouted in as sober a voice as he could manage.

"Hello Shirley" he slurred as Wallows made her way into Twead's office. "What can I do for you" he managed to say before releasing a drunken uncontrollable hiccup.

"It's more what I can do for you sir" she replied. Twead was a little confused. Was Wallows coming on to him? It certainly looked like it or was he even drunker than he thought. She certainly looked the part, she had obviously made an effort and was if he wasn't mistaken flashing a bit of cleavage something he had not seen from her before.

"Take a seat" he said pointing to the chair situated on the opposite side of his desk. Shirley sat down and smiled at Twead. She immediately realised that he was absolutely blind drunk and not far from being completely overcome with the drink and passing out. He was well known for this and he was often seen leaving his office in a dishevelled state by officers from the night shift and early turn as they were preparing to change over. It was common knowledge in the Station that he would drink himself into oblivion and end up slumped over his desk for the night then when he woke he could be seen staggering to the toilets to try and freshen up. Shirley reached in her bag and pulled out a half bottle of Grants Whisky. She could see that he had an empty whisky tumbler in front of him on the desk.

"I just wanted to say thank you for approving my attachment to CID and giving me, a chance and I wanted to give you this. It's only a bottle of Whisky and I'm not sure which one you normally drink but I think it's a popular one." She then walked around the desk, bottle in hand and unscrewed the cap and poured him a large measure and stood there next to Twead without moving. Twead noticed she was wearing a short tight quite provocative skirt. He was now sure that she was coming on to him and he decided to chance his arm and he put his hand on her bum and gave it a squeeze. She still didn't move or raise any objections but just smiled and let out a giggle. He pushed his luck a bit further and slid his hand inside her skirt and began to stroke the inside of her thigh, slowly edging his hand higher and higher up her leg and he still met no resistance from Wallows, in fact he was sure that she had opened her legs slightly allowing his hand to travel further up her thighs. Wallows lifted up his tumbler glass and handed it to him and said, "Don't forget your whisky."

He forgot how drunk he had begun to feel and downed the almost full glass down in one and put the glass back on the desk where Wallows once again refilled it. This continued on with Twead becoming more and more adventurous whilst Wallows continued to fill his glass until the bottle was completely drained. As Twead was sipping from his last tumbler full Wallows knelt down and put her head in his lap and undid his fly and removed his semi erect penis and started to give him oral sex.

Twead grabbed hold of the hair at the back of her head and forced her head down until she had the entire length of his still semi erect penis in her mouth. Twead had not had sex for some considerable time, oral or otherwise and it did not take long before he ejaculated whilst he was still inside her. With a mixture of sexual fulfilment combined with in excess of two and a half bottles of whisky Twead slumped back in his chair only just having enough energy to put his now flaccid dick back into his trousers.

Wallows stood up and reached for her handbag where she took out a tissue and wiped her mouth. Twead tried to thank her for the whisky but by now he was so drunk it just came out as drunken gibberish. Wallows knew what he was trying to say and offered to get rid of the empty bottle. Twead picked the empty bottle up and put it to his lips and upturned it to see if there was the slightest amount left in, when he realised it was completely empty he put it into Wallows handbag that she was holding open for him and with a smile she thanked him once more and left his office making her way back to the changing rooms.

She had decided because of the late hour to put her uniform back on for the walk home, she felt safer that way also she was in no rush to get back to her lonely little bedsit. She hated it, she felt so isolated there so after getting changed back into uniform she went back to Courtan's office and went through some more paperwork. At least in the Station she could hear other people in the office and she didn't feel quite as alone.

Twead stayed in his office he was conscious of the fact that he would shortly be asleep or passed out over his desk like he had done many times before but before that happened he mulled over what had just happened and thought what a fuckin cheap slag. Mind you they are all the same the useless bitches they will do anything to get on. They are worse than prostitutes; at least they are honest about what they do in selling their bodies for money. He then began to rapidly drift into a state of unconsciousness and he slumped forward over his desk head against his desk blotting pad and he began to snore.

21

Remember my Name

Karen and Jason were travelling south on the M6, they were feeling a little excited and also apprehensive at the prospect of shortly to be realising their fantasies. "I think we can come off the motorway at Stafford south and go through Wolverhampton to get there." Jason said.

"It's a good job you know where you're going; I haven't got a clue how to get there. We should invest in a satnav for the car, you can pick them up quite cheap now." replied Karen.

Jason laughed and blurted out "What exactly would we set the destination to; I don't think that dogging locations are included in satnav's places of interests." This then sent the pair of them into an uncontrollable fit of the giggles which they both realised was simply a release of the tense nervous energy they were feeling.

"How will we find the location when we get there?" asked Karen "I think the best thing to do would be to simply follow the signs for Stourbridge and just have a drive round the centre. I think the place is only small so we should be able to find a dogging spot somewhere. The news reports have mentioned the Oldswinford area a few times which I think is a small part of Stourbridge what do you think Jason?"

"Sounds like a good idea to me I mean we can hardly stop and ask someone for directions, can we?" Jason chuckled.

They had driven down from Littleborough, a small village just outside Rochdale. They had been hearing on the news about the murder of dogging couples in the Stourbridge area and had subsequently trawled the internet to find local dogging hotspots; they had been astounded at the sheer number of dogging websites and dogging locations named in the local area. It seemed totally out of proportion to the size of the place, it was like the unofficial capital for swingers and doggers. It was something they had tried when they were on holiday the previous year in Gran Canaria. One day after having a little too much wine at lunchtime they decided to take the thought of indulging in their sexual fantasies a little further and they had taken a wander around the sand dunes of Maspalomas.

They had managed to find some other couples who were indulging in various sexual acts and they watched for quite a while, but they could not work up the nerve to take part themselves. The whole experience had however ignited their sexual proclivity to participate in dogging. They didn't want to risk it anywhere near home, so the Rochdale area was out of bounds; they couldn't risk being seen because if they were recognised or found out then it would affect their jobs.

They drove around the area for a while looking for signs that might help them remember the areas and locations they had heard about in the national news but nothing seemed to ring a bell. They circled the main Stourbridge ring road a couple of times, the road signs giving directions to every location in or near Stourbridge but still no clue to the dogging sites.

"We'll have to find somewhere soon, remember we are both on earlies in the morning and it's a long drive back."

Jason replied "One of the dogging sites is the main park but we haven't passed a single one and there are no signposts for them. I did see a supermarket with a large carpark at the front, we could try there I suppose just for now and when we get back home we can look through the news reports and find out exactly where the best locations are and come back next week sometime."

After driving round for a short while longer they both decided to try the supermarket carpark. The access was on a one-way system off the main ring road, if they had been paying attention instead of being totally absorbed with what they were about to do they would have realised that the entrance to the supermarket carpark was directly opposite the rear entrance to Stourbridge Police Station just a few feet away. The carpark was fairly deserted but there were some suitable spots, they drove round a few times and then parked the car near the entrance adjacent to a slope that led from the access road with a wall either side of it. This provided a little cover, but anyone interested in having a look could still see if they got close enough. When they got out of their car they were both still blissfully ignorant of the fact that they were incredibly close to the main Police Station entrance. But time was running late so they decided to simply go for it straight away over the bonnet of their pride and joy, a silver BMW three series that they had both chipped in to buy together.

Jason looked around but couldn't see any occupant's in the few cars that were still parked there, and no one had driven on while they were parked up. "Perhaps the serial killer has driven them all away?" Jason joked.

"It's not funny" Karen replied, "remember some people have been killed, nobody deserves that."

"Oh God! He's got me, he's stabbed me from behind." shouted Jason.

Karen stifled a scream and instinctively twisted her body round to see Jason with a huge smirk spread across his face.

"You frightened me to death you bloody idiot, grow up."

Jason began to laugh and continued with what he was doing. Although no-one else was there they were both excited at the thought of what they were now doing and what could happen if they got caught and it gave them a heightened sense of sexual pleasure. Jason bent over and whispered in Karen's ear "I think there is someone skulking over there in the corner watching us." He then said with some urgency "Christ he's got a knife and he's coming straight at us."

Karen tried to stand up in panic but she couldn't, Jason hadn't moved and the weight of his body was pressed against her. He then began to laugh again.

"I've told you once it's not funny, you're just being childish now. Pack it in" Karen said with a bit of venom in her voice.

"I don't know what you're worrying about anyway, didn't you see the evening news they've caught the serial killer. It was one of the victims' husband. It would have added some extra excitement though if you thought there was the possibility of a serial killer out there that would put things on a knife edge and really spice things up."

Karen's face was beginning to get quite warm as it was pressed into the bonnet of the car the engine was still quite hot from the long journey so she turned her head around and faced the other way looking out towards the small side road and the entrance where they had drove in.

"Oh my god" she exclaimed.

"What's the matter?" asked Jason with a sense of panic in his voice.

"That building, a few yards away the other side of the access road. It's a Police Station."

"Oh, bloody hell that's all we need" Jason shouted in disbelief.

"Shush, not so loud someone might hear you." Karen said in a whisper "Just get on with it and be as quick as you can so we can get out of here."

They continued with increase vigour to speed things along but also because they were both a little excited and turned on by the added danger of doing it so close to a Police Station. They were now both nearing a climax and their movements and actions increased in their intensity until Jason began to cough and splutter as if he was choking and his thrusting movements stopped. He then lay motionless on the back of Karen and his frantic breathing began to subside, he still continued with his imitation of choking, but Karen decided to ignore his play acting until she eventually lost her temper and shouted at him.

"For fucks sake not now you bloody idiot, keep going." But Jason didn't keep going and remained still.

"If you've come get off me, in fact forget that just get off me anyway you've spoilt it now. It wasn't funny the first time and even less now."

When Jason didn't reply and continued to remain motionless she began to worry a little and started to struggle free and as she turned her body round she saw Jason was completely motionless and his face was completely expressionless. She began to realise that something was seriously wrong. To her horror she suddenly realised that they weren't alone, someone else was there and they were standing immediately behind Jason. She was engulfed by sheer terror and her face was panic stricken and for a few seconds she couldn't fully comprehend what was happening. But her panic-stricken face turned to a sense of relief when she saw who it was standing there; it wasn't a pervert or some sort of homicidal nutter but a uniform police officer.

Her breathing began to slow back to normal realising that help was there "thank god" she said "we need help, something has happened to my boyfriend he has just suddenly gone quiet. I think he's ill please help us. We're the same as you; we are police officers from Manchester. I know we shouldn't be doing this especially right next to a Police Station, but can you get us some medical help?" she pleaded.

The police officer stood there staring intently at Karen and shook their head in mock disapproval at the sight of the two of them half naked bent over the bonnet of a car in public.

"I realise this is not very professional of us and we could get into trouble for this but please help us."

The police officer stretched their hand out towards Karen and placed it behind her head which was still pinned to the bonnet. She breathed a sigh of relief now that they were being helped however

Karen's expression changed back to one of sheer terror when she saw what the police officer was brandishing in their latex gloved hand. It was a wooden handled instrument with a long thin steel blade attached and the officer was holding it aloft. The hand that had been placed behind her head now had a firm grip of her hair making it impossible for her to move her head in any direction. She tried to scream as the weapon was plunged with great speed and force towards her face but the scream never came. The metal spike that was now lodged in her brain having entered through her eye socket had beaten her to it and killed her instantly. Her boyfriend wasn't so lucky he was still alive and he had to endure watching through one partially opened eye the awful fate suffered by his girlfriend and had seen from a few inches away the metal spike penetrating her eyeball and being driven completely through until the butt of the handle was resting against her eyelids.

When the weapon was removed from Karen's brain the eyeball came with it still firmly attached to the steel spike. The officer looked at it curiously, this had never happened before. In all the other previous murders the spike had been driven clean through the back of the neck, even the practise ones on those dirty smelly drunken tramps but none of the others had managed to turn their bodies around so it had been easy. But what on earth should be done with the eyeball? It was never the intention to disfigure the female as they were not the focus of the slaughters just their boyfriends. The only reason they were murdered at all was to eliminate any witnesses. So carefully the eyeball was removed from the metal spike by sliding it gently to the end and then with some dexterity it was placed over the empty socket and then forced back in by applying pressure with the officer's thumb making a strange slurping noise as it entered the eye socket of Karen's lifeless face. There was no time to lose now if the plan were to succeed so the officer looked around and scanned the area to make sure they were alone. They bent over until they were face to face with Jason and with a sickly smile began to speak in low dulcet tones.

234

"You are a piece of shit, the metal spike that I forced through the back of your neck has severed vital nerves rendering you paralysed you cannot speak because I forced it all the way through to your vocal cords. You are now slowly internally bleeding to death but before you die I am going to cut off your pathetic little dick and force it down your throat. I want you to be on the receiving end for a change this is payback time."

Jason was fully aware of what was happening to him but he could do nothing, he was completely helpless. He couldn't even cry out when he felt the coldness of the blade as it began to slice off his manhood. He had in the space of a few minutes gone from having the most exhilarating experience in his life penetrating his girlfriend in a dangerous and risqué situation to being in such incredible pain that he was silently praying for death to come. His penis was now being dangled in front of his face taunting him with it as the officer began to speak.

"You are a bigoted evil bastard and this pathetic little cock of yours is at the root of it all and that is why I am going to reunite you with it by forcing it down the back of your throat. You will then be left here to die to slowly bleed to death lying on top of your dead girlfriend and that is how you will be reported in the news. The news that will be seen and read by your family and friends, I want you to think of that in the short time you have left to live but the final thing I want you to know the last thing in your memory is who I am I want you to know who the person is that has done this to you I want you to remember my name."

The officer then began to force Jason's penis as deep into his throat as possible and when it was fully lodged at the back of his throat the officer put their face close to Jason's and paused for a while admiring their handiwork. They then whispered in Jason's ear "The last words you will ever hear on earth is my name, the name of the person who has slaughtered you and left you to die in the most gruesome humiliating way imaginable so listen to my name and take it to hell with you."

The officer paused for a while revelling in the pain and suffering that their victim was enduring and then they bent down and whispered softly in their ear and said "My name is Shirley Wallows."

Wallows then looked around the carpark to make sure she was still alone and when she was positive that no one else was there she began to work quickly. She removed from her ever present handbag the empty half bottle of Grants whisky that Twead had drunk and carefully wiped the area just below the neck of the bottle where she had deliberately touched it when handing it to Twead and when she had poured him glass after glass until he was on the verge of passing out. She had practised several times where and how to hold the bottle so that she knew exactly where to wipe her fingerprints off. She had put her thumb on the Grant's crest on the front of the bottle and one finger on the label on the rear of the bottle, this way it was only her fingerprint that would be erased. Wallows couldn't believe her luck when after finishing the bottle Twead had picked it up and put the neck in his mouth and wrapped his lips around it to try and extract any remaining scotch and for him then to put it straight into her handbag without her having to touch it again was a dream.

If only he knew he was helping to stitch himself up. He thought he had been on a good thing and in control whereas in fact he was a stereotypical dumb bigoted male pig whose prick ruled his head, and this was being used against him. The bottle was them placed on the floor in a prominent position where it would easily be found by crime scene examiners.

She then removed a tissue from her handbag, the one she had wiped her mouth with after giving Twead a blowjob and unfolded it and with a clean sterile swab transferred what was left of Twead's sperm onto it. This was then inserted into Jason's back passage for a few seconds and rotated several times to make sure the evidence had been securely deposited. The swab was removed carefully and to make sure that Twead's DNA would be found she rubbed the swab

236

around the outside of his anus, something she had learned from the SOCO's at the post-mortem.

To make sure that the bodies weren't discovered too early Wallows gave the pair a slight push and they both slid along and eventually fell off the bonnet of the car. The bodies were now concealed between the front of their vehicle and the carpark wall. Jason was lying on top of his dead girlfriend; his head was facing upwards looking into the face of his attacker. She stared back at him with a smile across her face, she was pleased with the way things had worked out and she was enjoying watching the pathetic sight of the life slowly oozing out of Jason's incapacitated body.

She would have liked to have stood and watched for longer but she realised it was time to go. Wallows worked methodically, the swab and the scalpel were placed in a polythene bag to prevent any contamination of the inside of her handbag. The murder tool was placed inside a separate polythene bag and sealed; this would come in useful later. She scanned the area checking for any witnesses and when she was sure the coast was clear she so as not to attract attention to herself, walked casually away back home towards her bed-sit.

22

Room with a View

Pickes had now been forced to stand motionless for three hours, the muscles in his calves were burning, drowsiness was being to take over and the effort required to maintain his stance on tip toes was taking its toll on him. Every time the tiredness got the better of him he would lose his concentration even if only for a split second, but he would jerk back into life, when he felt the tension in the noose increase. The noose had now got tight enough to dig into his skin and he could feel the occasional trickle of blood coming from where the pressure was greatest on his neck near his larynx. This had also meant that he had been unable to call out for help. He tried to maintain his concentration by thinking about recent events, he realised he should have come clean with the police and told them about his real perversion something he had been too ashamed to tell anyone about he couldn't even tell the other people who like him, watched in secret as couples had sex. If he had told the truth and admitted his perversion to the police, then he could have told them who the real killer was and he wouldn't be in here.

He had watched as that policewoman stabbed both of them in the back of their necks while they were having sex. He had hidden in the bushes, in his normal hiding place where he knew he could not be seen and had waited there for a long time after the policewoman left before going over to them. When he did so and realised they were dead he didn't know what to do. He couldn't tell the police what he had seen without telling them why he was there. His wife and the bloke who had been fucking her were both dead and nothing could

239

be done for them, so he went home and waited for the inevitable visit from the police. He made up his mind now, he had decided that he would tell the court or police whoever spoke to him next about his fetish and what he was doing there, and this would explain why he hadn't told the truth before because he was so guilt ridden. He was thoroughly ashamed and disgusted with himself to admit to anyone that the only thing that satisfied his sexual cravings and fulfilled his sexual desire was to secretly watch his own wife being fucked by strangers.

The more strangers that fucked his wife the better the greater it turned him on. The fact that his wife was completely unaware of him spying on her added a heightened intensity to it all. He would watch and masturbate furiously during these sessions sometimes ejaculating two or three times in fairly quick succession. This would also explain to the police why he used to tell his wife he was working late whilst in reality he would follow her or try and locate the dogging spot where she had gone to. It was also the reason why he tried so many times to advertise in the contact magazine for like-minded people, he had hoped to find someone else who also liked to secretly watch their partner male or female fucking other people.

He continually kept going through the admission he would make and it didn't sound as bad as he thought it would as he repeated it over and over again certainly better than being accused of killing his wife and being remanded in this crazy hellhole. He could see the sunlight beginning to seep in through the window of his cell and he knew it would all be over soon one way or another.

Courtan was getting dressed in his girlfriend's bedroom, he had popped round for a quick one and that had been exactly what it was an extremely quick one. Sam didn't complain or say anything though she was more than happy with the extra money that Courtan was putting her way and it was a tidy sum. She knew more than to kill the goose that laid the golden egg as it were. She was staring out of the bedroom window as he got ready; he noticed this as he had done several times before curiously he asked, "You spend a lot of time looking out of that window, what it is that is so fascinating?"

Caught a little off guard by this question she replied after a short pause "It gives a good view of the park. I just like to look at the greenery, the trees, flowers and everything." She was secretly thinking to herself that he would be surprised if he knew some of the things she had seen from that window, the things that she kept locked away in her mind until she decided what to do with them.

Courtan took out the brown envelope given to him by Spenser Wark earlier from his jacket pocket and removed a wad of notes which he handed to Sam. He gave her a peck on the cheek and then made his own way out down the stairs and left shutting the front door behind him. Sam remained at the upstairs bedroom window and watched Courtan make his way down the street, past the entrance to the park and she kept her eye on him until he disappeared from view. She looked at the text message that she had just received from Latifeo. She typed in a reply which read 'Yes you can come around ten minutes xxx'.

As she walked along the landing she counted the money given to her by Courtan, it was another five hundred pounds. She picked up the pole that was used to release the loft hatch and hooked it round the ladders that glided down to the floor. She climbed up into the attic space quickly, it was fully boarded allowing for the storage of things that were only used seldom and some that were never used at all. A large tea chest was towards one corner of the loft; she moved it slightly and then lifted the secret hidden panel beneath it and reached in and took out a sizeable locked metal money box. She keyed in the five-figure digital number and opened the lid; it was full to the brim with varying denominations of bank of England notes. She crammed the five hundred pounds in and replaced it back in its hiding place and then went to get ready for the arrival of Latifeo. She rehearsed the latest sob story to give to Latifeo, he was a bigger sucker than Courtan and even easier to get money out of. The only problem was that he didn't have as much money but he was still worth using as a source of income.

Wallows had returned home to her small one-bedroom bed-sit that she hated. She was desperate to get out of the place and find somewhere decent but that would mean earning more money by climbing further up the promotion ladder. She was lying on top of her bed unable to sleep; she was a little worried about Pickes and couldn't help wondering if he had seen of the murder of his wife. The comment he made about seeing her lying prostrate over the bonnet of a car was revealing, it meant that he either saw the murder or turned up later when she was dead. There was a possibility he could identify her so she had begun to make arrangements to prevent this happening but she was unsure how long it would take. She eventually drifted off into a shallow restless slumber.

Pickes was now almost unconscious, the noose was severely restricting the amount of air intake and he was becoming light headed as a result of this lack of oxygen. He thought he must be hallucinating because in his mind he thought he saw the peephole open and close a couple of times but common sense dictated otherwise. It obviously hadn't he thought because the alarm would have been raised immediately.

He was now coming to terms with the fact that his life may soon be coming to an end and he regretted his decision to fake a pretend suicide to get put into isolation from other prisoners. His body was now completely exhausted with the strain of keeping completely still on his tiptoes to prevent the noose tightening but the reduced amount of oxygen his body was receiving was totally draining him of the strength needed to prevent him from simply relaxing and let the noose do its work and slipping to an untimely and completely unnecessary demise.

The paramedics arrived at HMP Birmingham at eleven minutes past six in the morning, seven minutes after receiving the call to an unresponsive prisoner. With the patient still breathing and a steady if weak pulse he was stabilised and transferred to City Hospital with blue flashing lights and sirens at maximum levels. Arriving at City Hospital at six-thirty-one, escorted by and in accordance with home office procedures handcuffed to a prisoner officer, a text book well executed procedure.

Within minutes Pickes was wired up to every imaginable piece of hi-tech monitoring equipment measuring all bodily vital signs. But after a short and frenetic few minutes the busy and highly rehearsed activity from the medical team slowed and glances and expressions were exchanged between members of the emergency medical response team.

The senior consultant looked at his watch and uttered a technical complex statement to the rest of the team that was immediately timed and documented. He then looked at and spoke with the prison warder who was still handcuffed to the prisoner instructing him that he could remove the restraints because although the patient was still technically alive he was for all intent and purposes almost completely brain dead.

23

You're Copped

The incessant ringing of the phone woke Wallows from her intermittent and uncomfortable sleep. She wiped the sleep from her eyes and sat on the edge of the bed and picked up the receiver. "Hello, Shirley speaking" she uttered in a quiet half-awake voice as she tried to stifle a yawn. The caller didn't identify themselves but in a cold calculated statement said "Job done, I let him strangle himself. I watched him do it through the cell peephole and it took him nearly all night to do it the poor bastard. He is now at City Hospital on life support, but he is now technically brain dead with no chance of recovery. He's going to spend whatever life he has left as a vegetable, so I have done my bit and I want you to complete your part of the bargain and destroy my DNA sample." She then heard the click as the caller hung up.

Wallows felt a lot better now this news had woken her up knowing that the only person who could possibly identify her was now no longer a threat and with renewed vigour quickly got ready for work. Before leaving her hated bed–sit and making her way to the station she opened her freezer and in a special compartment removed a number of DNA swabs including the one from the prison officer who had just phoned her. She read the details that she had carefully inscribed on each one using a special indelible pen given to her by the SOCO's. These swabs gave her fantastic power over a lot of individuals, all of them with one thing in common the one thing that made her hate them. They were all men and she would do anything to destroy them whatever it took to make their lives as miserable and as wretched as hers once was.

She had samples from police officers, prison warders and court staff including several senior solicitors and lawyers all of whom succumbed so readily to a quick blow job. The one she really wanted was from that condescending prat Dr Chuman, he had humiliated her at the first post-mortem and spoken to her as if she was worthless simply because she was a woman. She had been treated like this and far worse when she was a child growing up with arrogant pompous men using their power and influence to make her life a misery and she had vowed to repay the treatment handed out to her.

The first plan to get Chuman appeared to have failed, it had been muted in the office that he might be suspended because he had missed the penis that had been sliced off and placed in the victim's mouth but he appeared to have got away with it somehow. He hadn't actually missed the penis though because it simply wasn't there at the time of the first post-mortem. Wallows had placed it in there the day after when she was given the task of fingerprinting the body. The sliced off penis had been inside an evidence bag that she kept in her police handbag and she had been carrying it round with her since the murder deciding what to do with it. She had been given the perfect opportunity to discredit Chuman when she was alone with the body. Something still needed to be done about him though but it would require a bit more work and planning she thought but she was determined to get him somehow.

She examined the sample from the prison officer, she had got this one on a social evening arranged between police and prison staff. A quick blow job in the pub carpark then wiping her mouth with a tissue that she took out of her bag and then later transferring it to a swab and subsequently her freezer with the other samples. It had been so easy and every bloke had been the same, brains and common sense gone out of the window at the prospect of a quickie. She had agreed to destroy his sample in return for sorting Pickes out but she looked at it and studied for a while but instead of destroying it and with a big beaming smile across her face she replaced it back in the freezer together with the others, he was too good a contact to be let off the hook so easily. She looked at her watch as she shut the door behind her, it was still early and she wondered if the two dead bodies had been found yet. The supermarket would be opening up soon so it couldn't take much longer if they haven't already been discovered and she wanted to be there went the balloon went up.

The supermarket staff were busy getting the shop opened, the shelf fillers had completed their tasks and were getting the tills ready filling them with change and checking that they all had replacement till rolls available. One member of staff, a young trainee was busy restocking the shelves of several portable display stands containing potted plants which when full would be wheeled out to the carpark where people helped themselves on the way in to the store. She was humming a song in her head; she had heard it playing on the local Stourbridge radio. The radio station that had been named incredibly unimaginatively 'The Bridge'. She wondered how long it had taken for someone to think of such a lame title as that.

She continued humming the tune that she couldn't get out of her head as she started to push the first display trolley outside. She couldn't recall the title of the song but it didn't really matter she was in a great frame of mind and really happy with her new job. Although she had only been there two weeks she fitted in well with the other staff, she loved the work and it was well paid. She thought life is treating me great at the minute, there is nothing that could upset me, and everything is going along fantastically.

As she pushed the first display trolley outside and positioned it on the paved area next to the carpark she noticed a silver BMW car parked next to the wall near the entrance and thought it odd. She knew it wasn't a member of staff's car and the shop didn't open for another twenty minutes. She put it to the back of her mind as she returned for the next trolley. After ten minutes the last of the trolleys were in place and she looked at the parked car again, there was nobody in the car so it wasn't anyone who was waiting for the shop to open and if it had been parked there all night then the owner would be fined. There was a strict two hours parking policy and this was only for people using the store. She walked towards the car, it didn't look as if it had been stolen and then dumped there. She peered through the front passenger window and saw it was empty; there was a road map on the passenger seat that was open. How strange she thought, perhaps it was someone from out of town that had got lost. But why leave the car here? She walked round the back of the car towards the driver's side, that's when she saw them. Two pairs of legs were sticking out protruding from the front of the car; you could tell they were male and female and they weren't moving. Perhaps they were ill she thought or maybe drunk. She edged a little closer; it was clear that it was a man lying on top of a woman.

"Are you okay?" she asked timidly and, in that instance, it became obvious that they weren't okay, she could now see two lifeless bodies and that they were lying in a huge pool of blood. She let out an ear shattering scream over and over again and began to shake and cry uncontrollably. The pair where plainly dead and they seemed to have been killed in some sort of horrible manner.

Wallows was in the Police Station parade room when she heard the screams. She knew immediately that someone must have found the bodies; she waited for a while to allow other officers to get there first and then casually strolled outside.

She couldn't believe her luck from the previous night; her initial plan had been to get Twead totally drunk so that he would pass out in his office then go to the main park and butcher a couple of doggers and then plant the whisky bottle and Twead's DNA there. But when she walked out of the Police Station after leaving Twead almost collapsed over his desk and saw these two hard at it literally within a few metres from the unconscious drunken slob's office she realised that not only could Twead's trace evidence be left at the scene but Twead himself was also being placed in close proximity of the crime scene. It couldn't have been more perfect especially when she looked around the area and realised it was deserted, it was an opportunity that she couldn't refuse. To put the icing on the cake the final act to seal Twead's feat she mumbled anonymously amongst a group of officers that someone should get the detective chief inspector.

Immediately a young eager probationer constable ran the few yards back over the road to the Police Station to see if Twead was in his office. He returned to the scene a couple of minutes later telling everyone that the DCI had been asleep in his office but after waking him he was on his way.

Wallows smiled to herself knowing that Twead was totally and utterly stitched up when eventually his trace evidence would be identified, he would also have to admit that he had been just a few yards away from the murder scene on his own with no witnesses. The scene had been cordoned off awaiting the arrival of the SOCO's and the pathologist. The on call was Sally Drice, Wallows was pleased with this for she knew that Dr Drice was far more meticulous than Chuman and she would be certain to find the evidence that she had planted.

The supermarket manager voiced his concerns that the carpark was sealed off and that his customers couldn't get access to the store but he didn't get any sympathy from officers protecting the scene and the only response he got was a surly "Murder scene mate no one comes in or goes anywhere near." The young girl who had still not stopped sobbing was led away to the Police Station to make a statement.

When Twead turned up Wallows looked at him, he was and it was clear for everyone to see an absolute mess. He was dishevelled, unshaven and had quite obviously not showered or even had the briefest of washes. He was unsteady on his feet and eyes were completely bloodshot, it was a wonder he could focus or even see out of them they were that bad. He was still completely and utterly wrecked from last night's heavy drinking session. Twead was trying to clear his head and to think straight, this is a complete fucking nightmare he thought. He had been looking forward to sitting back and putting his feet up for a while but for god's sake another double murder and on the day, he'd got the biggest hangover for a long time. He knew he looked terrible and he hadn't got his wits about him, he needed to delegate responsibility until he could clear his head so he instructed Wallows to contact Grant Courtan and get him to take charge of the scene and to make sure the SOCO's got there as soon as possible.

Twead left the scene heading back to his office telling Wallows to keep him updated. His head was bursting and he badly needed a drink, he searched through his desk drawer then realised he had drunk all his supply of whisky last night shortly before he passed out. He left his office and walked the short distance to a local newsagent on Stourbridge high street, he was still that drunk he had difficulty walking and his eyes couldn't focus properly.

The newsagent fortunately was empty and Twead quickly bought the first bottle of whisky he saw on the shelf and hid it inside his jacket as he walked out the shop. As he passed Wetherspoons he saw that there were a number of early drinkers sitting outside on the pavement tables having their first drinks of the day, this was more temptation than he could stand so he looked around to see if anyone who knew him was in sight and when he couldn't see anyone he quickly went in. He ordered two pints of Thatcher's Cider and two large Famous Grouse Whiskies, his hands were shaking so much he had to pick his first pint up using both hands and even then, he managed to spill some all over the counter as he desperately tried to put it to his mouth.

The bar staff watched him as the cider glass eventually reached his lips and they saw him gulp it down. He finished the full pint whilst they were still pouring the second one, when the second pint arrived he paid for them both and the whiskies and finished the second cider off in a few huge swigs. He had chosen cider because he felt dehydrated and cider was stronger than lager and with the extra fizz the alcohol would work into his blood stream quicker than normal lager and together with the whiskies which he devoured each with one swig would speed things up even more and he could start to function. The cider and whisky combination had been an instant hit and he could feel the alcohol beginning to work its way into his bloodstream as he left the pub and slowly walked next door back to the Police Station. He looked at his watch, it was eight-fifteen and he had already downed two pints of cider and would soon be having a few whiskies whilst locked away in his office. He would be okay in a short time he thought when the full effect of the alcohol would kick in but he knew deep inside that his dependence on drink was getting considerably worse.

When he got back in his office he logged onto the force live incident log on his desktop computer and clicked on the incident in the supermarket carpark. He could see that the SOCO's were in attendance as was the pathologist Sally Drice. He also noted that the national press was there in large numbers and immediately thought of Latifeo as being the possible source of leaking inside information to the press and decided to ring his mobile number. The phone rang out for some time and when a sleepy voice answered it half stifling a yawn trying to say hello. Twead asked gruffly "Oli where are you?"

He replied a little bemused "I'm in bed sir, I've been asleep."

"What do you mean asleep in bed, why aren't you at work?"

Latifeo stuttered a little and said, "It's my day off sir; I was having a lie in until the phone rang and woke me up."

Twead thought for a moment thinking back to what Grant Courtan had said about Latifeo being the one responsible for leaking information to the press. He can't be right he thought, the press are there now so someone has tipped them off. If he is asleep in bed it has to be someone else.

"I'm sorry" he replied in a more controlled voice "Look there is something happening; we possibly have another double murder so I want you to come in to work and report straight to my office."

Latifeo agreed although in reality he knew he didn't really have a choice. He looked at Sam who was lying next to him "I have to go in to work, we've got something happening." She gave him a look and raised her eyebrows in a questioning manner implying that he ought to tell her what was going on and wouldn't let him go until he told her. He then explained how they may have another double murder which although the DCI didn't say would cause problems because the suspect we have is locked up on remand in Birmingham Prison so we may have a copycat killer.

Sam replied "Or you may have gotten the wrong man."

Latifeo shook his head and smiled "No, no way, we definitely have the right man for the other murders. There are lots of evidential things we have that I haven't told you about."

Sam thought to herself what a condescending prick you are, there are things I know that none of you incompetent idiot's in the force know. You haven't got a clue what is really going on but I think I do, I think I can work out who the killer is and their motivation for doing it. She didn't tell him any of this just smiled and said "Well you must know best."

Once he was dressed and ready for work Latifeo gave her a peck on the cheek and handed her a bundle of notes before leaving for work.

When he arrived at Stourbridge Police Station he went as instructed straight to Twead's office where Twead was in conversation with the pathologist Sally Drice. Latifeo was told to come in and sit down whilst the pair finished their conversation. Oli was thinking about the extra overtime this new murder would generate, he needed the money as Sam was repeatedly telling him that she was experiencing a hard time financially and subsequently he had been giving her more cash, in fact a lot more cash but he didn't have a lot of choice it was the honourable thing to do and she was a lovely girl.

Twead and Drice finalised the details on the arrangements for the post-mortem examinations that would take place that afternoon once the SOCO's had concluded their examination of the scene. Drice then made her way to the door where she stood and turned to speak with Twead, Latifeo had his back to Drice and didn't see her indicate with her head towards him.

"If you can make the necessary arrangements as we agreed for the appropriate staff" and again indicated with her head towards Oli behind his back and shook her head. They had both discussed Latifeo's performance at the previous post-mortems where he passed out cold and they had both decided that he was to take no part in the new examinations.

"Yes, I will sort that out" Twead replied meaning that Latifeo was not going to be used anywhere near the mortuary. This suited Twead as he had already unbeknown to Latifeo stitched him up to take the blame for what he thought was Chuman's cock up at the last PM.

Once she had left Twead said to Latifeo "I have a special task for you, it appears that the murdered couple in the supermarket carpark have been killed with the same M.O as the previous ones so we may have a copycat killer. I want you to contact the prison governor and arrange to conduct a further interview with Pickes; he may have information as to who would copy him or he may have had an accomplice. I need you to do it right away whilst I get some staff for the PM's, so off you go."

Twead opened his desk drawer and when he was sure he was on his own took out his recently purchased bottle of whisky, he would just have one more glass he thought just to finally clear his head and stop his hands shaking and then start to get things organised. As he unscrewed the cap of the bottle he realised how much he had already drunk even he was surprised when he looked at the amount left in. It was less than half full and it was still only half way through the morning.

Wallows had stayed at the murder scene watching the SOCO's work. She saw them recover the half bottle of whisky she had planted and place it in an evidence box. They had also very carefully and methodically taken swabs from the bodies including two from the anus of the male victim, it was normally the pathologist who

253

took these samples, but this procedure apparently had been agreed between the SOCO's and the pathologist Sally Drice. They had taken a lot more care and attention to the taking of these swabs than that useless twat Dr Chuman. This was all going to plan everything was working out perfectly exactly as I hoped thought Wallows.

One of the SOCO's examining the scene made a beckoning signal to Wallows, she was asked to write down two names in her notebook. When this was done she asked, "What do you want me do with these names?" the SOCO raised his eyebrows and with a serious look on his face that Wallows hadn't seen before he replied "Can you find the DCI and give them to him. Tell him they are serving police officers from Manchester, they both have their warrant cards with them."

Twead was just downing the last drop from his bottle of whisky when the knock went on his door; he put the empty bottle and his glass in his drawer and said "Come in."

Clutching her police notebook in her hand opened at the relevant entry she walked in. Twead sensed something was wrong by her demeanour so he invited her to sit down. Waiting for her to speak, Wallows took a deep breath and said, "It's about the two bodies in the carpark sir." She read out their names and paused before continuing. "They are both serving police officers from Manchester."

Twead was stunned and said nothing for some time he just stared unbelievingly at Wallows. When he did eventually speak, he simply said "Holy shit what an absolute fucking mess."

24

Strauss, Sadism and Sozzled

The incident room which had been partially dismantled after the arrest of Pickes was now hurriedly being put back in place together with the staff, some of whom had been stood down to return to their normal duties. In his office Twead had assembled his team for an initial briefing, his head having now cleared from his previous night's drinking. He was becoming increasingly worried at the amount of alcohol he had to drink simply to function and to stop shaking. It was midday and together with two pints of cider he had already polished off a complete bottle of Whisky. He tried to put it to the back of his mind as he attempted to concentrate on the job in hand.

The team consisted of Wallows, Courtan, Latifeo, and the SOCO's who had completed the scene examination. The SOCO's began with their input first; the crime scene manager Steve outlined the overall scene and began to detail the injuries to the bodies.

"It looks like they were having sex over the bonnet of the car and got attacked from behind, there were signs of an injury to the back of the neck of the male and this injury appeared to be consistent with injuries sustained to the necks of the previous victims. His penis has been sliced off with a sharp instrument and inserted into the back of his throat. The only difference between these murders and the previous ones was the injury to the female, she had obviously suffered some sort of trauma to her eyeball; there were no visible marks on the back of her neck as far as we could ascertain."

"Do you think she could have turned around as they were being attacked?" asked Twead.

"Very possibly" replied the CSM "It may be that whatever weapon was used it was forced into her head via her eyeball, but we will only know that once we have performed the post-mortem."

Twead mulled this over and then asked, "Have you recovered any trace evidence?" The reply was that a number of items and exhibits had been recovered and sent for fingerprinting and DNA profiling and that they were being fast tracked and results would be known early the next morning. The overall conclusion was that these murders were committed in the same manner as the previous ones in the park.

"Thanks" said Twead as he nodded towards Courtan to give his update. Courtan as he always did stood up to give his brief; he felt it gave him more authority.

"The scene examination is complete, and the bodies are now in the mortuary. There is no CCTV coverage of the supermarket carpark but I have requested a search of the automatic number plate recognition cameras on Stourbridge Ring Road. This will establish when the victim's vehicle arrived. Statements are being taken from potential witnesses and I have a team conducting house to house enquires at the addresses on the section of the ring road that overlooks the carpark. I have also received information from Manchester that a team of CID officers are on route from the victims' force; they are due to arrive sometime this afternoon."

"Okay" said Twead "I think what we need to do as a matter of urgency is to interview Pickes in prison. The M.O.'s is so similar it must be someone with first-hand knowledge. My personal theory at this moment in time is that he had an accomplice, if not it was someone close to him who knew exactly how he worked. How are we doing in making arrangements to see him in prison Oli?"

Oli looked disappointed and replied, "I have made contact with the prison governor and he has informed me that it won't be possible to interview Pickes or even see him."

Twead interrupted angrily at this point and shouted "This is a fucking murder enquiry, I am a detective chief inspector and I have more authority than that pissant little tin pot. If he wants to be an arsehole I will have his bollocks on a plate."

Latifeo managed to continue speaking "I'm afraid you have the wrong end of the stick sir; the governor is not being awkward. It's a problem with Pickes, he tried to commit suicide by hanging himself last night and although he didn't succeed the sustained lack of oxygen intake has left him with brain damage. His brain apparently shows very little sign of activity and he is and will continue to be in what the medical profession refers to as a persistent vegetative state. He is highly unlikely to ever regain consciousness and even if he did wake up he would be unable to communicate with anyone."

Twead let out a sigh of exasperation and shook his head in frustration. He then turned his attention towards Wallows. "Shirley, during the undercover operation when you and Pickes visited all those dogging sites did he ever mention anyone else? Somebody that might possibly accompany him either directly by name or some passing reference?"

Shirley thought for a moment and replied "I can't recall him naming anybody, but he did say concerning the ad that he placed in the contact magazine in order to meet someone who liked doing the same thing. He said it wasn't a one-off thing but he had done it several times so he may have met someone that we don't know about."

It seemed as if every possible line of enquiry was coming to a standstill before they even got going. The room went quiet all waiting for Twead to speak, with all eyes on him they could all see he was cogitating something through in his mind. He eventually addressed Courtan "What I want you do Grant is organise the following fast track actions." Courtan picked up his document case and prepared to take notes. "I want you to get hold of Peeves and Fergas and tell them to speak with the Oldswinford dogging club members with the specific intention of establishing the name of any associate or friend of Pickes. I want a team of officers to have with them a recent photograph of Pickes and show it to the residents in the houses directly opposite the first murders. Ask the residents if they have seen him and was he ever with anybody else again to establish an accomplice. I am aware that we shouldn't be doing this with his photo without the consent of Pickes but fuck him; he is never going to be in a situation to make a complaint. I suggest Shirley and Oli for that and I want it done now. I have arranged an eleven o'clock briefing for tomorrow and I want some information, something we can work on. SOCO's I want you to liaise with Sally Drice and help her with the PM and any exhibits with potential to identify a suspect are to be submitted immediately and you have my permission to have them fast tracked. You do not need to seek any other authority and I expect results tomorrow morning. No excuses, does everyone understand?"

Everyone agreed and started to make their way out of the office, they knew that Twead meant business. He was in a foul mood and it wouldn't do to get on the wrong side of him by dragging your feet. As Courtan got to the door Twead gave him a further task, this was to look after and babysit the officers making their way down from Manchester and tell them to be at the briefing the next day and also to keep them well away from him. He couldn't be bothered to brief them as well or even to meet with them.

When his office was empty he realised that he would need another drink soon and he was deciding where to go. He would give the Wetherspoons a miss because the press had reassembled there and he hadn't visited the Wagon and Horses since he and Chuman had drunkenly knocked the table over. There was a newly opened pub on the high street, it was built in an old bank and he was fairly sure that no other police officers or anyone that knew him frequented it. He would also stock up on a few bottles of whisky to replenish the supply in his desk drawer, ironically, he used to buy his whisky from the supermarket adjacent to the nick, the scene of the last murder but he daren't risk buying alcohol there now just in case the staff recognised him from the scene this morning. Damn it he thought, these bloody murders are playing havoc with my drinking. I can't wait any longer I need a drink, he put his jacket on and left the Police Station.

Wallows and Latifeo were knocking on the doors of houses opposite the park; they had a picture of Pickes with them. The photograph was one of the ones that Wallows had recovered when she had searched his van; it had been stuffed inside a notebook. The picture was a selfie, he was attempting to smile but he still managed somehow to look creepy and send a shiver down your spine. They had visited in excess of a dozen houses but without any success, nobody recognised Pickes from his picture let alone any accomplice.

They were now nearing Sam Gail's house and Latifeo was becoming a little concerned. He had tried to phone Sam and warn her that he would be knocking on her door whilst on duty but that he would be with another officer so she must make sure that she doesn't let slip that she knows him, but she hadn't answered her phone and he couldn't make an excuse for them not to visit the address because the location of it gave the best view over the park and an excellent view of anyone coming or going. He just hoped that when she answered the door to the pair of them she would have the wits about her to pretend she didn't know him, the last thing he wanted was for people to find out about her in case the gossip got back to his wife. As they walked down the path to Sam's front door Latifeo was praying that she wouldn't be at home, his heart began pounding when the door opened, and Sam stood in the doorway. Straight away before anyone else could speak Latifeo blurted out.

"Good afternoon Madam we are from Stourbridge Police. I'm Detective Constable Latifeo and this is my colleague Police Constable Wallows." He then went on to explain why they were there and showed her the photograph of Pickes which she studied for a long time. She eventually handed it back to him and she gave the same negative reply as all the other householders had given. They thanked her for her time and bid her good day. Oli felt a sigh of relief; he needn't have been worried at all. Sam must have realised straight away that she needed not to acknowledge Latifeo him and pretend she didn't know him and she had played the part perfectly. He would have to thank her later he thought, he then realised that he was stoney broke and Sam's idea of being thanked was some extra cash and he had already spent more on her than he could afford to.

He was hoping that this new murder enquiry would run for some time as he needed the money that the overtime would bring. They had almost finished their enquires at the houses that Grant had allocated to them but they both knew they would have to revisit the ones where no-one had been at home and they would have to complete them all before they returned to the station, so having done one complete run they went back to the beginning and started over again.

Twead was in the Bank pub downing a pint and a chaser, there was no-one in there that could recognise him, but he still felt uncomfortable and ill at ease. This was because the bar had big windows looking out into the high street and although they had some pattern etched into them it was still possible that anyone walking past could see right in and get a clear view of everyone in there and the lack of alcoves or booths meant he had nowhere to hide. He quickly finished his drinks and walked to the Mitre pub on the opposite corner. It was not a pub he had ever been in before, but it had windows with coloured glass that meant no one could see through into the pub.

Once inside after ordering his drinks he decided to ring his mate Dr Chuman to find out how he had got on with his meeting with the pathology delivery board and to invite him for a drink. He found himself a table in a back room that was empty and settled down to enjoy a few drinks. His massive hangover from the previous night had now completely disappeared but in reality, he was already three parts drunk again. His drinking was now spiralling so far out of control that he barely realised the effect it was having on him.

Chuman arrived about an hour after he had received the call and he bounded in with a spring in his step and a huge grin spread across his face. Twead realised immediately that all must have gone well and told him to sit down while he went to the bar to get some celebratory drinks. Chuman noted that Twead was already a little unsteady on his feet when he walked to the bar. He returned with two pints and two large whiskies as he placed them on the table.

"It obviously went well so fill me in with the details." They both downed their whiskies in one huge gulp and Chuman told him all about his meeting which basically exonerated him of all blame for the cock up at the post-mortem.

"The only slight down side is that the PDB are considering making a complaint to your chief constable against Latifeo and the SOCO's citing incompetence but still a great result for me so I'm looking to have a good drink."

Twead lifted his pint glass to his mouth and said in a celebratory fashion "Fuck em all" and began to laugh.

They clinked glasses together and in unison they both said "Cheers" and began to drink their pints which were downed in double quick time. Before the empty glasses were put down on the table Chuman was up on his feet making his way to the bar to get refills. Twead realising that Chuman was looking to really tie one on in celebration and that these were the pathologists first drinks of the day whilst he himself had already consumed several pints and a full bottle of whisky. He realised that this could turn into quite a heavy session even by his standards, he didn't want to go back to the Police Station if he was smashed so he called Courtan on his mobile and told him to look after the enquiry for the rest of the day and any problems Grant was to contact him by phone.

Courtan put his mobile phone back in his inside pocket; he could tell by Twead's slurred voice that he was halfway drunk. He looked at his watch it was only one-thirty in the afternoon, blimey he thought that's early to be pissed even for that drunkard. There was obviously no way Twead would return to the Station, so he decided to use it to his own advantage.

Wallows and Latifeo had completed their house to house enquires and had returned to Stourbridge Police Station. They went straight to Courtan's office to update him with their results. Courtan seized the opportunity and said to Latifeo "I have to go out on an enquiry; I am leaving you in charge, so you must remain in the Station. Any problems then contact my mobile."

Latifeo had no choice but to reluctantly agree even though he had plans for himself that afternoon, his intention was to go and see Sam but that was scuppered now. He decided he would send her a text later and ask if he could go around that evening. With Courtan gone he settled down in the detective sergeants' office which was a lot plusher than the one he shared with the rest of the detective constables. He made himself comfortable in a high-backed leather chair and put his feet up on the desk. Courtan's motive for putting Latifeo in charge served two purposes, the first it meant he could get out of the office and secondly it would keep Latifeo away from where he now was at Sam Gail's front door.

He knocked several times before Sam answered the door and when she eventually opened it she was somewhat surprised to see him "I wasn't expecting to see you today, I thought you were at work."

He walked in anyway "I've managed to get a few hours off, so I thought I'd pop round." Sam put her finger to her lips and whispered "You should have rung me I've got one of my music students here. You will need to come back in half an hour, go for a walk round the park or something."

Courtan whispered "it's okay, I'll sneak upstairs. They won't know I'm here" and went to make his way to the foot of the stairs.

Sam with some venom in her voice whispered forcefully "Look just do what you're told and come back in half an hour." She then half guided, and half pushed him out of the front door, she heard him mumbling something to himself under his breath but at least he was leaving. As the door shut behind him she gave a sigh of relief. She looked in the hallway mirror and ran her fingers through her hair and plumped it up a little, when she was satisfied with her appearance she hurried up the stairs back to her bedroom. Tied to the bed was her supposed music student, his wrists and ankles were attached to each corner of the bedstead using leather straps and he had a gag inserted into his mouth. She quickly took off her dress, the one she had hurriedly put on when Grant had knocked the door to reveal a black sadistic sex outfit, black boots, fishnet stockings and leather bra and knickers. She bent down and reached under the bed and retrieved the whip she had hidden there; she then stood at the end of the bed playing with the lashes of the whip. She slowly and menacingly approached the incapacitated snivelling naked creature on the bed.

"Now where were we you pathetic piece of human garbage." She gave an evil wicked smile as lifted her leg and put the heel of the black leather boot into his mouth "Now suck it, clean my dirty boots with your mouth you useless piece of shit."

He let out a loud cry which was muffled slightly by the stiletto that was inserted into his mouth and he began to writhe about. After a few seconds he exploded into a screaming orgasm and ejaculated. She kept the stiletto in his mouth until he had finished, he was panting franticly for breath for some time. When his breathing eventually slowed down and he began to relax. Sam said to him "and what do you say?" still slightly out of breath, he replied "Thank you mistress." She shouted back at him "Louder you fucking stupid little bitch, I can't hear you" he did as he was told and shouted loudly several times the phrase "Thank you mistress."

She carefully undid the restraints and released him and asked him if he wanted a cup of tea which he declined stating that he was in a rush. As he began to get dressed he reached into his pocket and pulled out a bundle of notes and as he handed them over. "That was fantastic, there is a little extra in there for you. I'll see you same time next week."

Once he was out of the front door Sam ran upstairs and looked out of the window to see if Grant was returning. When she had checked the approach and he couldn't be seen she counted the money she had been left, and yes there was something extra in there for her, a lot extra. She knew she didn't have a lot of time, Grant would be there soon so she didn't dare risk going up into the loft to stash it with the rest, so she hid it in her underwear drawer and quickly undressed out of her dominatrix outfit and got ready for him.

Wallows walked into the scenes of crime office. She had seen the SOCO's parking their vans in the Station after returning from the post-mortems. "Hi guys, how did the PM's go?" She was invited to take a seat and a cup of tea was placed in her hand.

The crime scene manager outlined the results of the PM. "It was pretty much as expected Shirley, the guy had something inserted in the back of his neck but this didn't kill him apparently. The cause of death was blood loss from the genital area but the pathologist estimated it would have taken a long time for him to die because although his penis was sliced off as in the previous murders he formed a small blood clot. Not enough to stop the bleeding altogether but enough so that it slowed the bleeding down to probably a small trickle. The pathologist reckons it would have taken him about eight hours to die."

Wallows took in a sharp intake of breath and put her hand to her open mouth in a pretend show of a mixture of horror and sympathy for the victim. In reality she was delighted that he had taken so long to die and she took a perverted pleasure in it. She was imagining him still conscious and for him to die in utter agony slowly bleeding to death. The thoughts and sheer terror that must have gone through his mind knowing that he was slowly dying and totally unable to do anything about it but just lie there motionless on top of his already dead girlfriend what a fantastic result Wallows thought even better than she had planned.

"Oh my god" she said, "that poor man and how about the female?"

The CSM continued "It sounds a bit strange but she was probably better off than her boyfriend because whatever weapon was used it didn't go in through the back of the neck it entered via her eyeball and straight through into her brain so she would have died more or less instantaneously."

Wallows was digesting all this information for future reference, she would have to make sure that the next chauvinist pig whose prick she chopped off died quicker. She couldn't afford for one of her victims to be found alive and possibly identify her but that instantaneous death when stabbed through the eye was interesting. "And have you got from your examination, anything that will help find the killer? She asked quizzically but casually.

"This is where it gets really interesting" he said. "I shouldn't really be telling you this before I see the DCI but when I took a swab from the guys anus there was what seemed to me to be semen, lots of it so it looks like he was buggered. So we took it straight to the lab before we did the PM and we should have a result first thing in the morning. So, if they are on any of the DNA databases then we will get our man."

Wallows gave the CSM a puzzled look "Databases plural are there more than one?"

The CSM replied "Yes, don't you remember I told you before. In addition to the normal database there is also an immigration database and then there is the police one that is not supposed to be searched. It is only for elimination purposes but believe you me in a case like this they will search it, illegal or not. It will be the same for the police fingerprint database that will also get searched. If we get any viable fingerprints but we haven't got a lot for the fingerprint lab to go at though the only thing of real interest was an empty bottle of whisky."

Shirley nodded her head and said "Yes of course I remember now, you told me at the last post-mortem. Is there anything I can do to help?" She was told that there was nothing that needed doing it was simply a case of waiting for results, so Shirley left and made her way back to Grant Courtan's office in the knowledge and incredible satisfaction that her plan was panning out perfectly.

The team had now reached an impasse, Wallows and Latifeo were sitting down kicking their heels in Courtan's office drinking endless cups of tea and coffee passing away the time by talking about everything and nothing. Latifeo was daydreaming about Sam and both were looking at the office wall clock every few minutes waiting for it to tick round to the end of their shift and home time.

Frank Fergas and Robert Peeves were in a pub where they had arranged to meet the Oldswinford swingers club. They had been chatting away to several members for a couple of hours but it became clear right from the outset that none of them knew of or had heard of any associate's or friends of Pickes. Never the less they had decided to stay, have a few drinks and join in with the dirty sexually oriented talk and try and get an easy shag. Peeves, as was his preference had homed in on the biggest and fattest one there. An absolutely huge woman, rolls of fat on display from every part of her body showing through her ill-fitting, way to small clothing. She knew the score though she appreciated that some blokes have a perverted obsession with fat birds and she was enjoying the attention and flattery. Fergas was trying his best with her mate who although not fat like her friend had the face like a back end of a bus but he mused to himself a fuck's a fuck.

Courtan was silently congratulating himself on what he thought was a great sex session, she must have loved it he thought especially with all the screaming and the moans of delight. He was lying naked in bed with his girlfriend or rather who he thought was his girlfriend. He hadn't realised that he was just another client but Sam had the wherewithal and the charm to twist most men round her little finger something she took great pleasure in and it was also extremely financially rewarding being able to manipulate them. As for the sex, she could have quite easily have dropped off to sleep and let him get on with it either way she knew she would be getting another wad of cash coming her way. It intrigued her where he was getting all the

266

money from; it certainly wasn't his police pay, that wouldn't cover the amount he had been giving her.

He wanted to have a sleep before going back to his office just to make sure that everything was okay and ready for the morning. He would make a point for someone to see him in the Station because it was past his finishing time and he liked to give the impression, albeit falsely that he was diligent and regularly worked beyond his shift even though he had hardly been at work today let alone done any work. He couldn't sleep however because of the incessant questions from Sam, she had told Grant about her visit from Latifeo and another female officer called Wallows and she wanted for some reason to find out all about her. Realising that he wasn't going to get the sleep he wanted and with an empty sac he decided to get out of bed and return to the office.

Twead and Chuman were still in the pub, Chuman by this time was totally plastered and being incredibly loud but this was nothing in comparison to the state of Twead. He wasn't far off from drinking himself into unconsciousness; they were the only customers in the tiny back room where they had parked themselves. Their noisy behaviour had driven away the other drinkers who had moved away to the main bar. The landlord was becoming concerned with their drunken antics, but he decided to put up with it for the sake of the vast amounts of money they were putting into the till, both of them had spent so much that each of them had to make an unscheduled trip to the automated cash dispenser at the bank opposite.

They were so drunk and there was so much fluid floating around in their stomachs that they couldn't take the physical quantity of beer anymore so they had turned their attention to and stayed on the whisky drinking full tumblers one after another. They had almost emptied the pub's shelves of their entire stock of expensive single malt whiskies and they showed no sign of slowing down in fact they began downing their tumblers even faster as they got drunker and drunker.

The pub landlord thought it was Christmas come early Twead and Chuman on their whisky binge had put more money in the till in the space of a few short hours than would normally be taken in three or four days, this was the only reason that the landlord tolerated their loud boorish behaviour. Chuman ordered another couple of treble measure whiskies clearing the last of the single malts off the shelf. It was obvious that they were nowhere neared finished drinking, so the landlord despatched one of his staff next door to Tesco's telling them to bring back six bottles of single malt whisky telling them to purchase whichever ones Tesco's had on special offer.

When the young barman hurriedly returned with more supplies Twead was already impatiently waiting at the bar ready to order more drinks there wasn't even enough time to stack the bottles on the shelf the first of the six bottles was taken out of the Tesco carrier bag and poured straight into the tumblers that Twead had put down on the counter. The pair had become something of a wonderment not only to the bar staff but the customers in the public bar who could see through into the backroom and were witnessing the bizarre sight of two middle aged men apparently in the middle of a hedonistic drinking frenzy. Most of the onlookers were astonished that the pair were still standing and were able to remain standing as they rapaciously downed bottle after bottle at an alarming rate, Chuman and especially Twead were so drunk they were oblivious to this and were unaware that they were the centre of attention as they continued to drink themselves into oblivion.

25

Lights Camera Action

The night turn duty sergeant and one of his constables were standing in the rear carpark of Stourbridge Police Station. It had been a quiet night and there were no prisoners in the cells to look after. He and the other smoker on the shift were both filling their lungs busily puffing away at their cigarettes in the night air. Both of them had at one time or another tried to quit the habit, but it was difficult to do when you were on night shift especially when nothing happens and the boredom of an eight-hour shift meant their resolve gave way and they usually succumbed to their habit.

They had been discussing recent events that had turned Stourbridge Town into a household name. The sergeant explaining to the young constable that Stourbridge had experienced more murders in recent days that he seen in his twenty years' service in the area. The town had been almost constantly the main headline news in the papers and national media coverage on television and most of it had not painted a complimentary picture of the local police and they had been portrayed as a bit of a joke to put it mildly.

"Let's hope we catch this second nutter pretty quick" the sergeant said to his officer. "Otherwise we'll get another slating from the press."

He was just finishing his cigarette when he saw in the corner of the carpark a drunk prostate on the ground fast asleep lying in what appeared to be a pool of urine.

"Look at the state of that drunken bastard lying in his own piss; I'm not having that stinking urine-soaked tramp in my cells. Go and get a couple of the lads and throw him into the supermarket carpark opposite" said the sergeant.

The young constable finished his cigarette, stubbed it out underfoot on the floor and replied "Okay sarge" and went in search of a couple of colleagues to give him a hand.

"Let me know when you've got rid of him, I'll be in the custody office. Make sure you and the lads put some latex gloves on before you touch him and make sure nobody sees you."

The custody office was abnormally quiet and unusually clean and tidy. On an average night there would be a number of prisoners being processed through there. Some drunk, some violent, most of them causing some sort of problems but this was one of those rare nights when you could catch up with the day to day things. The sergeant had used the free time to check and replenish stocks and supplies. The drawers and filing cabinets that contained the seemingly endless and ever-increasing number of forms that successive governments continue to churn out and the insistence upon their completion despite their so-called commitment to cut red tape had all been refilled. The prisoner property bags, security seals and every other consumable were now in plentiful supply; even the first aid box had been checked. It was time now to relax and let the hours drift by. He sat back in his chair took out his newspaper and perused the crossword. Two of his officers then walked in to the custody office, the expression on their faces showed that something was wrong.

"You'd better come and have a look at this sarge" one of them said. He put his newspaper down and saw the look of concern on their faces, so much for a quiet night he thought. He took an exasperated breath of resignation and followed them into the carpark. He could see one other officer standing over the stinking drunk in the corner of the police compound and walked over to him. As soon as he got there and looked at the pathetic creature on the floor he realised the officer's quandary. This wasn't a run of the mill down and out drunk that they were looking at, someone they could simply move elsewhere to let them sleep it off and forget about them. The drunken semi-comatosed wretch lying at their feet was one of her majesty's finest, it was DCI Frank Twead. The three young constables looked at their sergeant and asked, "What shall we do sarge?"

He stood there shaking his head wondering how someone in his position could get in such a state, everyone knew that he liked a drink and most realised he a drinking problem, but this was something else this was totally out of control. He knew what he was supposed to do in such circumstances, arrest him for his own safety, arrange medical assistance and then inform high ranking policers but that would most probably spell the end of his police career and he could kiss his police pension goodbye. They all stood there in silence listening to the intermittent snoring sounds mingled with the odd passing of wind that fortunately meant he was still alive.

"Right this is what we're going to do. Two of you pick him up and put him in his office. Sit him in his chair and lean him over his desk, that way if he is sick he's not going to choke on it and we'll let him sleep it off like he does most nights in his office anyway. One of you get the hose pipe from the car wash and hose down this pile of sick and piss and more importantly" he paused for a while and looked at all of them with a serious stern-faced expression then continued "this never happened, does everyone understand? Remember even though he's a chronic alcoholic he is still one of us and we all look after each other no matter what so whatever happens from now on, and as far as we are aware he must have made his own way into his office and we never saw him is that clear?"

A quick nod of heads from all concerned then Twead was lifted unceremoniously and dragged backwards by two officers holding him under each arm. He was bundled into his office where he was placed in his chair with his body slumped forward over his desk. They stood there and looked at the state of the drunken mess in front of them wondering how he had ever managed to obtain the rank of detective chief inspector and more baffling was how on earth he kept his position. They shook their heads in disbelief before leaving his office shutting the door behind them.

The evidence in the carpark had been washed away and the officers returned to the parade room where they received a reminder from the sergeant that this incident never happened, and no one was ever to mention it now or ever. They were all unaware that everything they had done had been witnessed and scrutinised from an upstairs window within the Police Station.

The onlooker had committed to memory the name of every officer involved and their individual actions had been noted. This information may come in useful later thought Wallows as she contemplated her next move. She had returned to the Police Station unnoticed for a specific reason and this could help her in what she was planning to do. She stood at the top of the stairs listening for the sound of any movement from down below. The shift when it was a quiet night would normally stay in the parade room playing cards or reading yesterday's newspapers.

She was able to see from the upstairs window the custody office and through the window she had seen the sergeant making himself comfortable with his crossword. She slowly descended the stairs, Twead's office was just a few doors along the corridor and there would be no reason for anyone else to be in that part of the building at that time of night. Once at the bottom of the stairs she stood still in the corridor for a while until she was confident that there wasn't anybody close by. Outside of Twead's office she put her ear to the door the low irregular breathing, and occasional snort and grunt could be heard. She had seen the state of Twead in the carpark and knew that he would not wake up as she walked into his office.

This could work out better than expected she thought as she opened her ever present handbag and removed the wooden handled metal spiked implement that had been responsible for the demise of so many bullying pigs and was now going to send this fat drunken bastard lying prostrate across his desk in front of her to prison. It had been her intention to simply hide the weapon in his room but the drunken state he was now in afforded greater opportunities. She put on a clean pair of sterile latex gloves and carefully removed the weapon from its evidence bag and took hold of Twead's right hand and gently wrapped it around the wooden handle, pressing each finger down firmly ensuring every fingertip made contact with the surface. She replaced his hand back on the desk and walked round to access the desk drawers and slowly opened the middle drawer and saw that it was completely empty, so she gently closed it and opened the bottom drawer. This was three quarters full of assorted papers and resting on top of the papers were two bottles of whisky.

Holding the weapon by the metal spike and not wishing to wipe off Tweads fingerprints she tried to slide it underneath the bundle of paperwork by slightly lifting the papers up. As she did so the two whisky bottles moved, and one fell to the bottom of the drawer with the other one landing on top of it. The sound it made in the quiet night atmosphere of the Police Station seemed to echo everywhere and she thought at first that they had smashed. Her heart began pounding, she was sure someone must have heard the sound she had to work quickly. She put the weapon under the papers and the whisky bottles that fortunately had not smashed were replaced on top of the papers and the drawer was closed quickly and she left the office.

In the corridor she could hear the sound of footsteps approaching and she heard someone say, 'I think the noise came from down here somewhere.' She had now reached the bottom of the stairs; the footsteps were very close and she began to climb up the stairs as quickly as she could without making any noise and manged to get out of sight before the footsteps entered the corridor. Wallows had a cover story prepared in case she was discovered but that was a last resort and she was hoping it wouldn't be needed. She remained at the top of the stairs listening for the voices downstairs, she heard someone say, 'It all seems fine down here, perhaps the noise came from upstairs shall we check up there?'

Wallows heart missed a beat; this was the last thing she wanted. She was trying to decide whether it would look less suspicious if she made her way down the stairs and met them halfway, it would be more natural than being discovered upstairs, it would appear then as if she was hiding. She decided to go down the stairs and as she put her foot on the first stair she heard one of them say 'It must have come from outside, everything's okay in here.' Wallows stood still now regretting her decision to make her way downstairs to meet them halfway because there was now a chance that they may not come upstairs, however she was now standing on the stairs in the open and if either of them looked up they would see her. She kept the sound of her breathing as shallow as possible and after what seemed an eternity she saw them both walk away without looking up. Allowing them enough time to get back to the parade room and return to their game of cards and when no sound could be heard she slipped out of the Station via the rear exit.

Once back at her bed-sit she made herself comfortable on the settee it was a bit too late to go to bed and the adrenalin rush of nearly being caught at the Station meant she wouldn't be able to sleep. She was also on a high in anticipation of what was to hopefully come tomorrow.

Fergas made his way along the darkened hallway, he was half drunk and he had woken up desperate for a pee. He realised that he was not at home, but he didn't know where he was. Someone was approaching from the far end of the hallway and as his eyes became adjusted to the light he saw that it was Peeves.

"Where the fuck are we?" he asked.

"Is that you Frank?" Peeves replied.

"Yes, it's me; do you know where on earth we are?"

"Yes" he replied "remember that great big fat bird I was with. It's her flat. We're somewhere in Lye. It's a bit of a shithole though but it's been worth it. She is a real dirty cow up for anything. How did you get on?"

Fergas nervously scratched his balls and replied "I think I shagged her mate, that ugly bird. At least I think it's her I just woke up and it was dark, so I couldn't see who was next to me. Let's get our clothes and piss off quick before they wake up."

They crept back into the bedrooms and as quietly as possible picked up their clothes and got dressed in the hallway then let themselves out of the flat. They couldn't remember where they had parked the CID car, so they walked along the high street continually pressing the button on the car key fob until they saw the flash of the indicator lights. As they neared the car they could see graffiti had been scrawled all down the near side in bright orange paint the words 'Fuck off pigs' in huge letters.

"Oh bollocks, how are we going to explain that? We can't let anyone know we were here" said Peeves."

They decided to drive back to the Police Station and if no one saw them or the car when they were parking then they would deny any knowledge of the damage and pretend it must have been done whilst in the Station carpark. They were pushing their luck though, the damage to the doors caused when they scraped the bollard in the pub carpark had already been passed off with that excuse. Fortunately for them no-one saw them arrive back at the carpark, so they parked the now ridiculous looking battered car quickly and left straight away making sure no-one was watching.

Next morning the team assembled in Courtan's office, they had all come in early to get ready for the morning briefing and they had decided to treat themselves to breakfast. A new sandwich shop called Butterfingers had opened in Stourbridge High Street and they delivered free, so they were all tucking into bacon and sausage sandwiches. They discussed between them the results of their attempts to find an accomplice of Pickes, all of them had met with a dead end. The conversation turned now to how the enquiry had escalated from a double murder to a serial killer and now it had gone up another level, a copycat serial killer.

The press was there in even larger numbers than before; this had gone from national media headline news to a global phenomenon. The huge press satellite trucks were occupying the majority of the parking places of the Police Station carpark each one crammed to the hilt with the most modern, high tech equipment that would even rival the resources of NASA. Wark had used his influence to secure his own personal parking space and his brand-new top of the Range Rover put all the other vehicles in the compound to shame especially the now battered CID vehicle which Wark had deliberately parked adjacent to. Most of the camera crews had noticed the damage to the CID vehicle parked in the back yard with the words "FUCK OFF PIGS" and had already taken their video footage in glorious technicolour these images would be splashed over television sets worldwide if nothing exciting or newsworthy came out of the morning's briefing.

The chief constable together with the chief constable of the slaughtered couples force was due to attend and it was almost impossible to walk round the Police Station without tripping over the television cables that would be transmitting the briefing live all around the globe. This made everyone feel a little nervous but at the same time excited in case they had a speaking part or simply had to answer questions from Twead which would mean they would be seen in real time on television and their every word would be broadcast live to millions of people. Everyone had one eye on the office wall clock watching it tick slowly and ominously round getting closer and closer towards the scheduled briefing time.

The crime scene manager and a couple of SOCO's entered the office and joined in the conversation. They asked the team if there were any updates with their enquires. When the team told them no and that they had met with negative results everywhere Latifeo asked "Is there any update on the forensics yet?"

The CSM replied that the results would be through just in time for the start of the briefing which put them under some pressure because they wouldn't have a lot of time to fully analyse them, but that they were very hopeful of some positive results. The conversation began to peter out and turned to general chit chat just to pass the time away prior to the eagerly anticipated briefing.

The atmosphere in the Police Station was electric with excitement, only one hour to go before the biggest most prestigious briefing this Station and Stourbridge had ever seen. Press crews were busy doing sound and lighting checks and the make-up artist was busy daubing the big named news presenters with powder to make sure they didn't have a shiny nose. Papers and pre-prepared notes were being shuffled and read through, introductions were being rehearsed and spoken out loud and then checked on their recording devices. Everything seemed to be highly professional and followed a polished laid out regularly practised routine unlike the slap dash approach used by the DCI. This became even more evident when Twead walked into Courtan's office.

The team could barely hide their surprise and disgust at the state of him. He had obviously slept in his clothes all night not only were they dishevelled and creased but they were stained with goodness knows what. His hair had not been combed and was a sticky mess; he had two days stubble on his face and clearly had not showered because he stunk to high hell. But by far the worst part of his appearance was his face, he resembled a zombie. His eyes were so red and bloodshot, and his complexion was so pale and lacking in pigmentation that he looked like something out of a hammer house of horror film.

He feebly managed to ask the team for any updates from yesterdays enquires and when he was told they were all negative he told the team that part of the briefing strategy would now include an appeal for information regarding Pickes associates. He asked if anyone had seen the SOCO's, the team told him that they had left to go and chase up the forensic results. Twead looked at his watch "Well there's no time now they will have to give their results during the briefing. I've got to go and get ready; I'll see you all at the briefing and remember the broadcast is going out live so be careful. I don't want any of you to say or do anything stupid because half the bloody world is watching." He looked at them all with a stern expression as if to emphasise the point and he then left the office.

They all shook their heads and looked at each other in utter astonishment stunned into complete silence. The first one to break the awkward silence was Latifeo. "What a fucking mess, I've seen him in a few rough states but nothing as bad as that. I've seen tramps look cleaner and less like a bag of shit as that, god knows what he got up to last night."

No one made any reply, there was no need to they had all seen it with their own eyes and smelt it. They decided to take their places in the briefing room early to make sure they could get a seat. A lot of the top brass were already there sitting at the table so that the cameramen and audio engineers could position and test their equipment. The two chief constables were at the head of the table flanked by Superintendent Gibbs and the press liaison officer. Twead had taken a seat towards the rear to keep out of the spotlight but he was signalled to by Gibbs to come forward and sit next to him. Twead did as he was asked and was now sitting square in front of the cameras, he looked a little better than he did a short time previous, but he still looked really rough.

Everything was ready to go now. Everyone was in place; the cameras were ready and all eyes were on the clock just ten minutes to go. A young constable not part of the briefing entered the room and approached the chief constable and whispered some sort of message in his ear. The chief nodded at the young officer he then gave his apologies to the rest of the other officers and left his seat and followed the officer out of the room. The go ahead was signalled from the press that they were now live and had to commence the briefing.

The chief constable had not returned to the room, but Gibbs realised that they couldn't wait because the briefing was going out live to television audiences and he started reading from his pre-prepared script, his image and voice being broadcast worldwide.

Wallows saw the door to the briefing room open and a deputation walk in consisting of the chief, the crime scene manager and someone she recognised as a detective chief superintendent from the professional standards department Bob King. His department which was universally despised throughout the force was normally referred to as the rubber heel brigade; they normally dealt with internal affairs and investigations. Not realising that the cameras were rolling and that they were broadcasting live Bob King walked up to Twead who was sitting directly in front of a TV camera.

He said loudly and clearly "Detective Chief Inspector Frank Twead, I am arresting you for murder. You do not have to say anything but it may harm your defence if you do not mention when questioned something which you later rely on in court. Anything you do say may be given in evidence."

The news crews couldn't believe their luck, they were witness to and filming live the arrest of a high-ranking police officer for multiple murders, this has to be the news scoop of the century. Twead hadn't said a word, he just sat there mouth wide open in shock as two uniform officers took him by each arm and began to guide him past the line of press and TV cameras towards the exit door. The chief constable whispered in the ear of Gibbs who nodded in astonishment and addressed the cameras.

"In view of recent developments the briefing is now postponed, I hope to be able to update you shortly with further news and the time for a re-scheduled briefing." He then hurriedly left the room in pursuit of the chief.

26

Lost Weekend

Twead in the space of half an hour had gone from sitting at the head of a table with other senior officers preparing to give a briefing and thinking of his next drink to sitting in a police cell in his own forces headquarters accused of being a double murderer. He even wondered if he was still drunk and was dreaming it all but the pain rampaging through his brain bought it home to him that this was real, he needed a drink and badly. This was the first time he had really seen the inside of a cell for more than just a few seconds and he realised how depressing and claustrophobic they were. He couldn't fully comprehend what was happening to him, this was the stuff of nightmares.

In a separate part of headquarters, a frantic and extraordinary meeting was taking place; the chief constable addressed the assembled officers. He began "Gentlemen, we have witnessed something that as far as I am aware is unprecedented in the history of policing. To publicly arrest a senior high ranking serving police officer live on television for being a suspected serial killer is undoubtedly unique. The eyes of the world's media are upon us, we must therefore ensure that every step of the way forward from now on is dealt with in a professional and meticulous manner. What I would like now is a short chronological run through of this morning's events starting with the crime scene manager."

The CSM stood up and outlined the course of action taken after receiving the forensic results. He explained how DNA in the semen sample from the male victim's anus had been a perfect match for

DCI Twead and how his fingerprints were identified on a whisky bottle recovered from the crime scene adjacent to the dead bodies. His SOCO staff had been the first to receive the results and they had informed him straight away and that he in turn had immediately informed the professional standards department.

The Detective Chief Superintendent Bob King then took the floor and detailed how he together with the CSM had contacted the DNA and fingerprint labs to double check and verify the results. Once this was completed they both attended the briefing room at Stourbridge and arranged for an officer to ask the chief to step outside to speak with him to relay the information.

"Obviously sir that was when it was agreed amongst us to arrest Frank Twead immediately. Unfortunately, none of us were aware that the cameras had started rolling and that Twead was being arrested in full view of a live TV audience numbering potentially millions."

The rest of the assembled group were the chief constable of the latest victims' force and Detective Superintendent Gibbs. The chief constable continued and outlined how he wanted the investigation to run, he thanked the visiting chief constable for his offer to supply a team of detectives to assist in the investigation and this had been gratefully accepted. This would help ensure impartiality and transparency. Detective Chief Superintendent Bob King would lead the investigation assisted by Tony Gibbs, they would both answer to the chief directly and all forensics would go through the crime scene manager again being fed back immediately and directly to the chief.

It was stressed that as a sensitive, high profile investigation that everything discussed, and any information uncovered would stay within the room and the only person who could authorise disclosure to any other individual or agency would be the chief constable himself.

"I expect everyone here to be back in this room at seven o'clock sharp tomorrow morning with updates, so gentlemen let's get busy."

Bob King briefed the crime scene manager and tasked him with searching Twead's office and collating together all the forensic evidence that had been gathered so far. King then began to go about assembling a skilled and trustworthy team of detectives.

The national press was having a field day; having a senior detective arrested on a live broadcast was a journalists dream. It had made the major headlines not only in the United Kingdom but throughout most of the western world with the actual film of the arrest constantly being replayed on the national and international news bulletins. It had even gone viral on social media sites. As far as news stories went Stourbridge was now the centre of the universe.

Back in his cramped cell Twead was just starting to feel the effects of alcohol withdrawal, it had been a few hours since his last drink. If he had not been in a cell he would have sneaked back to his office and had a good few swigs of whisky from one of the bottles in his desk drawer. But he couldn't do that and he knew that the cold turkey symptoms were on their way and he would start to feel them soon, he had heard of some real horror stories of alcoholics suffering the extreme effects of alcohol withdrawal and he realised this was the first time he had ever entertained the fact or admitted to himself that he had a real problem and he was without doubt a chronic alcoholic.

Wallows and the rest of the team were in Grant Courtan's office, they were still feeling stunned by the unbelievable turn of events all of them of course except for Wallows. She was feeling incredibly upbeat; over the moon with the success of her plan not even in her wildest dreams could she have envisaged that Twead's arrest would be broadcast live on television. She was making a good show outwardly of being shocked and bewildered but inside she desperately wanted to let her feelings of elation out.

They were all wondering what to do next without their leader. They were a little lost, they all knew Frank Twead was a bit of a twat but at least they would be told what to do. They were idly chatting amongst themselves to pass the time when Superintendent Gibbs walked in with some force headquarters detectives all from the professional standards department. Gibbs introduced everyone to each other and explained the reasons for Twead's arrest. He went on to outline what was to happen next. Courtan and the rest of the team were to co-operate with the FHQ detectives, answer all their questions and give them whatever information they had specifically in relation to the activity of Twead. They were also told that nobody was going home until they were given permission to do so even if they had to stay there all night and that was exactly what happened. The FHQ detectives went through every tiny scrap of evidence and information with a fine toothcomb recording everything on audio tape as well as making copious written notes.

It had been a long night for the team but even longer for Twead, he was now experiencing the full-blown delirium tremens most commonly referred to as DTs. The neuro transmitters were no longer being suppressed by the alcohol and he was experiencing a phenomenon known as brain hyper excitability. His hands were shaking, he was sweating profusely, and severe anxiety had kicked in. The cell was covered in foul smelling vomit, he had lost count of the amount of times he had been violently and gut wrenchingly sick throughout his long sleepless night and he felt as if his head was about to explode with the pain. He knew there was far worse to come in the next few hours and days if he couldn't get a drink. He felt so ill and was so terrified of what was to come that he felt as if it would be worth admitting to anything if it meant he could get a drink. He sat on his wooden bench that doubled as a bed, bent his head down and began to sob gently.

Bob King and his team worked diligently throughout the night as did the crime scene manager and by the next morning's meeting with the chief constable the schedule of evidence was ready to be presented and all the team were ready and waiting for his arrival. The chief constable entered the room, it was obvious he was under pressure and it showed on his face. He was normally as befits his rank quite unflappable and had the ability to deal with anything thrown his way, but this had been something extreme, what they were dealing with now was unique in British policing. He opened the meeting by thanking everyone for coming, he could tell by the tired look on everyone's faces that they had been working through the night, something he appreciated and would keep in mind for future reference. He always addressed a group of officers as gentlemen, something he had learnt from Bramshill senior officers training academy. This would give him an air of authority and give the assembled dross a feeling of importance which would encourage their co-operation. Bramshill was colloquially and derisibly known by rank and file officers as finishing school for the knobs.

"Gentlemen, as I pointed out yesterday we are dealing with something unprecedented in the history of British policing. This has attracted attention not only nationally but worldwide. I have spent a lot of my time answering to not only the police authority but also the home office, other government departments and even the prime minister. You can all see therefore how important our work is and how it is imperative that we leave no stone unturned and our methods are open to the strictest possible tests of scrutiny. Mr King we will start with you please."

DCS King stood up and opened a pile of papers and after shuffling them for a while he began his brief. "Detective chief Inspector Twead has not been interviewed as yet but I have checked with the custody sergeant and he has had an uneventful but apparently sleepless night, which is what could be expected I suppose. I have prepared a schedule of evidence pertaining to the latest murders and this will be the basis for his interview which will take place directly after this briefing. Due to obvious time restraints concerning the detention of prisoners we have dealt exclusively with the most recent murders we will deal in depth with the other related murders when and if the prisoner is remanded in custody and detention times are no longer applicable. The first focus point for the investigation is the physical timing and location of victims and suspect. Having scrutinised the automatic number plate recognition system we can place DCI Twead in his office at Stourbridge Police Station at the same time as the victims arrived at the supermarket carpark, which as we all know is a few short yards from the murder scene. When the bodies were found a young officer was asked to go to his office and inform him of the murders. This officer although somewhat reluctant to speak about another officer has stated that Twead was asleep in his office slumped over his desk and when he woke him to inform him of what had happened he appeared to be drunk as though he was suffering from a heavy drinking session the night before. So, we can place Twead near the murder scene from the arrival of the victim's car to when they were discovered dead. We also put out a force wide appeal for information in which we offered anonymity and no threat of criminal proceeding or internal discipline. It would appear that the suspect Pickes was illegally placed under covert surveillance, no authority was applied for under the regulation of investigatory powers act and in the circumstances would not have been granted. The initial reason for Pickes being a suspect was an anonymous phone call to DS Grant Courtan. The caller could not be identified because it did not go through the switchboard and could not be traced, therefore the caller must have access to DS Courtan's phone number. The voice was unrecognisable because the caller used a voice scrambling device, it was initially assumed it was an informant who did not wish to be identified. In a search of Twead's office a voice scrambler was discovered in his desk drawer along with several bottles of whisky and other items of significance that I will leave for the crime scene manager to fully brief us on."

King then reshuffled his papers and sat back down. Superintendent Gibbs was uneasy about the team finding out about the illegal covert surveillance as he had played just a big a part in it as Twead. He would just have to deny it if challenged on it, he would shift all the blame directly on to Twead; he was already totally fucked anyway he thought. The chief obviously impressed said, "Thank you for that, very informative and revealing you and your team have clearly worked extremely hard through the night. Please pass on my regards to the relevant officers now we will hear from the crime scene manager."

The CSM stood up and began his delivery. "The initial forensic evidence we have from the latest murder scene has been checked and rechecked. DCI Twead's fingerprints and only his fingerprints were found on an empty half bottle of Whisky recovered from the scene. The same bottle also revealed a DNA profile obtained from a swab taken from the neck of the bottle again matching DCI Twead. The swabs from the male victim taken at the scene have also revealed an identical DNA profile match of Twead. To be more specific one swab called a peri-anal swab was taken from the outside and near of the anus, this proved to be a match. The second swab is referred to as a high anal swab taken from deep inside the anus, this also proved a match and is of great significance because as we have all probably realised this would require some degree of penetration by the penis. The item of significance referred to by Mr King found in DCI Twead's office desk drawer is a wooden handled metal spiked implement. It is one normally used by officers to punch holes in their epaulettes to allow them to attach their collar numbers. This has been shown to the pathologist Doctor Sally Drice who has confirmed that the fatal wounds of each victim were inflicted by this type of instrument. It has been fingerprinted and DCI Twead's fingerprints have been identified on the wooden handle. The instrument is now at the forensic lab for DNA profiling from matter and staining that could be seen on the metal spike I am expecting a result very shortly."

The chief's P.A had been making notes throughout the briefing and the chief was now reading through them studying them intently. He then as always thanked the crime scene manager for his input and turned his attention towards and addressed Detective Superintendent King.

"Having briefly looked through the amount of what I discern to be quite damning evidence it would appear that there is more than sufficient evidence to charge DCI Twead with murder and rape. It will be interesting to find out what the crown prosecution makes of it."

King stood up to speak just as the CSMs mobile phone rang. He apologised and took himself to a corner of the room to take the call in a hushed voice. King continued "I have already spoken with the CPS chief prosecutor who is of a like mind that we already have enough to charge irrespective of what Twead may or may not say in interview."

The CSM returned to the table and remained standing indicating that he had further information to impart. The chief nodded towards him as a sign for him to speak.

"That was the forensic lab sir; they have an update on the metal spiked implement recovered from DCI Twead's drawer. So far, they have recovered the DNA profile from bloodstaining on the metal spike belonging to both of the two latest victims. In addition, they have also recovered matching DNA from the first victim Claire Pickes."

The room became visibly delighted and relieved with this news, this has vindicated and corroborated all their hard work overnight and put the finishing touch to their enquires so far. The CSM continued "there is also further DNA from blood on the metal spike but those samples require further work on them to identify and obtain a profile. The lab will update me when they have any information but the extra work is quite in depth and will take some time."

Looking extremely pleased with the outcome of the briefing and feeling much less pressurised now that he could give some positive news to the police authority and the home office he further addressed DCS King. "I expect you are now going to interview DCI Twead? Please inform my P.A of the results. Thank you in anticipation and once again thank you all for your hard work it will not be forgotten."

The team were feeling pleased with themselves as they watched the chief and his P.A leave the room. Bob King and Gibbs set about preparing an interview schedule concerning the two latest murders and rape. They decided not to mention the murder of Claire Pickes at this stage as far more enquiry work needed to be done let alone the fact that someone else had already been charged with the murder and that the person who had been charged was now to all intent and purposes almost dead. After drinking a quick cuppa to revive themselves they were now sat in the sound proof interview room awaiting the arrival of Twead.

When the uniformed officer walked Twead into the room both King and Gibbs could not believe their eyes. In the space of less than twenty-four hours an imposing figure of a man who had a presence about him had turned into a gibbering wreck. He could barely walk; his appearance was shocking and he could only be described as resembling a raving mad lunatic down and out dosser who was high on illegal drugs. The uniform officer placed Twead on a chair opposite King and Gibbs, but he may as well been a million miles away.

Twead was now deep into alcohol withdrawal, his body and his brain desperate for its normal daily intake of intoxicants that it needed to function. He was beginning to hallucinate, and he experienced the occasional tremor, sweat was oozing from every pore and unbeknown to them his blood pressure was off the scale. He was not even aware of his surroundings and even less aware of the presence of the two officers whom he knew well sitting two feet away across the other side of the table.

The tape recording equipment was switched on and Twead was asked if he wanted a solicitor, he made no reply, but his head was moving from side to side. King took this to mean no and he said, "For the purposes of the tape the prisoner is shaking his head indicating he does not want a solicitor." They verbally recorded the time and date and persons present and then began the questioning, but it may as well have been in a foreign language. The only response from Twead was the occasional grunt or moan, nothing comprehensible. There was no admission of guilt or culpability, but neither was there a denial. King and Gibbs had both misread the effects of Tweads withdrawal symptoms as an attempt to blow smoke on their enquires.

When all their questions were asked they finished by giving Twead the opportunity to say anything he wished but there was still no response. Twead just stared vacantly up at the ceiling, the ceiling that in his mind's eye was now moving to and fro. King spoke into the recorder to formally finish the interview and the tape machine was switched off.

The rest of the proceedings were a matter of formality. Twead was charged with murder and rape and a special hearing was arranged at the magistrate's court where he was remanded in custody to appear before the crown court and ordered to be held in H.M.P. Birmingham. Twead was still unaware of what was happening to him, he was continuing to descend deeper and deeper into severe alcohol withdrawal and was experiencing all the associated symptoms that went with it. He didn't even flinch when he was searched prior to being placed into a single cell.

The body searches themselves were uncomfortable to say the least and some officers enforced the standard searching techniques more vigorously than others. In order to protect the searching officer from the possibility of assault the prisoner was made to intertwine his fingers and place his hands-on top of his head. The prisoner had to open his legs wide to keep them off balance and when patting down the front of the prisoner the guard would place the heel of his hand under the prisoners' chin and force their head backwards, so their face was looking up towards the ceiling.

This served two purposes, one was that they couldn't be spat at and second, they were safe from the possibility of a head butt, however some officers with a cruel bent would force the prisoners head so far back it stretched the neck muscles causing severe discomfort. Twead was a candidate for this type of treatment no one liked police in prison, not even the guards. They resented the fact that police were given automatic protection in prison, if it was up to the guards they would leave them at the mercy of the cons.

Twead was now lying on the bottom bunk in his cell still oblivious to what was going on. All he knew was that things were getting worse. The cramps in his stomach were intensifying, his heartbeat had now become rapid and irregular and he was spiralling down deeper into depression and together with the room spinning round he was now as bad as he thought he could possibly get. The hallucinations that he was unable to distinguish from reality were getting worse in their frequency and their terrifying nature. He was now seeing snakes crawl out of the walls and floor; he pulled his feet up onto his bunk as the snakes got closer and closer hissing and spitting jaws wide open showing long bare fangs. He began to scream and climbed onto the top bunk breathing and panting for breath for all his might. He looked down on the floor to see the snakes climbing up the legs of the bed, so he lay on his back to turn his face away from them hoping they would go away. But then to his horror he saw them begin to crawl out of the ceiling, he screamed again and again as they dropped from the ceiling onto him. They were all over him, he kept trying to beat them off but more kept appearing.

They were now completely smothering him, biting him some of them trying to slither into his mouth he started to cough and spit to get them out but they came faster and faster he was unable to do anything to stop them, so he curled up into a ball and began to cry and asking for his mommy until he fell into an exhausted almost coma type like sleep. The night turn landing guard had been witnessing this through the security grill and found it quite amusing until Twead fell asleep and it was no longer entertaining, and he continued with his rounds.

In the morning a metal food tray was shoved under Twead's door, he wouldn't be eating with the other prisoners as had been automatically been placed on regulation 45 for his own protection so he could look forward to spending twenty-three hours a day or even more confined in his cell. He was still unable to consume food, but he realised that he was incredibly thirsty so ignoring the food he picked up the plastic beaker of fluid. It smelt foul, but his body was telling him he needed to drink something and he began to gulp it down. It tasted like piss, in fact it was actually piss but he continued to drink it his body demanding fluid. When he'd finished he was immediately sick all over the floor. He lay back on his bed and the hallucinations that he couldn't distinguish from reality returned with greater ferocity. When the next and subsequent meals appeared, they followed the same routine, unable to consume food but forced to drink piss. After three days of sheer hell Twead's cell door opened and the guard walked in. "Come with me, you have a visitor."

Before he was allowed to leave the cell, he was subject to the obligatory search, fingers intertwined and hands on head, legs spread wide apart and head forced painfully back. He was shown into a room where opposite him sat a pinstriped suited professional looking person with a briefcase, he introduced himself as his solicitor. It was now four days since his last drink and the worst of the withdrawal symptoms were over and he was beginning to focus a little.

His police federation appointed solicitor said he wished to discuss the case and how they were going to proceed. He outlined the evidence against him and paid great attention to the wealth of incriminating forensic evidence and said he expected a guilty plea from Twead and they would mitigate as best as they could. Twead continually protested stating he was innocent but with the evidence as overwhelming as it was, even his own brief was recommending a guilty plea. Despite this he still maintained his innocence to the extent that the now frustrated brief once again ran through the evidence against him, especially the forensic evidence in the form of fingerprints and DNA from the whisky bottle and the DNA swabs. His brief was getting tired of Twead's continued protestations of innocence and decided to leave asking Twead to think about the evidence and consider pleading guilty and that he would return the next day to talk further.

Twead was taken back to his cell, the withdrawal symptoms were still there but the effects were lessening and Twead was now despite the stomach cramps and constant headache he was able to think, and he tried desperately to piece together the events of the last few days.

27

The Mist Begins to Clear

Twead had begun to regain some composure and when his next meal arrived he was able to complain to the guard that his drink contained piss and demanded it be replaced. He realised that the replacement drink would also contain some other obnoxious substance probably spit but at least it wouldn't be piss. He had not eaten since his arrival in prison and he guessed he had been there about three days. He looked at the pile of slop on the segmented tray in front of him and moved it around the plate trying to find some morsel or scrap that was edible. He was glad he did so because hidden in the putrid pile of mashed potato he could see something glinting, looking closer at the tepid pile of muck he saw it was ground up glass fragments. He dissected some soggy vegetables and couldn't find anything that shouldn't be there, so he decided to eat them. It was the foulest, most tasteless insipid food he had ever eaten but strangely it seemed to make him feel a little better, he ate as much as his stomach could take and not wishing to throw up anymore called it a day on the food and lay back on his bed.

His brain was as clear as it had been for some time and he began to analyse the evidence against him. He couldn't remember a thing from his interview with Bob King his head had been in such a mess, but he could recall a little of what his brief had said to him and he ran through the details outlined to him by his brief concerning the DNA and fingerprint trace evidence. He said to himself let's start from the beginning; firstly, I must have been set up. The evidence had to have been planted but how was that possible. My fingerprints were found on an empty half bottle of whisky yet I never buy half bottles I always buy and drink from full size bottles. He then remembered the half size bottle that Wallows had given him, and he wracked his brain to try and remember what happened to it. If he recalled correctly then she took the bottle with her to get rid of it, so that could explain the fingerprints. If Wallows had dumped the bottle in the rubbish skip in the back yard of the Police Station then anyone could have picked it up.

Now we are getting somewhere he thought, the DNA was more difficult to explain. Could it have been someone swabbing the neck of the whisky bottle? That would work he thought, he needed to speak with Wallows to find out where she dumped the whisky bottle. Then he thought again but the DNA couldn't have originated from the whisky bottle, he ran through the words of the brief, he recalled him saying that the DNA profile came from a semen sample. He then began to doubt himself, perhaps I was so drunk I did it without knowing, maybe I did murder that couple in a drunken mindless stupor. His mind was racing with different thoughts and ideas; he weighed up the pros and cons of each thought and theory. He couldn't get the thought out of his head of him murdering the pair without realising. Then it hit him, but I couldn't have raped the guy. I would not have been able to get a hard on, I can never get fully erect if I have been drinking certainly not hard enough for penetration so again it has to be a plant but how on earth could anyone get a sample of my semen.

He suddenly sat bolt upright on his bunk, it had hit him like a thunderbolt it must have been that bitch Wallows. She had given him a blow job and after he had ejaculated in her mouth she wiped it with a tissue. It would then be a simple process to transfer that to a swab. She already had the whisky bottle with his trace samples on, the possibility is that that she came across the pair in the carpark who were already dead and then planted the samples, of course it was so easy it all made sense now.

He knew he had a police welfare visit scheduled for that morning; he would demand that they make arrangements for him to see the senior investigating officer and the prison governor. He would detail how he had been framed and who has framed him. Twead had been through complete and utter hell in the last few days but he knew he would soon be out because of what he had to say should give him grounds for immediate bail. This was the first time in ages he had been sober, probably decades he thought. He still felt ill and was still suffering from some withdrawal symptoms, but he could now see the light at the end of the tunnel and his spirits were lifted beyond belief. He lay back on his bed and tried to get some sleep, but his mind was buzzing with excitement and he simply drifted in and out of a mild semi relaxed state.

At Stourbridge Police Station a press briefing was being conducted. DCS Bob King updated the press with the current state of affairs including the charging of a serving high-ranking police officer with two counts of murder and one of rape of a male person. He outlined that further extensive enquires were being undertaken into recent murders in the Stourbridge area and it was expected that further charges would be brought.

Inevitably the main antagonist from the press Spenser Wark asked the much-anticipated awkward question.

"Does this mean chief superintendent, that the original suspect Trevor Pickes is innocent of all charges and that you have arrested the wrong man who has now tragically attempted suicide whilst on remand and as a result of that is now permanently and severely disabled?"

King had been ready for this and replied "As previously stated we are conducting extensive enquires into the recent murders and Pickes will form part of that investigation. When we have examined all the facts and evidence we will of course be updating you as soon as we have finished and evaluated those enquires."

Wark then asked, "Can you confirm that the latest victim was killed by inserting a metal spike into her brain through her eyeball?"

Bob King was fuming internally and did well not to outwardly show his anger. No details had been released of the circumstances of the method of killing to prevent any possibility of copycat murders, but he had obviously got an inside source. Trying his utmost to hide his anger King replied, "No details of the circumstances of the cause of death have been released and for operational reasons they will not be disclosed so I am unable to confirm or deny your question."

Wark smiled, he knew he had got the chief superintendents back up, something he took great pleasure in. I will have to give Courtan an extra bung for that bit of info he thought. Wark decided to wind King up further.

"Can you tell us if you are looking at or searching for any further suspects? Did Twead have an accomplice or is he the only bent perverted serial killer in the Stourbridge force?"

King knew full well that Wark was trying to provoke a reaction from him so he calmly replied, "I am unable to comment on specific details of the enquiry."

Wark realised that King was much more professional than Twead and it would prove more difficult to get him to react and lose his cool, so he thanked him for answering his questions and sat down.

The door to Twead's cell opened suddenly and a guard walked in and said "For some reason you are popular today you have two visitors. You will be allowed ten minutes with each one."

Twead stood up and began to walk to the door. The Guard said, "Hold it right there you know the routine by now."

Twead adopted the regulation pose, he spread his legs intertwined his fingers and put his hands on his head which was then forcibly pushed backwards with such force he was now looking directly at the ceiling. He knew the force used was excessive and a lot of the guards overstepped the mark in the use of force simply because they wanted to. It gave them a sense of power, especially with old bill to be able to treat a police officer in such a manner was a perk of a somewhat unrewarding and mind-numbing career. Twead thought to himself, I will remember you for the future you officious prick.

Searching complete he followed the guard through a series of corridors until they reached the visitors room. As he went in he was reminded that he would have ten minutes with each visitor and no more. He sat at a small wooden table in the centre of the room with his eyes concentrating on the door in front of him wondering who his visitor would be who had drawn the short straw and had the unenviable job of being his liaison officer.

It was a soulless cold room; the walls were painted a dull grey and the only furniture was the table he was sat at together with two plastic chairs. There were no fixtures or fittings and no windows, the light was provided by a ceiling strip light that was encased inside a metal grill. Twead now that he was coming to his senses realised he knew this room well; he had used it several times before. This had been when he was in charge, when he dictated to everyone what would happen and he would be in control even the prison guard would follow his instructions. This was where he had interviewed numerous prisoners and persuaded them to admit to being responsible for several un-cleared crimes this would be achieved by getting prisoners to agree to have offences taken into consideration or TIC's as they were better known as and sign the appropriate documentation.

In reality none of the prisoners had committed any of the crimes they were admitting to and they would only agree to take the blame for them safe in the knowledge that they would receive no extra punishment for the crimes and Twead would reward them with a sleeve of cigarettes. Even if the con didn't smoke themselves they would be greatly received as cigarettes were very valuable and highly prized commodities in prison. They were as good as currency and could be swopped or exchanged for other things such as drugs or alcohol and two hundred branded cigarettes was the equivalent of a fortune. This was how Twead as a detective inspector had manufactured grossly misleading inflated crime detection rates and it was this high crime clear up rate that had been instrumental in his promotion to chief Inspector. It was a win win situation all round, even the prison officer standing in the corner of the room maintaining a guard benefitted from a backhander of a twenty-pound note as he looked the other way when the illegal contraband was handed over. Tweads bosses the hierarchy at divisional command received their share of the spoils also as they could proudly coo and gloat at the expense of other divisions that they had the highest crime detection rates, they knew full well that the figures were being falsely manipulated but this knowledge was something they would utterly refute if it ever came to light so they simply ignored the practise and turned a blind eye. This was when Twead ruled the roost when he was top dog but things were different now the tables had been turned and he wasn't top dog anymore, he was however in a dog fight the most important fight he had ever been in it was a fight for his life for survival he knew full well what lay in store for him if he couldn't escape from this hellhole.

He pushed these thoughts to the back of his mind as he saw the first person walk in through the visitor entrance door, it was Latifeo who seemed a little cautious a bit on edge. He didn't really know what to do or to say as this was unknown territory for him indeed it was also something Twead had not been party to in his career. But Twead was anxious to tell Latifeo that he had been framed and start the process of getting himself out of this god forsaken squalid shithole. Twead told Latifeo to sit down, he said that he had something important to tell him and it would require urgent action by him. Latifeo was confused, he had expected this to be a sympathy visit to offer his support and to ask if he needed anything doing such as look in on his house or anything like that but this was different, he had never seen Twead in such a positive manner before, he was a completely different person.

Twead stared straight at Latifeo to ensure his full and immediate attention and said "Right now listen carefully we only have a short time, I know everyone thinks I'm guilty, even my brief thinks that way and I can understand that given the type and weight of the forensic evidence. But I can assure you that I am not guilty, I did not murder those people or take any part in their murder, I was framed. Since sobering up I have worked out how the forensic trace samples were obtained, how they were planted and more importantly who planted them, and I am able to prove it. I will blow the lid clean off this investigation. What I want you to do is arrange an interview between me, the prison governor and the senior investigating officer who although I was in a state of delirium at my interview is I believe Detective Chief Superintendent Bob King. You need to do it with immediate effect, tell Bob King that the enquiry will be compromised if I do not get that interview immediately, is that completely clear? Do you understand the urgency?"

Latifeo hesitated for a moment before replying, "Yes sir, I get it. I will do it as soon as I get back to the station but who do you think has framed you?"

Twead replied sternly "It is not somebody I think has framed me, it is someone whom I know has framed me and the first person to be given this information will be Bob King."

As soon as he had finished the door opened and the guard walked in stating that visiting time was over and told Latifeo that he had to leave. Twead gave him a last reminder as he was leaving and he nodded back in acknowledgement. Twead felt upbeat now he had done something positive, he settled down to receive his next visitor whoever it may be. He was pleasantly surprised when he saw his best mate Hubert Chuman walk through into the room, he approached him and gave him a hug, this was something neither of them had ever done before but these were extraordinary circumstances. Chuman said "I bought you a bottle of whisky, I hid it under my coat, but they searched me and confiscated it." This was the first time since he had figured out who had framed him that his thought had turned to drink, he would have given his right arm for a good drinking session and just thinking about it started the cravings off again.

He replied, "I could murder for a good drink."

Chuman smiled "Not really the most appropriate thing for someone in your position to say" and they both began to laugh at the ridiculousness of his statement. "I believe we only have ten minutes and they are quite strict on time so is there anything that you want me to do?"

Twead replied "No thanks, I have a feeling I will be out of here fairly soon."

They continued chatting for a short while until in what seemed to be only a couple of minutes they were told that their time was up and Chuman was ordered out of the room wishing Twead all the best as he left.

When Latifeo got back to the station he went straight into Courtan's office looking for a senior officer. Wallows and Courtan were in there, they had been given the job of getting all the relevant statements from all of the murders in chronological order so that Kings team of detectives could go through them.

"Cup of tea?" Wallows asked with a smile towards Latifeo

"No thanks" he replied, "I've got some work to do for Twead, does anyone know where there are any senior officers Gibbs or King preferably."

Courtan said in amazement "Work for Twead, are you mad, what do you mean work for Twead, you do realise he has been charged with murder and rape?"

Latifeo said "Of course I do but he reckons he has been set up and he knows and can prove who set him up, so he wants me to arrange a meeting between him, the prison Governor and King so he can tell them who has framed him."

Courtan shook his head and asked "Was he still drunk? I spoke with the custody officer about him when he was in custody; apparently he was in a terrible state with the shakes and sickness etc., I bet he has still not sobered up yet."

It was Latifeo's turn to shake his head "No, quite the contrary actually. I have never seen him so sober, he looked like he had been through a rough time, but he was very alert and with it."

Wallows was listening with interest to their conversation, Grant then said, "Did he say who has supposedly framed him?"

Latifeo shook his head and left in search DCS King.

Wallows said to Courtan "What a strange twist to events."

Courtan with a mocking expression on his face said, "It's just going to be some load of bollocks he has dreamed up, the last throw of the dice of a drunken psychopath" and returned to his task of sifting through murder statements.

Twead was lying on his bunk running through in his mind how he would tell King and the governor of how he had been framed and how to word it so they would take immediate action. He would also tell the governor about the piss he had been given to drink and show him some of the mashed potato impregnated with shards of glass that he had been given to eat, he had the nous to keep a sample of it for evidence and wrapped it in a napkin. Let's hope that useless twat Latifeo had done what he was asked he thought. He received his answer almost immediately, the cell door opened, and a guard walked in saying "Come on, you're going to see the governor."

A surprised Twead stood up and automatically adopted the position, fingers intertwined, hands on head and legs spread wide apart. He was impressed with how quickly Latifeo had managed to get the ball rolling, perhaps he wasn't the lazy good for nothing useless twat I had given him credit for thought Twead. His spirits were now lifted, and he didn't even mind when his head was pushed forcibly back even more than normal, he was on a high and couldn't feel a thing. He didn't even feel the razor-sharp blade that then cut him from ear to ear slicing his neck and his jugular vein wide open. The guard was now standing behind him, yanking Twead's head further back to allow the blood to gush uncontrollably like a fountain from his now sliced in two jugular vein. The blood loss was so dramatic and so rapid it had completely covered the far wall in an instant. Before Twead had time to realise what was happening it was too late to do anything. The blood loss had been so dramatic his brain had already been drained of all life-giving oxygen and the guard released his grip on him. He began to slump towards the floor and was dead before he hit the ground. His lifeless body was now lying in a huge pool of his own bright red sticky still warm blood. The homemade razor-sharp knife was placed in Tweads right hand and his fingers were wrapped around it and some pressure was applied for a few seconds. The weapon was then removed from his hand and placed next to the body. The guard checked his uniform for any staining and walked to the cell door and took a quick glance outside, seeing that the landing was empty he took a last look at the slaughtered poor bugger on the floor and then left closing the cell door behind him.

Courtan was handing Wallows a pile of statements for her to sort through when her mobile rang; she pressed the answer button and put it to her ear. The call only lasted a few seconds and she did not say anything, but she was unable to conceal a contented smile; she pressed the end of call button and replaced the phone back in her pocket.

Courtan asked with a puzzled look on his face "Who was that?"

Wallows simply replied "I think it must have been a wrong number" she then continued with her work feeling totally relaxed safe in the knowledge that Frank Twead would not be telling anybody anything ever again.

When news of Frank Twead's suicide in prison was received it changed the entire approach to the murder investigation. It simply became a paperwork exercise to tie up loose ends and blame everything on Twead. Anything and everything got pinned on him, not only the murders but the illegal covert surveillance and the botched investigation. Whatever had gone wrong in recent months, even missing property and poor crime detection rates were written off to him he had become the ultimate sacrificial lamb.

28

Coffee Cake and Friends Reunited

The media had a field day for a while especially when they trawled the bars and pubs in Stourbridge. Nearly every landlord or local drinker in every pub had a tale of drunkenness relating to Twead that they could sell to the press and if they didn't have one they weren't averse to making one up after all a dead man can't refute it or seek legal redress so why not make a few bucks at his expense. After exhausting every conceivable avenue possible to destroy the memory and reputation of Twead it gradually began to be yesterday's news and so was the town of Stourbridge.

The Town quickly returned to being a quiet sleepy small Midlands slice of suburbia where very little happened. Its fifteen minutes of fame was over and gone for good. The press machine had left town with all its entourage leaving vacancies at the previously rammed to the hilt Premier Inn. Chequers the Weatherspoon's pub that had been constantly full of big spending reporters from dawn till late evening had quietened down and the town was now returning to normality it was no longer headline news.

Stourbridge Police had acted speedily to restore public confidence and a number of high profile commendations were dished out amidst a blaze of publicity. A number of promotions were given out immediately to change the dynamics of the force. The only member of the team who didn't get a promotion was Latifeo; because he was known to be a bit dense and incredibly lazy, but it also suited him not to get promoted as it lessened the chance of him having to do any work if he was left as he was. It was the intention to bring in a new detective chief inspector from an outside force to act as the proverbial new broom and reinforce public confidence.

The newly promoted Detective Inspector Grant Courtan strode confidently into Stourbridge Police Station and said "Good Morning" to the newly promoted Detective Sergeant Shirley Wallows. She returned the greeting as she opened the door to her new office. Once inside she sat down on her brand-new state of the art leather office chair and admired the new décor. She had placed her recent commendation for outstanding police work in pride of place on the wall behind her desk so that everyone saw it when they came into her office. It had taken some hard work and she had taken a lot of risks to get where she was, but it had been worth it and she was now beginning to get the respect from male officers that she hadn't had before, even though they were low ranking constables it was a start.

She ran through the events of recent months in her mind. She had practised her slaughtering techniques on local tramps; she had tried inserting the murder weapon in various parts of the body. She had initially aimed for the heart but soon realised that quite often the ribs got in the way. She had then tried ramming it straight into the back of their skulls, but this needed several attempts and a lot of effort to get the spike through into their brain and all of the time those smelly tramps were screaming their heads off. It had given her a sense of satisfaction when exacting her revenge by inflicting the utmost horrific pain imaginable upon these worthless dregs of humanity and she took great pleasure watching their suffering and shrieks of terror. But she realised that although as much as she wanted to extend their suffering and witness their terrifying last moments on earth she needed to despatch her future victims in a quicker more efficient manner. This would lessen the chances of her being caught in the act, but it still needed to be one hundred percent effective. She eventually after several attempts managed to perfect the technique of driving the spike through the back of the neck. This method worked perfectly on several levels; firstly, by inserting it all the way through the neck into the vocal chords it prevented them from screaming or making any noise at all. It also had the effect of severing vital nerves which paralysed them immediately. It was also easy to insert as the tissue was reasonably soft there and it didn't require a great deal of physical effort.

She had chosen the wooden handled spike because she could keep it in her handbag and if for whatever reason it was discovered or seen in her bag then it wouldn't be a problem because it was the tool that was used by police officers to put holes in their epaulettes, so they could attach their collar numbers. The idea of giving blow jobs to obtain semen from as many men as she could came from the SOCO's, they were the ones who told her to always keep sample and evidence bags with her together with swabs the stupid idiots thought they were being nice to her when in fact they were helping and giving guidance to her on how to become a serial killer. They had even told her how to store them, by keeping them deep frozen. And knowing that blokes think more with their cocks than their brains it had been easy, and no bloke ever refused a quick no questions asked blow job. This had given her the power to arrange the execution of Twead in prison before he could implicate her. A randy prison guard whom she gave a quick knee trembler to in a pub carpark at a police social event who was later so petrified that his wife would find out that Wallows could get him to do anything. The same fate would have befallen Pickes but the poor bastard had saved them the trouble by turning himself into a vegetable by putting that noose round his neck.

Wallows thought back to her childhood. She had been brought up in an orphanage; this was where she developed her hatred of men. For years she had been subject to sexual abuse from the very people that were supposed to be looking after her. From a very early age, so young when the assaults began that she didn't know exactly how old she was she had been constantly raped and abused several times a day by a number of men. There was no one she could tell, no one she could turn to for help. She was alone, a young frightened girl who

307

couldn't understand why these big men wanted to stick their penises into her and up her bum until it hurt. The thing she hated the most was when they put them in her mouth and shoved them in so far, she almost choked; if she complained or began to cry then they would beat her and then continue doing what they were doing. She hated the taste and the smell of them and the sticky mess they made in her mouth or sometimes on her face. She had been passed round like a commodity much in the same way that someone would casually pass round a packet of cigarettes and everyone would help themselves. They even ridiculed her name with all the connotations that S Wallows conjures up, she hated this name but was determined not to change it to anything else because it served as a reminder of what she went through for all those years and it spurred her on in her quest for revenge.

She had sworn revenge on men, all men, any men the more the better. She would continue to do so with all her might and slaughter as many as she possibly could and in the most humiliating manner. But she needed to be a bit cute for the present. Twead had taken the fall for all the recent murders so she would have to put the spike through the head technique to bed otherwise it would reopen the enquiry. She needed to research a different method and find someone especially chauvinistic; some big mouthed condescending pig to be the first recipient. She wracked her brains to think of someone suitable but whom?

She came around from her day dreaming when the door to her office opened and Gibbs walked in with someone she didn't know. "Hello Shirley, let me introduce you to our new detective chief inspector. I'm showing him round the station, he has been brought in from an outside force and he will become after DI Courtan your second line manager."

Wallows stretched out her hand smiled "It's nice to meet you sir, I'm Detective Sergeant Wallows."

The new DCI didn't shake her hand and looked her up and down with contempt. "Bloody hell, women sergeants whatever next. Be a good girl and go and put the kettle on I could murder a cup of tea when I've finished the tour."

Without saying another word to Wallows not even as much as a goodbye they both left the office. Wallows heard the new DCI shout back down the corridor at her derisorily "And don't forget two sugars darling."

Wallows smiled and thought to herself. That was easy, I didn't even have to go looking, this one was going to be easy and especially worthy of my special attention.

She sat back down at her desk and looked at the pile of incoming mail and opened one meaningless memo after another, most of which went straight into the bin. The next letter she opened however sent a shiver down her spine, she read it twice and then looked towards her office door to make sure nobody could walk in and sneak a look at the letter. She walked over to the door and put the catch on and returned to the letter. She checked the envelope, it must have been sent by someone who knew her, and the name and address were all spelt correctly. The letter inside consisted of letters cut out of a glossy magazine and pasted together to form words which read. I KNOW WHAT YOU DID AND WHY. MEET ME IN THE COFFEE LOUNGE AT TWO O'CLOCK. SOMEONE ELSE ALSO KNOWS YOUR SECRET I CAN HELP YOU.

Wallows was stunned, and she sat back in her chair and stared at the letter and began to try and digest the implications and what she should do. She racked her brains to try and work out who the author could be and how they knew. If indeed they did know what she had done. It was now midday she had to decide if she was going to meet whoever it was in the café or simply just ignore it. The ramifications of each decision were weighed up against each other and she realised that she had no real alternative but to go to the café at the appointed time.

The Coffee Lounge was the new café in the park and was just a short distance from the initial murder scene. She wondered if this meeting place had been chosen specifically for that reason. She arrived a few minutes early and ordered a coffee and sat down; she scanned the room to establish if she recognised anyone, she felt sure that as soon as she saw the author of the anonymous letter she would know who they were. The café had only been open for a few months and she had visited it several times for coffee and cake and in all that time she had not seen anyone in there whom she knew.

She checked her watch, it was now exactly two o'clock and no one had entered the café for a few minutes. She scanned the room again with a little more intensity paying more attention to each individual face. As she did this she caught the attention of someone she had spoken to recently, it was the occupant of one of the houses opposite the park. She and Latifeo had spoken to her when they were doing house to house enquires; she remembered that they had showed her a photograph of Pickes and asked her if she remembered seeing him or anyone else with him. Wallows recalled that she had politely considered the question for a while gave it some thought and replied that she had not seen him. She then noticed Wallows looking at her and smiled; and she then picked up her cup and made her way over to join Wallows at her table.

Sam Gail sat down with Wallows and said "Hello there my names Sam, I thought I recognised you. Were you one of the police officers that I spoke to recently?"

"Yes, I was" she replied courteously. "Myself and other officers were making enquires in the area but it's all sorted now."

Sam said, "This is a lovely café, I come here quite often as the cakes are delicious, a bit fattening though but it's nice to have a treat every now and then."

Wallows was still scanning the room, she knew she needed to get rid of this woman or the author of the letter would not approach her, so she said to Sam "It's nice speaking with you but I am waiting for someone to arrive, we have an important meeting shortly."

Sam looked Wallows in the eyes and said "I am the person you are waiting for, I know what you did."

Sam let the statement sink in for a while before speaking again. "You don't remember me do you Shirley? I recognised you as soon as I opened the door to you and Latifeo."

Wallows replied "As I said, I remember speaking to you recently. You live in one of the houses opposite."

Sam shook her head "No, I don't mean recently. I'm talking years ago when we were children. We were both in the same orphanage. I was a little younger than you that is probably why you don't remember me, but I know what you went through. We all suffered at the hands of those bastards, some more than others. I know you had it particularly rough because you were passed from one abuser to another, you were a bit older that the rest of us and you were a bit more developed which made you more appealing to them. I was normally only abused by one of them, he kept me for himself, but I still had it incredibly rough. At eight years of age I had been raped and sodomised so many times that my reproductive system was totally ripped to pieces and damaged beyond repair leaving me unable to have kids. Even before I was old enough to have periods I used to have to wear sanitary towels to soak up the flow of blood from my collapsed rectum. So, I know the reason why you have done what you have."

Wallows replied, "And what exactly is it I am supposed to have done?"

"Shirley, I know you murdered those people. I saw you do it from my bedroom window and I have seen you stalking couples for a long time waiting for the right opportunity. I would see you two or three times a week but don't worry I'm not going to turn you in. We are both the same you and me. We share the same hatred of men and want the same thing, revenge. We want payback; the only difference is I destroy them financially whilst you destroy them physically. However, there is someone else who knows what you did, and they need to be taken care of or they will bring you down. It won't affect me, it will only impact upon you, but I am prepared to help. Now before I continue with the details I need to know if you are in or out do you want my help?"

Wallows considered this for a moment; she hadn't in her wildest thoughts imagined that this would be the scenario that she would be presented with. She had prepared herself for some form of blackmail, certainly not meeting a like-minded ally who would be offering her help in her violent and hatred filled vendetta against men. Her mind was racing unsure what to do, she decided to stall for a while to give her time to think so she replied, "I don't know what you are talking about, the person responsible for those murders has been caught and they killed themselves in prison."

Sam shook her head and replied with more urgency "Look you need to trust me; I know you killed those people and I also know that most of them were a smoke screen for your real intended victims Adam Dores and his evil bitch of a wife, they were the resident care workers at our orphanage. I can remember when you shared a dormitory with me and some other young girls. I used to lie awake at night and I saw the depraved cow get you out of bed when she thought the rest of us were all asleep and lead you away by the hand. We all knew where she was taking you and what for, it was so that bastard husband of hers could abuse you because you were the oldest and your body was starting to develop. You got led away in the night a lot more often than the rest of us. We all suffered this abuse but not to anywhere near the extent that you did, I can still picture you in my mind's eye when you were bought back. Sometimes you were in such a state you were so weak you could barely walk, and she would have to lift you up into bed and put her finger across her lips to tell you to keep quiet. I have already helped you out once without you knowing it. When the police said they were looking for sightings of the council van that I know was driven by Pickes I said that I had seen it there on the night of the second murders, but I hadn't seen it because it wasn't there that night. The only thing I saw that night was you. But someone is about to expose you and they are going to do it soon, I can help you, but you need to tell me if you are in or out."

Wallows stared at Sam for a moment whilst contemplating what to do, if she was right about someone exposing her then she didn't relish spending the rest of her life behind bars and this woman obviously knows a lot more about what had really happened to the victims.

It began to dawn on Wallows that she had no real choice she had to co-operate with this innocent looking girl sitting in front of her. A petite stunningly attractive woman whose life had also been ruined by those bastard perverts. She had obviously suffered at their hands as well and endured the same degrading treatment year after year without being able to tell anyone or turn to someone and ask for help. Her mind flashed back to those days in the home when they shared a dormitory and the memories began flooding back, she began to speak quietly and slowly with a deep heavy sense of sadness in her voice.

"He used to rape and sodomise me nearly every night, it used to hurt so much but I used to fight back the tears of pain because I knew it would do me no good crying I used to console myself with the hope that one day I would be able to inflict the same pain and suffering that he had put me through on him it was the only thing that kept me going that was the only thing that stopped me from killing myself."

Sam listened in hushed silence whilst staring into her eyes. She knew Wallow's was remembering and reliving the past and the torment in her face was plain to see. A solitary tear began running down Sam's face she could feel the pain and anguish that she was going through. Wallow's continued "and do you know what the worst bit was? It was her, that fucking bitch of a wife of his, she used to help him. She would hold me down and force my legs apart; sometimes she would hold her hand over my mouth if I cried out in pain. Then at the end she would put her fingers deep inside my mouth and pull it wide open, so he could put his penis in and come in my mouth. It didn't even finish there because then she would lead me along the corridor to be abused all over again by whatever care worker was on night shift. When all of them had their fill she would clean me up to make it appear as if nothing had happened and before she bought me back to the dorm she warned me that if I ever spoke of it to anyone then she would tell the police I had stolen from them and that I would go to prison for a long time and no one would ever want to adopt me and that I would eventually go and burn in hell for all eternity, but she could have stopped it all not only for you and I but for all the other girls there but she did nothing, she deserved to die along with her husband."

Both of them sat there without speaking for several minutes reflecting on their upbringing and the loss of what should have been a magical time filled with happy memories but instead it had been stolen from them, a childhood gone forever never to be replaced.

Wallows took a deep breath and replied "Okay I'm in, now who are we talking about? What do they know and what are we going to do about it?"

Sam asked, "Do you know a pathologist called Chuman?"

Wallows sat upright in her chair her attention now fully focused "Yes I know him well and he's a condescending chauvinistic pig."

Sam realised by her response that she had hit a nerve and there was obviously a lot of friction between her and Chuman.

"Well he's the one we need to deal with; he has apparently received information from a senior police officer whom you framed for murder. This officer is now dead and Chuman intends to pass this information onto a senior detective."

Wallows said "That makes sense, his best mate was a detective chief inspector called Twead and yes I did frame him for murder. I think he had figured it all out while he was in prison and he had said to a detective that he knew who had framed him but how do you know all this?"

Sam looked around the café and checked to make sure that no-one was within earshot and also looked behind her to make sure nobody had moved near them. "I know through one of my music lesson customers, he is a mortuary technician and he often works with and also has a drink with Chuman. It was whilst they were having a drink recently that his tongue loosened a bit with the effect of the amount of alcohol they had drunk and he let it slip out and he told him all about it. Now we have to work fast, apparently he has arranged a meeting with a senior detective called King sometime tomorrow."

Wallows nodded and said "Yes I know King, he is the most senior detective in the force and he is in charge of a department called professional standards so your information appears to ring true. On a lighter note though it must be nice to teach music what instrument do you play?"

Sam began to laugh "I can't play a frigging note, I can't even read music and the lessons are just a front for my customers."

Wallow's asked enquiringly "Customers?"

Without showing any emotion Sam replied "Sex, I sell them sex and I use it to bleed them dry of money. That's how I exact my revenge; this particular guy has a weird intense fetish. It's what's known as extreme masochism and I exploit it for my own benefit. He would do absolutely anything I tell him to and I mean anything at all no holds barred. I have asked him to get Chuman to the mortuary tonight at six o'clock when it will be shut. He has used the pretence that he has found some evidence concerning the dead detective whose body is still in the mortuary. We will need to be there waiting for him."

Wallows said, "Are you sure this guy can be trusted, is he going to help us with Chuman?"

Sam replied "I've told you before this guy will do anything I tell him to, it is part of his weird fetish. He is what you call an extreme submissive masochist, the things I have done to him and the gross disgusting things I have made him do would blow your mind. I have beaten him senseless, electrocuted him, burnt his penis with lighted cigarette's, tied him up for days on end inside a tiny bedroom

315

ottoman; I have pissed on him and pissed in his mouth. I have even shit on his face and made him eat it and then made him say thank you to me for the privilege. I have financially bankrupted him, I have forced him to re-mortgage his house three times, the house which he and his family will shortly be evicted from, that'll be a nice surprise for his wife and kids. Financially his usefulness is coming to an end because the banks and the money lenders are closing in on him. It seems that the more severe and the more ultimate extreme things I subject him to the better he likes it whether it's emotional, financial or physical there is no end to what I can make him do. So, you can relax Shirley, just think of him as my obedient little lapdog. Now I want to know something from you."

Wallows replied curiously "What is it you want to know?"

Sam looked intently at Wallows staring straight into her eyes and said with an air of excitement in her voice "What I want to know is what it felt like when you murdered those two child abusing bastards. How did it feel when you shoved the weapon into in them?"

"It was fantastic, absolutely unbelievable. All those years of abuse those years of hiding the pain and the shame deep down inside me, it was like everything came flooding out in that moment when I stabbed them but I wanted it to last it was all going to be over too quick for them I wanted them to suffer longer like I did and the rest of the girls they defiled and whose lives they ruined so I pushed them off the bonnet of the car so that they were both on the floor still alive looking up at me and I told them who I was. They couldn't answer but I could see in their eyes they remembered me. I told her that It wouldn't be me who was going to burn in hell forever but the pair of them were and very shortly and I also told them who my next victim was going to be. It was to be their son Cambion. I said I already knew where to find him, he was studying at Durham University and I had already made contact with him using his weakness. He had the same problem as his paedophile dad he thought with his cock and that was going to be his downfall. I was going to chop his cock off whilst I killed him but I wouldn't be shoving in his mouth like I had done with his dad, but I was going to find their grave and bury it with them, their own sons cock would be buried with them for all eternity. The tortured look on their pathetic dying faces when I had finished telling them made it all worthwhile, the satisfaction of exacting my revenge was utterly exhilarating like no other feeling I have ever experienced it felt as if a massive burden that I had been carrying on my shoulders all my life had been lifted."

After a further half an hour of swapping stories and experiences suffered from their time in the orphanage they finished their drinks and arranged to meet with the mortuary technician at five-thirty.

Wallows returned to her office to prepare herself for what was to come tonight, she had been greatly impressed with Sam. She especially liked her determination to inflict as much possible pain and suffering on men as herself and she had a sense of empathy with her. Only someone that had suffered like they had both suffered could fully appreciate that. To be sexually brutalised from such a young age meant that their entire childhood memories consisted totally of nothing but abuse. A complete irreplaceable childhood gone, stolen by those evil vile excuses for human beings not one of them deserved to have been given birth to and they warranted everything that she and Sam could do to them to make their pitiful existences a living hell. She watched the hands tick by on the wall clock getting ever closer to the time she needed to leave for the mortuary. She relaxed with copious cups of coffee and her reflexions on what had already been an extraordinary day.

When the time came Wallows checked for any messages on her office phone and her mobile but there were none. She had no outstanding e-mails and crime wise it was all quiet on the streets, a normal Stourbridge humdrum day. She locked her office and made her way to the mortuary. Sam was already there when Wallows arrived, and she opened the door to her and took her through to the mortuary technician's office which also doubled as a rest room and introduced her to the technician. This was the room where she had been before when Latifeo had tried to frighten her with his description of a post-mortem. It had ended with Latifeo being placed unconscious into one of the office armchairs having passed out cold during the examination. They all waited in there pending the arrival of Chuman.

The appointed time of six o'clock came and went with no sign of Chuman. The technician looked out of the window several times but Chuman was nowhere to be seen. After half an hour they decided to call it a day and were preparing to leave, Wallows had her hand on the door handle and was just about to open the door when they heard a knock on the outside and in a slurred voice heard Chuman shout "Come on I haven't got all pissing day open the bloody door."

Wallows looked at Sam and put her finger to her lips and pointed back towards the technician's office, then as quietly as possible they tip-toed back along the corridor leaving the technician to open the door. When the girls were out of sight the technician opened the door to an increasingly impatient Chuman who half stumbled through the door almost falling over the doorstep he had obviously had a few drinks. He was greeted by the technician and the girls heard Chuman loudly and indignantly ask "What's this supposed suspicious evidence you think you've got regarding Frank Twead?"

The Technician replied, "I'll show you, I've already got the body laid out."

Wallows and Sam were looking through a gap in the door and saw Chuman being led into one of the examination rooms. Not the main one where Wallows had been before but one further along the corridor. After a short while Sam and Wallows as silently as they could made their way along the corridor until they were outside the door to the examination room. The door had been deliberately left slightly ajar and they could see in. The body of Frank Twead was laid out on a huge examination table; it was twice the size of the ones Wallows had seen before. It was a specialist table that was used to examine extremely obese cadavers and it had a body hoist adjacent to the table. When they were sure that Chuman who had his back to the door was engrossed looking at the body of Twead they both without making a sound entered the room and tiptoed towards the examination table behind the unsuspecting Chuman. Not daring to make a sound, getting closer and closer.

"There's nothing here" shouted Chuman angrily towards the technician "You don't know what you're talking about you bloody idiot. You've got me here for nothing you're just wasting my time."

The Technician who was standing directly opposite Chuman could see Sam and Wallows approaching out the corner of his eye and on a nod from him when they were directly behind Chuman they grabbed hold of him and forcibly grappled him to the ground. The Technician ran around the table and jumped on top of him and together they applied leather restraining straps to his arms and legs. Chuman who had been caught completely by surprise barely put up a struggle caused in part by the shock of what was happening but mostly because of the amount of alcohol he had consumed lunchtime that had dulled his reactions. He was now quickly coming to his senses and he began shouting and screaming until a gag was forced into his mouth. Then using the hoist, they lifted him up onto the examination table and applied further restraints which secured him to the table next to the corpse of his dead mate.

The cold lifeless arm of Frank Twead was placed under and wrapped round Chuman's neck as if in an embrace. The look of shock and sheer terror on his face was a pleasure to behold thought Wallows especially as we were in his domain, his little kingdom where he usually cracked the whip and shouted out his orders mostly in a condescending sexist and bigoted manner. He didn't look so cocky now as they saw the wet stain on his trousers where he had pissed himself with fright. The technician began expertly to cut Chuman's clothes off and in a couple of short minutes he was lying there totally naked. Chuman could feel the coldness of Twead's body against his skin and he tried to move away but he couldn't budge an inch, the leather harnesses were holding him firmly in position.

319

Chuman tried even harder to break free when he saw the Technician approach him menacingly with scalpel and a syringe in hand in hand. The razor-sharp blade was held with the point against Chuman's neck just below his chin; in his other hand the technician emptied the contents of the syringe into Chuman's arm.

"What's he doing with the needle?" Wallows asked Sam.

"He's injecting him with a drug it's called a psychostimulant. It's designed to keep a person awake no matter what happens because we wouldn't want Dr Chuman to pass out and miss all the fun now would we?"

Wallows and Sam looked into the terrified eyes of Chuman; they were almost bursting out of their sockets with sheer panic and fright. Then with a smile from Sam and a nod of her head, the technician with the deftest of touches began to open up Chuman.

Starting as one would in a post-mortem with the first incision made just below the chin and then continuing slowly and methodically down the throat towards the chest. Wallows noticed that the technician was being especially careful not to cut the jugular vein as this would obviously cause extreme and rapid blood loss and despatch Chuman much too quickly. The depth of the incision was carefully controlled so as to go just deep enough to cut through the entire outer layer of fat but not as deep as in a post-mortem to make sure that no vital organs were breached; every effort was being made to prolong the living hell that Chuman was experiencing.

The technician meticulously and studiously extended the incision across the breast bone and continued down towards the stomach. Chuman was trying to scream for all his might but no sound was forthcoming, the gag in his mouth was doing its job. When the full length of the cut was complete it ran from Chuman's neck all the way down the length of his torso and finished just above the genital area. When complete the technician stood back and admired his handiwork he seemed pleased with the results so far.

Then using a different knife with a long flat blade, he turned his attention to Chuman's abdomen where he skilfully inserted the long

320

flat blade and gradually began to prise open the stomach cavity just enough to carefully and gently remove his intestines. They resembled an extremely long endless string of sausages covered in blood. Wallows was impressed with the skill that this butcher possessed in keeping Chuman alive during this process. The still attached and working intestines were carefully eased out of Chuman's stomach cavity and placed into his hands.

Wallows felt sure that if Chuman's hands weren't tied down securely then he would have instinctively tried to shove them back into his stomach, but he couldn't, all he could do was lie there and feel them pulsating in the palm of his hand. A hand-held mirror was then produced and held aloft above the grotesque sight of this partly disembowelled still alive body. It was held in such a position that Chuman could witness the macabre sight of himself holding his own still functioning internal organs in his hands. Wallows looked on in amazement the whole scenario had obviously been pre-planned between the technician and Sam she thought because they had hardly spoken to each other and again with a simple nod from her he continued with the next stage. Sam changed the angle of the mirror so that Chuman could see what was about to happen next.

His penis was grabbed hold of and stretched out to make it easier to cut; the scalpel was placed against the base and held there for a while so that Chuman could get a good look at what was about to happen to his manhood. Wallows tried to imagine what he was experiencing, what thoughts were going through his mind. He was completely sliced open totally gutted, his still working internal organs had been removed from his stomach and placed in his hands and he was now about to watch as his own penis was being cut off. After allowing enough time for him to contemplate and fully realise the horror of what was about to happen to him then Sam nodded once more then slowly and deliberately the scalpel began to slice into his penis until it was completely cut all the way through. After it was sliced off the technician brought it round to the head of the table and handed it to Wallows.

She took hold of it and examined this tiny piece of useless flesh, this little flaccid pink thing that ruled men's brains and made them do the most horrendous acts of abuse especially against the young and vulnerable. They had caused her so much pain and suffering for so many years she detested them. This pathetic thing in her hand wouldn't be causing her or any other female any pain or abuse ever again. She didn't need to be told what to do with it.

Wallows held it in front of Chuman's face and taunted him with it. She then carefully moved the gag in Chuman's mouth to one side and dangled his bloodied penis over his mouth. He tried to move his head away and close his mouth, but it was no good he was now extremely weak from the blood loss. Sam held his head still and the technician put his fingers inside Chuman's gums and yanked his mouth open. Wallows then began to shove Chuman's penis into his mouth forcing it in as deep as possible. She looked into Chuman's eyes and said, "You are not going to scream, or faint are you my dear."

Wallows then looked at the technician and indicated towards Twead with her head, he immediately understood what she wanted and turned to Sam to seek her permission.

Sam smiled and nodded her head to give consent and the technician turned his attention to Twead and using the same scalpel sliced off his lifeless penis and as he had done with Chuman's penis handed it to Wallows. She again taunted Chuman with the detached penis but the expression on Chuman's face hardly changed, he was now beginning to come to terms with his impending fete. He knew full well that his deceased best mate's penis was now going to be forced into his throat and that's exactly what Wallows did whilst grinning from ear to ear. She was somewhat disappointed at his complete lack of show of revulsion, he just seemed to accept what was happening to him so she aggressively forced the penis as far as possible down the throat of Chuman to try and get a reaction but he was past the resisting stage, there was no fight left in him he was merely succumbing to whatever was to happen before his impending death which he prayed would come soon.

His blood was now beginning to pool everywhere, his life slowly coming to an end, the blood loss had slowed considerably and although there was no hope left for him he would have to endure the agony and terror for some time to come. Nothing else needed to be done to him; they could all just relax and enjoy watching him endure the most painful, terrifying, slow death imaginable. Sam then told the technician to use the pen and paper on the adjacent examination table and write the words 'I'm sorry for everything.' The technician did as he was told in silence without question and when he had finished he placed the note together with the pen back down on the table and he then turned back to face Sam.

She was now holding a large beaker filled with the foulest smelling pungent clear liquid. It was a smell Wallows was familiar with; it was the smell of the mortuary, the smell associated with death but a thousand times worse. Then it struck her, she remembered what it was and what it was used for. It was formaldehyde. She told him to hold the knife that he had used to butcher Chuman with in his right hand and then handed him the beaker and told him to sit down on the floor in the middle of the pool of his blood. He did so willingly without offering any resistance and simply looked up towards Sam with big puppy dog eyes as she nodded to him as a sign to drink what she had given him.

Wallows was totally transfixed at the power that this woman exercised over this perverted sick wretch, he was now being ordered to end his own life in what must be an incredibly painful death and he obviously knew it. He looked like the lapdog that Sam had referred to earlier; she could just imagine a trusting loyal dog looking with big frightened eyes up at his master as he was being put in a sack ready to be thrown into the canal.

Sam stood over him legs apart, hands on hips in a dominatrix fashion and glared at him intensely urging him to do what had to be done. The expression on his face was a strange combination of sheer terror and utter exhilaration at being forced to do the ultimate submissive act of masochism. He then took a deep breath and put the beaker to his mouth knowing that his life would be over shortly and that this was the ultimate most extreme submissive masochistic act and his last ever. He smiled at Sam and then quickly swallowed almost the entire contents in one enormous swig. The effect was instantaneous, and he began to shout and scream in agony clutching his stomach. He began to retch uncontrollably for some time then suddenly began to shout, "Oh my god what have I done, help me, help me for god's sake do something help me please."

Sam made no attempt to help but instead stood there and began to laugh gently "You pathetic stupid little man you deserve to die, now stop crying like a baby and shut up."

His screams and pleas for help went unheeded and he continued to beg for help until the poison began coursing through his veins and he was unable to move; all his internal organs were beginning to shut down with the effect of the poison and he was unable to scream anymore. He sat there in the pool of sticky blood still clutching the scalpel in one hand, the blood from the still alive Chuman on the table above him dripping onto his head and running down his face. The slimy blood-soaked intestines had slipped out of Chuman's hand and were now resting on the technician's head.

The Technician was now quiet and still, the damage caused to his nervous system had dulled the pain and he stared at Sam with a strange vacant stare. Sam hadn't moved she was still standing in the same dominant manner directing her sadistic gaze towards her now muted forlorn submissive; she then said to him "Almost done now just one last thing to do and then it's all over."

Wallows said nothing but watched in awe at the total and utter control that Sam was still wielding over the dying technician and wondered what on earth is she going to do to him now what else could there possibly be for him to suffer. She didn't have to wait long to find out as Sam said, "You know what to do now get on with it."

The Technician obeyed and with his left hand moved aside his plastic apron and rested his hand on his lap, his actions were now slow and laboured. Sam screamed at him "Get a fucking move on you piece of shit."

He slowly and clumsily took hold of his trouser zip and gently slid it all the way down he then stopped and looked up towards Sam.

"That's better that's a good boy now take it out" Sam shouted with venom.

He pulled his manhood out from his trousers and stretched it with his left hand exposing the full length of his flaccid penis and with his right hand which was still holding the scalpel he put it at the base of his penis with the razor-sharp edge touching the flesh and he waited. Sam said nothing for a while she just stared.

Wallows now began to realise why Sam remained quiet it was to increase and prolong the terror that must have been racing through his mind. The tension and silence in the small examination room was spine tingling until eventually Sam raised her right arm in the air, her hand had been made into a fist and her thumb was pointing upwards reminiscent of a roman emperor who was about to decide the fate of a gladiator or some other wretch who had been defeated in battle. The hand remained motionless with the thumb continuing to point upwards and Wallows saw the beginning of a smile emerging onto his face.

One last act of compassion for a dying man she thought, then Sam quickly inverted her hand so that her thumb pointed downwards and in a flash the technician with one swift movement had sliced off his own penis. He looked down at his hand that was now holding his bloodied and detached penis and then looked back at Sam seeking her approval. She smiled back at him and held her arm in the air as an indication for him to do the same, he did as he was ordered and fully extended his arm into the air as far as it would go and held his penis aloft his gaze now firmly fixed on Sam awaiting his next instruction.

Sam made him wait for what seemed an eternity until she finally nodded her head towards him as sign to continue, he then tilted his head back and opened his mouth and then slowly inserted his penis, he then let his arm drop down to his side his bloodied penis now half in and half sticking out of his mouth. The two barely alive, miserable excuses for human beings who were now suffering slow lingering and agonising deaths looked into the faces of Wallows and Sam. Their eyes pleading with them to end their lives quickly and put them out of their misery and the girls realised what they wanted and knew they were begging for a swift death. But neither of them had the faintest desire to show them any mercy and put them out of their misery but instead they both stood and watched enjoying the last little vestige of power that they held over the pair, their pathetic faces pleading for clemency for an act of compassion, but the girls remained impassive both wishing there was some way that they could extend their suffering, they both realised however that they now needed to act quickly to erase all trace of their presence get out..

Sam looked around the examination room, the apparent murder confession and suicide note was on the table and the incapacitated technician still had hold of the scalpel. Wallows and Sam stood in silence and surveyed the scene and the carnage they had created. A dead dickless, murdered high ranking police officer with his arm wrapped around his dying best mate who himself had been gutted like a pig with two penises jammed into his mouth with his still attached and working intestines spilling out of his stomach. A pathetic sexual deviant sitting beneath them in a pool of blood with intestines resting on his head and his dick in his mouth who would be leaving his wife and children destitute with the impending visit from the bailiffs but moreover he would forever be remembered and infamous as the mortician who went berserk and slaughtered the pathologist Chuman before committing suicide.

All that was left to do was for her and Wallows to take off their protective clothing which they would take away with them leaving no trace of either of them having been there. They took one last look at the slaughter and carnage they were leaving behind as they left the mortuary examination room. After removing their protective clothing and placing it in a bin liner to take away with them to be destroyed later they both checked their makeup and hair and casually left the building after checking through the window that the coast was clear and stepped back out into the street. As they closed the mortuary door behind them Sam said with a confident satisfied air "Our work here is done."

Wallows looked at Sam and studied her face for a while, she realised at that moment together with Sam that their actions had forged a deep and unbreakable bond between them. One that had initially been born out of their past shared experiences and now cemented together for all time by their vengeful act of retribution on the two tortured souls who were enduring the most painful and gruesome demises imaginable.

Then with a wicked smile and an evil glint in her eye she replied "Yes, it is" and then added pointedly "for now anyway."

As she walked Wallows began to reflect on recent events. The number of tramps she had murdered in order to practise and perfect her killing art, the dogging couples she had mercilessly slaughtered and the penises she had sliced off and shoved down their male chauvinistic throats. The females had never been her target initially but in hindsight they all still deserved to die because they were allowing themselves to be abused by their male counterparts allowing the cycle of male domination to continue.

The years of pent up anger and pain that she had kept hidden away for so many years and had begun to eat away at her insides were still present but now she was able to deal with them, the retribution she had inflicted especially on the husband and wife abusers from the care home where it had all begun had lifted her confidence and self-esteem and the added bonus of meeting and pairing up with Sam a like-minded strong woman who had suffered just as much as her all those years ago. She knew as did Sam that this was the beginning of something big and there were no limits as to what they could achieve together.

Sam broke the silence and said "I'm feeling peckish, what do you say we go to the coffee lounge in the park and get something nice? My treat."

Wallows smiled and replied, "That sounds lovely I could just murder a coffee and something tasty to nibble on let's go."

They strode purposely along together with a spring in their step and with a feeling of euphoria and why not, by their joint actions they had just formed a deep unbreakable bond between them and they had just committed and got away with the perfect crime, another two evil male pigs had been slaughtered and dispatched to meet their maker and they were now off for coffee and cake both of them completely and blissfully unaware that their every movement had been monitored and still was. Someone was watching.

The End

Printed in Great Britain
by Amazon